T0035518

"Carla Malden's memoir about her husband and screenwriting partner Laurence Starkman is a haunting story of love and loss, and a demonstration of the courage required to put a broken life together again."

—**SUSAN COOPER**, AUTHOR OF *THE DARK IS RISING*

"All I can say is WOW! I read for a living [and] never has one made me cry until I read this manuscript. Although this is a book that will tug at your heart, it is like the tug on a fishing line when you know you've got a big one. I can't wait to share it with others. This is more than a book, it's a blessing for anyone who reads it."

—**BARRY KIBRICK**, PRODUCER AND HOST, *BETWEEN THE LINES*

"Emotionally raw from start to finish, the story...also celebrates a rare and profound love that transcended death. A brutally candid memoir of the 'all-consuming and profoundly uncomplicated' power of grief."

—*KIRKUS REVIEWS*

# Search Heartache

a novel by

# Carla Malden

Rare Bird
Los Angeles, Calif.

THIS IS A GENUINE RARE BIRD BOOK

Rare Bird
6044 North Figueroa Street
Los Angeles, Calif. 90042
rarebirdbooks.com

Copyright © 2019 by Carla Malden

FIRST PAPERBACK EDITION 2023

All rights reserved, including the right to reproduce this book
or portions thereof in any form whatsoever, including but not limited
to print, audio, and electronic.

For more information, address:
Rare Bird Books Subsidiary Rights Department
453 South Spring Street, Suite 302
Los Angeles, CA 90013

Set in Dante
Printed in the United States

10 9 8 7 6 5 4 3 2 1

Publisher's Cataloging-in-Publication Data

Names: Malden, Carla, author.
Title: *Search Heartache: A Novel* / by Carla Malden.
Description: First Paperback Edition | A Genuine Rare Bird Book | New York, NY;
Los Angeles, CA: Rare Bird Books, 2023.
Identifiers: ISBN 9781644283608
Subjects: LCSH Marriage—Fiction. | Los Angeles (Calif.)—Fiction. |
Man-woman relationships—Fiction. | Divorce—Fiction. | Women—Fiction. | BISAC /
Fiction / General
Classification: LCC PS3613.A4335 S43 2019| DDC 813.6—dc23

# PROLOGUE

I MUST HAVE BEEN twelve years old when I first heard the joke.

I know I was in the seventh grade, because at the Ridgepoint School for Girls, the seventh graders were entrusted with carrying out the flag salute ceremony every Friday in all its pomp and patriotism. The entire Lower School, kindergarten through grade seven, lined up in our crisp white cotton uniforms. Monday through Thursday, the bucolic campus swarmed with girls in pink, yellow, and powder blue, as though scattered with prepubescent Easter eggs. But white on Friday. Always white on Friday. These traditions had kept the crème de la crème of Los Angeles young womanhood on the straight and narrow for nearly a century. And you never broke the rules. At least Maura Locke didn't. Not me.

I was standing in the flag salute line, staring down at my saddle shoes. They were so caked with white polish that it looked like the creases across the instep were smiling up at me. I was glad it wasn't my week to perform the actual raising of the flag. That was nerve-wracking. The unfolding, the clipping of the hooks through the brass rings, the hand-over-hand on the rope. I hated the pressure. No, this week all I had to do was march out, stand there, and slap my hand over my heart.

I would keep an eye on Miss Zipser, my teacher, a study in adamant spinsterhood (even then an old-fashioned word, but so excruciatingly appropriate). Miss Zipser had a thing for patriotism, especially now that her dream-come-true was in the White House—a wavy-haired movie star pledged to safeguard the conservative values she held so dear. On flag-salute Friday, Miss Zipser conducted the proceedings. She stood ramrod straight, as though steel encased the fibers of her every nerve, if indeed nerve fiber existed at all in this woman who passed her years, one after the other, holding court in front of a roomful of girls on the brink of life. She would place her hand on her heart—right on her anatomical heart, between her conical breasts, beneath her pearls. Sometimes we bet on whether Miss Zipser would manage to squeeze out a few tears as we pledged our allegiance. She loved her country that much.

On this particular Friday, Betsy Nagle stood behind me. She leaned in close to my ear, breaching the mandated nine inches of air space between Ridgepoint girls standing in line. I could smell the sickly sweetness of the pomade Betsy used to slick back her ponytail, a ponytail so tight it gave me a headache just to look at her. I never would have thought I'd hear a dirty joke from Betsy Nagle. It wasn't dirty really. I knew that. But still, it was about sex. Or something like it anyway.

"These groupies are hanging around backstage at a concert," breathed Betsy. "One of them says, 'I slept with Jon Bon Jovi last night.' And another one asks, 'How was he?' 'He's good,' she says, 'but he's no Mick Jagger.'"

"The next day, the first one says, 'Last night I slept with Bruce Springsteen.' 'How was he?'"

(That was the part that struck me. The notion that a girl would actually ask another girl that question. How was he? So matter-of-fact. It punched a hole in my romantic notion of an out-of-body, swept-away experience. It sounded more like comparing hamburgers.)

"He was good, but he's no Mick Jagger." (Not enough ketchup.)

"Then they run into each other a few days later. The girl says, 'You'll never believe who I slept with last night! Mick Jagger.'"

"'Well? How was he?'"

"'He's good. But he's no Mick Jagger.'"

Betsy Nagle's joke made no sense. *How could Mick Jagger not be Mick Jagger?*

We had recently finished reading *Alice in Wonderland*. While Miss Zipser highlighted figures of speech, and the hipper girls mined the text for hidden, drug-related meaning, I liked the story precisely as it read, even if parts of it confused me. This Jagger joke reminded me of the line: "I can't go back to yesterday, because I was a different person then." Weren't you always yourself? Wasn't Mick Jagger, by definition, as good as Mick Jagger? If Mick Jagger didn't define Mick Jagger-ness, then who did?

I suspected there was some sort of irony at play. We had recently completed a unit on irony in English—verbal, dramatic, and situational. I had aced the end-of-unit test, but I was glad this joke had not been one of the questions. I would have had a hard time categorizing which type of irony applied and would have had to go with "All of the Above," an option that always made me feel uneasy, if not outright defeated.

I nodded a silent "that's a good one" to Betsy as I noticed a tiny splotch of white polish on the navy saddle of my right shoe. I hoped the line monitor wouldn't give me a demerit. Demerits were so humiliating, not that I had ever gotten one.

At lunch, my best friend, Gwen Kadison, told me the same joke. It was going around. Gwen substituted The Who's Roger Daltrey and Marty Balin of Jefferson Starship. So that was it. Not really a joke so much as a game. A game where you slipped in different names.

Carrot stick half-chomped, I proposed, "He's good but he's no Weird Al." Gwen laughed so hard that her Tab came out of her nose.

Gwen countered, "He's good but he's no Captain."

"Huh?"

"And Tennille." Good one.

We went on like that through lunch.

The game would run all the way through our high school years. The game where you could talk about having sex with the pantheon of rock stars, swapping one for the other willy nilly. Eventually I realized that the joke wasn't about rock stars. It wasn't even about sex.

It was about promise and hope. It was about greener grass. Mostly, it was about disillusionment.

# CHAPTER ONE

"I'M GOING TO HAVE to start wearing my glasses on one of those chains," I said. I was sitting on the bed, propped against four pillows, filing the rough spot on a fingernail I had been fidgeting with all day. I stretched my arm out straight, willing my fingers six inches farther away. "You know," I said to Adam, "those chains you wear around your neck?"

"Like an old lady?"

He was slouched on the foot of the bed in his underwear, remote control in hand, adding the latest channels to the box. Netflix, Prime, Hulu, HBO. Behind these icons, neatly arranged on the screen, was a new generation of media tycoons, flush with cash and buying shows like drunken sailors. My husband was an agent in the motion picture/television department of a major talent agency—his father's. It was part of his job to make sure the agency was selling what the "entertainment providers" were buying, though entertainment value often seemed the least of the transaction.

"I beg your pardon," I said. *Old lady?*

"Nothing," he said as he added the CarChase Channel to the lineup.

But I knew perfectly well what he had said. *Old lady. Old. Lady. Old.*

I thought about filing the rest of my nails to match the newly shortened one, but that seemed several fingers too many to cope with right now. Especially since I couldn't see.

"Would you turn down the air?" I asked. It was barely early spring, but the temperatures had been late-summer-high the last several days—calm and still, what people in LA sometimes call earthquake weather. I had turned on the AC for the first time since last summer.

Adam didn't answer. He was watching a promo for the new Ken Burns documentary. This time out: the Dust Bowl. They were hyping it as the worst manmade ecological disaster in history. "I wonder if that's true," Adam said.

"What?"

"About the Dust Bowl."

"People thought it meant the end of the world," I said, uninterested.

"Maura, people always think everything means the end of the world."

"It's blowing right on me," I said. "Would you turn off the air?"

Adam got up from the edge of the bed and studied the thermostat. The AC shut off with a troublesome click. "That doesn't sound good," he said.

"No," I agreed.

Adam resumed his channel reprogramming. I picked up my book. I had decided that twice a year I was going to read one of the classics that had slipped through the cracks of my education. I was currently slogging through *The Great Gatsby*, not really enjoying it, but determined to finish.

*"No amount of fire or freshness can challenge what a man will store up in his ghostly heart,"* I read silently. I read the line again, hoping to commit it to memory, along with the Faulkner, Joyce, and Proust I had stored in the hope chest in my brain that I doubted would ever be opened.

"You better call the air conditioning people," Adam said as he climbed into bed.

I nodded. Done.

Adam rolled onto his side, his back to me, and let out a sigh that said how good it felt to finally be in bed...or, more likely: another day, another dollar. I read to the end of the chapter, then turned out the light.

◆◆◆

WHEN I WAS A small child, I had a recurring nightmare of being chased by a witch. I ran but could not escape, opened my mouth but could not scream. I looked over my shoulder and there she was: the witch, behind me, closer and closer. Until she was close enough to reach out and run a long, pointy fingernail down my back. I would wake up, the last tingle of sharp nail bursting at the base of my spine.

That witch hadn't made an appearance in forty years. But this particular night, she paid me a call. And when I awoke at 2:00 a.m., nightmare heart thumping, Adam's side of the bed was empty. I didn't hear him in the bathroom. I waited a few more minutes, assuming he would appear with a glass of water and, most likely, smelling of Oreos or something else chocolate. I had picked up a pint of Ben and Jerry's latest concoction, Fifty Shades of Chocolate. If the middle-of-the-night munchies hit, Adam wouldn't be able to resist.

I knew there would be no falling back to sleep after my nightmare, so I headed down to the kitchen to join Adam, hoping there would be a shade or two left for me. As I passed Adam's study, the light from his computer caught my eye, its eerie glow a sort of technological Cheshire cat grin suspended in the darkness.

On screen were two bodies. A man and a woman. Naked. Legs entangled. Arms entangled. Flashes of thigh. Flashes of breast. Flashes of who-knows-what, who-knows-where. A man and a woman having sex. As if in a horror movie, from out of nowhere, Adam's chair rolled slowly up to the desk. I knew the witch would be sitting in it.

I was still trapped in my nightmare. *Don't scream. Don't wake Adam and Stephanie.*

But it wasn't the witch after all. It wasn't a nightmare. It was Adam sitting in the chair, his back to the door, his sandy hair matted where a half-hour earlier it had been wedged into his pillow. Something about Adam's demeanor stopped me from going in, from uttering a word. He sat there, quite still, right elbow on the desk, chin in hand, left hand hovering over the mouse.

I held my breath and took a silent step backward. This was a different kind of nightmare. My husband was watching porn.

On screen, nothing extraordinary seemed to be going on between the sheets. Nothing acrobatic or gymnastic. Barely aerobic. There were no stilettos, no leather, no handcuffs or silken restraints. Just two people in a slightly grainy video. What there did seem to be was a surprising tenderness between these two players, an intimacy that made me look away for a moment, that made me feel like a voyeur. This didn't feel like a spectator sport. This felt like intruding.

The woman was young, barely more than a girl really. The camera was not stationed at the foot of the bed, but rather off to the side, trained more on her than him. The girl turned her head, opened her eyes, and looked straight into the lens. The man's shoulder pressed against her cheek, but when he propped himself up, lifting the bulk of his weight off of her, I could make out the girl's face—deep-set almond eyes, broad forehead, a hollow sculpted by her cheekbones that no amount of cosmetic contouring could create. Her lips were wide and full. They curved gracefully into an upturned smile as she gazed into the camera. I had no idea that porn stars came with such finishing school features. I was about to say something to Adam, something cutting that would make him wither. But just then, on screen, the rhythmic intakes of air and their throaty replies—a sort of guttural call-and-response—were interrupted.

"Oh my God," said the man's voice. An involuntary utterance. "Oh my God! Minou…"

Why was Adam talking to the screen? And then the voice spoke again. "Minou."

Yes, it was definitely Adam's voice. But it was not coming from him. Not from the Adam sitting there at the desk. But from the man on screen.

Yes. It was Adam on the screen.

Yes. It was Adam on top of the beautiful girl.

Yes. It was Adam making love to another woman.

Yes. It was Adam calling this other woman "Minou"—the French word for "kitten" that he had called me when we were young.

That's why the scene seemed so intimate. Because the man was my husband. A vise tightened around my chest. I was seized by an urge to leap to Adam where he sat in his hydraulically controlled desk chair and pound him, to grab the closest, heaviest, object—

the Waterford clock perhaps—and shatter it over his skull. I tamped down the impulse. Not only because I was, by nature, no murderer, but because at that moment, the on-screen Adam shuddered. The words "God, yes" escaped from his lips with that very particular coital huskiness. Then he laid his cheek against the girl's—gently, ever so gently—and ran the back of his index finger along her quite perfect jaw.

I caught my breath long enough to see that this was not exactly my Adam, but an earlier Adam. A younger Adam. As young as when I had first met him. No, even younger. I could see it now. His on-screen face, at least what I could make out of it, was fuller and unlined. His hair was thicker and longer, flipping at the back of his neck. As if to prove the point, the girl reached around and twirled a lock around her finger as though this was something she did regularly, as though she had done it a thousand times. It was a gesture of ownership.

My stomach flipped.

Then the camera caught Adam opening his eyes. They looked softer than I had seen them in years. How they looked was full of promise.

Adam—the Adam seated right there right now at the computer—rested his head in his palms and covered his eyes with splayed fingers. His entire upper body sank into his hands, not with shame, but with the weight of insupportable loss. He remained slumped there, eyes covered, so that when I slipped away, he never knew that I had been standing in the doorway watching.

◆◆◆

BACK IN BED, I lay awake, trusting the darkness to calm my heart. No chance. Soon, Adam edged back in next to me. I pretended to be asleep. It was either that or unleash the fury ignited by the scene in his study. But I didn't want to do that. I wanted to imagine a scenario that made it all right, to come up with the twist that explained the crazy misunderstanding that had sent the second act spinning, but made everyone hug and laugh before the final credits. I had not come up with one by the time Adam began to snore.

I stole back down to Adam's study and stared at the computer. Only now there was no skin on skin, simply the screen saver, a chronological jumble of photos of our daughter. Stephanie as a toothless seven-year-old; then fourteen, dressed as a beatnik for Halloween; an infant babbling at a merry-go-round mobile; and last year, at sixteen, waving her driver's license.

I slid my hand along the side of the iMac, but detected no slot. I used both hands, running them around the perimeter of the thing. No slot anywhere. Adrenalized, I'd forgotten this evolutionary step. Could it have been that long since I'd slipped a CD into a computer for Stephanie to build SimCity or dance along with *Kids In Motion*? Of course Adam's new computer—already a year or two old—was slot-free. Everything was in the cloud, including his past, it seemed.

I scrutinized the desktop for an icon that might lead to the video. Nothing. I opened files inside of folders. More files. More folders. No clues. No "Sex Tape." Nothing unusual. I clicked on History. It had been wiped clean. Why would Adam erase his History? And why was he suddenly compelled to revisit it? I was out of luck. But then it came to me. The saga of The Incredible Vanishing Term Paper.

It had been last December, the week before winter break, when Stephanie's epic essay, "At Play In The Field of Roald Dahl's Mind" had evaporated into thin computer air. How-to manuals are anathema to me, but I had sat at Stephanie's side, a collection of "Dummies" books on the desk in front of us, until we recovered the treatise, safe and sound. "Just stay calm," I had repeated to Stephanie throughout the e-cheological dig. "Just stay calm." I said it to myself now. "Just stay calm, just stay calm." Then I clicked on the Finder icon.

I would not have believed the steps to retrieval had actually been filed away in my brain, but there they were. I opened the Spotlight window. When the computer asked what kind of file, I typed in "movie." I clicked on "within last day." Like magic, one title popped up. Only one. "A & A." Closed—2:47 a.m.

It took me a second to realize this was it, like staring at the winning numbers on a lottery ticket. I had missed the beginning of the tape earlier. Now, here it was. On screen, the bed was empty, waiting. The covers were thrown back, the sheets already rumpled. The camera swished onto target, *Blair Witch* style, accompanied by a soundtrack of giggling. I could hear Adam's voice, but could not make out what he was saying. Then the girl—unspeakably lovely, devastatingly young—entered the frame. She lay down on the bed, fully naked, as though she did this every day. Had I ever been that comfortable with my own nakedness in my whole life? No. I had not.

The camera racked into focus. I pictured Adam's face pressing against the eyepiece. Had they planned this for days or was it spontaneous? Had it been her idea? His? Was it commemorating a beginning or an end? Or was it just for fun?

I clicked on the little diagonal arrows at the bottom right, expanding the picture to full screen. Adam was there now, too, lying naked next to the girl. I stared at the screen: the two young lovers facing each other side by side, her leg draped over his, kissing and laughing. I could hear them laughing. Then the giggling dissolved, replaced by breathing—shallow and increasingly urgent. I hovered over the pause button. I knew I should click on it—stop right now—but could not. Impossible to click. I was held captive. This is where I had come in, as it were, as though it were a movie whose beginning I'd missed at the multi-plex: the moment when the girl turned to the camera and smiled. I steeled myself for what came next. "God, yes."

By the fourth time I played the video, I was mouthing the words along with Adam. By the seventh, I said them aloud with him. Like the flying monkeys in *The Wizard of Oz*, like Benjamin rattling the church window in *The Graduate*, like Sophie making the choice to hand over her daughter—the on-screen image of my pre-husband and this girl was now a part of my DNA.

I pushed back from the desk and wondered if I could let that be the end of it. Did I have it in me to keep my mouth shut?

♦♦♦

I WAS SILENT AT breakfast. I stared at the Ezekiel sprouted-grain English muffin on the plate in front of me. (I preferred the traditional white brand with its nooks and crannies, but always felt compelled to buy the healthier alternative.) I spread a thick coating of all-fruit apricot butter on the thing, though I could not bring myself to take a bite.

Adam sat across from me, spooning oatmeal into his mouth. I made it for him every morning, the long-cooking steel cut kind.

Monday through Friday, I stood at the stove stirring for fifteen minutes to keep his arteries Roto-Rootered. My reward? Finding him in the middle of the night, seated at his desk, watching himself fuck another woman. I resented how this episode had changed me overnight. I was never that girl who could use the word "fuck," especially as an active verb.

I stared at him, my head cocked slightly to the left. He knew what that meant. He was chewing too loudly. I had a thing about chewing noises and he knew it, had known it for twenty years. He made a show of the next bite—silent as could be—and I smiled in return. That was my part of the routine. And this morning, I didn't want anything to be off. My marriage was supposed to be like that Buddhist adage about hands—how we have a right hand and a left hand and they never fight or take credit. The left hand doesn't say, "I wrote that word." The right hand never says, "I turned that page." They simply help each other. When one hand is injured, the other takes over. My marriage was like those hands, intertwined so that sometimes you couldn't even tell which finger belonged to which hand. But this morning, I was the hand that stirred the oatmeal, and Adam was the hand on the mouse of the computer, and they were bodies apart.

Stephanie slouched in, grabbed a carton of yogurt from the refrigerator and plopped herself down at the table. Mornings were not her friend. "I can't pick a topic," she said. She was six months away from college applications, but there had already been great debate about the topic of a topic.

"We'll figure it out," I said.

"They're all so…" She rolled her eyes in exaggerated frustration.

"Are you with us or against us?" Adam said.

"With you," she said.

That was their morning routine. As always, he smiled at her response. I was still a sucker for my husband's smile. It had the power to transform everything. In an instant, the hand gripping the wooden spoon and the hand guiding the mouse found their way back to the same body. Our morning routines were intact. Our life was good. Everything was going to be okay.

◆◆◆

BUT IT WASN'T. No matter how I tried to execute a soul-deep count to ten, there was a buzzing inside me that I couldn't swat away.

I tried to stem the adrenaline with housework. I watered the cacti in the greenhouse window. I hunted in the back of the broom closet for the special cloth meant for cleaning electronics and ran it over every television and computer in the house, except the one in Adam's office. It produced a tiny effervescent crackle of static that sounded like the frayed edges of my nerves. I cleaned the coffee maker with a solution of white vinegar and water.

Once a year I took the time and care to dust my snow globe collection. I'd been collecting them since I was a little girl and they lived behind beveled glass doors in a cabinet in the den. I had dusted them seven or eight months ago, but there was always something meditative about the task, so I gathered a few shammies and a bottle of spritz. I removed each globe from its particular spot. Heading backward in time, there was Mickey Mouse, reminding me of Stephanie's first trip to Disneyland; a palm tree from an anniversary trip—our third—to Hawaii; and from a Ridgepoint School trip to DC, the tower at Dulles International with a jet taking off in the foreground, angling adventurously into the sky. There were probably thirty of them by now. It felt good to shine them up. It felt good to hold them. Their cool smoothness reassured me. I shook one or two, watching the minute bits of glitter snow swirl down. I loved the moment when the initial snowstorm abated and you could begin to glimpse the scene inside.

When I picked up the Big Apple—the Chrysler Building, the Empire State, the Statue of Liberty—I noticed something running along the outside, bisecting the Brooklyn Bridge. I dabbed at it with a rag, thinking it was a bit of schmutz, but there it stayed. I ran my finger along it, discovering a hairline fissure no more than an inch long, but deep enough to feel—a bona fide crack in the making. I poked a fingernail into the crack, causing it to grow a fraction of an inch. I stopped cleaning and set New York back down in its spot on the shelf, crack to the wall. But that left me staring at the back of the Statue of Liberty. I turned it around and walked away. The rest of the collection would have to wait. But then I turned back, opened the cabinet, removed New York with its ruinous crevasse, and stashed it in the drawer with all those CDs that hadn't been touched in forever.

I had killed a good hour and a half. Then I made a second pass through the house. I ran a cloth over the Caesarstone countertop in the kitchen. Marjoram was its official color. I passed through the den with its massive television where Stephanie channel surfed but no one ever really watched anything with any real attention. I glanced into the guest room where the plantation shutters needed to be dusted, but decided they could wait. I could not resist any longer. No amount of household spit and polish would scratch the itch that originated at the base of my spine, the very spot where that nightmare witch had poked me, and scattershot through my nervous system.

I was pulled to Adam's study. My fingers rested on the computer, settling into the keys' subtle scoop. Adam had left his email open. Why wouldn't he? He had nothing to hide. Not my husband. Despite last night. I scrolled through Old Mail. I did this without a second thought, without guilt. We were not the kind of couple who kept secrets from one another, or so I had believed. I recognized most names: his sister, assorted friends, online vendors he used often. I opened a few at random—a director thanking Adam for his painstaking attention to his first major deal and for believing in him long before; two from fellow agents concerning the fine points of a couple of deals—back-end participation, above the title credit—that sort of movie business thing; one from Sam Fielder, Adam's father and the eponymous head of the agency, advising him to drop the very client who had sent the thank-you email.

Farther down, there were a series of invitations to join LinkedIn. "Will you connect with me?" The question came, again and again, from one Aimee Laroche using the screen name ALAmateur D'art. Aimee. "A & A"—that's how the file had been labeled. Ridgepoint young ladies had been encouraged to study French as our foreign language, and I had followed the recommendation. However, after all these years using only the occasional culinary term, this is what I knew about that screen name: it had something to do with love and something to do with art. You could throw up. Adam had spent a summer in Paris during college. This French girl must have been a relic of that time, now begging him:

"Please connect with me."

"Please connect with me."

"Please connect with me."

She had to be the girl in the video, the girl with whom, it seemed to me, a fairly decent connection had already been made. At least Adam had not responded. Otherwise, I assumed, the requests would have stopped. Okay, that was good.

I clicked into Adam's Sent Mail, scanning for corresponding dates to the LinkedIn requests, but could find none. He had not sent any emails at all to ALAmateur D'art. I exhaled. I was mad at myself for cultivating an avowed disinterest in matters techno. If only I knew how LinkedIn worked. Maybe she wasn't badgering him. Maybe requests were generated automatically by a program that trawled contact lists. Maybe it was a coincidence that he'd been watching the video and she appeared on LinkedIn. *Calmez-vous*, I told myself, *calmez-vous*. Maybe he had watched the tape only to remind himself of exactly who she was, to jog his memory. To arouse nothing more.

I came up for air, having exhausted Old Mail and Sent Mail. But then, inevitably, my eye landed on Saved Mail. Of course—that's where something like this would be stashed. I opened the file and dragged the cursor down like a child following a line of text with her pointer finger. No Art Girl...no Art Girl...Then, there she was. I clicked on her name, desperate—possessed—but even so, I closed my eyes, instinctively aware that my old life hung in the moment before I opened them again.

My heart stuttered as I read. There were a few, rather formal confirmations that yes, this is really that Aimee—yes, this is really that Adam, from long ago. Then reintroductions containing the CVs of their lives since.

I had never heard of this woman, though I knew the names of the girls who had preceded me in Adam's life. There had been a Carrie and a Diane and a Trish. Their names had appeared in wacky stories that made me feel all the smarter, all the saner, all the more perfect for Adam. But never an Aimee.

Aimee. A name Adam had never spoken to me. That could only mean one thing. Unlike Carrie and Diane and Trish, Adam had been in love with this Aimee. Fuck.

I managed to exhale: Adam had immediately declared himself married. Aimee was not. *"Pas surprise,"* she had written, "I never marry."

*Pas surprise* indeed. Email after email. Then, there it was. "Remember your last night in Paris? I gave you our petit souvenir. These days one could have made a copy, yes?"

So that was it.

I set about searching Adam's cluttered office. The tape had to be there somewhere. I rummaged in the closet. In one corner were stacked file boxes I had last seen in our Public Storage locker years ago. Several had been slashed open. This mademoiselle had sent Adam on quite the scavenger hunt. I wondered if his heart went pitter-pat when he spotted it, labeled "Last Night in Paris" or simply "Adam and Aimee"—perhaps only with a crimson "X."

Behind Adam's desk sat a Japanese antique—a Sony Betamax— squatting on its own eBay shipping crate. Rigged up to the computer by way of a fistful of adapters and connectors were cords no doubt required to transfer the ancient tape to something he could watch on his computer in the privacy of his study in the middle of the night. Adam had been on a mission.

I dragged the file containing the video to the bottom of the screen and watched the trash can slurp up the eleven minutes. I hit Empty Trash to make sure I could not watch it again—not now, not ever. Of course, Adam could never watch it again either. Maybe I wanted to make him lose something the way I suddenly felt I had lost something, something irrecoverable. Maybe I wanted to leave him to wonder what human error—his own human error—had sucked the video into cyber oblivion. That would be the end of it.

I had been married for twenty years. I had swallowed hurt before. It comes with the territory. For richer and for poorer, in sickness and in health, in humiliation and disappointment. You vouch for some of it ahead of time; you discover some of it along the way.

# CHAPTER TWO

WHEN THE TELEPHONE RANG when we were kids, my sister and I would race to the nearest extension, shouting, "I'll get it!" We couldn't wait to find out who it was. "It's for you!" "It's for me!" Those days were over. Caller ID ruined the surprise.

As the computer was asking me if I was sure I wanted to permanently erase the items in the trash, the phone rang. Yes, I was sure. I clicked on Empty Trash and, as it did its thing, checked the Caller ID. I didn't feel like talking to anyone, but when you're a mom, you always check. It was, as Stephanie had programmed it, Mom's BFF.

"Meet me at the Country Mart," said Gwen.

"Not today."

"What's going on?

"Bad day."

"What?" Ours was a friendship way past extraneous words.

"I can't even…," I trailed off.

"One of those. But listen…I've got to buy a bathing suit." Gwen allowed me as long a silence as I needed.

"I'll be there," I said. *Maybe I should get out of the house. Out of my head.* No matter what you just saw…over and over…on your husband's computer, there are some things you don't make your oldest friend do alone. Like confronting the naked torture of a three-way mirror.

◆◆◆

GWEN WAS WAITING ON a bench at one of the picnic tables in the south patio. I knew she would be there. That had become our rendezvous spot.

We had grown up going to the Brentwood Country Mart, eating chicken baskets and licking the swirled peaks off soft-serve cones. As children, we made fun of the cantankerous old man who ran the candy store, though his crabbiness never stopped us from handing over piles of coins for Abba-Zabas or Bonomo Turkish Taffy. We stuffed our allowances into our pockets for trips to the toy store and deliberated in front of shelves of Barbie outfits, trying to decide between Garden Party and Solo in the Spotlight.

But now the Mart had outgrown us. It was no longer the neighborhood hangout, a rambling red barn with a separate grocery, produce and fish-and-poultry emporia. There was no longer a bakery with a bench for kids to stand on so they could peer inside and watch frosting smoothed onto a layer cake while waiting for the nice lady to hand over a sprinkle cookie.

It never ceased to amaze me. Now, in the space once inhabited by the mom-and-pop deli, there was a Chi-Chi restaurant that served a twenty-five dollar lobster roll. Now, there was an ice creamery delivering "small batches of happiness" in flavors like Thai iced tea and fig jam with goat cheese. Now, where the cubbyhole of a bookstore once stood there was a jewelry store where chunky pendants and studded cuffs were secreted away in velvet-lined drawers opened only upon request by a leggy girl with an Australian accent. Now, the toy store carried only handcrafted wooden toys imported from Germany. Now, paparazzi lurked in corners hoping to snap a shot of Reese Witherspoon or Jennifer Garner clutching an oversized Frappacino.

The Brentwood Country Mart had gone to its own head.

So, over the past few years, Gwen and I had relocated to the back patio, out of the fray.

Gwen waved when she spotted me approaching from the main courtyard. "I've been sitting here breathing the smell of the chicken. Want to split a basket? What am I talking about?! I've got to wear a bathing suit this weekend. Can you believe it? A pool party? Before June?"

"We can do this," I assured her, always at the ready with the pom-poms. That's me.

"First tell me what's going on with you," she said. "What happened?"

"Nothing," I lied and she knew it. She gave me a look. "Nothing important. It's just me being me."

"Do you need me to talk you out of being you?"

"No," I said, "I need you to find you a bathing suit."

We headed for the tiny beachwear store where you paid dearly for the privilege to mix and match tops and bottoms.

"Let's go in here for a sec," Gwen suggested as she entered Calypso, one of the boutiques that opened onto the patio.

"I think we should do the bathing suit thing first and get it over with," I said. Getting things over with is my MO.

"No. Not yet. I have to build up to seeing my thighs."

I nodded. Who didn't get that?

I followed Gwen into the shop. Each rack was devoted to a single color palette. I fought the attraction of the gray and black, forcing myself to explore the blues and pinks. Maybe it would feel like summer was on its way if I bought something pink. Maybe it would make me feel like the video had never happened, or at least like it would one day soon be a funny story.

"My name is Heather." A teenaged salesgirl appeared at my elbow. A necklace with her name written in rose gold script shone against her golden skin.

Gwen emerged from the dressing room in a diaphanous celadon tunic.

"Can I wear this over my bathing suit?"

I circled her, scrutinizing from all angles. "I think you can."

"Thank God."

"You're crazy," I said. "You look great."

"I know I pay you the big bucks to say things like that, but I look like the Pillsbury doughboy."

"Come on, Poppin' Fresh. Let's go get you a bathing suit."

Gwen studied herself in the full-length mirror. I suspected it was tilted at some trick-of-the-trade boutique angle. It made her look an inch taller and absolved her of a good three pounds. She wiggled her toes. "I like this polish color. It makes my toes look skinny."

I had never considered the slenderness of my own toes. But before I could contemplate toe chubbiness, there came the sound of brushes dusting a snare drum. Gwen leapt to her phone as Marvin

Gaye crooned: "Ooooh, baby." Tammi Terrell joined in. "Ain't nothin' like the real thing, baby..."

Gwen held the phone in her hand, watching it sing.

"Go ahead," I said. "Take it."

"I don't want to. I like it when he leaves me a message."

"Nathan?"

"Nathan's over. Done and dusted."

"Who's this?" I nodded toward the phone. Marvin and Tammi stopped singing.

"Bernard," she said, disappearing back into the dressing room.

"Bernard? I don't know Bernard."

"He leaves the best voice mail." Gwen's arm shot out from the dressing room, handing me the tunic. "He gives great email, too." Gwen was dressed in her own clothes again. "If only when I was actually with him, he could make me feel like I do when I read his email."

We stood at the register as the salesgirl struggled to make the computer accept the number that identified her as her. "It thinks I'm supposed to be at lunch," she explained.

"Once," Gwen continued, "I left him in bed and went in the other room to read the emails he'd sent me to remind myself of why I was in bed with him in the first place." Even Heather looked up from her task. Gwen went on. "I slept with him on the second date. I'm having standards issues," said Gwen, not even sotto voce. "And..."

"And...?" I prompted.

Gwen raised her eyebrows and hunched her shoulders in an exaggerated shrug. "I sort of..."

Heather handed Gwen the credit card slip to sign, but couldn't find a pen. I produced one from my purse.

"You sort of what?" I asked.

"You know."

"I don't know. You sort of what?" I asked again.

"She faked it," said Heather, taking the signed slip from Gwen.

"What she said," said Gwen, cocking her head toward Heather. "Actually, not quite." She was talking to Heather now, as much as to me. "Let's just say, I allowed myself to be misinterpreted."

"Gotcha," said Heather. "Have a good one!" she said, handing over the bag with the tunic nested in yellow tissue.

Gwen and I left Heather folding scarves. We headed through the south patio around the corner to Malia Mills. "I'm warning you," she said, "I've grown back fat."

I had no way to spin back fat. I knew only that French Girl certainly did not have any.

# CHAPTER THREE

WHEN I GOT HOME, I did what I had stopped myself from doing earlier. I Googled the name: Aimee Laroche. I wondered what I would have done if I had found myself embroiled in this scenario fifteen, even ten years ago. Would I have hired a private detective to track this woman down? Would I have passed sleepless nights waiting for him to hand over a manila envelope containing long lens black-and-whites of a femme fatale smoking Gauloises at a sidewalk café? Probably not. But Googling was irresistible. Like everything on screen, it required no effort. It was so easy.

I chased the "click" trail like a storybook waif following breadcrumbs. Within minutes, I found myself face to face with the vital statistics of the life belonging to one Aimee Laroche. The woman owned a gallery on the Rive Gauche. Of course she would be a Left Bank kind of woman, still steeped in the art scene that had attracted Adam so long ago. I clicked on the gallery website and scrolled through examples of the work shown there, largely tired reimaginings of Abstract Expressionism. This Aimee probably touted them all as the second coming.

How could I compete, I wondered. I felt so…bourgeois. Of course, the word for how I felt had to be French. Of course, it would evoke everything Adam and this girl would have disdained when they were young. Of course, this Left Bank Gallery Girl would have known things at nineteen that I still didn't know, even as I sat here, a middle-aged woman, in my husband's study in my home on the west side of LA. This Left Bank Gauloise Gallery Girl knew French things.

Staring at the list of Google results for Aimee Laroche, I willed myself to stop scrolling, but could not resist the siren lure of the screen. It gripped me in a kind of narcosis. I clicked on files I'd already opened ten times. Then something caught my eye: under My Folders, there, along with Finances, House Stuff, and all the rest, was a folder named ALR. I'd noticed it before, in passing, but I'd thought Adam had made a charitable donation to a disease. Now I got it. Aimee Laroche. ALR. The charity known as Ancient Lover Revisited.

I clicked on it. A string of emails, seemingly endless, assaulted me. A quick scroll to the bottom traveled back in time, nine months to be exact. Nine months. Three quarters of a year. A whole pregnancy. As in the creation of an entire human life. That's how long the string of emails was. Back and forth, forth and back, from her to him, from him to her. Between my husband and another woman. This couldn't have happened. This wasn't happening. Not my life.

I started with the one at the top, the most recent, dated a mere eleven days ago. It was from her. It began: "Mon Chèr Adam…I am wondering if perhaps it would be possible for us to meet."

My lungs tightened like an asthmatic's, the room drained of air. My stomach spasmed. My heart ricocheted off my ribs like a pinball. But I couldn't stop reading. Every nerve inside me had fired, but my body was dead weight in the chair, powerless against the screen.

There was no response from Adam to her question…not yet.

I scrolled down to the bottom of the email chain, going back in time, month after month to the beginning. My finger, icy and damp, clicked on the first one. It picked up where the emails languishing in Saved Mail had left off. Adam must have neglected to scoop those few into this special folder. How sloppy of him. But why bother? Why would his loving wife be sifting through his email? She wouldn't. But she was.

The first exchange was innocent enough, if innocence could pertain when another woman was involved, a woman who had once arched her back with pleasure at your husband's touch. French Girl wrote that she was delighted to be back in touch. Adam wrote that he was, too. She said she thought of him often, more often than he could guess. He said that he had thought of her, too. He didn't say how often. Did that mean he'd thought of her once or twice in thirty years or that he thought of her every single day of his life? Was she always lurking in the way-back of his brain?

"Remember that night? Our last night *ensemble*?" Somehow she knew precisely which word would be more alluring in French.

"I remember," Adam wrote.

"Our last night," she responded. "We made that *petit souvenir*." So the tape had been their last night. The night before Adam returned to college, to meet me, to the rest of his ordinary American life.

"I might still have it somewhere," Adam wrote. "Stuffed in a box."

And then, a few weeks later, a subject line from Adam: FOUND IT!! Two exclamation points—as though he were not the powerful man who, day after day, fit together the jigsaw pieces of major motion pictures to build blockbusters, but instead a teenaged boy unable to contain his exhilaration after actually having had sex. I had never got an email from him with even one exclamation point.

"I hope it makes you smile to see us together," she said.

"It does..." he wrote, "very much."

More back-and-forth followed, both of them trying too hard at black-and-white movie banter. A longish email thread dealt with their careers, how each of their professions demanded they keep artistic egos buoyed. She talked about an artist she represented who insisted on wearing a patch over one eye when he painted so that he could reinvent perspective. Adam threw out some amusing anecdotes about the movie stars on his roster. He even trotted out an old favorite from his father's heyday—how, when asked by a director to smoke for a part, a young Richard Gere assured him, "I can smoke without smoking."

"Like you," wrote the French Girl. "That is how I remember you. Smoking without smoking." Now my husband was a movie star.

She asked if Adam was still painting. He said, "Not much. Life gets in the way of the things we think we want to do the most." Is that how he felt? Our life was getting in the way? I was in his way.

She segued into asking about his marriage.

"My marriage," I actually said out loud. "That's *my* marriage."

That might have been the moment when I could have stopped. It was probably the moment when I might have known I should have stopped, that if I kept reading, there would be no un-reading. There would be no forgetting. The next word and the word after that and the word after that would become part of me, would reshape each and every cell, warping them malignantly. I had enough—more than enough—to confront Adam about what had happened here, what was happening here, with this other woman. I had plenty. Any more would be suicidal. But of course I would keep reading. There would be no stopping until the last word had been read. And read again. I might have pretended I needed all the facts, a prosecutor building her case. But I was beyond needing. I craved the next email like a junkie, so propelled by anguish that I had to have more—torment as narcotic. Only every last word could somehow set me free from the torture unleashed by the word before it. It was that moment when you see an accident coming—when the inevitability of the crash hits you as hard as the car itself—but you can't do anything to stop it. When your heart is thump-thumping against your ribs and your nervous system sparks, insanity piggybacks onto the adrenaline rush and gets a free ride. I had no psychic surge protector.

I kept reading.

Adam wrote, "You know how marriages are," then leapt quickly to: "I have the most wonderful daughter." A non-answer followed by a non-sequitur—a politician sidestepping a question by clicking into a sound bite.

"I do know how marriages are," wrote the French Girl. "That is why I never marry!" And then she did that semicolon, colon, parenthesis thing to show that she was winking.

She continued to probe. Finally, Adam gave her what she wanted. He wrote, "To be honest, I am so disappointed."

And she was off. "You mustn't be," she stroked him. "You are so talented. Gifted, mon chèr."

"That was a long time ago," he insisted, but only so she'd keep going.

She wrote back. The time stamp showed it was mere moments later. "Talent like yours does not go poof. I remember your work. And I remember how you made me laugh. I remember everything of our time together," she wrote. "Every little thing. And as I recall, every little thing was not so little!"

Adam didn't write back. I hoped he had the decency to be embarrassed.

A few weeks went by—nothing. She had to try harder: "Chèr Adam, I hope you do not think me too forward, but I am wondering, how is your intimate life? *La vie sexuelle?*"

Again, he didn't write back.

She tried again. "Do you remember what we were like together? I would pass the entire day thinking about you so that by the time the night came and we were together, *ensemble—toi et moi*—I was already…" The ellipsis needed no translation. The words left off were the same in English or in French.

I thought long and hard about reading his response—a good nano-second or two—even though I knew that opening the next email would probably lead to sudden death, as in Coroner's Report to read: Death by discovery of husband's opinion of marital sex life.

"I always loved that you were a little too forward," he wrote. Winky face. Honestly—a grown man, a powerful man in a business full of powerful men, using a winky face. He went on. "Getting to know each other's bodies is exciting. The unfamiliar is an aphrodisiac, isn't it? Then it becomes something different. It's comfortable."

"I suppose comfortable is nice," she said. The bitch. "Do you ever imagine what it would be like between us *encore*? To discover each other all over again? New but full of wonderful memory. The best of all worlds, *n'est-ce pas*?" And I saw her face—her dewy, teenaged face—daring me, "Go ahead. Make him feel like I can." I saw her staring straight at me the way she had gazed directly into the camera lens—fearless, shameless, secure in her own magnificence.

"Of course I imagine," he wrote. "I imagined even before I found the video."

"And what do you imagine?"

"Part is imagining. Part is remembering," answered my husband. "I remember your taste."

"The taste of me…where?"

"Everywhere. I remember how every inch of your body tasted. Like oranges and the sea."

I closed my eyes and pressed the heels of my palms into my eyelids, willing my eyes to recede into my head to a spot somewhere far behind my mind's eye. But there was no such spot. There was nothing left of me but my mind's eye.

I opened my eyes and kept reading.

"I dreamed of you last night," she wrote.

He wrote back. "I've dreamed of you, too. More than once."

And there I was, back at the top of the chain with French Girl seducing my husband, "I was wondering if perhaps it would be possible for us to meet."

My pinball heart went TILT.

◆◆◆

FOR THE NEXT SIX hours I sat in the easy chair in my bedroom, motionless. I did not answer the phone. I did not go to the kitchen. I did not go to the bathroom. I sat.

At one point I tried to move an arm, almost as an experiment— to see if I could—but my brain could not rally the electrical impulses needed to flex the muscle required for this simple act. My body was detached from me—a puppet, a marionette, whose strings had become tangled, if not cut entirely.

There was nothing I could do, let alone wanted to do, other than sit in that chair. No television. No music. No book. Even sleep required too much effort.

I might have reread the emails, but there was no need. Every word was etched into my brain—branded there, molten and deep. I might have managed to budge from the chair to look at the video again. But the video no longer existed. How close were we to a remake? *French Girl—Part Deux.*

And what did it matter? She had invaded his subconscious. He was dreaming of her. Maybe I was, too. Maybe she was that witch who'd been lying in wait for me since I was a little girl.

I wondered if some fresh air would rouse me from my torpor. But that was impossible. Moving would require figuring out that baffling brain-muscle communication thing. Besides, what if the pool man showed up? Or the gardener? Or even the meter reader? I would have to engage in small talk, at least say hello. I could not do that, not today. The very thought of making chit-chat produced the same butterflies that had afflicted me at Ridgepoint when I had to read a book report in front of the class.

No. Staying in my chair was the only option.

I realized my pinky had gone pins-and-needles. An elastic thread had unraveled from the cuff of my sweater. I had been wrapping the thread around my finger unconsciously. My pinky had turned white, but I could not find the end of the thread, having coiled it around itself too tightly. I stared at my finger for several minutes. Finally, I opened the desk drawer, my muscles tight and stiff. I rummaged for a cuticle scissor and tried to slide the tiny blade under the thread. But I couldn't see clearly enough at this mid-range. No pair of glasses hung around my neck at the ready.

I had to navigate the scissor under the thread by the feel of it against my skin and hope for the best as I snipped. When I freed my finger successfully, the sight of color rushing back brought tears to my eyes. I was alive after all.

For the first time since discovering Adam in front of the computer—on the computer and *on* the computer—I cried. The tears empowered me, a small victory over paralysis. They fueled me enough so that I could stand from my chair, walk into Adam's closet, take down his largest suitcase, throw it open and jam it full of his clothes.

# CHAPTER FOUR

ADAM HAD LEFT FOR work assuming he would return home that evening to his regular wife. But she was no longer there. She had been swept out to sea by a cyber undertow and deposited on the distant shore of how things used to be. He found me sitting at the kitchen table, hands wrapped around a mug of hot coffee. It tasted of acid. I held it only for warmth against the chill that had started in my trembling fingertips and snaked its way along my limbs before settling in my core.

"What's wrong?" he said, alarmed.

I'd had all afternoon to come up with an answer to that question. But I didn't have one.

Adam took the mug from me and placed it on the table. "What happened?"

"I had a nightmare last night."

He held me in his arms, guiding my head to his shoulder with one hand. "That spooked you this much?"

"I couldn't go back to sleep."

"You're exhausted."

"I'm not exhausted."

"Are you sick?"

Adam leaned back and looked at me. "What happened?" he asked again.

"I couldn't fall back to sleep, so I came downstairs. And there you were."

It took him a minute. Then his head dropped. It took another minute before he nodded. "Okay," he said. "It's just a stupid video I made a thousand years ago."

"Don't lie to me."

"I'm not lying. Honestly, I knew her that summer in Paris. I was nineteen years old, for Christ's sake." He reached for me again, but I pushed him away. "I'll delete the thing," he said. "I'll burn the original. I'll make it gone forever. Okay?" He wasn't mad. He simply wanted to make this conversation go away.

"I already did," I said.

"You went onto my computer?"

"I did."

He recalibrated. "Okay," he said. "Good, it's gone."

"That's right. The video is gone."

"Over with," he said. He took a sip of the coffee to punctuate the declaration.

"Except for one little thing," I said.

"What's that?"

"The emails."

I could tell that for a minute, he considered asking, "What emails?" but he had the good grace not to. Instead he said, "I'm sorry you found them."

"You're sorry I found them," I repeated.

"I am."

"Not sorry you wrote them?"

"That, too. Of course that, too."

"Just not sorry enough not to write them in the first place."

"You wouldn't understand."

"Oh, I understand perfectly! You're having an affair."

"I am not," he said. "I am not having an affair." He said it as though this was a conclusion he had reached, as though he'd already had that conversation in his own mind.

"What do you call it?"

"I call it stupid, childish fantasy."

"I'm supposed to be your fantasy." By now I was on my feet.

"You're supposed to be my wife."

"Well, thank you for that," I said.

"Maura…"

"Let me get this straight. You're upset that you got found out, not that you've been writing to another woman. About how she tasted—how she *tasted*, Adam—and I'm supposed to be your good, little, real life wife."

"C'mon," he said. "You're overreacting."

Short circuit of the brain. I scrambled to retrieve a few random words before it fully exploded, synaptic fireworks, and would have to be scraped from the interior of my skull with a spatula.

"Overreacting!" I screamed. "I am not overreacting. By definition, I cannot be overreacting because this is the way I'm reacting. My reaction is my reaction. This situation—the situation you created, the situation I came downstairs in the middle of the night to find in my house with my husband—calls for exactly the reaction I'm having. In fact, I'm not sure I'm reacting enough. If I knew how to have a bigger reaction I would. I think I might try for spontaneous combustion! Overreacting? You wish I were overreacting. If only I were overreacting!"

I threw open the hatch at the back of the Gevalia coffee maker and retrieved the soggy paper funnel full of Peet's French Roast. I yanked it from its compartment with such force that it split open, sending wet grounds across the countertop and onto the floor.

Adam went for a roll of paper towel, but I grabbed it from him and began ripping off sheets, wadding them up, swiping at the grounds. Then I chucked the whole mess back onto the floor. We both stared at the pile of coffee grounds scattered across the save-the-forest bamboo.

"Look," he said, suddenly calm. "Sometimes I can't sleep. Like you. I go downstairs. One night, there she was. I was curious. You can understand that. The past was…well, the past was so long ago. I admit it, okay? I wanted to remember what it felt like to be young and in love…."

"You have to be reminded of what it's like to be in love?"

"That's not what I said."

"That's exactly what you said."

"That's not what I meant. Don't twist things."

"If you can't remember how something feels, it's because you don't feel it anymore."

"Of course I know what love feels like. I love you every day of my life. It's the young part that's gone missing."

"Because you're stuck with someone who needs to wear glasses on a chain."

He snapped his neck like he'd been whiplashed. His gesture of *What the hell…?*

"You told me that's what old ladies do," I said. "Wear glasses around their neck."

"I don't know what the hell you're talking about. All I know is my life is half over—more than half over—and it's not the life I thought I was going to live. That's all. It's just a fact. I thought I was going to live one life and now I find myself sitting in an office in a building with my father's name on it. Aimee reminded me of that other life." The sound of him saying her name sent bile rising in my throat.

"Why didn't you say these things to me?"

"I don't know," he said. "It was easier, I guess. Safer."

"If you're not safe here with me, where are you safe?"

He shook his head. He couldn't figure it out either.

"She wants to see you."

"That's not going to happen," he said.

"You're lying."

"It's the truth. I didn't write back. I was never going to write back."

"Why should I believe you?"

"Because I'm telling you the truth. I've never lied to you."

"What do you call all those emails? They're a great big giant lie."

"No, they're not. This is going to sound crazy, but it was like therapy."

"Swell!" I said. "Now she's your fantasy *and* your therapist. Well, isn't she special?"

"I know it sounds crazy. Maybe I'm crazy. Maybe I should go to a real therapist."

"I'm driving you crazy. I've been driving you crazy for twenty years. Is that it?"

"No!" Adam took a deep breath. "It's just that… I'm not sure how to say this. I feel like I've lost my way."

"Give me a break," I said. "Surely you can come up with a better line. Call in the script doctor."

Adam stared at the coffee sludge on the floor. "It happens to be the truth."

"You've lost your way?" I pointed to the door. "It's right there."

He hefted the suitcase that had been glowering from a corner of the kitchen and headed for the door to the garage.

"Adam…," I said. He turned, hopefully.

"I was your Minou. I was supposed to be your one and only Minou."

◆◆◆

I IMAGINED ADAM CHECKING into a hotel for the night, one of those high-end beach getaways near the office. There was no way he would go to his father's house, overflowing as it was with his father's questions under the most ordinary of circumstances. I expected him to phone, waited for him to phone, but he did not. I wanted to apologize and make it better. I wanted to yell at him. I wanted to invoke the five second rule for saying hurtful things as though they were a cookie dropped on the floor. I wanted to haul out every thing he'd ever done to annoy me and throw it on the bonfire. I wanted him to come back so that I could beg him to hold me. I wanted him to come back so that I could pummel him with my fists. I wanted to make love to him. I wanted to kill him.

I roamed the house, always ending up in Adam's study, furious with myself for having deleted the video, relieved that I had.

As for the emails, now I deleted them, too. Not en masse, but one by one, reading each of them one last time. As if that mattered. As if I didn't already know them all by heart. As if they weren't going to reverberate in the echo chamber of my brain for the rest of my life.

# CHAPTER FIVE

THE NEXT DAY AT lunchtime Adam appeared with sandwiches from our favorite deli: one pastrami and one corned beef. A peace offering. I indulged my attraction to nitrates only once or twice a year. Today the smell of the rye bread reminded me of motor oil. I pulled a slice of meat from between the bread, held it for a moment, then put it back in its gray cardboard take-out box next to a squashy paper cup of cole slaw.

Next to the sandwiches, Adam had placed a piece of paper on the kitchen table.

I unfolded it.

Across the top was scribbled: "The Top Ten Reasons Why I Divorced My Husband."

I looked at him. What kind of a stunt was this?

"Read it," he insisted. He had to raise his voice to be heard over the gardener's leaf blower. It sounded like a plane was taking off in the backyard.

I read the list silently.

10. He was arrested for picking up a transvestite on Hollywood Boulevard.

9. The housekeeper was giving him blowjobs on Mondays, Wednesdays, and Fridays.

8. He cleaned out our savings for drugs.

7. He took my best friend to Big Sur.

6. What happened in Vegas didn't stay in Vegas.

5. He wasn't philanthropic enough. (Code: he didn't have enough money.)

4. He was having an affair at that sleazy motel on Ventura Blvd.

3. He had another wife and three kids in Cincinnati.

2. He was looking at a sex tape with a girl from his past.

1. He just pissed me off.

Adam didn't have to explain. Every single one of those things had happened in the marriages of people we knew. Except #2. Now that was the thing happening in this house, in this marriage. Not to mention that the video had come with its own Special Edition commentary in the form of a chain of emails.

"See?" Adam pushed the paper closer to me. He was trying so hard to be both contrite and cheery that I could not look at him. My eyes darted around the Tuscan Yellow kitchen. Getting the yellow right had been a saga. I had asked the painter if he could mix something less citrus, more butter. Then, once that was on the wall, I corrected myself. "I meant," I told him, "unsalted."

"We finally got the yellow right," I said.

"You've made a beautiful home," he said. "I don't thank you enough." He exhaled long and loudly, signaling the craziness was over.

"I don't want thanks. I want your respect. I want you to respect me enough not to be flirting with some French woman, not to be talking about your private life with some stranger! Our private life! Our intimate private life!"

"I do respect you," he said.

"You're just tired of me."

"That's not true."

"Then why?" I said. "Why, Adam? Tell me."

"I wish I could." He shook his head as though he himself were confounded. "It was simple curiosity," he said finally. "If some old boyfriend contacted you, you'd be curious. Anyone would be."

"Curiosity is one thing. Starting a relationship is another."

"It wasn't a relationship"

"What would you call it?"

"I don't know. A pen-pal thing."

A laugh shot out of me, more of a snort actually. "Come on, Adam. You may have convinced yourself of that, but I read those emails."

"Okay," he said.

Neither of us said anything for a long moment.

"I can't believe you ever made a sex tape in the first place." I said. "You never asked me to make a sex tape. Did you want to but you thought I was too much of a prude? Or did you not even care?"

"Don't start...Maura..."

"Was it too boring with me? Why immortalize something so ho-hum?"

"Okay," said Adam. "You want to go make a sex tape? You want to go upstairs and make one right now?" He grabbed me by the wrist. My pulse beat hard against his fingers. We both stared at his hand, astounded by this aberration: the sight of his hand gripping my wrist. Adam let go and looked down at the floor, shaking his head. He waited for me to say something. He picked up the list and forced a chuckle. Maybe I would laugh with him. But I didn't. He stared at the paper. "We're not anything like those other couples."

"That's what I used to think," I said. A tear slipped down my cheek. "You never say, 'God, yes' with me."

"I beg your pardon," he said.

"That's what you said with her. In the video. 'God, yes.' You've never said that with me. Never once in our whole life."

"I have no control over what I say at times like that."

"Bad answer," I said. "Clearly I never make you see God."

"You know you've lost your mind, don't you? Like...!" He whistled as his hand whooshed over his head to demonstrate my brain taking off for another planet.

"Don't make fun of me," I said. And then I hauled off and punched him in the arm. Hard. He did not even try to rub away the pain. "You're obviously madly in love with her," I said.

"Jesus, Maura! It had nothing to do with love." And then, "I was in love with her when I was nineteen. There. Okay? That was a long, goddamn time ago. Do the math."

"If you're not in love with her, why are you writing to her?"

"It's fun to pretend. And...she's nice to me," Adam said.

"She doesn't have to listen to you chew."

♦♦♦

I SAT ALONE AT the kitchen table and studied the Top Ten list lying in front of me between the uneaten corned beef and the uneaten pastrami.

I thought I believed in shared history, in riding out the bad times, in commitment. I knew those were all the right things to believe in. I had believed that Adam would always be worth the effort. I kept picturing the way he walked when he was young, the way he moved through space, his torso tilted forward ever so slightly. He looked like he had somewhere to go, like he was headed somewhere important and couldn't wait to get there. But what he had been leaning into turned out to be the wind of responsibility. So much responsibility—to his clients, to his father, to Stephanie, to me, to adulthood, to real life. I understood how a person could want to escape that.

I resisted the impulse to run after him. I got it. Who didn't want to escape real life? But that didn't make actually doing it all right, even if it was only online. Betrayal was betrayal, online or off.

Suddenly, I was starving, sick with emptiness. I stood at the kitchen counter and wolfed down the sandwiches. Both of them. All four halves. I dunked the last half in Russian dressing bite by bite until there was nothing left but a string of peppered fat.

◆◆◆

I GOT INTO BED early, reminding myself that I often luxuriated in a night alone when Adam was at a screening. Of course this was different, this pajama party for one had a new wrinkle. Adam was not going to be late. Adam was not coming home at all.

I distracted myself with reality television. I fell into a *Love It Or List It* marathon, caught up in the homeowners' dilemma: to remodel and stay or to give up on a lost cause house and move. When black mold was uncovered in a basement and the homeowners fled, I became too demoralized to watch another episode. I picked up my book and dragged myself to the end of *Gatsby*. I read the last line: "So we beat on, boats against the current, borne back ceaselessly into the past." I marked the passage with a yellow highlighter, then closed the book, weighing whether Fitzgerald's use of alliteration was too heavy-handed or just right.

I turned on *The Late Show* and set the sleep timer for ninety minutes, hoping I would be soundly asleep by the time the TV clicked off. I still yearned for David Letterman. They could do all that pushing-the-envelope stuff on cable—full frontal, F-bombs, chic lesbianism—but when Dave threw it to commercial, slid his chair in close to his guest and whispered in her ear, it was the sexiest moment on television. *That* was compelling. The wondering. The surmising. The unquestionable cleverness of Dave's private remark. Stephen Colbert was too ebullient to conjure even a whisper of sexual tension. You have to be something of a tortured soul for that. I missed Dave.

I clicked the sleep timer button on the remote again. Six minutes had elapsed and I wanted them back. I was going to have that much trouble falling asleep tonight. I would need every minute of opiate flicker.

I could not slow my mind. Over the years, when I had needed to focus, I had developed the habit of telling myself the story of Stephanie's birth. I began, hearing my own voice in my head.

I moved through the details, one after the other. The slightest trickle of water down the inside of my thigh awakening me at 5:00 a.m. Realizing I had forgotten to make Jell-O for the day of clear liquids ahead. The all-consuming urgency about Jell-O readiness. Getting out of bed. Being so careful not to disturb Adam who would need all the rest he could get for the coming hours. Creeping into the kitchen. Four boxes of Jell-O waiting. Filling the kettle, waiting for the water to boil, thinking, *This is it...this is it...*Making all four boxes. Red, green, yellow, and orange, as if preparing for a new life of primary colors.

I continued telling myself the story. How Adam steadied me when we took a walk around the block to hasten my labor. How he set a pink stuffed rabbit on top of the TV in the labor room as my "focal point." And, finally, how Stephanie slid out into the world, eyes wide open, ready to see everything there would ever be to see.

I kept going, segueing more into subvocalized incantation than story. I kept going, past the point of Stephanie's birth. I had never done that before. But that night I kept going, conjuring an image of Adam cradling the tiny thing in his arms and trundling her off to her first bath. I remembered bringing Stephanie home, Adam carrying her into the house, still strapped into the car seat with all those harnesses that flummoxed me for weeks. "Baby in a bucket," we called her, as though she were so many wings and thighs from KFC. I remembered Adam carrying her into the waiting nursery, all sea foam green and gingham. I remembered going into the kitchen and finding every bowl we owned—ramekin, soup bowl, cereal bowl—filled with Jell-O, uneaten and encased in a springy skin.

By now, I had nearly fallen asleep, but not quite. So I started over. "Her water broke at five in the morning..."

Without realizing, I switched to the third person, slipping out of my own life long enough to fall asleep.

# CHAPTER SIX

EVEN BEFORE I OPENED my eyes, I knew something was off. If it had been a few years earlier, I would have assumed I was getting my period, but that hadn't happened for nearly eighteen months now, so the likelihood was slim. I wondered how long you can milk the concept of perimenopause before having to drop the "peri" and declare yourself wizened.

I rolled over onto my left side and opened one eye. A strand of hair clung to my eyelashes. A silver thread was woven into the auburn. When I tried to flick it away, I felt the tug at my scalp. It was coming from my own head. The room began to spin. A sadist at the wheel on the teacup ride. I closed my eye and tried to regain my equilibrium; how does equilibrium even come into play when you are lying in bed? The spinning continued deep in my head, followed by a wave of nausea so intense that it caught me by surprise, like a sudden burst of morning sickness when I was newly pregnant and had not eaten breakfast soon enough. I should have known, had I been able to think, that nausea would accompany dizziness this ferocious.

I lay there for a while, twenty minutes maybe. Then I rolled onto the floor like a child trained to escape a smoke-filled room and crawled to the bathroom. I was drenched in sweat. My nightgown clung to my chest in patches. I tried to focus on the grout lines between the limestone tiles on the bathroom floor, but my pupils were fibrillating. Eyes closed, I inched toward the toilet on my hands and knees, bumping into the claw-footed tub once or twice along the way. By the time I bent over the bowl, sweat saturated my hairline and collected in the creases of my elbows and at the backs of my knees. I grabbed onto the toilet to steady myself, holding on for dear life. I vomited until there was nothing left. Then I vomited some more.

Even so, having my face stuck in the toilet bowl was, in so many ways, easier than having it stuck in my husband's computer.

I grabbed a towel and wadded it into a pillow. I was going to be spending some time here on the bathroom floor. I tried opening my eyes and caught sight of the inside of my left thigh. It was smooth, even relatively firm—all the yoga saw to that—but a network of purple squiggles, slender as silk thread, seemed to have appeared since I'd last caught a glimpse of this patch of leg. When had my skin grown tissue-paper-thin and transparent? When had all these capillaries exploded to form a sort of close-up from a Thomas Guide, roads stopping abruptly and leading nowhere?

After a while—I had no idea how long—I began the crawl back to bed. I paused in front of the sink closest to the toilet—Adam's sink—and managed to brace myself against the counter. We'd gone for the Costa Esmerelda granite, quarried in Sardinia. Who cares? I knew only that the stone was cool where my belly rested against it. Momentary relief. I splashed my face. Unable to reach for a towel, I raised the hem of my nightgown to dry my face, locking eyes with myself in the mirror. The whites were shot red and the skin underneath appeared bruised. I wondered if I'd hit my face without remembering, but no—blood vessels had burst from the force of the vomiting. Talk about insult to injury. I panicked—could this be a permanent condition?—and tried to focus in the mirror to better evaluate, but the room began to spin.

I retreated back to bed—holding onto the counter in the bathroom, then pressing a palm against the bedroom wall. If I could make it back between cool sheets there might be a reprieve. That's the good thing about throwing up. You always feel better afterward.

Not this time. It turned out that vomiting was only a sideshow of the dizziness. If only I had learned how to spot properly in ballet class. I could not think about it now—executing all those châiné turns with my body spinning at one speed and my head snapping around at another; the thought of it made me sicker, both conjuring the sensation and remembering that I'd never been any good at it. Instead, I thought about the measured box step I had learned at cotillion. The nice, steady tracing of a square on the floor with my patent leather feet. Back together, side together, front together, side together. That I could do and do quite proficiently.

Lying in bed after my sojourn on the bathroom floor, I mapped out a box step in my mind, summoning Randy Cochran, the best dancer at cotillion. He was not like most of the boys who steered me around the ballroom—sweaty palm on my back, sweatier one gripping my gloved hand, pumping my outstretched arm as though trying to draw water. This kid could dance. He was all good things.

Randy Cochran was my first date. He took me to a movie—a scary movie. At the moment when the young doctor visits the deserted morgue, my hand twitched ever so slightly in Randy's direction. He grabbed hold and held it through the rest of the movie. It was different, I had to admit, than holding hands while fox-trotting, something like the difference between executing that elegant box step and the rock and roll "free dance" at the end of every Thursday afternoon class.

My mental box step with Randy Cochran calmed me for a while as I lay in bed attempting different positions, different angles of the head. When I finally opened my eyes, they fell on a ceramic box in the shape of a heart that sat on the dresser across the room. Stephanie had made it at Color Me Mine when she was six. I stared at it as though I were that woman in labor fixed on that fluffy pink rabbit focal point. Then I edged my gaze from the box to the bookcase to the photos in the silver frames. Wedding pictures: a posed portrait of Adam and me flanked by our parents, a photo of Adam and me dancing, a shot of us laughing. Pictures of Stephanie: poised to blow out five candles on a birthday cake, elementary school graduation, middle school dance.

Thank God, the room was no longer on a turntable.

I had survived my second night without Adam. Barely.

I stayed in bed reveling in the stability—not only a relief, but an accomplishment. The phone jerked me from my trance.

*Adam?*

"I can't believe you didn't tell me." It was my sister, Barbara. She often called first thing in the morning with the news flashes of the day. I didn't usually star in them.

"Tell you what?"

"About your fight with Adam."

"What fight?"

"Oh, come on. Adam called me."

"What did he say?"

"I'll tell you at lunch."

"Tell me now."

"I'll tell you later."

"I can't go out. I had the night from hell. I was so dizzy. Beyond dizzy. Dr. Seuss would have to come up with a word for it, it was so beyond dizzy. I was throwing up all night."

"So you'll do the BRAT diet," Barbara advised. An acronym from Stephanie's childhood. "Bananas, rice, applesauce, and toast. It's what you have after an upset stomach." Barbara knew these things even though she had no children.

"This was no ordinary upset stomach. I'm sick. I must have some weird combo platter of viruses. Swine flu, Hong Kong flu, SARS, Legionnaire's Disease…"

"You're not a Legionnaire. You're coming to lunch." Barbara was the big sister. She could make proclamations like that.

"The Gardens at noon," she said, adding, "What is a Legionnaire anyway?"

◆◆◆

SUNLIGHT SLICED THROUGH THE domed skylight of the restaurant. The hostess led me to a banquette built into the curve of brick wall. Glare bounced off a water glass. My heart raced. Sweat beaded at the back of my neck. The room was on the verge of spinning. My eyes fell on the breadbasket. I worked to focus on the intricate crackles in the crust of sourdough until the room stopped pulsating. My heartbeat slowed. I wiped my hand across the back of my neck, mopping the sweat. The fine hairs felt icy. I breathed. And waited for my sister.

Adam would not have told Barbara about the tape. Would he? Nor the emails. If he had, he would have spun it to make me look like a lunatic. Maybe he made something up altogether. Would Adam do that? I didn't know what Adam would do anymore.

In my mind, I played and replayed the tape loop of Adam in front of the computer as compulsively as I had rerun the video itself. By now, I thought of him as having a full-blown affair, but I didn't want Barbara—or anyone—to know. More than the humiliation, I didn't want anyone else to think less of Adam. I would guard Adam's integrity with my silence.

I knew how Barbara would hear my tale. Stupid, at worst; provincial, at best. If there were one thing I could not take it would be Barbara saying, "Oh, was that all? Are you out of your mind?" Barbara would disparage me and call me a big baby, like she had when we were kids, then quite possibly haul out an old story of a tape she herself had made in her heyday or correspondences between her and old boyfriends rivaling letters out of *Penthouse* magazine. Knowing Barbara's past, her story would include details I did not feel like hearing, details that would make Adam's online foray seem like *Sesame Street*.

Besides, Barbara had always adored Adam. She would take his side if he had axe-murdered a dolphin.

The sight of Barbara never ceased to give me a start, even though she had been putting herself together like this for years. She had reinvented herself over the course of her thirties. When we were kids, I had tried desperately to emulate my sister's style. In her early teens, Barbara was shopping at cool boutiques while I was stuck with Mom in the children's department at Bullock's, buying crisp Florence Eiseman dresses and white ankle socks. Barbara had worn Landlubber jeans practically spray painted across the thigh and flaring to a foot in diameter where they brushed the ground. Ribbed poor boy tops. Cork platforms that made her tower over most of her boyfriends. And there had been many.

But something happened when Barbara hit thirty. The sea of boyfriends began to dry up. She slid into a style intended to beat life to the punch in declaring her an old maid. If she was going to eschew trendiness, she was going to do so flamboyantly. She started appearing in frocks. Dresses that climbed up her neck and extended down to her wrists, often including bizarre leg-o'-mutton shapes or some other odd puffing at the shoulder. None hit short of mid-calf. Sometimes she fastened lengths of lace around her shoulders with a rhinestone brooch as though sealing her fate. She often appeared in cabbage rose prints, as if to hide a multitude of figure flaws, though in fact, Barbara's body was long and slender.

I never could have guessed that the sister who once tossed a honey blond mane with devastating elan would one day pull her hair, now a mousy no-color, into the half-ponytail we both had worn as little girls and secure it with a serviceable tortoise shell barrette. Both the coif and the fashion forward wardrobe of Barbara's youth had gradually been replaced by a style that could only be called Amish wannabe.

So, when Barbara entered the restaurant, I shook my head ever so slightly at the sight of her. She wore a navy dress punctuated by pink stalks of some kind and shoes so sensible they managed to possess neither curve nor angle. By the time Barbara arrived at the table, I had fully remembered that yes, this was my sister now. The coltish teenager was gone. This odd librarian from another time and place had swallowed her.

"You look better than I expected," Barbara volunteered, taking the chair across from me.

"I don't feel so great." In fact, I had worked hard to look fine. I'd rinsed and repeated with the shampoo, trying to wash away the night before, then spent more mirror time than usual. I had always battled my hair-to-face ratio—my long, narrow face, a slit down the center of a thick, wavy triangle. Today, I blow-dried my hair straighter, closer to my face, and even put a dab of highlighter at the inner corner of my eyes to make them appear wider set. I wanted to look like a person getting her life together, not like someone whose life was falling apart. This was LA after all, land of fake-it-till-you-make-it. I took a sip of water, careful to replace the glass on the table well out of the shaft of sunlight.

I waited Barbara out. I wanted to hear what she knew before I said a word.

Barbara pretended to study the menu. So did I.

"Do you think they roast the turkey for the turkey sandwich on the premises?"

"No, they import it from Istanbul." I couldn't take it. I cracked. "What did he say?"

"Let me hear what you have to say first."

"I don't know where to begin."

"How about at the beginning?" Barbara said.

"Okay. It begins with the summer Adam went to France."

"What summer was that?"

"He was still in college. He was nineteen. Adam had a girlfriend that summer that he never told me about."

Barbara started to speak. I shot her a look. *Shut up and listen.* Barbara mimed zipping her lips, locking them, and throwing away the key.

Now that my sister's mouth was locked shut, I didn't know what to say. There was a long silence. Too long for Barbara. She mimed a crowbar cracking open her mouth.

"Let's cut to the chase. Adam said you saw a photo on his computer. Him and that girl from France, I gather. An innocuous photo. He didn't go into details. And that there were a few emails, too. 'How are you?' 'How's your life going?' That kind of thing. Happens every day. Facebook, all that stuff. You took it out of context, made a big deal of it, packed his suitcase, and showed him the door."

"First of all it wasn't a photo. It was a video. Second of all, it wasn't innocuous. Third of all, I gather he neglected to be entirely forthcoming about the nature of the emails. Ongoing emails, I might add. As in still going on. Like an affair. Like something on Dr. Phil. That's what my life has come to. I'm a heartbeat away from Dr. Phil telling me the best predictor of future behavior is past behavior..."

"Emails do not necessarily qualify as behavior," offered Barbara.

I wasn't done. "And fourth of all, Adam knows where the door is, he didn't need to be shown, and he didn't need to pick up his suitcase and walk out unless he felt completely guilty. Or maybe," and this came to me on the spur of the moment, "he has been waiting to be found out so that I could kick him out and he could be the victim. Or run off to France and be with this woman for real."

Barbara held up her fingers—one, two, three—to tick off her responses. "Sorry, he may have said 'video.' 'Innocuous' was my word. As for the emails, he said they were a stupid fantasy. We all have stupid fantasies, Maura. And you're the one who packed the suitcase. But the point is, just call him up, tell him he can come back through that door, unpack his suitcase, and have some really great make-up sex."

For a moment, I thought my big sister was right. (I hate it when that happens.) But then I went global: I thought about the state of my marriage. Maybe we would have great make-up sex, but then what? Would we have to go through the next twenty, thirty years fighting in order to inject passion into our marriage? And would Adam always have his nose pathetically pressed against the window of a computer screen, looking jealously at the life he would have had if…if…if some butterfly hadn't flapped its wings and sent his life on an entirely different course? That's no way to live. That's not a marriage. Not my marriage.

Or had Destiny brought us together? Could no amount of butterfly flapping ever have kept us apart? If so, what was our destiny *now*? Did it even matter what choices I made? Did it matter which one of us packed the suitcase and which one of us picked it up? And what about *my* nose pressing? Didn't I also have windows to press up against? Careers I could have had. Men I could have been with, if only. If only.

I didn't know what to do. Flip a coin? Diagram my marriage on a blackboard like some compound-complex sentence overburdened with dependent and independent clauses? Barbara started humming the theme to Final Jeopardy. I was taking too long to respond. Of course I was. I was mentally diagramming my marriage, only to find that I had marital participles dangling all over the place.

The waitress arrived to take our order, saving me from considering whether it was Adam or I who was the other's direct object…and of what?

"What do you have that's white?" asked Barbara. "I'm trying to eat white."

"What does that mean?" I asked.

The waitress shifted her weight, pencil poised.

"It means," Barbara explained, "mostly food that's white. Turkey, chicken, tofu…."

"We have a white chili," the waitress suggested.

Barbara shook her head. "I'll have the Chinese chicken salad."

"I'm sure that's a lot of green," I said.

"But the protein's white. I'm focusing on the protein."

I went for the soup called Bowl of the Sun. Maybe it would light me up from the inside.

The waitress scribbled the order and retreated toward the kitchen.

"I've got to say, Maura," said Barbara, "this is so you."

"What's so me?"

"To make a big deal out of this."

"And it's so you to be an authority on relationships? I don't think so."

Barbara didn't bristle, though she could have. "It's Adam we're talking about here. Adam would never act on anything. He's just..."

"What is he, Barbara?"

"He's a man."

"I know that," I said. "But he's different. He's not your ordinary man."

"I know," Barbara agreed. "That's why we love him. But still, Maura, he's a man and that means he needs to take his mojo out for a test drive every now and then. He's got to remind himself he's still got it. It has nothing to do with loving you. Which he does. You got off lucky. He was writing to a woman in France, that's all. It doesn't mean anything."

"I'm so tired of everyone telling me that."

"Everyone who?"

"You and Adam. If it means something to me, why doesn't it mean anything? Why do you and Adam get to say what means something? That's so not fair. I get to say what means something in my own life. And this means something! This is not okay with me."

"I get it. And so does he. Case closed."

The waitress returned with our food. Barbara studied her salad. "I should have asked for the dressing on the side." She began hunting out wonton strips and setting them to one side of the plate.

I dipped my spoon into the Bowl of the Sun. It was nothing more than a pasty mass of navy bean beige stabbed with a petrified parmesan spear. I raised the spoon to my lips and blew. No need. The soup was barely lukewarm, more overcast than a midsummer day.

◆◆◆

When I got home, I called Adam at the office. I didn't know what I was going to say. I didn't know what I wanted to hear. I guess I was hoping that Adam would know just what to say—just what I needed to hear—to make things better. He would read my mind, better than I could myself, and know how to apologize in just the right way. He would know how to tell me he loved me with just the right words.

One of his assistants put me on hold. This was why I rarely called Adam at work. In a typical day, he fielded a hundred calls, popped in and out of a half-dozen meetings, and hosted several drop-in visits from A-list talent. He was like a plate-spinner at the circus. I hated to be one of those plates. More to the point, I did not want to be the one wobbly plate that made all the others come crashing down.

After a few seconds, I hung up.

The phone rang immediately. It was Adam. His voice shot through me like morphine, taking away all pain. The more he talked, the better I felt. He was saying all the right things. He was winning me over...until it occurred to me that winning people over was what Adam did for a living. He was a goddamned theatrical agent. Was I being agented? I couldn't tell anymore.

I stopped him mid-sentence and asked him, point blank, "What about our marriage? Is it as good as you wanted it to be on the day we were married?

Without hesitation, Adam replied, "Even better."

*Yes, Barbara, I have make-up sex in my future. Sex that will make him say, "God, yes."*

Then Adam broke his own cardinal rule of deal making. He kept talking.

"We have a great marriage..." His voice trailed off.

"But...?" I asked.

"There's no but... There's sort of an asterisk," Adam added.

"An asterisk?"

"You have a picture in your mind of how things are supposed to be and when real life doesn't match..." He stopped himself.

"Go ahead," I prodded.

"It doesn't matter."

"Oh, but it does. It so does." Maybe my big sister was going to be wrong after all.

"You get upset."

"People get upset, Adam."

"I know. But you hang on to the upset. So sometimes I don't tell you things. That's the asterisk."

"Like what things?"

No response.

"Like what things?" I said again.

"Like...now listen to everything I have to say... Like, as long as all this nonsense has come out—which I'm really glad about, actually—I saw Aimee at Kevin's funeral five years ago. You were there. You were right there a few feet away. And I said hello to her. And we chatted a little. And then I said goodbye."

"And you didn't introduce me?"

"That's what I'm talking about. It would have been more trouble than it was worth."

"I'm more trouble than I'm worth?"

"Maura, that's not what I said."

"So that's when you started sleeping with her again?"

"No! I never slept with her."

"You've got a video that says otherwise."

"I mean since then. Not since we were kids. Honest to God, Maura. I hadn't seen her in forever. Then I saw her at the funeral."

"And that reminded you of her. Lit the old spark."

"Not at all. It's just how life works. People from the past just pop up now and then."

"What was she doing at Kevin's funeral anyway? She lives halfway around the world."

"She's done business with Daniel over the years. And she had an artist with an opening here around then so she made the trip. An opening at the Jean Marc Gallery on La Cienega."

"You remember everything she said awfully well."

"You asked me why she showed up. I told you. That's all."

"Until you suddenly remembered how she tasted!" I shrieked:

"Oh please, that's so stupid. It's nothing," Adam said. "I admit it. It's embarrassing, but it's embarrassing because it's so stupid. Beyond that, it's nothing."

"It's not nothing!"

"It's nothing that means anything. It's make-believe."

"You don't make a date to meet when it's make-believe," I said.

"I didn't make a date. I never wrote back. I was never going to write back. I was done."

I could hear the click of computer keys.

"Are you writing to her right now?"

"Of course not. I'm at work. I'm doing business."

"Well, thanks for giving what may be the final gasping breath of our marriage your full attention."

"Let me say it again. I was never going to make a date," he said. "I was never going to see her. Never ever. You have to believe me."

"Why should I?"

"Because," he said, "I'm telling you."

"So, to be clear...you could have introduced me to her—old girlfriend meet wife. Then you could have told me after the fact that you saw her at the funeral. Then you could have told me she contacted you. Then you could have told me you'd started writing to her. For over nine long months. You could have told me she wanted to see you, but you turned her down. But instead of picking door number one, two, or three, what you did was drive to Public Storage, dig through a ton of boxes, find an old video tape, buy a Betamax on eBay, transfer the tape, and sneak downstairs in the middle of the night to watch yourself doing it with another woman for fun, to refresh your memory, so that you could tell this other woman how disappointing your life is and how you still remember how she tastes. How she tastes, Adam. Everywhere. Just to be clear."

"I know that doesn't sound good," he said, "but if I hadn't been worried that you'd..."

"Don't even finish that sentence," I said. "And fuck your asterisk."

# CHAPTER SEVEN

ADAM CALLED THE NEXT day. His voice was calm. *No plates spinning in the background.* "Tell me what you need to make this better," he said.

"I don't know what I need," I said. I thought that maybe a few days to get some perspective was all I needed, but it turned out I was wrong. I had thought of nothing but the video and the emails, reciting them over and over in my head, a litany of misery. Even though I believed Adam when he swore his love for me, there was a woman in Paris—the Left Bank of Paris—who thought otherwise. She thought Adam didn't love me. She thought Adam was ready to end his marriage. She thought that Adam would be tasting her again and that she would be tasting him. Adam had to be lying to one of us, and at this point the odds were 50-50 that he was lying to me.

"I don't know what I need," I said again.

"That's not helpful."

"But it's the truth."

"Maura, I can't fix this by myself."

"You broke it by yourself."

"One day you're going to be really sorry you did this," he said, his voice strangled with frustration.

"I didn't do anything. You were the one who did something."

"We've had this conversation," he said. That's the way he ended a conversation he wanted over. Hanging up without hanging up.

But he kept calling, every two or three nights. Something in me looked forward to the calls, but the conversation always went in the same direction. Downhill. Any buoyancy at the hellos quickly wilted. I stopped looking forward to those hopeful hellos, and soon, like a self-fulfilling prophecy, the hellos were no longer hopeful. And then I stopped looking forward to the calls altogether...so much so that one night I didn't answer at all.

Instead, I stared at Adam's name on the caller ID, certain that he was picturing me staring at the phone but not reaching for it—a telepathic standoff. I couldn't face the aftermath of the call as much as the call itself. I knew how it would leave me—precisely as all the previous calls had: flattened, wishing my husband would say anything other than what he was saying, wishing I could unearth the desire to say anything other than what I was saying, and having no magic wand to make any of the wishes come true.

Around then, time began to blur. Everything began to blur. The frequency of the calls dwindled to every three days, maybe every four. And then they stopped altogether, leaving me wandering the no-man's land between wishing Adam would call and resolving that I would never speak to him again.

There was this pesky itch to call him myself, if only so that we could riff on the same dialogue that had gotten us nowhere in all the other calls. My pride arm-wrestled that urge, night after night. After all, wasn't the boy supposed to call the girl? Hadn't we been trained to sit by the phone, making a fine art of waiting and cultivated nonchalance? Sometimes I got in the car and drove, precisely because I knew that I would never allow this to be a Bluetooth conversation. I headed for areas with known dead spots to make sure.

On those evenings when Stephanie stayed late at school for swim practice or to work on the school newspaper, I drove the five minutes from Holmby Hills to Westwood to pick up a two piece chicken combo from El Pollo Loco.

"You get to pick two sides," said the pimply boy behind the counter.

I stared at the menu lit up on the wall behind him. Corn cobbette, french fries, mashed potatoes. Beans, cole slaw, mac and cheese.

"Cole slaw and beans," I said to the boy. But then I noticed "fresh vegetables" on the list. I hadn't eaten one of those in a while. "No," I said, "Cole slaw and the fresh vegetables." But that seemed redundant. "No," I said again, "Vegetables and mac and cheese." But the mac and cheese would cancel out any good done by the vegetables. "Not mac and cheese," I said. "I shouldn't have mac and cheese. Make it the vegetables and Spanish rice." I hate Spanish rice. They used to serve it to us at Ridgepoint for lunch under dried-out clumps of stringy chicken. "No," I said again, revisiting the bean option. But that came with its own rock-and-a-hard-place: black versus pinto. I stared at the colorful photos meant to whet appetites. They strobed before my eyes.

The woman in line behind me couldn't stand another second. "Excuse me," she said, "maybe I could go while you make up your mind."

I stepped aside to let her place her order like a normal person.

And then I walked out. Even if I could decide on two sides, the tortilla choice lay ahead—corn or flour.

I sat in the car with my eyes closed, relieved to be out of there. I knew when to admit defeat.

Soon I abandoned the pretense of dinner altogether. I stood over the kitchen sink popping the top of a single serve can of tuna while the television news burbled in the background. Often I didn't even wait for the national broadcast and ate to the drone of the local five o'clock, riddled with guilt for leaving Stephanie to forage in the kitchen when she got home.

I tried to convince myself that the situation was providing valuable practice for Stephanie. In no time, she would be away at college and would not have her mother to do everything for her. But the argument was specious, even in my own mind, which happened to be where I was spending most of my time, alone and unsupervised.

Ever since Stephanie had entered high school, I had projected myself into the year-of-Stephanie-leaving. Often, I awoke in the middle of the night, heart knocking, thinking: *I'm not done with her yet. I might be one discussion short of a fully developed value system.* Habitually, I conjured images of the house without her. How would it feel to have effectively been handed my pink slip? I steeled myself against the emptiness by envisioning it. Over and over. A mental tic. But I could not have known how empty the house was really going to be. How utterly empty. I understood that emptiness only now, with Adam gone.

So I holed up in my sweats, hobbled by both physical inertia and mental overdrive, savaging my daughter's last year at home.

An image haunted me: An advertisement I had seen in a magazine—even then, a very old magazine at the bottom of a pile—when I was a very little girl. A woman lay on the floor, a sweeping holiday gown billowing behind her, one hand caressing a shiny red vacuum festooned with a green bow that matched the sash encircling her Scarlett O'Hara waist. In festive candy cane cursive, the ad promised: "Christmas morning she'll be happier with a Hoover." Suddenly, I found myself in the clutches of some atavistic, pre-feminist yearning. I longed to be the woman made happy by a brand new vacuum cleaner. Maybe that woman got the hearts and flowers she had been begging for. Maybe that woman's husband told her he loved her, that he loved her more than he had ever loved any woman on any continent, that he loved her so much he splurged on a Hoover.

The woman in the ad floated before me often during those days, taunting me as if she had won a contest I forgot to enter. I batted the housewife away as I sleepwalked through my day, looking forward to nightfall as though it marked some sort of victory.

◆◆◆

THE SECOND BOUT OF vertigo hit like the first, while I lay in bed, which was a great deal during this time.

I struggled for a deep breath. My breath had been shallow and quick for what seemed like so long. There was an acrid smell, but strangely sweet, too, almost cloying. I realized it was coming from me. My thin flannel nightgown was sour with sweat, but still slightly scented with the clementine-and-bergamot sachet tucked into the back of my nightgown drawer. Vertebra by vertebra, as though getting up from a bed where I had lulled a child to sleep with a good-night story, I maneuvered my way up and over to the dresser. It was made of spruce. The saleswoman at the Design Center had touted its whorled knots. I took care not to look at them now. They might start spinning like the free-floating pinwheels at the beginning of *The Twilight Zone.*

I rummaged for a fresh nightgown. My hand encountered something satin in the depths of the drawer. I removed it, took off the drenched, rumpled flannel thing clinging to me, and let it lie where it dropped. I slid the satin over my head. Then I made my way back to bed.

Gwen had given me the negligee at my bridal shower all those years ago. I had worn it once, on our honeymoon in Paris, but rarely again. It was cool, almost refreshing, but I needed to take it off. It was an instrument of seduction, and seduction had not figured in my game plan for longer than I could remember. It didn't feel like me any more. And these days I needed all the help I could get remembering exactly who that was. I pulled an oversized T-shirt over my head and crawled back into bed.

Not until this moment, lying there, windmill tilting, did I realize that Gwen's gift had been a sort of call-back. She and I had gone shopping for something seductive, something satin, for me to wear for my night with her cousin a century or two ago. We—meaning Gwen—had decided I couldn't enter college as a virgin. It was something of a challenge, like an extra credit trig problem. Gwen's cousin, John (a.k.a. Gorgeous John) was spending the summer in her family's guesthouse, taking a course at UCLA. Anthropology, archaeology, sociology…one of those "ologies" that separated the college men from the boys. Gwen told him the "situation," as she put it. I would not have to feign experience.

So one August night, I slept with Cousin John who, with his Jackson Browne hair and dark brown eyes, was, as advertised, gorgeous. When we finished (when *he* finished), he raised himself onto one elbow and smiled at me. I was a goner. Later, in Gwen's room, the post mortem ended with a declaration: "I'm in love with your cousin."

We peered through her bedroom window at John lazing in the pool, elbows propped up on the side of the shallow end, legs extended out in the water. He was smoking—*oh*, I thought, *that was the smell of him*. The way he sliced the air with his cigarette as he raised it to his lips, with such grace and cool, made me want to be lying under him again. It was an urge I had no idea what to do with—a jolt of something crazy somewhere, everywhere. *So this is what it's all about.*

A few days later, once again gazing out of Gwen's window, I saw a girl emerge from Cousin John's guesthouse, zipping up the fly of her 501s. I cried. Gwen consoled. And suddenly, just like that, I felt grown up, more grown up than I had those few nights earlier. A mournful sort of jackpot.

It occurred to me now, lying in this bed alone, that I had never worn that other satin nightgown, the first one. What could we, Gwen and I, have been thinking in buying it? That I was going to slip into the bathroom like a girl on her honeymoon and pause in the doorway, candlelight glinting off of satin, for Cousin John to take in the vision that was me? Hardly.

# CHAPTER EIGHT

IT TOOK THREE TRIES, but Barbara finally managed to coax me out of the house. The latest offering at the Geffen Playhouse had not done it. Nor had Judy Collins performing at UCLA's Royce Hall. "I hear she wears sequins now," I said. "Like a lounge singer. That's just more than I can bear." The idea of sitting still in a theater filled me with panic.

But I could walk. Moving was good. So Barbara hit paydirt when she mentioned the new cupcake ATM in Westwood. "I think I've got to go make a withdrawal," she declared, her voice sugar-speedy with anticipation.

Twenty minutes later, we stood in front of a machine in a wall. I stared at the screen. It introduced itself in all caps: "Sprinkles Cupcake ATM."

"Genius," said Barbara. Maybe it was. Twenty-four hour cupcake-on-demand machine.

Barbara touched the monitor and scrolled through the flavors. Red Velvet, Chocolate Marshmallow, Black and White. She kept touching the screen; the options kept appearing.

"Toasted coconut," she finally announced. The monitor lead her through the purchasing steps: selection, confirmation, credit card swipe. We gazed behind the mesh grill as a robotic claw removed the cupcake from its shelf and placed it in a small, brown cardboard box.

There it was. Delivered into Barbara's hands. I peered into the box as she unfolded its flaps.

Then it was my turn.

"I'm not hungry," I said.

"What's hunger got to do with it?"

"Yeah…" I said, "what's hunger but a secondhand emotion?"

I had hardly eaten in I didn't know how long. The last thing I wanted was something sweet, something meant as a treat rather than sustenance, but I went with the Red Velvet to avoid an argument. Cupcakes in hand, we set off to stroll Westwood Village. The area bore no resemblance to the quaint college town of our girlhood except for the two old movie theaters across the street from one another—the one with the spire, the other with its Deco marquee.

They used to be landmarks: "I'll meet you at the Village." "The coffee shop down the street from the Bruin." Now they were relics of another time. A time when Adam and I stood in line to see first run movies because you couldn't buy tickets online. We had taken turns dashing across the street to Stan's Donuts to fuel ourselves during the two hour wait to see *Titanic*.

"You've got benign paroxysmal positional vertigo," Barbara proclaimed as we passed Stan's, one of the few places from that time still standing (though it had sacrificed the definitive Orange Julius to boba tea).

"No," I said. "I've got the end-of-my-life-as-I-know-it syndrome."

Barbara rolled her eyes. "I Googled it. There's a maneuver."

"To get your old life back?"

"To get rid of the vertigo. You know, a manuever."

"Like a military thing?"

"There's a little crystal BB that gets unlodged in your ear," Barbara explained.

"Dislodged," I corrected.

"Whatever. The thing isn't where it's supposed to be. In the inner ear, I think. Or middle. I forget. There are some exercises you can do to get rid of it. Actually, they have to be done to you. It's not painful or anything. You just lie there while they move you around."

"Sounds like New Age voodoo."

"You have to get the BB thing back in the hole. Like in those little puzzles."

"I've lived with a screw loose this long…" I said.

"I think you should try it," Barbara nudged.

"I think I shouldn't."

"Be that way."

"I will."

"Fine."

"Fine."

I had eaten the cupcake in spite of myself. I pressed my finger against the crumbs stuck to the bottom of the little cardboard box and licked them off, wondering if anyone worried about red dye #2 anymore. Barbara was still picking flakes of coconut off the frosting and eating them one by one. We shook our heads in unison as we passed three vacant storefronts in a row.

I felt like a tourist—out of sync, without reference points. Lost in a soulless version of my hometown. Every several yards, I spoke the name of a long-gone shop or restaurant as I passed its former site, as though the place were still standing right there. Barbara joined in.

"The Yesterday's," Barbara remarked. She knew I would remember the story of the boy who took her there and proceeded to hit on the waitress.

"The Chatham," we said in stereo. And then, again in unison, "Moment of silence." So many sandwiches, so many squares of gingerbread, so many family stories. Enough said.

"Mario's," I said.

"No pizza like it," said Barbara. Its primo corner had been usurped by a California Pizza Kitchen.

"Like Mario's would ever have stood for a barbecued chicken pizza," I said.

"How about pear and gorgonzola?"

"How about Jamaican jerk?"

Barbara shook her head. "I could go for a piece of Mario's pepperoni pizza pie."

"It's not white."

"Yeah, and no one says pizza pie anymore, but that doesn't mean I can't want one."

"Yeah. You can't call broccolini on a whole wheat crust a pizza pie. I'm sorry, but it's all wrong, so wrong," I said. I could no longer rely on the landscape to provide what it was supposed to provide: a sense of my own history. More than that. I took this watered down Westwood as a personal insult. It felt like my hometown had breached its contract, its agreement to maintain the landmarks that allowed me to measure my life. My city had morphed into something unrecognizable, something ordinary and impermanent, even cheap. Worst of all—generic. Metropolitan infidelity.

"Westwood hasn't aged gracefully," I said.

"No. It hasn't."

"Of course, I don't know how you're supposed to do that in this town," I said.

I glanced at my watch. Right on schedule: two twenty-three. I had not picked Stephanie up from school for a couple of years now. Adam and I had decided that Stephanie would not get a car until senior year, but Volkswagen Jettas and Honda Civics had appeared in the driveways of her classmates. Carpools had formed. I was unceremoniously retired as chauffeur. I had not, however, managed to reset my internal alarm clock—the one that went off at two twenty-three every afternoon, the one that signaled me to drop everything so that I could be first in line at carpool. (Two-thirty would be too late, could put me ten cars back.) On cue, this alarm sounded. Only now, there was nothing to do about it but hit the snooze button.

"How did Stephanie get to be so old?" I mused.

"It happens," said Barbara.

I veered into the beauty supply store. The place was chronically under new ownership. "I need conditioner," I said, "I'm not properly conditioned." Barbara followed me in, pausing to test various hand lotions on her way to the hair products.

"How is Stephanie?" Barbara asked, nonchalantly, as she dribbled a sample of cuticle oil along her nail bed.

I heard clearly the unspoken second half of my sister's question: *How is Stephanie...with everything that's going on?*

"She's good," I answered.

"Good."

"Yeah," I reiterated, "Stephanie's good. Busy. With school and friends and after school stuff. We were never that busy when we were kids. It's kind of ridiculous."

"That's what everyone says," said Barbara.

"Too busy," I said. "But maybe that's a good thing." *Maybe it was a good thing Stephanie is so busy...with everything that's going on.*

I bought It's A 10 Miracle Conditioner and we headed out, drawn to the easterly reaches of the village where the architecture had been less compromised.

"Nesselrode Bula," I said. Barbara snorted. An in-joke. An old-timey ice cream parlor had stood on that spot. Nesselrode Bula was one of their flavors. We never knew what was in it. We certainly never ordered it. But we loved to say it. The space, as places were now called, had moved through many incarnations, but to me it would always be the ice cream parlor of my childhood. Home of the world's best sundaes—served with a tiny macaroon nestled in a wax paper envelope imprinted with a picture of an angel and the words, "It's heavenly."

When I was in the seventh grade, if you scored one hundred percent on your weekly spelling test, Miss Zipser took you there for one of those sundaes on Friday afternoon. Usually, four or five girls crammed into her Buick Skylark and headed for hot fudge. I was always one of them.

But there had been the week of "inexhaustible." The silent "h." "Ible" versus "able." "Inexhaustible" was tricky. "Inexhaustible" tripped up everyone but me. So "inexhaustible" put me in the Skylark's front seat, then all alone at a wrought-iron table across from that woman with the pointy bra and the helmet hair. I could not stand on this spot without remembering the mortification of that one-on-one afternoon with Miss Zipser.

"Look for the bean in the cream," I said to Barbara. The motto had been written across the top of the menu. Despite the crazy Nesselrode Bula, the establishment was mighty proud of its homemade vanilla.

We had weaved our way through most of Westwood Village without mention of Adam. Some conversations you don't need to have out loud.

# CHAPTER NINE

I RAN MY FINGER along the shelf in the den designated for the "somedays": Dostoyevsky, Melville, Tolstoy. Nothing appealed. Hemingway—not today, probaby not ever. I was fantasizing about going on a date with Adam. Getting dressed up, sitting across from him at Valentino's, reaching out to touch his hand, pretending we had never lain next to one another drooling onto the pillow, open-mouthed and fetid.

When the phone rang, my heart hiccuped. It must be Adam. I would invite him on a date. I would be coy and tell him it was Sadie Hawkins Day. I would make it all better. But it wasn't Adam. It was Don Gilder. A name from the past—the soccer era to be exact. I carbon dated acquaintances according to Stephanie's age—a method that placed Don in the early AYSO Period. I remembered chatting with Don on the sidelines, distributing orange segments at half-time, joking about how aptly the team had named itself: the Bumble Bees—a passel of little girls buzzing around the field in their tiny black and gold uniforms.

"I thought maybe you'd like to have dinner some time," Don said.

"I beg your pardon." I used the tone I normally reserved for telemarketers.

"I'd like to be your training wheels," Don offered as if he were doing me a favor.

"I don't think so," I said.

"Let me give you my number in case you change your mind."

I pretended to find a pencil to jot down his number and actually mimed writing it as though that made it less of a lie. Then I hung up the phone and ran to the bathroom to vomit.

Calls from two others followed: Alex Burke from preschool (Stephanie's) and George Samson from elementary school (also Stephanie's). And finally, there was Peter Lafferty on the line. I struggled to put faces to the first two—Mr. Preschool and Mr. Elementary. But Peter Lafferty I knew. There was history with Peter Lafferty. Couples history.

◆◆◆

CINDY, PETER'S EX-WIFE, AND I had met cute in the produce aisle at Gelson's. We were both pushing carts containing bananas and sweet potatoes—foods easily mushed for babies' first forays with solids—as well as the babies to go with them. I smiled at Cindy's baby. Dressed in navy, it seemed to be of the boy variety, though you could never be sure. Cindy smiled at baby Stephanie, who, dressed in pink with lacey socks, was less mysterious.

On cue, we both said, "How old?"

And, again, in stereo, we both answered, "Seven months."

The conversation quickly included birth dates or, more precisely, a single birth date. Stephanie and baby Joshua had been born on the same day, October 17, both at Santa Monica Hospital.

The babies hit it off right there in front of the romaine. Stephanie reached for Joshua's hand and Joshua held out a slobber-soaked book. By the time we cruised on to frozen foods, we had exchanged phone numbers and even made a playdate for the following day.

Over the course of those early playdates, Cindy and I circled each other. I wondered if the friendship would take. It did. Within a few months we were splitting the cost of a babysitter on Friday nights. Dinner and a movie. I sat across the table from her husband, Peter, wondering what it would be like to be married to a man like him. Not that I really had the slightest idea what kind of man he was—only that he was different than Adam.

My Adam. Just-right tall—six-one—with a thick crop of sandy hair that reminded me of Robert Redford's in The Way We Were. I sometimes reached out and brushed a straw-colored lock from his forehead the way Barbra Streisand did in the last scene of the movie, half-expecting Adam to grab my hand mid-sweep the way Hubbell grabbed Katie's. Peter's hair was dark, nearly black, and silky. I realized that it was still all about the hair. Must have been that early rock star imprinting. There was no escaping the atomic wallop of first hormones colliding with guy-with-guitar.

But it was more than the difference in their looks, Adam's and Peter's. Peter had a detachedness that was contrary to everything about Adam. I always felt like Peter was thinking something he wasn't saying. I wondered if other people, other women, might suppose the same of Adam. Was he exotic to them? Was it because I knew my own husband so well that I could tell what he was thinking from the curl of his lip or the slight rise of an eyebrow? Was mystery intriguing simply because it was mysterious? Did familiarity take the oomph out of every relationship? Of course, as it turned out, Adam had been a mystery to me. While I knew every gesture, every intonation, the timbre of every silence, I hadn't known the secret landscape of his psyche after all. My Adam would not have been sitting at his computer at 2:00 a.m., and yet, there he was.

◆◆◆

PETER AND CINDY HAD been divorced for ten years now. They had set the bleak trend that mowed through our circle of friends during Stephanie's middle school years. Husbands turning in their wives for newer models—often, in this town, actual models. Paunchy men believing a new wife would make them look cool rather than just plain silly. Wives turning in their husbands for personal trainers with chiseled six-packs and a nearly completed screenplay on their laptop. Husbands turning in their wives for the same trainers. The occasional wife leaving her husband as a preemptive strike against the inevitability of being replaced.

As I understood it, Peter and Cindy's marriage had melted away, or sweated, really, like a glass of lemonade on an August day, leaving nothing but a ring of condensation in the form of two sons. Cindy had remarried quickly, within two years, and moved with "the new guy," as Adam always referred to him, to Hancock Park. My friendship with Cindy faded until even the jollity of Christmas card catch-up was nothing more than a tedious chore.

Peter sidled through a series of relationships, but none caught fire. Occasionally, Adam met Peter for lunch, but gradually, those lunches fell by the wayside, too.

I had not spoken to Peter in well over three years when he called.

"Maura?" His voice was a tad thin, almost breathy. It sounded like he was nervous, which was not like him. "Peter Lafferty here. I heard…"

Of course he'd heard. LA was such a small town.

"I guess everyone's heard," I said.

"We never thought you guys…," he said.

"I know. Nobody did." *We never did. I never did.*

"I just wanted to let you know I was thinking about you."

"Thanks," I said. "I'm sure Adam would love to hear from you. He's always saying it's been too long."

"But the thing is…" There it was. I could hear it again. That case of nerves. "The thing is, it's not Adam I want to take to dinner."

"Oh…" I managed. "What did you say?"

"I'd like to take you to dinner."

"Just the two of us?"

"That's what a date usually is."

"A date?" I was equal parts horrified and thrilled. "I'm not dating."

"I'm sorry," Peter said, "Adam told Scott Crawley at WME that you were separated, so I…"

"Adam said we were separated?" I interrupted.

"Yeah, I heard you were a free agent," he chuckled at his own joke; it was my husband who was the agent.

"Separated." I double checked. "Adam used that word?"

"That's what I heard," Peter said again.

"Separated." A declaration of fact. "You know," I added with determination, "I'd like to have dinner with you."

# CHAPTER TEN

IT TOOK A MOMENT for my eyes to adjust to the darkness when Peter and I entered the restaurant, a clubby affair with retro-hip aspirations, a place that served frilly shrimp cocktails and to-hell-with-it sixteen-ounce steaks. The hostess asked if we preferred a table or a booth. Peter Lafferty deferred to me.

"A booth would be great," I said, picturing Adam and the French Girl pressing thigh against thigh in a charming booth in a charming *bôite* off a charming rain-glistening alley. So it might have been spite that drove me to opt for the booth. And spite probably had something to do with it when I slid along the dark red leather and stopped halfway around, so that I was not seated across from Peter, but something resembling next to him.

There were a few false starts at chit-chat before Peter and I landed on the comfortable territory of the kids. Josh was not getting along with his stepfather and was lobbying to move back in with Peter. Peter worried that the boy was not likely to get along all that much better with him. Wasn't not getting along with your father, step or otherwise, part of the job requirement of being seventeen? More nerve-wracking still, Josh wanted to take a year or two off before college after graduating. It was the "or two" that had Peter worried.

"Don't you think it means he's never going to go?" he asked me. "One year off is a plan. Two years off is something else. Two years off turns into three. Turns into never."

"Not at all. It means he's not ready to go now, that's all." I tried to be reassuring, but wondered what I would do if Stephanie had that attitude. There might be throat-slitting involved. Laissez-faire was an art I could never master.

By the time the cappuccinos arrived, Peter had to apologize for not having asked about Stephanie.

"There's always a reason to worry," I remarked. "Stephanie's obsessed with getting into the right college, whatever that means." I knew precisely what that meant, but felt the need to dilute Stephanie's drive.

"She won't have any trouble. Not that one," said Peter, sipping his coffee. A few dots of foam clung to his upper lip. I tapped my own to indicate where. Peter wiped the foam with his napkin, but missed a bit. I inched closer and reached over—not with my napkin, but with my index finger—to dab the last smudge from his lip. And I stayed put, not bothering to slide back along the booth.

Once, when I was about Stephanie's age, I had been riding in a car packed with kids coming home from a Ridgepoint mixer—one of those events where the girls' school girls huddled against one wall and the boys' school boys strutted back and forth against the other. I found myself in a massive boat of a car—a Chevrolet or Chrysler—with an expanse of front seat. I ended up in the middle, pressed between another girl and the driver, a boy whose name I never knew. I remembered only that he asked me to steer so he could take off his jacket. For a moment, our arms tangled as he slipped his out of a sleeve and I reached mine over to grab the wheel. When the girl squishing me against the driver was dropped off, I didn't know whether I should slide to the right or stay plastered against the boy. There I was, left hip nudging his right. I may have wanted to stay put, but I slid to the right, all the way to the official passenger seat, leaving a gulf of tuck-and-roll between us. I was a Ridgepoint girl after all.

It may have taken thirty years, but I was not going to slide back along this booth. Not tonight.

I studied Peter's face. He wore glasses now. He had not in our previous life. Our couples' life. The frames were perfectly round and gave him an owlish look. The gray at his temples made him appear untended rather than distinguished. He was not aging like George Clooney. When I parsed the conglomeration of his features, I realized he was not good-looking. But the way he looked at me was good.

He leaned in and said, "Do you want to talk about it?"

"About what?"

"Adam. Your...situation."

"I'm not sure it qualifies as a bona fide situation," I said. It sounded snarky. I hadn't meant for it to.

"I'm sorry," he said, sitting back against the booth. "I just thought...you know, sometimes it helps to talk about these things."

"No, I'm sorry," I insisted. "I don't know which end is up."

"It gets easier," he said. "I promise."

"I don't think I want it to get easier. My whole life has been flipped over like a pancake."

"It'll get easier whether you want it to or not. That's just what happens."

I shook my head no, like a petulant toddler. Peter Lafferty smiled like an indulgent parent who knew better. I didn't care what he knew or thought he knew. If your marriage falling apart didn't call for suffering, what did?

Adam's ghost lingered with us at the restaurant for awhile, but retreated once Peter and I found our conversational groove. It was such a relief to feel Adam float away that when Peter suggested we go to a movie, I accepted.

It was one of those "living room" theaters, no armrest between us. Peter inched closer on the loveseat. I lowered my head onto his shoulder. I didn't think about it. I just did it. I nearly forgot that it wasn't Adam next to me until my head hit Peter's shoulder; it didn't feel familiar. A shoulder with a different slope. A stiffer, narrower wale of corduroy than the cushy, velvety one of Adam's well-worn jacket. Something shot through me—something like arousal. Or was it wistfulness? After the attendant's speech reminding us which movie we were there to see, after the previews, after the animated announcement admonishing us to turn off our devices, I dug in my purse for my phone. Before I could locate it, Peter kissed me.

One kiss. One kiss that made concentrating on the movie impossible.

I stared at the screen, wondering if I ran into an old friend in the lobby, would I look different now that I had been kissed by another man?

◆◆◆

ON THE LAST DAY of tenth grade, Gwen and I burst out of our Latin final, catapulting ourselves into summer. Mrs. Talbot had instructed us to stretch a rubber band around the declension chart at the back of our books so it would be inaccessible during the exam, while still allowing access to the vocabulary glossary as permitted. Once the test was behind us—our last final of the year—Gwen and I threw open the classroom door and snapped those rubber bands into the first trashcan we passed.

"We're juniors!" said Gwen.

"We're juniors," I said. "Do you suppose we look like juniors?"

"I don't know." Gwen thought about it. "It's not like when you lose your virginity, I guess. Everybody can tell then, you know. Especially guys."

"Really?" I didn't have to pretend to know these things with Gwen. That was the beauty of our friendship.

"That's what they say."

"Who?"

"You know," Gwen said, "the people who say those things."

"And we assume they wouldn't say them if they didn't know them to be true."

"Exactly. That's our part. Ours is just to believe."

Gwen's mom was waiting for us in her wood-panelled Caprice wagon in the roundabout at the front of the school. She dropped us off to wander Westwood Village and spend our allowances in the last-gasp-of-Woodstock "head shop," though no one had called it that in ages.

We sifted through incense and crystal prisms. We felt deliciously full of ourselves, having finished finals and now able to call ourselves juniors. We chatted with the cute guy behind the counter, discussing astrology and the I Ching. I twirled a strand of hair at the nape of my neck, twisting it into a long corkscrew. I had the kind of hair that held a soft wave when I did that, and I did it whenever I was nervous.

He eyeballed our uniforms. "Girls' school girls..." he mused cryptically.

We spent the rest of the day dissecting his remark. Did he mean that was a good thing or bad thing, being a girls' school girl? Was he lusting after us in our starched cotton regulation issue with the filigreed "RS" embroidered on the collar? Or, God forbid, was he mocking us?

We were on our third free sample at Baskin-Robbins when I asked Gwen, "How can they tell if you've done it or not?"

"They just can," Gwen assured me. "Something about the way...I don't know...Just something."

Now, thirty-some years later, I wondered if Gwen had been right. Had something shifted when Peter Lafferty kissed me?

I emerged from the theater into the lobby, attempting to recalibrate, Peter at my side. And then I spotted Barbara. Would my sister know that I had just been kissed by another man, by this non-Adam? A kiss, especially at my age, could not rank cosmologically with losing one's virginity. All the same, at this point in my life, it felt seismic. Barbara would know.

Miraculously, exactly then, Barbara turned her attention to the butter dispenser. Things like popcorn-to-butter ratio were important to Barbara. The task absorbed her for several seconds—enough time for me to slide my arm under Peter's, nestle in close so as not to be spotted and lead him quickly through the lobby out into the fresh air. We walked in silence to the parking lot.

Peter drove a Bentley convertible. The car must have come as part of the single-life package. He opened the door for me, and when I got in, he leaned down and kissed me again.

For a minute, I thought: to hell with Adam, which was probably not the healthiest form of psychological foreplay. It seemed to do the trick nonetheless. Suddenly, I was threading my fingers through Peter's hair as he drove, touching his shoulder, reaching for him when we came to a stoplight. It wasn't like me. Who was this woman? This person who was not, at the moment anyway, Adam's wife?

I was dizzy, but it wasn't the same old vertigo. Had I been ordered to, I was not at all sure I could walk a straight line.

Suddenly my surroundings snapped back into focus. Peter was heading straight on Pico instead of turning left onto Beverly Glen which led to my house. He had drawn the logical conclusion based on my behavior. It just happened to be wrong.

"Where are we going?" I asked.

"My house."

"How come?"

"Isn't Stephanie home?"

It took me a long beat. "Oh," I said finally. And then again, "Oh."

Peter looked at me. "I thought...I mean...You know, you've been..." Finally, he spat it out. "You want to come home with me, right, kiddo?"

"I don't know."

"I thought...," he said again. "I'm sorry. I'll take you home."

"I think that's a good idea."

The rest of the ride was silent—back down Pico onto Beverly Glen, up past Wilshire Boulevard, and then onto Strathmore, my street. Boys had a name for girls like that. Did it apply to grown women, too? I didn't know how to do this whole thing as a grown woman. Honestly, I hadn't known how to do it as a girl.

I got out of the car, hurried up the steps to the front door, and disappeared inside.

Stephanie jumped up from the kitchen table when she heard my key in the door.

"Oh my God, Mommy, where have you been!"

"I went to the movies."

"Why didn't you have your cell on?"

"I guess I forgot to turn it back on after the movie."

"You always make me have mine on."

Stephanie burst into tears, the way you do, even when you're seventeen, and you've been holding it in until you lay eyes on your mommy.

"What's wrong?" I asked. "What happened?"

"Grandpa."

# CHAPTER ELEVEN

SAM FIELDER HAD GROWN a business based on one simple tenet: "Sell it, don't smell it." Making a living became the name of Sam's game when he was fourteen years old and his father dropped dead while filleting a flounder behind the fish counter.

Young Sam set out from the Bronx with the Help Wanted section stuffed into the pocket of a jacket two sizes too small. He had circled some thirty ads in red grease pencil and was headed for the first one on the list: finisher/presser at a dry cleaner. He had no idea what that meant, but he had a finished a thing or two in his time and figured how hard could pressing be.

Though it was only a bridge away, Sam did not know Manhattan. He reversed the street and avenue numbers and ended up several neighborhoods north of the dry cleaner, finding himself instead at a talent agency which also, as fate would have it, was looking to hire.

They stuck him in the mailroom that afternoon. Once ensconced, he wheedled his way into the business by hip-pocketing clients everyone else rejected. It turned out that Sam Fielder had a gift for booking acts no one else could sell. Before he hit twenty, he was a junior agent. He quickly made stars of a ventriloquist in the Catskills and a ballroom dancing team—Velez and Yolanda—in Miami Beach. He worked his way up to full-blown agent.

It was required by the laws of New York grammar that every sentence contain a subject, a verb, and an intersection. Sam's particular dialect also required that he drop a name or two before he hit a period.

"The Colonel and I were at the corner of Broadway and Fifty-Third when we decided to let Elvis go on Sullivan."

"It was when the Morris office moved to Sixth Avenue by Forty-Second street that I closed the deal for Marilyn with Fox."

"So Frank comes walking down Lex past Sixtieth with his Oscar in one hand and a slice in the other..."

When other agents passed on this singer, Sam signed him. When other agents wouldn't go near that actress, Sam signed her. When the rest of the business declared that act dead, Sam stuck with them.

"Sell it, don't smell it" moved Sam Fielder to Hollywood, launched him in the movie business and, finally, opened FCM: Fielder Creative Management.

The business grew. The legend of the man grew. Larger than life, they called him.

But tonight, there he was, Sam Fielder lying in a hospital bed looking remarkably small. He smiled and nodded when Stephanie and I pushed open the door to poke our heads in, then raised a hand from the rumpled sheet to beckon us to his side. Stephanie moved toward the bed and perched on the edge, lowering her head to her grandfather's chest. The old man stroked her hair. She had her father's hair—sandy and thick. (Of course she wanted it to be sleek, Asian if possible. Every time a commercial came on for volumizing shampoo, I pointed out: "See, that's what you've got naturally.")

Sam looked jaundiced in the greenish light of the room.

"I'm fine," he said. But it didn't sound like his voice. A gurgle punctuated his words.

"I'll have you know I'm lying in a fifteen thousand dollar bed."

"You're kidding," said Stephanie.

"I kid you not. Nothing but the best for your old grandpa."

I studied the numbers on the monitor: blood pressure, pulse rate, something else, I wasn't sure what. The numbers gave me something to focus on, to gather myself. I had been expecting to see Adam here. Of course Adam would be here. But he was not. And if he wasn't here, where was he? Who was he with? Was some woman nuzzling into his shoulder in a dark movie theater or reaching over to him in the front seat of his Prius? That damn thing was so small anyway—more like a cockpit than a car. It would take nothing for this other woman to lean over and kiss him on the cheek or on the neck. He could be easily distracted while driving. What if this other woman distracted him and he crashed the tiny car that barely afforded sardine can protection from the Escalade barreling headlong toward him? What if Adam were lying downstairs in the emergency room of this very hospital right now? Was I even supposed to care about any of this now that he was out of the house? Now that he was calling us separated? After what he'd done? What was it again that he had done? Oh yeah—the taste of the French Girl. There it was.

"Your blood pressure looks good," I said to Sam.

The old man had not been known as a deal-making shark for nothing. He could read faces like the veteran poker player he was. He watched me glance from the monitor to the door.

"He went to the Starbucks. Coffee from the cafeteria's not good enough for that one."

"I'm sure the cafeteria's closed at this hour, Sam."

"He would have gone to the Starbucks anyway."

I smiled and leaned down to kiss him on the forehead.

"Well, this was very dramatic of you," I said.

"I thought it was gas." He shook his head. "That's what people always say, and it turns out to be true. Funny, huh?"

"Funny," I said.

Stephanie was sitting up on the edge of the bed now. "It's a good thing you called nine-one-one."

"I figured everyone needs to ride in an ambulance once in their life. It was kind of fun. Felt like I was in a goddamn movie. Honest to Pete."

There had been several ambulance rides when Adam's mother was dying of cancer. Knowing Sam, he meant it was now his turn to be the special guest star of the episode. Out of a sense of obligation to my mother-in-law, I almost reminded him of these earlier rides, but Sam heaved a sigh and said, "In any event…" That's what Sam Fielder said when he wanted to make it clear there was nothing more to say on the topic.

"Can I get you anything, Sam?" I asked.

"No thanks, sweetie. Adam's bringing me a scoop of Jamoca Almond Fudge from the 31 Flavors."

"Is that a good idea?" Stephanie asked.

"Sure, honey. A little ice cream never hurt anyone."

"Sam..." I was ready to argue cholesterol. But when I looked at him, lying there, I thought better of it. Let the old guy eat what he wants.

"Maybe we should go," I said. "You'd sleep if we went, wouldn't you?" I didn't want to see Adam now. I had thought that I did, that I really did want to see him, but I was wrong.

"Maybe I would," Sam said, closing his eyes.

Stephanie and I kissed him on either cheek and said goodnight.

I was pretty sure I spotted Adam's back rounding a corner at the opposite end of the hall. But I didn't call to him. I convinced myself I was not one hundred percent positive it was Adam, though I knew every curve, every sinew of his back as well as my own. Better.

# CHAPTER TWELVE

I AWOKE ON MONDAY morning with a mission: I needed to get bumped up to third grade. That's what I told the principal's secretary when I walked into the administration office at the school where I volunteered once a week. I'd had a good run in second, but it was time for third. I didn't mention that I could not bear to say goodbye to Ernesto. But that was the truth, the truth that gripped me when I opened my eyes that morning and realized that my hours with Ernesto were numbered.

I had been spending one morning a week at Saint Christina's Elementary ever since Stephanie started middle school. The sudden impulse toward community service had blindsided me. I dropped Stephanie off at Seaview that first day of sixth grade and found myself driving south on Lincoln Blvd. to Venice to sign up.

I walked into the office and announced, "I want to volunteer."

Gwen lived not far from there, on the canals, and had mentioned that a flyer had circulated her neighborhood begging for volunteers at the local elementary schools. If only she had the time she would do it, Gwen said. Well, I had the time. Plenty of it with Stephanie slip-sliding from tween to teen.

The process felt more like applying for a job, but I didn't mind. It swabbed the whitewash off the volunteerism. I filled out forms. I got fingerprinted. I had a TB test and delivered proof of my good health.

Finally, I was escorted to a second grade classroom. The full name of the school was Saint Christina the Astonishing, and thirty-five little heads swiveled to gaze at me with all due astonishment.

I was assigned one child per semester to tutor in reading, though I usually stayed through recess to work with another child or two or to read to a small group. I sat on the floor and made them laugh with the tales of Amelia Bedelia, the wacky housekeeper with the overly literal bent. They smiled when Amelia "dressed" a chicken in a frilly apron. They tittered when she "pitched" a tent by throwing it across the yard. They belly-laughed when she baked a "sponge" cake. Each week, the semicircle around me grew. My Amelia Bedelia Club.

As Stephanie moved from sixth to seventh to eighth grade, I carved out a place for myself on a rug depicting the United States in a second grade classroom not really all that far from Stephanie's school, but as far away as the east coast from the west. It was a school where many of the children did not learn English until they arrived at kindergarten. I stayed in the second grade when Stephanie went on to high school. But as this, Stephanie's eleventh grade year pushed into spring, I did not think I could find the heart to stay in second grade any longer. I could not go to college with Stephanie, but I would to go to third grade with Ernesto.

It had been love at first sight. From the moment Ernesto sat down next to me at the squat, square table in the corner of the room, I had been enchanted by his moon face and swooping black eyelashes.

"Are you the reading lady?" he whispered on our first Monday morning.

"I am," I said. "And you must be Ernesto." I had received the usual background info from his teacher, Ms. Barcraft. Occasionally over the years, Ms. Barcraft had provided the additional tidbit. Consuela's father had been killed in Afghanistan. Teresa knew her two and three times tables already. Frankie wasn't very bright. Ms. Barcraft had actually said that: "You're getting Frankie. He's not very bright."

I had spent the entire semester trying to prove Ms. Barcraft wrong, but in the end, I had come to the conclusion that Frankie was not, in truth, very bright. If he had been at Seaview with Stephanie, some expert would have slapped a label on him—ADD, ADHD—to explain away his underachievement. But here at Saint Christina's, Frankie was allowed to be just plain not very bright as though it were simply another one of his traits, like the small white streak in his hair or his pear-shaped torso.

If Frankie wasn't so bright, then Ernesto was clearly special. His struggle with reading made no dent in that fact. I watched him push his chubby index finger along a line of text, pausing not just under each word, but under each letter as he searched his memory for its sound. I watched as his mouth strung the sounds together until they became a word. And I watched his enormous brown eyes look up at me, from under those swooping black lashes, when he transformed the squiggles on the page into an actual word. At those moments Ernesto reminded me that reading was no small accomplishment, that it was an alchemical leapfrog from squiggle to word to meaning.

I needed to be there to see his face next year as he deciphered all those third grade words. So many words lay ahead. Double consonants. Contractions. And what would his face do when he mastered a bonus word like "amazed"? My throat clenched when I thought of some other volunteer sharing those moments with him. It was no fair, not after I'd gotten him through all five of the short vowels.

When Ernesto returned from the Christmas holiday, he told me that Santa had gotten lost this year. Ernesto figured that Santa must not have known he had a new foster family. My heart split wide. I cornered the fourth grade volunteer in the girls' bathroom and asked if she had ever given a child a gift. The answer came back loud and clear. No.

Regardless, I arrived the next week with a book for each member of the class—each one wrapped in New Year's paper. I had gone to four different shops before finding any, and it had taken two more to find a roll that did not feature martini glasses.

I handed one to every child so that Ernesto would not be singled out, but would still have the thrill of opening a present. I even made sure that Ernesto's was not the only pop-up book in the batch, though his was the most elaborate. Even so, Ms. Barcraft took me aside.

"Please do not do that again. The children," she warned, "should not get in the habit of expecting things."

"But this was a surprise," I said. "The whole point of a surprise is that you don't expect it."

"Don't do it again," said Ms. Barcraft. "It's against policy."

Maybe the third grade teacher would see things differently. Maybe she would see what was special about Ernesto. How he studied the pictures so intently before giving me a nod to turn the page. How he drew illustrations when I read him a book that did not have enough pictures. How he looked off into the distance, not out of boredom or inattentiveness, but because his imagination could not be contained by the classroom. And how, in all my years at Saint Christina's, he was the only child to say thank-you every single Monday.

I couldn't go back to being just another boring grown-up who commandeered forty minutes of some kid's time, helping him sound out words before he could go outside to throw a dodge ball.

So this Monday, I arrived fifteen minutes early and marched into the office to have a chat with the principal's secretary.

"Third grade is spoken for," the woman said.

"But I've been really loyal to this school," I countered. "I've never made a request before."

"I'll see what I can do."

I knew she wouldn't. Keeping things the way they were was always the easier option. I would have to figure out how to say goodbye to Ernesto without crying. Crying was bound to be against policy.

# CHAPTER THIRTEEN

"I HATE YOU!" STEPHANIE's voice, shrill and charged, blasted through the rhythmic rumble of the washing machine. I was folding wash in the laundry room off the kitchen when Stephanie burst in after school. I clutched a towel to my chest as though its warmth could protect me.

"I hate you!" Stephanie shrieked again. As if I didn't quite catch it the first time.

I had escaped those three words until now, cruising through the legendarily brutal middle school years and landing in high school smugly unscathed.

Barbara predicted the three words when Stephanie was no more than a few days old. "When she's thirteen, she'll tell you she hates you."

But Stephanie never said them. Not my Stephanie. Until today.

"What brought this on?" I asked.

"You've ruined my life." Of course, the two invectives would launch as Siamese twins. "I was sitting there eating lunch with Mallory and a bunch of other people and Andrea Fine walked by and patted me on the shoulder."

Andrea Fine—the school psychologist. *Got it.*

I finished folding the towel, in thirds then in half, still pressing it against my chest. Stephanie grabbed a Diet Coke from the fridge and rummaged for the bottle opener in a drawer. There was something in the washing machine that shouldn't be there. It clanked against the interior—metal against metal—an angry, persistent metronome. Stephanie must have left something in a pocket, but I let the thing, whatever it was, rattle.

"I'll call Andrea Fine tomorrow," I said.

"Don't you dare."

"Okay, I won't," I assured her. "What do you want me to do?"

"I want you to put things back to normal," said Stephanie, her eyes cool with determination. They had my heavy lid, but were Adam's precise steel gray.

"Sometimes things aren't that simple," I said.

"That's not what Daddy says."

Stephanie waited for a reaction, but I said nothing. She had spent the past weeks following the rule, not mentioning one parent to the other. Suddenly the door cracked open to all she'd locked away. The gale force of accumulated fear and fury and sadness blew it off its hinges.

"Daddy made me promise not to get in the middle. He says it's not fair to me. But what's not fair is that I should have to keep my mouth shut. I know, some things happen between two people…" I suspected Stephanie was quoting her father there. "But we happen to be a family of three. I'm in this family, too. Nobody's thinking about me. Especially you. You're not thinking about me or Daddy. He's stuck in some stupid hotel room. I mean, honestly, it's all so completely lame. What's Daddy doing in a hotel? Like, what's wrong with this picture? Everything! And you don't even care. You're not thinking about anybody but yourself. You're so selfish! You're so selfish, you won't even tell me what's really going on. That's just… that's just…rude!"

Stephanie found the bottle opener, popped the cap off her Coke and took a swig. I didn't move. Give in to the crash of a tidal wave instead of stiffening against it.

"Daddy's waiting for you to snap out of it. He may be able to wait forever, but I can't. This is not supposed to happen in our family. I'm sorry if you and Daddy had a stupid fight. Who cares? Get over it. I mean, honestly, grow up."

She paused for me to respond, to react in some way, any way. But I said nothing. I had no air left to speak. It hissed out through the pinprick in my heart, sealed until now by the Band-Aid notion that Stephanie was handling all this with aplomb.

After all, Adam was not absent from Stephanie's life. The past weeks had been filled with brunches and dinners and long walks on the bluffs overlooking the ocean during which, I imagined, father and daughter had heart-to-hearts about the future. I told myself that Stephanie's relationship with Adam would flower. But I knew better. Their relationship had never needed extra watering.

Stephanie gulped the rest of the Coke, swallowing hard against the carbonation. Even so, a cluster of bubbles gathered in her esophagus. She tapped the spot beneath the hollow at her collarbone. I winced, feeling the pressure of the bubbles in my own throat.

I willed her to keep going, to hold nothing back. *Say it all. I deserve it.*

"I'm sorry if you're having a hard time," she said, more accusation than empathy. "I'm sorry for everything I ever did that disappointed you. I'm sorry for everything I ever did wrong. I'm sorry! I'm sorry! I'm sorry!"

She dropped the empty bottle into the recycling container under the kitchen sink. It clinked against another bottle. Both of us shivered at the sound of the crack.

"You could never disappoint me," I said. "Never ever."

◆◆◆

THAT NIGHT—ANOTHER VISIT FROM the vertigo. It grabbed me by the scruff of the neck and swung me around like a lasso. But this time, no vomiting, no sweats, no headache. Only the spinning. As though my body had shooed away the supporting players and let the above-the-title star run the show.

"I hate you," Stephanie had said. I could live with that. "You've ruined my life"—that was the tough one. Because maybe I had.

The day's mail lay beside me where I had tossed it on the bed. I propped my head up on three pillows, angled just so, and sifted through it. Magazines kept coming that I had never subscribed to. Several had arrived today. I opened one and was smacked by a fragrance sample. Not my mother's Jean Nate, nor Miss Zipser's Jungle Gardenia. More masculine. Like English Leather.

My first official boyfriend had worn English Leather. Jeff Bonham—devoted, kind, thoughtful. He'd had some gentleman training drummed into him, that Jeff. He always complimented my attire. He always walked on the curb side of the sidewalk as though to protect me from the gutter splash of a passing carriage.

He always held me for a long moment after kissing me good-night. Jeff Bonham was all good things.

I saved mementos of our dates in a box covered in lavender silk. Ticket stubs, menus, play bills. The stuff of a proper courtship. A respectable courtship. But not a sparkly courtship. No sparkle. No spark.

I began to invent protean versions of Jeff, morphing him into someone I knew he was not so that I could manufacture a decent case of butterflies when he was on his way to pick me up. But then I would look out the window and see him getting out of his car and walking up the path to my door, and the butterflies would turn into something else, something more like a brick. So when, one night over Number 11s at Hamburger Hamlet, nice enough Jeff Bonham said, "I've been thinking that maybe we should...," I breathed a sigh of relief. *Thank God*, I thought. *Next*.

These days, they'd call Jeff Bonham a starter boyfriend. Gwen called her sixteen-month marriage a starter marriage, though she had never moved on to the next category, whatever that was. It was like she learned all her lines, but decided she didn't want to be an actress after all. She kept tossing out boyfriends like first pancakes. Had I been in a starter marriage all these years? Surely there was a statute of limitations on starters that my marriage had long outrun.

I tossed the smelly magazine onto the floor. The perfume was stinging my nose, stinging my eyes, so much so that my right eye began to twitch. I closed my eyes tight, but the twitch was too deep to care. So deep that it crossed my mind that it might never stop.

# CHAPTER FOURTEEN

BARBARA ARRIVED WITH VENTI Frappuccinos. It was one of the many "in-service" days that popped up on Stephanie's Seaview School calendar with surprising regularity. Translation: no school. Stephanie was halfway through her Frappuccino when I came downstairs.

"Bopper and I are going for a hike," said Stephanie.

Stephanie had called her aunt Bopper since she was three years old. She was strapped into her car seat as the Beach Boys sang, "Ba-ba-ba-ba-Barbara Ann." "Who's Bopper?" she asked.

"What do you mean?"

"They're singing about Bopper Ann."

"No, sweetie," I explained. "It's Barbara. Like Aunt Barbara." Barbara was Bopper ever after.

"Want to come?" Barbara asked me as she slathered her arms with sunscreen.

"I'm exhausted," I said. "I was up all night."

Stephanie shot me a look, yesterday's rage replaced by the slightest tinge of remorse.

"I was worrying about Sam all night," I added. I didn't want Stephanie to feel responsible for my insomnia. "He didn't look good when I saw him yesterday."

"That old coot's going to be fine." Barbara had never been a fan. "He's going to live to be a hundred out of sheer stubbornness."

She was probably right. "You two go without me," I said.

"Are you sure?" asked Stephanie.

"I'm sure." I was not sure. Lately I was never sure if I wanted to be alone or with other people. The only thing I knew for sure was that whichever choice I made, it was bound to be wrong.

Barbara and Stephanie scurried out, chirping "See you!"

A second later Stephanie stuck her head back in the door. "I volunteered you to come on the field trip to the Hollyhock House. But you have to sign up online."

"Okay."

"Thanks, Mamasita." And she was out the door. Yesterday's explosion had served its purpose: she felt better, I felt devastated.

My laptop lay closed on the built-in desk next to the swing-out pantry. I flipped open the computer and logged onto the Seaview School site, navigating my way to Stephanie's History of Los Angeles elective. I looked forward to these field trips, both because I found learning about my city's backstory reassuring and because chaperoning a field trip reminded me that, even though the kids on the bus were now hormonal grenades, motherhood was still my raison d'être. At least for another year.

As I read the information—date, time, location—my concentration evaporated. Staring at the screen invited other images to barge in. Body parts. Young, smooth body parts. And, most searingly, the tenderness in Adam's eyes when he looked at the girl lying beneath him, the smile he could not contain as he leaned down to kiss her.

I was jonesing to watch the video and reread the email chain, but they were gone forever. I had made sure of that. Thank God. Godammit. It hardly mattered. Thinking of them made my chest tighten. A Pavlovian asthmatic.

I added my name to the chaperone list. But the computer had taken on a permamently creepy aura. Something had frizzled its way through the Ethernet. The virus of virtual infidelity.

A perky pop-up materialized on the right of my screen. TODAY ONLY—a sale on shopbop.com. Stephanie had requested a flouncy top from the site for her birthday last fall. I suspected that most of the clothing on the site was too young for me, but I clicked on the link anyway.

The possibilities were thrilling. Shop by designer, category, trend. Troll the sales—thirty, fifty, seventy percent off. Have a peek at "What's New." Peruse the style guide known as the "Look Book."

I stared at the screen, considering the possibilities. I clicked on "Designer Index." An alphabetized list, plus the promise of free worldwide delivery within three days or less. Amazing—they could get a Lauren Mirken handbag to Antarctica by Tuesday. I scrolled down the list of designer names. Some I knew. More I did not. Poised on the mouse, my hand suddenly took on a mind of its own. I clicked on Marc Jacobs, rolling the cursor over the pictures to enlarge them one by one. The girls in the photographs stared into the camera lens as if to say, *This is how you wear this skirt, these pants, this top*, their hipbones jutting forward, their knees akimbo to show the diameter of thighs no bigger than a soup can. Page after page of these girls. Fashions. Accessories. Shoes.

I clicked on "View All." I moved on to other designers: Anna Sui. Nanette Lepore. Theory. The clothes, the purses, the jewelry rolled by. I communed with the screen.

When I stood up from the little desk twenty-five minutes later, I had spent eight hundred fifty-three dollars and sixty-seven cents and had a cyber hangover of guilt.

I would atone in the safer harbor of the kitchen, cleaning out the fridge and the cupboards. I tossed expired yogurts and bottles of salad dressing that contained oil slicks floating atop congealed glop. I progressed to the pantry where I jettisoned old rice pilaf mixes and quinoa studded with tiny black specks that might have been alive. I moved on to drawers and cupboards and finally came upon the old Crockpot at the back of a corner cabinet.

Inspired, I spent the rest of the afternoon assembling a mixture of chicken, tomato, peppers and onion that smelled like a family still lived in this house—an Italian family, not mine, but a family nonetheless. The whole enterprise so energized me that I passed much of the next several hours running into the kitchen to peer into the Crockpot, defeating the purpose of an appliance specifically designed for neglect.

◆◆◆

OVER THE NEXT WEEK, I continued to cook. I sat in bed surrounded by old friends from my newlywed days. Jacques Pepin. Charlie Trotter. And, of course, Julia Child. I made new friends with Giada De Laurentiis, Ina Garten, and Curtis Stone. The Sub-Zero filled with all shapes of Tupperware. Leftovers pushed aside the usual half-pints of tuna or egg salad from the deli counter at the supermarket. When a wave of olfactory nostalgia washed over me, I scouted for the bread-maker long retired to a cabinet in the garage. Surely the smell of home-baked bread would calm the chatter that looped in my brain. The chatter that kept echoing, *Where's Adam? How did I get here? How did this become my life? What happens now?*

On Thursdays, Stephanie's post as photo editor of *The Seaview Current* kept her at school until eight or nine o'clock. This Thursday, I was fidgety. I had already flipped the flank steak so that both sides would absorb the marinade of soy, ginger, and honey. I fluffed the basmati rice and turned down the flame. I made a salad dressing of extra virgin olive oil and fig balsamic. When there was nothing left to do, I gathered the silverware to set the table. I had already set out the placemats before I realized that I had grabbed three forks, three knives, three spoons. I was placing one of each back into the drawer when the doorbell rang.

The sun had set some time earlier, but I felt no need to turn on any lights. I preferred moving about the house in the semidarkness. I put my eye to the peephole. There, under the porch light, stood the UPS man. I opened the door and scratched my signature onto his tablet, but could not imagine what he was bringing. Only after I had carried the box into the kitchen and sliced open the tape did I recall that just the other day I had logged a second session trolling the shopping sites. If only I could remember what it was that I had bought.

The skirt was shorter than it looked in the picture. I had assumed the model was eight feet tall and that her flamingo legs accounted for the length of the skirt or lack thereof. Apparently not.

I didn't feel like trying it on. The skirt disturbed me. Not so much the skirt itself, but the fact that I didn't remember clicking on it. That's the way I thought of the moment. Not shopping. Not buying. Just clicking. What had prompted me to click on this item: an acidic, head-turning purple with diagonal zippers at the pockets?

When Stephanie arrived home a few hours later, she wandered into my room brandishing the skirt.

"Thanks, Mom," she said. "This is really cute."

It was too embarrassing to admit that I had bought the thing for myself, a supposed grown-up. This online shopping thing was not going well. If only I had a hobby, something I could do with my hands when I felt myself shifting into hyperdrive. Something like crocheting or playing solitaire that would unplug my mind. I had toyed with knitting when it had been the rage a decade or so ago, but the pastime never took. Though Barbara had a bit of the Martha Stewart in her, I had no patience for crafting. And painting was Adam's domain. Never mine.

# CHAPTER FIFTEEN

I HAD NO ARTISTIC ability whatsoever.

That I knew. Ever since the third grade at The Ridgepoint School when I was asked to draw a tree. Mrs. Kanin, the doughy art teacher, stood before the class, the buttons of her smock straining against her paunch. She gestured toward a photograph of a sprawling maple pinned to the bulletin board at the front of the room and instructed us to begin with the trunk of the tree, then to construct a network of branches, and then, finally, to fill in the leaves with a series of tiny lines—hatch marks—attaching to the limbs at a just-so angle.

Caroline McCardle created such a stellar example of this technique that her maple was hung not in the art room with the other efforts, but in the school's main corridor, the artery that led from the porte cochere to the Great Hall, a stately room redolent of rubbed mahogany. It was the room where every major all-school gathering took place. Caroline's tree got to hang in the corridor on the way to that room. As the school year progressed, it was joined by other perfect art works: a still life of two lemons and a bunch of grapes, a portrait of a girl playing the cello, and a watercolor of a sunset over the ocean.

Adam was the only person I ever told about the tree with the hatch marks and the corridor with the examples of the perfect still lifes and the perfect sunsets. And how I longed to have something of mine hang alongside them.

I met Adam my sophomore year at the University of Southern California. I was taking a survey course in Art History. Although I could not for the life of me paint a tree, I could make it my business to memorize the names and dates of every painting of significance— profile, urn, and, yes, tree—throughout western civilization. Toward the end of the semester, the professor posted a sign-up sheet for term papers—a list of paintings, some iconic (Mona Lisa, Starry Night, The Birth of Venus), some less so. I wrote my name next to Chagall's "The Birthday." So did Adam.

That afternoon I ran into Adam in the quad outside the art building. He wasn't one of those guys in chinos and loafers, nor one of the guys in ratty jeans. His hair was neither jock short nor long enough to be tied back with a leather cord. He looked like someone who was meant to look exactly the way he looked—not like so many kids on campus who looked like they were temporarily trying on an identity for size. "You're doing the Chagall, too," he said.

"Yeah," I said, "but I don't know what I'm going to write." There was nothing scholarly about my choice. I simply could not resist the vision of a man performing acrobatics to prove his love with a kiss. His face blurred with passion. Love eschewing gravity. Floating. That was Chagall.

"I know he said his wife was the great central image of his art," I said. "But that's about it so far. I've barely started my research."

Adam looked at me quizzically. "It doesn't have to be a research paper, you know," he said. "Look at the painting and write about what you see."

I shook my head. "I don't think so. There wouldn't be enough."

"I bet there would be plenty."

*But would it be right?*

Then Adam reached over—casually, as though we'd known each other for years—and brushed my hair behind my shoulder.

Three months later we were in his bed.

◆◆◆

Now, WITH ADAM OUT of the house, I kept rewinding to the string of rainy afternoons that descended that year, the kind of rain that's business as usual in other cities but brings LA to its knees. There were street closures and Sigalerts—a continual downpour that provided a happy excuse for us to stay in bed.

The story that began that February was not supposed to be derailed by this plot twist—such a pedestrian plot twist at that. Husband's mid-life crisis drives him to revisit young love. That

February so many years ago, I believed I was his only love, as we lay in bed, working the New York Times crossword puzzle, and eating Jiffy Pop for dinner.

Adam licked the salt from his fingers, then slowly traced my spine, lingering at the small of my back to rest his palm there. One finger circled the dimple to the left of my spine. There was no dimple on the right (as I had learned during a scoliosis check performed by the Ridgepoint nurse). Adam didn't seem to mind the lack of symmetry. "This spot here," he said. "It makes everything right with the world."

Now, lying alone in bed, I ran my finger across the small of my back to see if it was still there. I had to arch my back to feel its indentation, but there it was. If only it hadn't stopped working its magic.

We moved in together six months after that first night in Adam's bed. It seemed fast for me, but I needed to move out of my apartment. Because of the duck incident.

In an effort to step up our sophistication quotient, Gwen and I had decided to throw a dinner party. Adam and I had already coasted into being a couple, and Gwen had her eye on a guy in Brain and Behavior. (He was the only other non-biology major in the class, and they forged a connection from a shared ignorance of semipermeable membranes.)

Gwen and I scoured our mothers' cookbooks, landing on a full-page picture of a high-gloss bird. The caption identified it as Muscovy Duck with Cumberland Sauce. The recipe looked complicated.

"It's long," I told Gwen, neglecting to mention that it was, in fact, so long as to be subdivided into four sections, beginning with instructions to pluck any stray pinfeathers with tweezers. Gwen was relieved when the man behind the poultry counter assured us that step had already been taken care of, but I was disappointed. I did not like shortcuts. I did not want to cheat in any way. We proceeded nonetheless—piercing the mallard's skin, stuffing its cavity with oranges and onions, roasting and glazing the bird with a reduction of grapes and citrus and wine. The duck glistened. I carried it to the table on a meticulously garnished platter.

The boys ate every morsel. Even though the post-feminist era held full sway, I could not help but wonder if the most direct way to a man's heart was indeed through his stomach every bit as much as through parts farther south. To prove the point, Gwen and Timothy retreated to her bedroom, the lingering aroma of duck fat hanging between them.

Adam and I turned to the kitchen for clean-up. I opened the oven door and closed it immediately, like a surgeon stitching up a patient upon discovering a tumor more widespread than predicted. I headed straight into my room, ignoring the noises coming from Gwen's, and began to pack.

"What are you doing?" Adam asked.

"I have to move."

"How come?"

"Did you see that oven? It can't be cleaned. It will never be the same."

"Okay," said Adam, "move in with me."

So I moved in with Adam. He sketched a duck—waving its wing from inside an oven—and hung it over the bed.

After graduation, Adam began weaving bedtime stories from our days.

"Today was a great day," he would say. And then he would tell its tale. How we had read the morning paper. How we each went off to work or, on the weekends, to run errands. How we returned to the apartment where we spent the early evening watching an old movie on TV, *The Philadelphia Story* or *To Catch A Thief.* How we went to dinner at that little place on Pico, where he had the short ribs and I had the chicken. No detail was too small to be included, as though reciting them all would permanently store them in his brain. He was tucking in the day. And then would come the happy ending: now, here we were, together.

"You and me," he said, wrapping his arms around me, as though it were more than the title of the story of our day. As though it were a complete sentence.

Gradually, I felt safe enough to tell him stories, too. At first, I told them like they were about someone else. That girl who wore knee socks only when the temperature fell below sixty-eight degrees as prescribed in the Ridgepoint student handbook. The girl who presented her fingernails for bi-weekly inspection, making sure they were neither bitten, nor extending beyond her fingertips more than the slightest crescent moon. The girl who took her PE uniform home every Friday and never neglected to bring it back, washed and pressed, on Monday. A Ridgepoint girl. I made the stories funny and ironic.

But when I told him about my struggle to draw that maple tree in art class, my eyes welled with tears. I confided for the first time in my life how desperately I had wanted to have a picture hang in the Ridgepoint corridor that led to the Great Hall.

"Now," he said, "you draw that tree and we'll hang it right here." He patted the hunk of empty wall next to his drawing of the duck.

But I never did. Adam's art filled the walls instead.

◆◆◆

WITH ADAM GONE, I found myself waking up before the sun. Five am. Then four. My motor idled too high to sleep. Like a scientist obsessed with a formula that works theoretically, but simply does not in the real world, I kept telling and retelling myself the story of our life to find out where the chink first appeared.

Early on, Adam sold several large canvases for decent sums of money, and then better than decent. At least two artist reps fought over him. He landed one commission and then another. He had a show at a gallery on La Cienega. It seemed like he was going to be able to make a living at this.

Maybe we could buy a house. We spent a year's worth of Sunday afternoons exploring open houses—a year of Sunday nights with me despairing we would never find anything that met my criteria. I wanted a house with EGGS: Elegance, Grace, Geniality and Style.

"It shouldn't be that hard to find," I cried.

Adam held me in his arms. "Maybe we could try for three out of four."

"I've thought about that," I said. "But I can't figure out which one to let go. I can't seem to let any of them go. I just can't."

We held out, leaving six realtors in our wake, and sacrificing all our free time to scouting favored neighborhoods for For Sale signs.

"This is it," I said as we pulled up in front of a two-bedroom, one-and-a-half-bath single story craftsman. My instinct was right. We put a bid in on the place that afternoon.

Later, over moo shu pork, Adam said, "You know what we might as well do now that we're buying this house?"

"What?" I asked even though I already knew.

And so we got married. Why not? All the pieces were in place. We were going to be homeowners. We were building a life together. And we still couldn't get enough of each other. One afternoon, when Adam reached to change a light bulb in an overhead fixture, a slice of skin between rib cage and hipbone was revealed, and I nearly swooned. That had to be a good sign. To still feel that rush even though we'd been together four whole years.

I freelanced as an "author's liaison," wrangling writers on book tours from appearance to interview to signing. But I knew my passion would lie in motherhood, the gooey center I felt compelled to coat in the hard candy shell of career. When it seemed like Adam might swing a life as that rarest of creatures, a working artist, I came to believe I might win the luxury of being a full-time mom. Cocktail party chit-chat be damned.

But as quickly as it had begun to glow, the aura of promise surrounding Adam's career started to fade. After five years, he was no longer the new kid in town. His rep got him a few commissions, one for a small hospital in Mar Vista and another for a restaurant in Tarzana.

"It's come to this," Adam told me one night in bed. "The owner of some steakhouse is telling me what colors he wants for the painting over the bar."

By then, I was pregnant, very pregnant.

Normally, Adam's father pestered him on a regular basis about his plans for the future. But Sam kept his mouth shut for the duration of my pregnancy. Even with the baby coming sooner and sooner, Sam remained mum. I figured he had finally taken a giant step back—parental Simon Says.

But Sam Fielder knew the art of negotiation. He had put the offer on the table many times. Why didn't Adam come to work at the agency? "You know how many guys would give their eye teeth for a job in the mail room? You know how many more would give their left nut not to have to work their way up from the bottom?"

Now, suddenly, Sam's silence was deafening. With nothing, no one to battle against, Adam's arguments for staying away from the family business seemed little more than childish obstinacy.

So one morning, exactly three weeks before Stephanie was born, Adam woke up, put on a suit and tie, and drove to Santa Monica.

Thirty years earlier, his father had chosen to house the agency at the beach. All the other prominent agencies staked their claim in prime West Hollywood and Beverly Hills real estate, on the Sunset Strip or Wilshire Boulevard 90210. Not Sam Fielder. He stayed at the beach.

"Why the hell would I want to move? Look at that..." the old man once said to me as he stretched his stocky legs onto a massive rosewood desk and nodded his square head toward the wall of glass and the ocean beyond. "Out there...that's what keeps you grounded."

I had glimpsed the shred of a soul. Either that, or my father-in-law's eyes were puddling because the place was finally paid for. Maybe he loved seeing his moniker on the front of a building. An edifice complex, people joked. Even though the name was bastardized all over town. Mostly, Fielder Creative Management— FCM—was known as Fuck Creativity, Man.

"You look so handsome," I said to Adam as I stood at the back door June Cleaver-style, waving him goodbye like a princess on a parade float. Adam was about to get into his Saab when he turned back to me.

"You know what?" he said. "I know how to do this." He was astonished by the epiphany. "I can be an agent. All those years with my dad—I learned it by osmosis."

"Of course you did," I said.

"How about that? I can do this."

"You're doing it," I said. "And you're going to be great at it."

Neither of us knew whether that was a compliment or an insult.

Adam slid behind the wheel, backed out of the garage, and went to work. Just like everyone else's husband.

And though Adam drove west like a creature drawn to the glimmer of the Pacific, he was really headed for the intersection of art and commerce, a juncture so precarious that it would require Cirque du Soleil skill to keep his balance there.

Within the year we moved to the house on Strathmore. It felt like so much house to me, embarrassingly so, but it was walking distance to Holmby Park where I could send Stephanie down the slide and chat with other mothers about bedtime meltdowns and first visits to the dentist. But, as it turned out, I was out of sync with the neighborhood. Few other mothers came to the park. Homeowners walked their dogs around the perimeter while nannies tended to the children, punching straws into juice boxes and flicking sand from scraped knees.

More than a little wistfully, I thought, *our salad days are over*.

Literally speaking, they lay ahead. Lunches with friends meant nothing but salads in the years to come. So many salads. Salads composed of overpriced greenery, often bitter and curly, with a stray tendril inevitably poking its way out of your mouth. Salads decorated with glazed walnuts or dried cranberries and a sprinkling of feta. Salads featuring heirloom produce in rainbow colors that surely must confuse preschoolers taught to identify a tomato as... say, red. My salad days had actually been my burger-and-fries days, and I missed them in the same nagging way that I sometimes craved an In-N-Out double-double.

# CHAPTER SIXTEEN

OCCASIONALLY I FELT LIKE I had stepped off a boat, but the vertigo did not hit full force for several weeks. I had resorted to that foolproof method of banishing an ailment: I made an appointment with the doctor. Even so, I was at that age when various body things started to go wrong. I needed to eliminate the nagging thought bubble that popped up whenever the vertigo struck—the one containing the words "Brain Tumor."

That thought bubble hovered as I drove into Beverly Hills for my appointment. I distracted myself at a red light by checking out the window at Barney's, but a homeless man caught my eye instead. I generally calloused myself against these guys, but I had to give this man points for creativity. He clutched a sign: "I am God's next of kin."

I dug out two singles and handed them to him. Our fingers brushed as he took the bills. Then he said, "Have a wonderful day, sweetheart." I couldn't remember the last time someone had called me sweetheart, let alone the last time I had felt like someone's sweetheart. Tears streaked my cheeks.

On my way into the medical building, I dabbed my finger on my tongue and wiped at the Pierrot stripes of mascara. I was about to snap my compact shut when I noticed something disturbing… at the outside corner of my left eye: a line. To make matters worse, it had a few tiny offshoots. My finger flew to the spot. It was deep enough to feel only at the very corner of my eye, but still, that didn't bode well. I shifted the mirror to my right eye. There was something there, too—but nothing like the left. I was an LA girl. Now I was an LA woman—with driver's window grooves.

My internist had recently moved. I studied the directory for his suite number, trying not to stare at my reflection in the glass, at this awful etching around my eyes (which now appeared as deep as the San Andreas fault). And then I spotted it. The name of another doctor. One Howard Grossman. The man responsible for making half the mothers at Stephanie's school look like they'd been to the Mauna Lani over Winter Break. Right here. On the first floor.

I had ten minutes to kill. I strode into Dr. Grossman's office before I could think twice. The waiting room was full, his eager patients falling into two categories: rookies striving for nonchalance as they leafed through pamphlets, and returning customers, giddy with the anticipation of addressing a whole new sector of face or body. If there were women in LA who didn't care about how they looked, they were not in this room. Probably not in this building, or in Beverly Hills, or west of downtown. Who was I kidding? No such women exist anywhere. Even those women who seem devoid of romanticism and awash in, for example, the wonders of astrophysics must hope for a sprinkle of stardust when they study their reflections.

But the women in this waiting room were not looking to vanish an imperfection here and there. They were held prisoner by a very particular phantom—perfection itself. Maybe I needed a dose of that. Maybe the tiniest remodel would have made my husband look at me the way he looked at that girl on the computer screen. Maybe if Dr. Grossman had erased three-year-old Stephanie's bout of pneumonia from my forehead, Adam would never have gone chasing that French phantasm. Come to think of it, maybe the good doctor could give me back the body of a woman who had never given birth at all. Is that what Adam wanted? I never thought so, but maybe Barbara knew better—maybe he was just a man. Maybe the illusion of immortality resided for him not in plain old everyday family life, but in new, young flesh. I didn't necessarily want him back, but I wanted him to eat his heart out. I looked at the women in the waiting room. *I'll have what they're having.*

I approached the receptionist window; the young woman was talking on the phone. I waited, gathering an assortment of brochures. Most pictured women preternaturally aglow, smiling the youthful smile of a debutante from a countenance serene in its linelessness. One brochure sung the praises of an injectable hyaluronic acid-based filler designed for the mid or deep dermis. It could be used for either dynamic or static wrinkles. I wondered which kind I had. Static, probably. They didn't seem to be doing anything remarkable, just sitting there ruining my day. The pamphlet assured me the substance was "basically harmless" and was particularly effective for areas like nasolabial folds. That's where they get you. The instant I read that phrase, I had to get mine fixed at once. There could be no going back to thinking of them as part of my face now that they had a medical name.

I read on, fascinated by the possibilities of facial remodeling.

"Ever wake up in the morning, had a good look at your face, and then backed away from the mirror with a shudder?"

"Yes!" I wanted to scream. Especially since becoming acquainted with Young French Girl.

The receptionist turned her attention to me. "I'd like to make an appointment for a consultation," I said.

"Certainly. Are you a new patient?"

"Yes."

I thought the receptionist smiled at me, but I couldn't be sure. Her lips protruded stiffly, revealing a glimpse of pink underside that I found disconcerting, almost obscene. She reminded me of the stuffed platypus that Stephanie used to sleep with when she was a toddler. The girl tapped her high-gloss manicure on her keyboard as she scanned the screen.

"He has an opening on January twelfth," she said.

"Next January?" I was confused. Hadn't January come and gone not long ago and wasn't the next one really far away?

"Yes," said the receptionist, "next January. Shall I book you?"

That was so far away. Adam could have moved to France by then. I could be staring at the side dish offerings night after night, driving myself more loco than the pollo.

"I can put you on the waiting list, but you have to have an appointment for me to do that," the girl said.

I fingered the corner of my eye where time and the sun had done their plowing. "Sure. I guess so." I gave the girl my name and phone number as a patient emerged from an examining room. She looked like she'd gone five rounds with George Foreman. And his grill. Bruises swelled around her lips and along her nasolabial folds. She kept making strange faces—scowling, scrunching, and stretching wide the corners of her mouth in a silent "Eek!" She caught me staring at her and said, "Twenty-five times," as though that constituted explanation enough.

I nodded as if I were a member of the club.

The receptionist handed me an appointment card and said, "See you in January." Then she added, "Need any products today?" She gestured toward a glass case behind her stocked with vials and bottles and pumps...oh my.

"I don't know," I said. "Is there something I can't live without?"

The girl nodded knowingly. "The new one with coffeeberry extract. It's a miracle worker."

"I could use one of those," I said. And before I knew it, I had bought the rejuvelixir. I wished it had been one of the ones that came in an amber glass bottle, like from an apothecary, glowing with magic.

On the way out of the office, I overheard one patient saying to another, "You know, they call it a lunchtime procedure. And that's exactly what I do. I mean, I always book mine for lunchtime. Might as well force myself to skip lunch. That way..." At that point, the woman leaned closer to whisper conspiratorially, "That way, I'm not only getting rid of my wrinkles, but I lose half a pound!"

Absorbed by this woman's secret of fabulousness, I bumped smack into a young lady—an actress, I thought—with skin so polished I could almost see myself in it.

"I'm so sorry," I said.

"No worries," said the girl.

I could not help but laugh at the ridiculousness of that suggestion.

# CHAPTER SEVENTEEN

SAM LOOKED BETTER TODAY. Or maybe it was my clean bill of health from the doctor. No brain tumor. He had sent me on my way with a prescription for Antivert and the name of a book about meditating. More time alone with my mind? No thanks.

Whatever the reason, Sam's color was better and he had managed to shave. When I entered his hospital room, he smiled at me so sweetly it broke my heart.

"There's my girl," he said.

He never spoke to Adam's sister, his own daughter, that way. He was a man who was hard on himself, and he saw too much of himself in Kathy to eye her with anything less than the sharpest scrutiny. But he could relax with me, his daughter-in-law. Blood ran thicker than water, but sometimes the flimsier trickle made relationships less fraught. I was so grateful for that right now. No inquisition.

He asked only, "How you doin', baby doll?"

"Good."

"Can I ask you something?" He didn't wait for an answer. It was a rhetorical question. "What's so bad about this life my son has given you?"

I grabbed the pitcher on the side table—rose-colored plastic—and refilled it at the bathroom sink. I wondered what Adam had told the old man, stunned that he had told him anything. I could be sure it had nothing to do with Penpal French Girl.

"Don't get me wrong. I know it takes two. One to talk, one to listen...Old joke..." Sam rasped. "But honestly, Maura, what do you expect?"

I replaced the lid on the pitcher and stood there, staring at myself in the mirror. I'd be damned if I'd share the answer to that question with my father-in-law. Especially since I had no clue what the answer was.

Sam coughed. Hard. I poured him a glass of water, but he shooed it away, managing a wink—his way of saying everything was going to be okay. Turn out in the end, as he would have put it had he been able to catch his breath.

He nodded toward the flat-screen mounted high on the opposite wall. He was watching the late morning news. The anchor threw it over to the arts critic, that guy who always wore outlandish vests. Today, it was a brocade number befitting his review of last night's premier of Wagner's Ring Cycle at the Music Center.

Sam shook his head, struggling to inhale. "I guess that proves it," he coughed. "Who cares what those New York pricks say? We've got ourselves culture up the ying yang. The deal is, you got to take the 405 to the 10 to get to it." Always with the intersections.

His voice was reed thin. He fumbled for the remote, its cord ensnared in the bars at the side of the bed. I untangled it and handed it to him. He clicked off the television.

"Is there anything you need, Sam?" I asked.

"I'd kill for a hunk of meatloaf from the Ivy."

I hopped up.

"Not now. It doesn't have to be right now."

"I've got nothing else to do," I said, heading for the door. "Anything else?"

"No, baby doll. That'll do it. "

"I'll see you in a bit." And I was off.

It took less than five minutes to get to the Ivy from Cedars-Sinai, but I circled for another ten looking for a parking spot. I refused to wind my way through the narrow, coiled passageways of a structure. The doctor may have assured me that my symptoms were consistent with garden variety vertigo (benign paroxysmal positional, just like Barbara said—goddammit), but I wasn't going to chance corkscrewing through a parking structure.

I finally found a spot in front of a new, high-end furniture store on the corner of Beverly and Robertson. The room vignettes in the windows looked like they'd been lifted from an Italian movie circa 1966. I could see Marcello Mastroianni lounging on the vanilla leather chaise. It occurred to me that this is the way Adam and I would have decorated our house when we first moved in had we been able to afford it. But that was nearly twenty years ago. The urge to infuse our home with ultra chic had given way to the Fisher-Price invasion. Sleek gave way to slouchy, cool to cushy. Adam and I had nested, and a nest is feathered, not faddish.

As I walked the few blocks south to the Ivy, I caught sight of a man getting out of his car. He was about fifty—Hollywood handsome, fit, impeccably dressed. He stepped out of a black BMW and grabbed his jacket from the back seat. I watched him slip on the herringbone sport coat, finessing that little flip men do to the collar when they put on a jacket, forcing it to lie flat in the back. The maleness of the move made me ache—so subtle, nearly imperceptible really, yet so deeply rooted in some sort of masculine muscle memory.

It was like the thing Adam did with his tie when he arrived home. He did it automatically, without thinking, but there was something so personal about the wriggle of the knot. The tie would relax. The knot would slip. The real Adam would be home.

In the last few years I had noticed that the tie made no difference. Adam never completely disengaged from his day. The specter of office-Adam had set up shop in his face, not merely in his wardrobe.

I surveyed the patio at the Ivy. It was still a little early for all the men in ties, the expense account lunch crowd. Although I phoned from the car as soon as I left the hospital, the order was not ready. I chatted with Albert, the maître d', for several minutes, telling him the order was for Sam Fielder who was at Cedars following a minor cardiac incident.

I had tightroped around the edges of the movie business long enough to know that one always made light of such things, things like illness and hospital stays. Odd, I thought, given the fact that PR honchos all over town were rolling out the red carpet for their clients going to rehab. But coronary events, cancer, diseases with multi-syllabic names—they were a different story. Rumors were spoken in hushed tones over breakfast at the Fountain Room, circulated wildly over lunch at The Grill, then squelched by agents and managers over drinks at Bar Noir, permitting them all—agents, managers, and clients alike—to easily digest their filets at Mastro's come dinner time. Of course, Sam was retired, seven years now. Even so, I knew he would want me to play the game, partly as a nod to tradition and partly because, as he would say, you never know.

Albert patted me on the shoulder reassuringly. For my ailing father-in-law and to acknowledge he was on the case with the meatloaf. Then he sashayed off to the kitchen.

I stationed myself between the patio and the dining room. I had cut through a swarm of paparazzi on my way in, bumping against a lens the size of the giant rain stick Stephanie had made in kindergarten. Now I scanned both sections, indoor and out, for their target. There was a buxom brunette eating her grilled vegetable salad with her fingers, corn niblet by corn niblet. There was an overly tanned man in a cream linen blazer yukking it up with the waiter. There was an emaciated girl, no more than nineteen, emptying packets of Splenda into her Diet Coke. None of them was the telephoto target.

The shutterbug frenzy kicked in when the ladies' room door opened and Victoria Beckham stepped out in seven-inch platforms and an Herve Leger bandage dress. If Posh Spice were to eat a blueberry, you could track its way down like a boa swallowing a mouse.

Albert returned with a bag containing, along with the meatloaf, Sam's favorite dessert—a wedge of white chocolate lemon torte. On the house. I thanked him profusely and walked back to the car past the minimalist Italian room in the shop window. I thought about how pleased Sam was going to be when he heard that the mere mention of his name had earned him a free hunk of cake.

As I made my way through the hospital corridors, I wondered, as you would when dealing with a small child, if I should open with the big news of the cake or save it for after Sam had eaten some protein. In the end, I couldn't stop myself.

"You'll never guess what's in this bag!" I blurted out.

But Sam was asleep.

I sat in the chair at the foot of the bed. The smell of the meatloaf made me hungry, so I pulled a piece of bread out of the bag. I made an exception about bread when it came to the Anadama from the Ivy.

I had almost finished it when Sam opened his eyes.

"I've got white chocolate lemon cake," I said. "On the house."

He smiled and nodded.

And then the line on the monitor went flat.

# CHAPTER EIGHTEEN

STEPHANIE WASN'T SURE WHAT she wanted to be when she grew up. Clearly, she wished everyone at the funeral would stop asking—first a few guys from the agency during the mingle before the service and now everyone back at the house during the catered shebang.

After much talk, Adam and sister Kathy decided that the official Fielder residence was the best place to have the after-party (as Stephanie called it). It would be less confusing for all of Sam's aged pals. The ones who still drove could get there on automatic pilot. There had been fifty-plus years of poker games and dinner parties and barbecues and, more recently, deathbed calls on Adam's mother, Eileen. The rest of the old-timers would arrive with a driver—either hired by the hour or in the form of dutiful offspring.

Once back at the house, Kathy retreated upstairs to her childhood bedroom. This left Adam alone to greet the onslaught. I stationed myself at the buffet, but kept an eye trained on the front door. Adam opened it with his right hand as he reached out with his left to flip on the light in the tubular brass casing affixed to the Renoir. The painting hung on the small width of wall next to the door. Adam had been a little boy when his father had "scored" the piece at auction, as Sam had put it. *Picnickers in the Bois de Boulogne.* Sam had hung it just there, to the side of the front door, so that all visitors would spot it on their way out.

Adam glanced at the painting, trying to make sense of the idea that it might belong to him now. Of course, there was also the possibility that Sam had left it to a museum so that his name would be engraved alongside it forever after. "Donor." Or better yet, "From the collection of."

Often, in this house, Adam wore adulthood like a suit of clothes that was supposed to be his size, but in some undetectable measurement, did not quite fit. But not today. Today he looked like a genuine grown-up. Despite his grief (which was layered and complicated), Adam appeared in charge.

*Is that how it works?* I wondered. *You're finally an adult when you are no longer anyone's child?*

Roger Zimring was the first to arrive. He had recently been named head of packaging. ("I want to be in packaging," Stephanie used to say when she was little, picturing an elf workshop with shiny rolls of wrapping paper and mountains of rainbow satin bows.) Adam shook Roger's hand and kissed his wife on the cheek.

Not that long ago, it seemed, Adam used to cram for social gatherings. In the car on the way to this dinner party or that screening, he would say, "Okay, tell me everyone's name." And I would rattle them off, adding informational tidbits—children's ages, recent vacations, new redhead on so-and-so's arm replacing previous blond. But now that I thought about it, that was ages ago. Adam was doing very well, thank you very much, at the door without me. He greeted everyone from the boys in the mailroom to Bradley Cooper. From D-girls (did they still call them that?) to network heads. From Julia Roberts to Wendell Tucker.

Wendell had been Sam's driver for the last thirty years of Sam's tenure. He had arrived at the Fielder house every morning by eight, decked out in creased black trousers, a crisp white shirt and a solid, burgundy necktie. "Look sharp, feel sharp, be sharp," he used to say.

This philosophy extended to the vehicle in his charge. Every morning Wendell spent a good fifteen minutes rubbing perfect circles across the surface of Sam's black Eldorado. Then he drove Sam to the building at the beach and drove him back down Sunset Blvd. to Beverly Hills in the evening. He drove Sam to lunch as well, departing the office at 12:30 and returning him at 1:45. A different restaurant was assigned to each day of the week, culminating in Friday's drive twenty-seven blocks down Wilshire to the Pacific Dining Car. Ensconced in a red leather booth, Sam would order a rib-eye, medium rare, with a side of creamed spinach and potatoes au gratin.

When his cardiologist prescribed Lipitor twenty years ago, we all begged Sam to, at least, substitute steamed spinach for the creamed. "Baby steps," I had submitted. But Sam said no. Why bother now? The little pill was on the job. The family pressed Adam to have a word with Wendell, the one person who might be able to talk some sense into Sam. Wendell reported back that Sam insisted he join him for lunch and taste the creamed spinach for himself. Wendell had to admit spinach got a lot of help from that butter and cream. From then on, Wendell joined Sam for lunch on Fridays. As if to prove a point, Sam added creamed corn to the menu.

I hadn't seen Wendell in years, since my mother-in-law's funeral now that I thought of it, but he looked the same.

"You look wonderful," I said when it was my turn for a hug.

"Black don't crack," said Wendell.

Adam kept an arm around Wendell's shoulder. "I don't know what we would have done without you," Adam said.

Wendell smiled. "Mr. F. was so much company," he said. "You got to know that's a fact."

"That is a fact," I said, and I hugged him a second time.

Wendell glanced from me to Adam, testing the temperature between us. Wendell put no stock in gossip. He'd heard his fair share, more than his share, invisible as he was, behind the wheel in the front seat. But today, when he locked eyes with me, I knew he had heard about us. And he was disappointed. Disappointed and sad.

"Where's our girl?" he asked.

I nodded toward the dining room. Stephanie had stationed herself there, handing out Villeroy and Boch strawberry pattern plates as guests arrived at the buffet. There had been a brief conversation about the pros and cons of paper versus china, but Adam and his sister deferred to Stephanie when she reminded them of what Grandpa always used to say: "Even Beluga tastes like shit off of paper."

Everything else fell in line: linens, cloth napkins, crystal. It would be a send-off Sam Fielder could never have imagined as a boy in the Bronx, but which, he would surely have insisted, he had spent the rest of his life earning. You're darn tootin'.

I watched Stephanie hand a plate to Edgar Resnick, the first agent Sam had hired. Edgar asked her what she planned to do with her life. By this point in the proceedings, she had declared herself on the road to social work, graphic design, and in response to one particularly deaf old woman, logrolling.

To Edgar she said, "I'm going to be a lawyer."

He asked Stephanie why on earth she would ever want to become one of those.

"So I can wear a pencil skirt and stomp my foot."

"Your Grandpa had a lot of friends," he said, gripping a knife with arthritic fingers to spread pate on a cocktail rye.

"With friends like that, who needs family?" said Stephanie, quoting her grandfather. There would be no more quotable Sam-isms.

I led an old-time comedy writer to the buffet. His toupee slid halfway down his forehead as he leaned over to pick up a bagel. "You know how you keep bagels from being stolen?" he said to me.

"How?"

"You put lox on them."

I laughed and watched as Adam left his post at the door to chat with an A-list producer—female and stunning. I wasn't accustomed to being aware of Adam's every move; my hypervigilance unnerved me.

I continued to chat with guests, accepting condolences, chuckling at Sam stories. Everyone had one. But it was Wendell's I wanted to hear.

He shook his head, "We had ourselves some good talks in that car."

"I bet you did," I said.

"May not have seemed like it, but Mr. F. knew what was what. He couldn't have kept the whole operation going without Adam, you know. He told me that himself. More than once." News to me. "My boy, he used to say...he's something."

# CHAPTER NINETEEN

No MEAT OR MEAT by-products to be served in the dressing rooms or any area designated within the "backstage area." Aromatherapy candles in sandalwood exclusively. Private meditation area painted sage green. This was the grunt work of a fledgling entertainment attorney. That's what Peter Lafferty was when we first met him.

Adam and I shook our heads and laughed at the wacky demands he was forced to stipulate in contract riders for the rock acts he repped. If a rogue M & M showed up backstage—a brown one for one group, a red for another—Peter could be out of a job. Finders, minders, and grinders, they call them—the pecking order of attorneys in major firms. Back then, Peter was in his grinder phase.

Now his name was on the letterhead. Now he was a finder.

Peter phoned the day after Sam's funeral. "You're going to want to go to this show tonight," he said.

"What is it?" I asked.

"It's a funeral."

"What could be more fun? Another funeral."

"Funerals are the new raves," Peter joked.

"I hear all the finer people are having them," I quipped.

"It's for the guy who founded The Whisky. Actually, it's the anniversary of his funeral. He died, like, ten years ago. But it's going to be really star-studded. All those people who got their start at the Whisky. Johnny Rivers. The Byrds. The Doors."

*He's good but he's no Mick Jagger.* "That'd be a good trick if Jim Morrison shows up."

"Listen," said Peter, "I don't have to go to this thing. We could do something else, but it's the hottest ticket in town."

♦♦♦

I HAD NEVER BEEN a club girl. I hated the cigarette smoke. I hated the smell of cheap booze. I hated being packed into a room full of chests and shoulders blocking my view of the stage. You might as well stay home and listen to the record as far as I was concerned, except for the vibe. And I was never convinced that the vibe was all it was cracked up to be.

When we arrived at the Whisky, Peter was immediately sidetracked by a posse of middle-aged men in Hugo Boss suits. I smiled and nodded, shooing him off. I was content to hold my Pinot Noir and take it all in.

The room oozed star power, but most of the heavyweights had retreated upstairs. It was far too dark up there to identify anyone, but they were there. Or at least their ghosts were. All those guys who had spent the sixties and seventies chiseling the LA scene out of dreams and sex. Robert Evans and Lou Adler. Jack. Warren. Men who charged the air around them.

Downstairs were the aging rock stars and rock star makers. No one immediately recognizable. I rifled through my mental index of album covers, envisioning how those faces might have aged. How many lithe young men, lean of thigh and thick of mane, now stuffed themselves into jeans a size too small and debated whether to lose the comb-over?

Peter was trapped across the room. He held up his index finger: one second. That was fine with me. I didn't mind being on my own, observing. Old friends greeting old friends from another time.

And the groupies. Also aging. Many already aged. Girls more heartbreaking even than the aging rock stars who might still claim some talent. (The groupies might possess a certain talent as well, or with the passing years did a girl lose her finesse for plaster-castering?)

These girls—it was impossible to call them women—dotted the crowd in clumps like junior high besties. One wore a pixie cut and a long, flowing skirt that gave off a cloud of Topanga Canyon. Another wore a band of purple satin around her throat, a beaded sunflower dangling from it. A third had wiggled herself into a tawdry black velvet number and glitzed it up with ropes of rhinestones. Black satin gloves stretched above her elbows and a cowboy hat slung around her neck. It slapped against her back as she bobbed her head in animated conversation.

When the speeches began, Peter made his way to my side. He stood close as we listened to tales of the early days. Dancers in cages with fringed dresses. Unknowns transformed into rock gods on this very stage. Everything-a-go-go.

Then Glove Girl climbed the stairs to the stage.

"I'm here to represent the wild babes of the seventies!"

The crowd whooped, mostly the other wild babes.

Glove Girl continued. "I went to lunch with Elmer a few years before he died. He was already losing it a little. We talked about old times. And then, finally, he said to me, 'Did we ever do it?'"

Huge laugh.

She milked the moment, peered out into the crowd from under shaggy bangs and batted her Twiggy eyelashes.

"I'll never tell," she said coyly. The place went wild.

I laughed. That was the girl I had never been. A girl who'd had fun for the sake of it. Consequences be damned.

Was I like any of the women here? I was not one of the old guard record label wives in Chanel suits with diamond brooches in the shape of dragonflies and peonies. I was not one of the new guard company wives with *Real Housewives of Beverly Hills* hair. I was not one of the groupie girls with a history in this place. I was not even Peter Lafferty's girlfriend.

But when Johnny Rivers took the stage, none of that mattered. I felt like I was seventeen. I was moving to the music. I was singing along. Maybelline. Summer Rain. Poor Side of Town.

"To him you were nothin' but a little plaything / Not much more than an overnight fling / To me you were the greatest thing this boy had ever found / And girl it's hard to find nice things / On the poor side of town."

Glove Girl turned to Beaded Sunflower and said, "Can you imagine if you could have a song like that written for you?" The two collapsed into each other's arms like a couple of fourteen-year-olds. I could almost remember that yearning—aching and delicious—from another lifetime. Was it still buried there?

One by one, other musicians took the stage. "So you want to be a rock and roll star...," sang one of the Byrds. Peter grabbed my hand. We were sharing something wonderful.

He nodded toward a couple dancing at the foot of the stage. The guy, at least sixty, had British teeth and a sallow complexion. His girl—twenty-two, tops—was spectacular. The world would gladly heap itself onto a silver platter for a girl like that. But here she was—with this guy with the yellow teeth and the pallid skin. Go figure.

The man followed the girl to the ladies' room and waited outside the door for her to come out. He must have had something. Money, power, connections. But bubbling beneath it all, insecurity so crushing that he didn't want this lovely young thing to have to make her way through the crowd to find him. Not this crowd full of other men—better looking men, men with more money, farther reaching power, tighter connections, better teeth. He didn't want her alone in this place for even a minute. He didn't want her to have the chance to trade up.

Johnny played the James Bond riff. Everyone screamed along: "Secret Agent Man...Secret Agent Man..." I sang the chorus at the top of my lungs: "They've given you a number and taken 'way your name." Rock and roll could do that to you—make you succumb to the backbeat and the thrust until you forgot everything but the here and now.

When Johnny finished, I whooped and cheered and clapped wildly, arms high above my head.

"Thank you so much," I said to Peter as he took my elbow and led me toward the door. "This was really something."

"You're welcome," he said.

I paused to watch the coffee klatch of groupie girls say their goodbyes. Embraces all around. One wiped a tear from another's cheek. They noticed me watching them. I smiled. And they smiled back, as though I were a member of the club, before Peter guided me out.

A stream of headlights assaulted me as I stepped out of the darkness. I glanced away from the street, but their glow stayed behind like the tail of a comet. A wave of vertigo washed over me.

I braced myself against the ticket window and breathed against the panic.

"Are you okay?" Peter asked.

"I get this vertigo sometimes." It shamed me to admit it. Like a weakness. "It's a pain," I added dismissively.

Peter slung an arm around my waist to steady me.

"Maybe you need something to eat?"

I shook my head no.

Finally, I looked up from the ground. The sidewalk appeared reliable enough, though I had learned not to trust any appearance of stability.

"I'm okay," I said. "I'm okay."

Peter kept his arm around me just in case.

*So here I am,* I thought, *walking down the Sunset Strip on a Monday night, of all things, with some man's arm around me.* But Peter's arm felt less like an overture than support, as though I were an old person with a bad hip.

The vertigo lifted quickly—false alarm—but a buzz persisted. I thought it was the rock and roll. All that bass in such a small room. And so much adrenaline, so few powers of thought. Wasn't that the way this new single lifestyle was supposed to be—so *Sex and the City,* all impulse and rush?

Once in Peter's Bentley, he headed west on Sunset. He caught a red light at Sunset Plaza Drive and glanced at me. Straight would take us on to my house. Right would mean his.

"Right," I said without looking at him. "Turn right."

# CHAPTER TWENTY

"THESE ARE THE BIRD Streets," I said, redundantly, as we passed Oriole, then Skylark, and Blue Jay Way.

"That's right," said Peter as he turned onto Thrasher Avenue. He pulled into a driveway on the left. "I moved here in oh-seven."

*That's a man thing,* I thought. *Anchoring events to years.* I myself remembered everything, excruciatingly, but never by the year attached, only by the emotion, like an actor calling on sense memory.

"It's beautiful up here," I remarked. It seemed the required reaction to the jetliner view of the city spread out below in all its twinkle.

"It's too hazy to see the ocean tonight," Peter commented as we stepped out of the car, "but it's there." He nodded to the west.

There was a bucket by the front door, an insulated cooler. "My food," he explained. "I have it delivered."

I nodded. Of course he did.

"Wow," I said, again somewhat redundantly.

The house was indeed a wow—a steel, glass, and cement study in minimalism. A stark contrast to the cottagey Lego repository Peter had shared with Cindy and their little boys. Cindy had gone with soft blues and grays. This place was all about black and white with the occasional pop of sour green. "Pippin apple green," some decorator probably enthused. Glass cylinders of varying sizes were clustered everywhere, bunched with lilies and orchids.

"Pretty flowers," I commented.

"The plant guy changes them twice a week."

Of course he did.

"I don't have good luck with orchids," I said.

"It's kind of silly," said Peter. "I'm not home very much. But it's nice for the housekeeper," he joked. "And she keeps a nice house for the plant guy. They've got a good thing going."

He crossed the living room and slid open the glass doors. The backyard was mostly swimming pool—zero-edge infinity. Peter flipped a switch and the underwater lights glimmered on. Another, and a waterfall cascaded to life.

"Wow," I said again.

There was something so Hugh Hefner about it that I nearly laughed. I glanced at Peter to make sure he was still himself, the man I had known when we were both new parents. He stretched out on one of the sculpted lounges, more like unfurled ribbons of molded resin in pippin apple green. He patted the spot next to him, but I pretended not to notice. The music, particularly the vibration of so many bass guitars, had left me unsettled—at once aroused and sort of drugged. I would have to touch him if I sat there next to him beside this pool without borders here on top of the City of Angels.

Peter stood from the lounge, took me by the hand and led me back inside, wordlessly, through the living room with its white couches, through the dining room with its ebony table, down the hall lined with gold records, and into the master bedroom.

Here, the decorator must have said, "Let's go Portobello." Where bachelor pads were concerned, portobello was the chocolate brown of the new millennium.

"Your house is spectacular," I said.

"Thanks, kiddo." His voice was softer now, its register lower. He took my face in his two hands.

"All those gold records…Really impressive." I was still pretending we were going to have a conversation.

"It's not like I earned them. The labels hand them out to people like me. Sort of like thank-you gifts. My decorator thought they'd make a cool statement piece."

He kissed me on my right cheekbone, under my eye. I closed my eyes. He kissed me again. On the lips.

This was it. Peter was no longer the other husband in a foursome enjoying an evening away from the kids. Suddenly he was mine for the taking. I took a step closer to him. Closer. I pressed my hipbone against him. And when he kissed me again, it was I who pulled him to me. When his lips separated from mine and his head drew back for a moment, it was I who leaned into him.

The next kiss lowered us to the bed. Peter ran his hand down the side of my body, methodically, as though he were counting my ribs. As his fingers trailed along my waist, I reflexively sucked in my stomach. I wished I could somehow inhale an inch or two off my hips as well. I told myself men didn't care. "If you're naked, they're happy." I had heard Barbara say that to a friend once when we were teenagers. Even so, I was relieved when Peter reached over and turned off the light.

*Unfamiliarity as an aphrodisiac*—that's what Adam had written to the French Girl. Didn't magazine articles advise wives to cure the marital ho-hums by greeting their husbands dressed in Saran, like a pile of leftovers? No tricks needed here. Peter Lafferty's body was entirely new. For a minute or two I felt new, too, like I had shed myself, like I was all in one place instead of performing my particular, exhausting brand of multi-tasking: worry and obsession.

*New equals exciting*, I thought. The calculus of desire. New fingertips. New lips. New.

I opened my eyes. The swimming pool light cast a silver-blue glow on the bed. The exact same silver-blue glow of a computer screen. The silver-blue glow of decades-old video. And just like that, the drive to quell my craving—to dissolve and to merge and to be anything other than my singular self—flickered out, snuffed by the images seared into my brain and all those email words that went with them.

But it was too late to cry wolf. If there were an etiquette for handling this moment, it escaped me. It had not been part of the Ridgepoint curriculum, I was pretty sure. It was time for the old Hollywood standby: fake it till you make it.

Surely I could do what French Girl had done. I could do it better. If only I knew what it was. As I lay there under Peter Lafferty, I realized that French Girl had simply been enjoying herself. What she had been was fiercely present. And that, I could not manage.

I remembered the look the girl had presented to the camera, a look of profound satisfaction—not just her own, but Adam's too.

Something exquisitely mutual. I rested an open hand on the pillow behind my head expectantly. Adam would have interlaced his fingers with mine. Not Peter.

Peter was taller than Adam. As he lay on top of me, my mouth could only find its way to his shoulder. I kissed it. Because it was there. By now he was fully on top of me. I reached a hand around to his back. I wasn't sure what I was aiming for, but my hand landed at the crease where back of thigh meets ass. I found it to be more pronounced, less gradual, not to mention hairier than that particular patch of real estate on Adam.

I wished Adam would leave the room. I wished that French Girl would leave the room. Courtesy of a funhouse mirror of memory, projection and obsession, this was turning into a bigger party than I had signed up for. I strained to use the images jump cutting in my brain as a sort of How-To video, but I could not concentrate, could barely catch my breath in the tangle of limbs, half of them phantom.

# CHAPTER TWENTY-ONE

"I HAVE A HEADACHE," Barbara said. She was sitting across from me at the long communal table at Le Pain Quotidien in Westwood. A group of Asian students from UCLA sat at the other end, intent on their laptops. It was hard to tell if they were together, an actual group, or just happened to be sitting next to one another.

"Want some Advil?" I fished in my purse.

"Too hard on the liver. It probably wouldn't work anyway. It's one of those barometric pressure headaches. I get them when the June Gloom comes in."

"It's May," I said.

"You know what I mean."

"They call it May Gray now. So much for sunny Southern California. We're lucky if we have blue skies by the Fourth of July. I swear to God the sun has retired," I mused.

Gwen rushed in. "Sorry I'm late. Traffic."

Barbara and I nodded. It was always the traffic these days.

The waitress arrived with the lattes and Gwen ordered café au lait with a shot. Barbara coated her spoon with the thinnest film of almond milk foam skimmed from her latte. She licked it off, poised to spring should the young barista have mistakenly given her soy or, heaven forefend, something from a cow.

"I have a horrible headache," Barbara filled Gwen in.

"Drink your coffee," I said.

"The caffeine will help," Gwen agreed.

"You know what was great?" Barbara asked. "When my girlfriends and I would roll into Mel's Diner at two a.m. and the host there…What was his name? Ron? Rich…?"

Gwen and I exchanged looks. *Here we go.*

"Anyway," Barbara continued, "he'd make us homemade Alka-Seltzer. Without even asking. He'd take one look at us and know that's what we needed. I'm not sure what was in it. Baking soda and something else. Anyway, he'd bring it over and we'd drink it and we'd feel better instantly. Then we'd eat steak and eggs and hang out. Frank Zappa would be holding court in the booth at the back. I sat on his lap once..." Her voice trailed off, trapped in the net of nostalgia.

Whenever Barbara dove into one of these reveries, my competitive streak prickled. When we were kids, I had remained the dutiful daughter while my sister loitered on the Strip and got into cars with boys she didn't know. I shielded my parents from the rumors whispered between classes in the Ridgepoint halls, especially the rumor that Barbara Locke had been dancing in a cage at Gazzari's... that she'd been shaking her groove thing, shaking everything.

I had envied my sister's wild-child days and parsed all their details with Gwen, but by the time it was my turn to live my own, I made the somber discovery that I did not seem to have the right stuff, the wild-child stuff. Introductory Sex, Drugs, and Rock 'n' Roll sounded like fun. But I knew it could turn out to be the prerequisite for Advanced Sex, Drugs, and Rock 'n' Roll. And that was scary. That meant losing control. No thanks.

Look where it had gotten Barbara. She had led multiple lives, waiting for one to take. Ultimately she threw herself into respectability the way other kids hurled themselves into cults. Only occasionally—like right now, lost in the Zappa story—did I see my sister long for the old self she had armored in polished cotton.

"Sometimes it would take us three hours to make it a couple of blocks down the Strip." Barbara savored the tale. "It was so thick with cars and people. After a while, there was no point in trying. It was easier to hang out or go to some guy's house nearby and wait till the sun came up before going home."

"Yeah, and I'd be home telling Mother and Daddy not to worry while they argued about whether or not to start phoning the hospitals."

Barbara waved a hand dismissively. Parental concern—whatever.

"It's not easy, you know, being a parent." I bristled. "Actually you wouldn't know." That was hitting below the belt. Though we never discussed it, never once, I knew that Barbara lived with some measure of regret for trading in motherhood for three abortions.

The waitress placed Gwen's coffee in front of her. "I'll have a muffin, too," Gwen decided. She squinted at the list on the chalkboard on the far wall. "No, make that a croissant. Chocolate. A chocolate croissant." Gwen turned to me. "Barbara's right. Stephanie's a great kid. You really shouldn't worry that much about her."

"Who said anything about Stephanie?" I said. *What would I do if I stopped worrying about her. That would be too huge a space to fill.*

I had not intended to tell them about Peter Lafferty, specifically last night with Peter Lafferty. But I itched to prove that I could do something besides worry. More than that. It was all that talk about the years when Barbara was on a first-name basis with the host at Mel's. I could be buoyed by a devil-may-care wind, too. Last night I had needed to prove it to myself, and now I needed to prove it to Barbara, and to Gwen, too, for that matter.

"I slept with another man last night," I said.

"You what?" shrieked Gwen.

"Besides Peter Lafferty?" Barbara asked.

"No! Peter Lafferty. That's who I'm talking about. How did you know?"

"Peter who?" Gwen was so confused.

"I saw you two at the movies," Barbara said.

"You did?" I said. "And you didn't say anything?"

"What movie?" Gwen kept trying.

"Obviously you didn't want me to," countered Barbara. "Say anything, I mean."

It clicked for Gwen. "Peter Lafferty? Like from a million years ago. Weren't you friends with his wife?"

"Ex-wife," I clarified. "Ten years. At least."

"Whatever," Barbara rolled her eyes. The chocolate croissant arrived and Barbara ripped off a piece.

"So what happened last night?" Gwen asked.

For once I was actually the purveyor of the lurid details.

"Well, we went to this really cool thing at the Whisky. A memorial for the guy who ran it forever."

"Elmer Valentine," said Barbara. "I practically lived there, you know."

"We've established that." I wanted my moment back. "Anyway, we were driving home and I basically said, 'Your place.'"

"You actually said those actual words?" Gwen asked.

"No. But he got the idea."

"Well, look at you…" Gwen handed me the primo hunk of croissant, dense with chocolate.

Look at me was right.

Barbara said nothing. One of the eighteen buttons lining the forearm of her sleeve had come undone. It was self-covered in a chipper little Liberty print. She struggled to slip it back through its tiny loop.

"I need a button hook," Barbara said.

"That's a sentence you don't often hear," I said.

Gwen added, "…these past few centuries."

Barbara secured the loop around the wee button. "Go on," she said.

"It was weird. He wasn't Adam. There was so nothing Adam-ish about him." I shook a brown paper packet of raw sugar, stirred the crystals into my coffee. Gwen leaned forward. Barbara leaned forward.

Their impatience tickled me. I may never have laughed—full-throated and uninhibited—in the back booth at Mel's Diner, but now, finally, I had this one night to spin however I pleased. I came up empty. In fact, I was sorry I'd ever mentioned it. There could be no pretending it hadn't happened now that I had told my sister and my best friend.

"I'm sorry," said Barbara. I wasn't sure for what.

"I know," Gwen agreed, "we always think we can vet a guy with his clothes on. When he's naked…that's when, you should pardon the expression, the rubber meets the road. Men get lucky…when they get lucky, I mean. We wax and we tweeze and we slather. Not that they even care."

"It's true," Barbara concurred. I wondered if my sister were waxed and tweezed and slathered these days.

Gwen was on a roll. "We go to all this trouble, and they don't care one wit if we yank off our Spanx and everything oozes out all over the place. It's bare skin! Hooray! There's no up side to all that false advertising for us…We see a cute little rear in tight jeans and it turns out to be covered in fur. Fabulous broad shoulders—nothing but clever tailoring. An Armani suit that makes you think he's got class and *je ne sais quoi*? Underneath? Chicken legs."

"Sleight of stitch, you might say," I suggested.

"Correct," Gwen asserted.

But my next-day queasiness had nothing to do with Peter Lafferty's body. My salient memory of the whole episode had nothing to do with him really. It was the moment when, lying beneath him, my eye was captured by a rainbow dancing on the opposite wall, a prism created by a patio light striking, just so, the diamond in my wedding ring.

Recalling it now, tears sprang to my eyes.

Barbara reached across the table and took my hand. "He's a jerk?"

"Not at all. He was very…nice. When we were lying there…you know, afterward…he talked a lot about when he was first single and how hard it had been to 'get back in the swing.' That's what he said. Oh my God—he said, 'get back in the swing.' How could I have been with a man who says 'get back in the swing'?"

Gwen shrugged. She'd heard lamer.

"Do you want to see him again?" Barbara pressed.

"Not really." My index finger circled the rim of my cup, scraping the drying dregs of latte foam. "No. So no."

"Okay," Gwen rallied, "on to the next?" She raised her coffee cup.

Barbara said nothing. Nor did she raise her cup to future men.

I propped my head in my hands and closed my eyes. The restaurant had begun to spin.

"The vertigo?" Barbara asked.

"I'll be fine in a few minutes," I said. "Shit."

"Let's get you some air," Barbara suggested. She grabbed one arm and Gwen the other. Together they led me outside. They deposited me on a café chair and sat in silence for several minutes until I nodded. The spell was passing.

"I'm okay," I declared. "I'm sorry. It's so stupid."

"Are you sure you're better?" Barbara asked.

"I think I am."

"I'll go get the car," said Barbara and she headed down the street.

"I'll pay the check," said Gwen. "I'll be right back."

I breathed, and breathed again. Then I heard it—the crack of skull against pavement. An elderly woman had tripped on a patch of uneven sidewalk. The woman's husband struggled to lower himself to his knees—a laborious task since even while walking, his torso was already parallel to the ground. The old man and woman wore matching skipper blue windbreakers. By the time her husband raised her head off the ground, a rivulet of blood trickled from the back of her head.

"Silly me," I heard the woman say. "Silly me. I don't know what happened."

"It's all right," her husband said. "You're going to be fine."

"Of course I'm going to be fine," she insisted.

The old man cradled his wife's head as though it were a Faberge egg. I hurried over to help, digging out my phone to dial 911. But a passer-by beat me to it.

The old man reached into his pocket and shook two aspirin into his palm. He handed them to his wife whose head, by now, was propped on someone's wadded-up sweater.

"Don't give her that," I said.

He looked at me, his eyes cloudy.

"Excuse me. I'm sorry, but you shouldn't give her aspirin. It's a blood thinner. She's bleeding."

"She's right," said the old woman.

The EMTs rushed in. In a heartbeat, she was on a stretcher. One of the medics cleared the way, spreading his arms in a sort of breaststroke as though he were parting seas.

As they carried the woman away, she smiled at me. A gauze bandage was now wrapped around her head, sending out a spray of white hair. "Thank you, dear," she said to me. "Don't worry. I'm fine. Tell her, Fred."

Fred had caught up with the stretcher. He reached for his wife's hand, raised it to his face and pressed it against his cheek. "She's fine," he said to me.

I nodded to the woman. Her husband would not let go of her hand. I patted him on his hunched shoulder as he passed. He forced a smile, then raised his wife's hand to his lips and kissed it.

# CHAPTER TWENTY-TWO

THE ROSES WERE EGGSHELL in color, each petal rimmed with fuchsia. They arrived in an impossibly long gold-foiled box like in the movies. It was tied with hot pink satin ribbon. When I untied the ribbon and lifted the top, I counted a full two dozen. They scared me to death.

Not as much as the card. "I'm so glad this has happened. Love, Peter."

I thought about phoning him—no, texting him—asking him to define "this." But before I could do anything, I had to get rid of these long-stemmed souvenirs of my temporary insanity.

What I didn't tell my sister and my best friend was that I hadn't been able to get out of Peter's bed fast enough. It was a real struggle to find the patience to lie there. Basically, the whole escapade had not been worth the effort. Why had it taken so much effort anyway? But if, like Alice in Wonderland, I could not go back to yesterday, I most certainly could not go back to the day before yesterday. I was so many removes from the person that was me. When could I stop proving my point? It was no fun anymore.

I carried the flowers out to the trashcans at the side of the garage and tossed the box into a bin. Although I needn't have worried that Stephanie would ever take out the trash unprompted, I went back into the kitchen and grabbed today's newspaper as well as the crushed bag of trash from the compactor. Then I carried them out and dumped them on top of the flowers and their shiny gold box. If only I could pretend they had never been delivered. If only they had *not* ever been delivered.

Ever the Ridgepoint girl, I sat down at the kitchen desk, slid Peter's card into one of its cubbies, and pulled out a monogrammed note card from another. (Every time I pulled one out, I regretted my font selection—a girly script with too many rococo frills. I could not bring myself to order a new batch until I worked my way through this one. Given email's assassination of the handwritten letter, there was a good chance I'd be stuck with these forever.)

"Dear Peter," I wrote.

*How to combine a thank-you note with a Dear John letter?*

"I beg your forgiveness for my lapse in judgment."

"I'm afraid I have made a most amusing, if heinous, error."

"Oops."

I gave up on the thank-you note idea. I would deal with the niceties of a thank-you later. For now, I found myself compelled to go back out to the side of the house. I reached deep inside the trashcan and pulled out one of the roses. It was partially crushed; the blossom hung off its stem dejectedly.

I carried it back into the kitchen and pulled the thickest Martha Stewart cookbook off a shelf. I opened it at random, landing among the fishes, between Pan-Sautéed Trout and a Coulibiac of Bass. I had no clue what a coulibiac of anything was. My cooking mania had been short-lived anyway. There was something far too sad, pathetic really, about cooking elaborate meals for Stephanie and myself. I placed the rose between the pages, closed the book, and returned it to its place on the shelf.

Only I would know that a rose was stuck there, fading between the trout and the bass. Sometimes it was good to be able to put your hands on a reminder that someone had once found you…whatever it was that Peter found me. As Sam (may he rest in peace) would have said, "You never know."

♦♦♦

I SPENT THE NEXT several days in bed pretending I had a sinus headache. Given the last few months, it might have made more sense to invoke the vertigo, but I feared bad karma. Better to invent an ailment that did not actually stalk me.

It was late May and it had been an unusually rainy winter. Weathermen were already including the pollen count in their forecasts. An allergy related malady would work.

For the first time ever, I phoned in sick at Saint Christina's. I tried not to picture Ernesto's chubby face as he squinted with concentration over *The Adventures of Taxi Dog*. I had been lying in bed for so long my voice had a nasal quality that made my sinus excuse convincing. The school secretary thanked me for not coming in and spreading germs.

The fact of the matter was I was suffering from post-one-night-stand chagrin. I could feel my cheeks flush, even alone in the privacy of my darkened bedroom, when I recalled how Peter had whispered to me afterward.

"That was nice," he said, his words embarrassing me as much as what the two of us had actually done. This was a strange new world—the world of singles angling for a next time. It was just plain creepy, not to mention tepid. He might have at least gone for "sensational" or "terrific." But it hadn't been.

I avoided thinking about Peter Lafferty by drifting in and out of sleep. Adam had told me, many times over the years, that the thing I feared most was losing face.

"You're terrified of being defaced," he would tease me. He was right. Embarrassment was anathema to me. Now, I had taken to my bed just to save face with no one but myself.

The television segued from daytime chatter to nighttime drama. Normally I had no patience for all those initial shows: NCIS, SVU, CSI. But now they were just the ticket. I watched as cops with expensive haircuts combed through crime scenes in search of what had gone wrong in the life of the person lying in a pool of blood spiked with the telling pinch of someone else's DNA.

# CHAPTER TWENTY-THREE

WHEN I FINALLY GOT out of bed on the fourth afternoon, I had no idea whether it was Wednesday or Thursday. In fact, it was Sunday, which I realized only when I picked up the newspaper from the driveway and discovered its bulk. I blamed my disorientation on my supposed illness, which I now thought of as a hybrid of vertigo and imaginary sinus problems. But the truth was I had been free-floating in time for a while now.

True, school days clicked by one by one. But Stephanie's after-school activities varied from week to week. One Tuesday, she volunteered at a local senior center; every other Wednesday, she made sandwiches distributed to the homeless; and she spent the odd Saturday morning at the beach, rubber gloved to her elbows, stabbing garbage with a sharp stick and chucking it into a bio-hazard bag. Stephanie was rarely home, busy with this college application collagen, designed as it was to plump her extracurriculars into an admissions department version of an irresistible pout.

With Stephanie so self-propelled, I was at loose ends.

And Adam had taken the workweek with him.

What was left of its structure, that is. As Adam had signed more and more A-listers, his weekends had become less and less his own. He spent most weekend hours reading scripts and making pacifying phone calls to clients.

Adam's particular gift for handholding had distinguished him early on. If a producer went with another director, Adam took it personally. If a studio put a script into its seventh turnaround, Adam took it personally. If a writer took one too many Vicodin while staring at a blank computer screen, Adam took it personally. What made him extraordinary for the job weighed him down. Sometimes he couldn't sleep. He often wandered down to his study.

On this Sunday afternoon, finally out of bed, I wandered, too. Downstairs in the living room, I pulled the curtains aside to double check that there was still a world beyond my house. It may have been spring, but the sunset was particularly vivid, like those usually reserved for November in Southern California. I stood at the window watching the sky streak itself lavender and coral. I wished that I could call Adam to this window, to this sunset, and watch him watch the sky with his painter's eye. Instead, I cut across the backyard to his little studio.

The last time I'd ventured there must have been two, maybe three, years ago. I had gone to tell Adam his father was on the phone. I found him reading a screenplay—not painting. Even so, he snapped at me.

"How can I get anything done in here when you keep interrupting me?"

I snapped back. "He said it was important."

Adam marched past me toward the house. "Between the two of you, I might as well never pick up a paintbrush again." He said it to himself, but so that I could hear. Nothing would cut deeper than suggesting even the most farfetched alliance between me and Sam.

"Yeah," I said sarcastically. "Stop painting."

And he had.

As far as I knew, Adam had not stepped foot in the studio since. Even so, today, as this sunset suggested a special nuance of color and light, I was drawn there.

The smell of turpentine and sour rags smacked me.

The room was a mess. It was Adam's turf; I was not allowed to tidy up. Canvases were stacked along each wall three and four deep. Only a bold swatch of color on some. Others near completion, I guessed. How could Adam have walked away from those?

Careful not to disturb anything, I circled the room, running my hand over the edges of the canvases, fingering the bristles of the brushes. Some were supple and silky like mink. Others were stiff and brittle, probably beyond hope. I was tempted to throw those away, but never would.

A shirt lay tossed on the seat of the ladderback chair in the corner. Cream-colored chambray—worn and splotched with paint. I picked it up, examining it as though it were a Rorschach test. What I found was Adam. The old Adam. The one who retreated to this space before showrunners and spec scripts distracted him, drained him. I held the shirt close. It was stiff where the thickest patches of color had dried. Otherwise it was soft in the way that only the most favored shirts can be.

I slipped into the shirt, wrapping the front around me. It was oversized on Adam—he had intentionally bought it a size too big. On me, it hung to my knees. The sleeves extended well past my fingertips, but I didn't roll the cuffs. I wanted to dissolve into this shirt completely. If I closed my eyes, it felt like Adam's arms around me, like his body covering mine. Safe and easy. Connected. And there it was. The whoosh of swept-away I had nearly given up on when I was so young. The something-came-over-me that had never come over me that night with Peter. The free-fall I had discovered all those years ago on a rainy afternoon in Adam's arms. Surrender.

Wrapped in Adam's shirt, I stood in front of his easel. Various notes were tacked to its edges. Business cards from art supply stores. Stephanie's locker combination from middle school when she was always forgetting it and calling home in a panic. And Daniel Lilliani's phone number.

◆◆◆

DANIEL LILLIANI HAD BEEN Adam's teacher—his mentor, really. I had heard about him from the start, this avuncular character who figured in Adam's life but who, unlike real family, came with no strings attached. Adam had told me the story of Daniel Lilliani as though he were telling a child about Santa Claus.

Adam met Daniel during the summer between his freshman and sophomore years of college when Sam handed him a box of Trojans—"Don't come home with a dose"—and sent him off on the obligatory European grand tour.

He flew directly to Paris. As it happened, the grand tour began and ended there. Now, after all these years, I knew why. He struck a deal with the proprietor of a small hotel on the Ile Saint-Louis: room and board in return for painting the pension's peeling exterior. The arrangement left Adam his nights. Now I knew how he had spent them. I felt like such a fool to have always believed it was the art scene that had attracted, then kept him there, the painterly version of the philosophy world that lured Audrey Hepburn in *Funny Face*.

As early Parisian June turned into later Parisian June, daylight lingered until ten o'clock. Many evenings, before hitting the jazz clubs in the arrondissements less frequented by tourists, Adam would poke his head into the grimy kitchen at the back of the hotel. The cook would nod toward the baguettes and cheeses lying about as if waiting to be a still life. Adam would carve himself a few hunks to enjoy in the courtyard. Inspired by the light there, he splurged on tubes of paint and canvases. Before long, he was spending all his spare time in a corner of the shabby courtyard, painting.

It was there that he met Daniel Lilliani, fellow artist and temporary ex-pat. Thin, with sharp cheekbones and a Fred Astaire penchant for threading silk scarves through his belt loops, Daniel was at least thirty years older than Adam. At first Adam assumed Daniel was coming on to him. Maybe he was. But Adam pretended to be oblivious because Daniel seemed genuinely interested in his work.

"You're afraid of the void," Daniel would say.

Adam didn't get it. What void? And besides, he thought, like all nineteen-year-olds, I am afraid of nothing.

Gradually, however, Adam began to understand. He needed to fight the instinct to fill the canvas. He needed to allow it breathing space. He needed to resist showing off. Less could be more.

Daniel told him to paint the light, not what the light hit. Daniel told him to paint what he saw, not what everyone else saw. Daniel gave him the courage to develop a style he could almost call his own.

"You've got what it takes," Daniel told him. "You really do, my boy."

By the time Daniel returned to the States, Adam had graduated from college. Daniel was folded into the Fielder family, gradually earning Sam's reluctant stamp of approval. (This, upon Sam's discovering that Daniel possessed an uncanny eye for pieces undervalued at auction.) Regardless, Sam could not hold his tongue when Adam informed him that Daniel was going to be his best man.

"You want that old queen to stand up for you?" Sam spat.

"Yes," Adam answered simply.

When Stephanie was born, Daniel became Uncle Daniel. He visited the hospital and cried when he laid eyes on the tiny pink bundle. Adam fished inside the blanket and pulled out a minute hand for Daniel to study.

"It rather makes one want to rethink atheism, doesn't it?" Daniel said.

Daniel hunted down originals of children's book illustrations and presented baby Stephanie with piece after piece. Eric Carle's Hungry Caterpillar. Garth Williams' Stuart Little. Even Eloise herself as imagined by Hilary Knight.

But as the years went by, we saw less and less of Daniel Lilliani. Family life hummed along at a frequency that often didn't keep time with the metronome of old friendships.

Today, in Adam's studio, I peeled the post-it with Daniel's phone number off of the easel and returned to the house. Back inside the kitchen, I dialed the number.

"Daniel, it's Maura."

# CHAPTER TWENTY-FOUR

DANIEL HAD ALWAYS WANTED to paint me. It had become a sort of running gag between the two of us—a someday we both knew would probably never come. But by the time our phone conversation ended, we had agreed that I would come over the next morning to sit for him at long last.

We flirted with the topic of Adam over the phone. Daniel had heard that Adam was "inhabiting other lodgings at the moment." I fretted all night that Daniel would dig for information. I almost cancelled, even dialing Daniel's number from the car as I turned into Santa Monica Canyon, but I hung up before he answered.

Daniel had aged. I had seen him only twice since his lifelong partner, Kevin, died, and some years had passed since then. The loss had taken its toll. Daniel had shrunk and his skin appeared gray and parched. His once glossy shock of silver hair now seemed to crackle when he ran his hand through it. The voice that had once been so resonant now faltered. Did this halting staccato indicate haziness of the larynx or of the mind?

He embraced me and whispered into my ear, "We shan't discuss Adam."

I leaned back, away from Daniel's embrace, to look him in the eye.

"I spoke to him," Daniel explained. "I rang him when Sam died. I was out of town. Positano. Adam filled me in."

I averted my eyes from Daniel's.

"I told you. Not one more word about that boy. Not even if you beg," Daniel said. I laughed.

He offered me tea but I declined. He puttered around the kitchen, pouring coffee into a dented aluminum thermos, asking about Stephanie with genuine interest. He was so delighted to hear every detail of her life that I felt horribly guilty for not having made a point of keeping him part of it.

The little house missed Kevin. It groaned with Daniel's stuff in a way that Kevin never would have allowed. As Daniel led me downstairs to his spacious studio overlooking the canyon, I worried he was on his way to becoming one of those hoarders you see on television with their ceiling-high columns of newspapers and used teabags fossilized along the window sill.

I was relieved to find the studio more orderly. Clearly, this was the only place that still mattered to Daniel. He instructed me to have a seat on a chair positioned atop a large rectangular riser painted the same green as the foliage in the canyon outside the plate glass window. I sat, crossing my right leg over my left and hooked my foot around my other ankle.

"Can you plant both feet on the ground, Maura dear?" Daniel asked.

"Oh sure," I said. "Sorry." I unpretzeled myself. Even so, I required further adjusting. Daniel gently edged my right shoulder back, then placed one hand on either side of my jaw and inched my face slightly toward the sliding glass door.

"You can look outside," he told me.

"It's beautiful."

"I've never tired of this view," Daniel said, "and I've lived in this house for fifty years. Except for those years in Paris when Kevin and I were…shall we say, on hiatus."

My heart lurched at the mention of Paris. I felt caught, as though Daniel had divined my ulterior motive in paying him the visit. He had known Adam that summer in Paris. And he had known the girl. He must have known Adam and the girl together. I had formulated questions on the drive over, clever circumnavigations around the heart of the matter that was quite simply: What was she like? Had Adam loved her? Did he love her still?

But now, here in Daniel's studio, I could not ask, even though Daniel had opened the door to the topic.

"Never," he said again. "I could never tire of this view."

"I can see why," I said, though the view I remembered from twenty years ago was now marred by McMansions that dominated the canyon rather than nestling into it like the homes they had replaced. Daniel seemed unbothered by the transformation. It was still his personal view, if fuzzied by a patina of dust on the sliding glass door.

"How many years were you with Kevin?" I asked.

"Forty-two," said Daniel. "Did I ever tell you about how we ended up in this house?"

He had told me. Many times. But I would never dream of depriving him. "Tell me."

"Well…" Daniel set about organizing his paints and brushes. "It was summertime. And we were walking along the beach. Can you imagine Kevin taking a walk on the beach with his fair skin? And no one worried about sunscreen in those days. Anyway, I was struggling. Financially. I mean, a painter with no other means of supporting oneself, can you imagine? So I thought, wouldn't it be grand if I moved in with Kevin and we could share the rent? You know, I'd contribute what I could. So I said to him, 'How about living together?' And would you believe it? He thought I was proposing marriage. So I thought, why not? And that was that."

"Maybe you were proposing marriage and you didn't know it."

"Maybe. It was a safe proposal in those days, more metaphoric than literal," he said. "Anyway, that was that. Then it was ten years. Then twenty. Then forty."

"And life with Kevin was always good, wasn't it?" I asked.

Daniel stopped squeezing paint from half-empty tubes onto the white enamel sheet pan he used as a palette. "Always," he confirmed. "Except on those days when it wasn't."

"I always thought you two were so madly in love."

"We were. But that has nothing to do with life getting boring. Not boring. That's the wrong word. Ordinary. They all go just as fast, the ordinary days and the wonderful days." He blew on his fingertips, then flung them wide to the air—poof—like a magician. The thick ridges in his fingernails were yellowed from the nicotine of unfiltered cigarettes and years of seeping pigments.

Finally, he lifted a huge sketchpad onto his easel, flipped to a fresh page, and said, "All righty then, my dear, the time has come."

With that, he fell silent and began to paint.

I worried that I would not be able to sit still. Not for more than a minute or two. Certainly not for as long as would be required.

"I will tell you when I'm done with your eyes and then you can look around," he said.

Until that time, I stared directly at him. Right into Daniel's eyes, grown rheumy with age and grief. It was strangely intimate, this sitting. In a weird way, it felt like I were entrusting myself to Daniel in the way that a woman does when she is about to sleep with a man. (It hadn't been that way with Peter. Maybe I should have paid attention to the distinct absence of connection, of any sort of sublime submission.)

At first, I was self-conscious. I had never shared such an extended silence with any man but Adam. But gradually, as the minutes passed—I had no idea how many—I felt as though nothing would be stranger than the sound of speech. I could barely recall the sound of the human voice. Especially my own. It began to feel perfectly natural that Daniel should be studying every millimeter of my face and saying nothing at all. He was not saying, "You are pretty. You have lovely skin." He was just looking at me. In a way no one had ever looked at me before. He was examining me for accuracy.

Finally, he said, "You can move your eyes now."

I looked at the pan where he was mixing his colors. I wanted to say, "Those are not my colors. I am not ochre and burnt sienna." But I didn't. At least he had gone for a rich green for my eyes. If nothing else, I would have emerald eyes.

The harder he concentrated, the more he manipulated his jaw from side to side as though he were trying to dislodge something stuck between two back teeth. Occasionally, he poured the coffee from the thermos into the cup that was its top. He sipped delicately at first, but as the coffee cooled, he poured it down his throat in great gulps.

I had no idea how much time had passed when he said, "It's finished."

I had been sitting still for so long that I wasn't sure how to move again. I tried to stand too quickly and lost my balance, stumbling off the riser.

"Oh dear, not so fast there," said Daniel. "That happens sometimes. You were probably in a sort of a trance and you didn't even know it."

"I think so," I said.

I crossed to the easel, but Daniel blocked me. "Not yet. It's not finished. I'll finish it in a day or two. That's my evil plan. You'll have to come back to see it." He stood back and studied his work. "There's something a little off with the eyes. I'm losing my touch, I think."

"I'm sure it's wonderful."

"You're beautiful, you know, dear," said Daniel.

I felt my face flush.

"That was the first thing Adam told me about you."

I looked askance. Adam was supposed to be off limits.

"Indulge me," he said. "I'm old. Besides, I was declaring a DMZ about present day Adam, not ancient history Adam."

I picked up the thermos cup and emptied the remainder of the cold coffee into the sink in the corner of the room. Daniel slid open the glass door. The scent of Hawaiian ginger hung heavy in the canyon.

"Maura?" he asked.

"Yes?"

"I have the feeling...That is to say, what is it you want, dear?"

"Something else," I said before I had a chance to think about it. "Don't we all?"

"Too much of the time, I suppose," he said.

He set to cleaning his brushes: dipping them in a container of dishwashing liquid, wiping off the detergent and residual paint, then repeating the process several more times. Each time he wiped the bristles, more paint appeared on the rag. Though the smears on the rag grew fainter and fainter, it seemed like there would always be more paint trapped in the bristles.

"Nowadays they're saying you should wrap your brushes in aluminum foil and store them in the freezer. It's greener apparently. But old habits die hard." He dipped another brush in the detergent— the rust color he had used, along with several other shades, for my hair. "I don't feel like I've been working unless I clean my brushes. We all need our little rituals, I guess."

Daniel cleaned the next brush in silence—dip and wipe, dip and wipe—while I scanned the canvases lining the walls. Some were stacked against one another, mostly face in, but a few faced out. I poked through a couple of stacks. "Whatever happened to that painting of...What was his name?...That handsome young man... Before Kevin?"

"Christopher?"

"Christopher." I remembered the painting well. A personality captured in remarkably few brush strokes—a dynamism capturing the passion between artist and subject.

"That was a nice piece," Daniel said. "I got rid of it. Gave it away."

"Why?"

"Kevin didn't like having it around. It was silly of him, of course, but what can you do?"

You could do what Adam had done.

I longed to tell him about the French girl and the video, about Adam and 2:00 a.m. I wanted to explain how I was still reeling from the sucker punch of seeing my husband making love to another woman, even if it had been through the time warp proffered by technology. I wanted to ask him how Adam had slithered so easily into an e-correspondence with another woman. I wanted him to agree that cyber relationships may be their own form of betrayal, but are betrayal nonetheless. I wanted him to convince me that cyber relationships don't count. I wanted him to explain what I had done so wrong to deserve the constant replay I could not stop in my mind's eye.

But I did not ask him. I was too embarrassed. I did not want him to know why I had come. Not to sit for him. Not to make sure he was okay. But to pick his brain about Adam's summer in Paris, about the first Minou. I wanted him to confess that he knew that Adam had been having an affair. I wanted him to assure me that would never happen.

Daniel finished with the last brush and placed it, bristles up, in a mason jar with the others. He turned to me. "You know what?" he asked.

"What?"

"I was wrong. That wasn't the first thing Adam said about you. It was the second."

"What was the first?" I wondered.

"He said he was going to marry you." Daniel cast his mind back and smiled. "'Daniel,' he said, 'I've met the girl I'm going to marry.'"

# CHAPTER TWENTY-FIVE

I GLANCED DOWN AT the gas gauge. Half-full. I became anxious if it dipped much below that, so I pulled into a station. The needle drifted back to that sweet spot beyond full, the spot where possibility lay. I pulled away from the pump and headed west on San Vicente toward the ocean instead of east toward home.

I cruised through the songs on my playlist, landing on Joni Mitchell. "There's a man who's been out sailing / In a decade full of dreams / And he takes her to his schooner / And he treats her like a queen." My cell rang, interrupting Joni.

"I have reason to believe," said Barbara, "that I might have MCS."

"You have MS!"

"MCS."

"What's that?"

"Multiple Chemical Sensitivity."

"Multiple Chemical Sensitivities?"

"Sensitivity. Singular. Because the multiple takes care of the plural part, I guess."

"What does that mean?"

"It's a chronic condition. Chronic. Condition. Having to do with nonspecific symptoms from exposure to environmental chemicals and things."

I weighed my words. "So...you have allergies," I said. "You've always had allergies."

"It's more than that. It's bigger. It's like...it makes it hard for me to be in the world."

"Join the club," I remarked.

"Where are you going?" asked Barbara.

"I'm on my way home." But she couldn't hear me. I'd hit a dead zone. Just as well—I wasn't on my way home. I was on my way to see Adam. It was time for us to talk.

I abandoned my playlist and spun the dial on the Sirius. I landed on Journey and cranked it up. "Just a small town girl, livin' in a lonely world...."

I felt like a teenager en route to a drive-by of a guy's house.

Though the true drive-by was a pairs sport. You needed a friend to squeal with. If the boy's driveway was empty, you launched phase two: Driving by all his friends' houses until you spotted his car—*the* guy's car. Then, the squealing. At some point, squealing would be involved.

And always, the music. So many songs etched into my brain, forever linked with a moment, with the euphoria and anguish reserved for teenagedhood.

"She stood there bright as the sun on that California coast...." There was Bram Wheeler's yellow Cougar.

"Ventura Highway in the sunshine..." Todd Sekulovich's battered Datsun Z.

"I wish they all could be California girls..." Michael Stone's black VW.

So many songs about California. It made us feel like we were the center of the universe.

Today, when I heard the opening strains of Journey, I was back in my mother's Volvo, Gwen riding shotgun, manning the radio. We rounded a corner and there it was. Scott Lawler's white Camaro. "Some will win, some will lose / Some were born to sing the blues / Oh, the movie never ends / It goes on and on and on and on...."

I circled the block that night, living dangerously. On the second pass, Scott came out of the house. I stepped on the gas and the car took off. I sang. Gwen sang. We sang together, "Don't stop believin'...Hold on to the feelin'..." Much squealing. It was the kind of night legends are made of.

And now, today, Journey was singing again. I sang along like I had all those years before behind the wheel of my mother's Volvo with my best friend at my side and our whole lives stretching out in front of us like...like Ventura Highway in the sunshine.

The music cut out when I turned into the underground parking of the ten-story, glass-walled building overlooking the ocean. Brass letters across the top declared: Fielder Creative Management. I wended my way down into the underground garage, gripping the wheel, willing my sweaty palms dry against its slippery leather. I circled down, down, farther down. The walls were scraped where drivers had miscalculated the sharpness of the spiral. My breathing grew shallow, but I concentrated on avoiding the wall instead of the sensation swirling in my cranium.

The guys at the valet station knew me. Hector waved me toward one of the reserved spots. More than one Prius occupied the designated employee area, a smattering of Little Tykes mobiles among the Mercedes tanks. But I did not spot Adam's. Stephanie had given him a "Baby You Can Drive My Car" license plate frame on her sixteenth birthday as a subtle hint.

I pulled into the spot, but did not shut off the engine. I kept the air conditioning running so that I could gulp its blast. Besides, I didn't want Hector to think I'd gone batty, driving in and driving right out like that. I would get out of the car, make a show of having forgotten something, then get back in and leave. But when I did get out, I spotted Adam's Prius being washed at the far end of the garage. He was there after all.

A few rows over, farther from the elevator, I noticed a colleague of Adam's—Henry Boswell from indie distribution—chatting with Tara, assistant to the head of the literary department. I watched as Tara threw back her head, laughing wildly, so that her mass of copper curls swung behind her shoulders. Her hand flew to her sunglasses to keep them from falling where they were hooked into the deep V of the button-down shirt she wore tucked into a high-waisted, curve-hugging skirt. Tara From Literary was the kind of woman who rocked the Brooks Brothers look in a men's shaving cream commercial sort of way. Her fingers lingered on her sunglasses, drawing attention to her cleavage. I wondered if moves like that were studied or if they came as standard issue, like a factory extra, with Tara's kind of packaging. It made no difference to Henry Boswell, especially when Tara reached over and brushed some imaginary lint from his lapel before getting into her car.

As I headed for the elevator, Tara slipped into her glacial blue Audi. The overhead fluorescents flickered off of the car's interlinking rings medallion. Tara backed out of the parking space. The tinted window slid down and she waved bye-bye to Henry Boswell, a one-finger-at-a-time ripple of a wave as though she were drumming her fingers in the air.

As the Audi screeched away, I caught sight of the rear bumper. To the left was plastered a decal. The Rolling Stones logo: Jagger lips and tongue.

◆◆◆

"YOUR HAIR LOOKS GREAT." I said. Patty, Adam's assistant, had let it go gray.

"Thanks." Patty brushed a strand from her forehead. "I figured, who am I kidding?"

"Absolutely," I said. "I mean, it really looks good." I was out of small talk.

"Stephanie looked so beautiful the other day," Patty said. "I can't believe how she's grown."

"Yeah, she's been doing a lot of that lately. I can't seem to get her to stop."

Patty chuckled.

I had no idea that Stephanie had stopped by.

I nodded toward the door to Adam's office. "Is he busy?"

"I'm afraid he's not here. There was a problem on the set of that pilot and he had to run over there." I didn't know about a pilot.

Patty had never given me reason to distrust her, not in all these years, but I had seen Adam's car downstairs in the garage. Being detailed no less. Patty must be covering for him. Covering for what, I had no clue. Was French Girl in town? Had she ignored his non-response? Or had he finally responded: *My wife has gone nuts. Come at once!*?

Or did Adam have a non-cyber, in-town girlfriend? Was he having a nooner with some young, dewy wannabe—an actress or a screenwriter or one of that new crop of female cinematographers? Could it be going on right this minute? Behind the door to his office?

Was that door not only closed, but also locked? My hand twitched at my side. I wanted to give the doorknob a twist.

"Oh well," I said breezily, no hint of the mania sucking the oxygen out of my brain. "I was over in Santa Monica Canyon, and I thought I'd swing by…"

"You just missed him," Patty said. "David Sweeney whisked him away a few minutes ago."

So that explained it. David would have driven. I exhaled.

"I'll tell him you dropped by," Patty went on.

"No, don't. I mean, you can if you want to. It was nothing. I don't know. Nothing important. I just felt like…"

Patty answered a call, "Adam Fielder's office." She held up an index finger: just a sec. When she hung up, she looked me in the eye and said, "Your husband will be so happy to hear you came by."

"Okay, then, by all means, tell my husband I was here."

I waved goodbye to Hector as I pulled out of the structure. To head east, away from the water, I turned onto Sunset Boulevard, activating some vestigial automatic pilot from when I first learned to drive. I used to find Sunset's easy-going curves exhilarating back then, but there was no chance of the road working its magic at this speed. Or lack of speed.

As I traveled from the beach through Pacific Palisades into Brentwood, traffic stopped moving. Stopped dead. I knew better than to take this route. These days, rush hour began at noon for eastbound drivers. Angelenos went miles out of their way to avoid this stretch. I felt trapped. I was trapped. Bumper-to-bumper claustrophobia. Sunset had no breathing room anymore.

# CHAPTER TWENTY-SIX

WHEN GWEN AND I were thirteen years old, we made a sleepover pact—midnight, a foot apart in the twin beds in my pink and orange room. My mother had appeared in the doorway three times to tell us to hush up and go to sleep. But we could not be hushed. There was too much to talk about: too many dreams to imagine, too many mysteries to unravel, too many plots to hatch, too many giggles to stifle. Thirteen—a time of too much, too many.

We crept downstairs to the kitchen to raid the refrigerator. Standing in the light of its open door, we turned to each other and made a solemn, if giddy, vow. Everything. Always and forever. That's what we would share. We sealed the deal with mouthfuls of Reddi-wip straight from the can, frothy and sweet as the pledge itself.

And then came ninth grade Geometry—the pledge put to the torture test.

A Geometry test had been filched. By students challenged in grasping the mysteries of the sine and cosine. (And observational skills as well. The test had been returned to the folder on Miss MacBurney's desk upside down.) The ensuing scandal rocked the school, dividing it into two camps: one intent on smoking out the offenders, the other waiting for conscience to mete out its own punishment.

I fell into the former, Gwen the latter. We argued for hours, Gwen unable to convince me that karma would do its thing, and I unwavering in my conviction that consequences must be paid.

I found an ally in Sydney Hight, a nice enough girl who was seeded in tennis. (*What does that mean?* I wondered. I pictured Sydney, already a head taller than most of our classmates, being watered and sending out shoots.) It turned out that Sydney had a sharper serve than wit. I found myself lobbing amusing asides over the net to my new friend; she let them thump like a dead ball.

After three weeks, the Geometry Girls turned themselves in. All three were expelled anyway, leaving many Ridgepoint young ladies wondering which camp had actually prevailed, that relying on karma or that demanding punishment.

As the news of the Geometry Girls' expulsion flowed down the halls, I said to Sydney, "I hope they had proof. I mean, it was a Geometry test." It took Sydney several beats to get it, and even then, she didn't even bother to groan. In June, Sydney scribbled something in my yearbook about having a bitchin' summer, but by then, I was back to having lunch with Gwen, our best-friendship having survived the great Geometry scandal of The Ridgepoint School for Girls.

I remembered that incident as I drove to meet Gwen at a new place on Abbot-Kinney in Venice. I remembered our vow, too. I could practically taste the Reddi-wip, feel its film on the back of my tongue. Sharing everything. Today that would mean no short-cutting the details of Gwen's latest infatuation. And there would be details. She lived for the can't-eat-can't-sleep fix of infatuation as though this time, each time, the infatuation would not ever lose its fizz.

I slid into the booth across from Gwen and ordered an iced tea. "You got it, babe," said the waitress, handing me a menu. It boasted locally grown produce, though I had not exactly noticed a farm wedged among the trendy boutiques and Bikram yoga studios.

"Too stripy, don't you think?" asked Gwen.

She had suffered a highlighting mishap. The strawberry in her blonde had been amped up to lollipop intensity and the undertones had gone maroon. The whole look was a tad Willy Wonka.

"It's edgy," I submitted.

"Truth," she demanded.

"How soon can you get an appointment?"

"Tomorrow."

"Take it," I said.

"But I have a date tonight," she said.

And there we were. Jet propelled into the land of Gwen's love life.

"Richard?"

"Richard's over."

"What happened?" I asked.

"He had the stomach flu."

"You saw him throw up." I knew a deal-breaker when I heard one.

Gwen nodded. "You know how some men say they can never look at their wives the same way after seeing them give birth?"

"Those men are useless," I said.

Gwen shrugged. Regardless, Richard was history.

"So tonight's contestant?"

"Nathan."

"Nathan," I repeated. I was about to ask, "Who? What? When? Where?" but stopped myself. Why bother? In a month or two, poor Nathan would have the misfortune of catching a cold. Gwen would see him red-nosed and watery-eyed, or he might put ketchup on his eggs, or reveal in casual conversation that he had once voted Republican. Let alone committing a faux-pas like the socks-with-sandals debacle known as "pulling a Clark." Some hiccup would provide Gwen with a deal-breaker that would allow her to abandon the tarnish of familiarity for the shiny newness of someone else.

But for the moment, right now, Nathan was divine and Gwen was chasing the rush.

"I swear to God," said Gwen, "when our fingertips touch, even graze, sparks fly. I bet if you had one of those special cameras like they use to detect paranormal activity, you could see them. Actual sparks."

I said nothing. It wasn't like me not to have a witty comeback for a line like that.

"How are you?" Gwen asked. "I mean, really."

I shrugged. *Everything—always and forever.* I wanted to uphold the pledge's mandate, but I had regretted telling Gwen about Peter Lafferty. I had developed the good listener muscle over the years as "everything—always and forever" had morphed into "everything, as long as it's about Gwen." I wanted to stick to my assigned part. I was comfortable there. I used to think I didn't like to talk about my life because it was fulfilling in a way that Gwen's was not. Now I didn't want to talk about it because it had gone askew. Wildly.

"You know what the real problem with Richard was?" Gwen asked. "He always wanted to sleep over."

"That's a switch. Who was the guy you dumped because he couldn't get out of there fast enough?"

"Barry. Like lightning. No decorum whatsoever. I mean, really."

"So Richard…?"

"He never came right out and said it, of course, but honestly, he started withholding sex. What kind of a guy does that? He didn't want to sleep with me unless he could sleep with me. I mean, really, like wake up in the morning, brush your teeth, whole long night spending the night."

"So?"

"It kind of spoils the romance, don't you think?"

"I wouldn't know," I said. "You mean there's an exact right amount of time to stay?"

"Of course. There's that hour or so for lying there and cuddling or drifting off or whatever, but before you have to get up and go the bathroom or wash your face and do all that ablution stuff. You know, the magic hour. You don't mess with the magic hour."

I fished a piece of ice out of my water glass with my fork and slid it into my iced tea. "You're sort of the Goldilocks of relationships… only I'm not sure…" I stopped myself.

"You're not sure what?"

"I'm not sure you want just right. Would you be happy with just right?"

"Just right…'" said Gwen yearningly. "I think that might be Nathan. I guess you can never really know for sure."

I nodded. Once, I had known what just right looked like. It looked like Adam. I wondered which was the sorrier state: the never knowing or the forgetting. Were they flip sides of the same coin? Flip sides of giving up?

"I can't stop thinking about him. It's like he's set up camp in my brain," she added. And then that look came over her. If she'd been in a movie, Gwen would have gone all dreamy and soft focus, the lens smeared with Vaseline.

Regardless, I knew that by the next time we met for lunch, or the time after, a tornado would have ravaged the campgrounds. Nathan's tent was destined to be flattened.

"Maybe," said Gwen as she wrung the last drops from a lemon wedge into her Diet Coke, "...maybe I have some sort of attachment disorder, like those babies from Romanian orphanages. What do you think? Do you think that's possible?"

"You don't have attachment disorder," I said.

There had been a time when I believed that I had some sort of attachment disorder, a reverse strain. In college and after, while my friends discarded boyfriends one after another, I had become attached to Adam with a vengeance. It wasn't just the sex. It was because Adam made me laugh. It was because Adam saw me cry. It was because I let Adam in. I wondered if what I had was too-attached disorder.

That night with Peter Lafferty maybe I was trying to prove that I didn't need attachment, that I could opt out of attachment, flip the attachment switch to the "off" position at will. There was glamour in that, at least the illusion of glamour. A glamour that was purported to outweigh the melancholy. But didn't.

"Are you sure?" asked Gwen.

"Of what?"

"That there's not something wrong with me?"

"I never said that," I said.

"Ha," she snorted.

"But you don't have an attachment disorder," I added.

"I want to be attached. I really do," Gwen insisted. "When I'm not seeing someone, I feel so out of it. Like I go to the movies and see people kissing on screen, and it's like I'm left out."

"It's like you've got your nose pressed up against the glass," I reflected. "The way people used to watch TV through the window of the hardware store, trying to imagine how wonderful it would be to have a television set in their very own living room. Well, guess what? Maybe what's going on in that living room is not so great after all. Maybe it only looks good through the window."

"Maura," said Gwen, "you're my oldest, bestest friend in the world and I love you. But that living room is your world. You're not a swipe right, swipe left kind of girl. You're not like me. Familiarity is boring to me. I like first dates. I like waiting for the second date. I like being in bed with someone who doesn't have a last name."

"I can be that person," I said. "I slept with another man."

"And how did that make you feel?"

"Like shit. But maybe feeling like shit is an acquired taste."

"You're so lucky," she said.

"Because I feel like shit and my life is in rubbles?"

"Yeah," she said.

"That makes a lot of sense."

"Because," said Gwen slowly, "it means something when your life falls to rubble. Most of us move from this pile of rubble to that pile of rubble."

"That's not true," I said.

"It is." She held a chunk of her hair out to the side so that she could study its color. "Maybe I should go dark."

I shook my head no.

"Forget it," she said. "I don't know what I'm talking about."

"You want me to get over myself," I said.

She shrugged again. "Yeah, I think that would be a good idea."

"So do I," I said. "I don't seem to know how."

# CHAPTER TWENTY-SEVEN

I RETURNED HOME TO four new voicemails. All Peter Lafferty. I deleted them, one after the other. I didn't want to hear what he had to say, his idea of what he thought the two of us might be. My own idea did not match his. There were oceans between our ideas. The difference between something and nothing.

I had tried to chuck Peter Lafferty into the way-back of my brain like a sweater tossed into the back seat while driving. I would compartmentalize, I'd decided, the way men seemed to know how to do, organizing their lives like a game of Scattergories, instead of the undulating mass that women's lives tend to be—lava lamps of feelings, desires, experience, analysis. All the retelling and the reliving.

I stared at the contents of the refrigerator. I should have been ashamed of myself. This was not the refrigerator that belonged in a house with a growing girl. I had no idea what I was hungry for. I found a brick of white cheddar and cut myself a chunk, then another. I gulped some orange juice straight from the plastic jug. I moved from the fridge to the pantry and foraged for something sweet. The best I could find were some stale Fig Newtons, whole wheat at that. No fun. With the last of the cookies and a dozen almonds stuffed in my fist, I headed for Adam's study. And the computer. The only way to channel the adrenaline that zapped through me was to return to the source.

Even though the video and the emails had been banished, who knows what I might have missed? I scoured for wayward folders, anything I might have overlooked in a corner of the desktop. I kept trawling, knowing the definition of insanity well: doing the same thing over and over and expecting a different result. Maybe I'd missed some tidbit of information the first time around. The first three or four times around. More like seven or eight. Twelve maybe.

I searched Aimee Laroche and scrolled down past the first several results. I was all too familiar with them by now. Clearly, some of these Aimee Laroches were not my girl. But I kept clicking anyway. "Next." "Next." "Next."

On the fourth page something caught my eye. Aimee Laroche, Actress: *La Folie D'Amour*. That much French I knew. *The Madness of Love*. I clicked on the entry. There she was. Provocatively posed. French Girl gazing over a perfectly sloping shoulder—naked shoulder—into the distance. An expression so vacant it was hard to know if she was being driven mad by love or if she was the one behind the wheel.

I started clicking. I Googled the movie: an unknown French film by an unknown director, a last gasp of New Wave iconoclasm described as "freewheeling." As far as I could tell, it centered on a group of teens predictably disenchanted with family, society, and love. Yada, yada, yada.

I IMDB'd Aimee Laroche. *Folie* was her only film. Clearly, Ingenue Girl had no talent and had been forced to give up her dream. Or had it been a one-time lark? Had a brooding, young director spotted her in a café and begged her to be in his movie, barely having to prod her into shedding her clothes?

I ferreted through Adam's drawers, but found no copy of *The Madness of Love*. I tried Netflix though I was certain this film would not be available. I was correct. I tried Larry Edmunds Books and Video, a Hollywood institution specializing in obscure titles. Still nothing. I hit eBay, wondering if an overzealous film student or committed Francophile might have a copy.

And there it was. One lone copy up for auction by a collector in Budapest. Minimum bid: 2,000 Euro. I didn't need to check the current exchange rate to know that wasn't going to happen.

I was out of options. *La Folie D'Amour* would remain out of reach. I popped the last of the almonds and clicked onto Shopbop.

By the time I pushed myself away from the desk twenty minutes later, I had ordered a heathered cashmere cardigan, a navy and white polka dotted dress (in case I was invited to the races at Ascot), and a silk blouse with French cuffs that required cufflinks. I bought another blouse described as having poet sleeves. It looked like something Barbara would wear, but seemed to carry the likelihood that I would hear a madrigal play the instant I slipped it on. Riding a high that was shameful, I also decided on olive suede Manolo Blahniks so drastically reduced in price that my finger simply had no choice but to click on "Add to Cart," even though the one remaining pair was a half-size too big.

No *La Folie D'Amour*, but guilt…in the form of an ever-expanding wardrobe for someone whose life had shrunk. I was horrified, though not enough to delete any of my purchases. Instead, I swung toward the pragmatic, quickly buying three pairs of Spanx—brown, black, and rose gold—in case the Fig Newton thing should evolve into a Milano thing or, God forbid, a thing with those rectangular French butter biscuits that are the delivery system for a quarter-inch slab of chocolate.

The Spanx gave me a second wind. I strolled more cyber boutiques. "What's New" presented dresses that looked like Ace bandages and parachute pants that looked like leftovers from Hammer Time. There was a feature promising eight ways to wear a white shirt—a headline that suggested images requiring contortionism. I pictured sleeves wrapped like a turban and shirttails tied into a cummerbund. I clicked on the link, only to find the white shirt paired with eight different bottoms.

I wandered through "Lookbooks," arriving on a series of images that made me do a doubletake. They were underpants. That's a look all right. Brand name: Hanky Panky. Picture after picture of thongs—shocking pink, leopard print, "after midnight." The captions hyped slits in strategic places. I clicked on a pair to enlarge the image. Three additional views appeared. How many angles were required to get a sense of a two-inch piece of stretch-lace?

I jumped when I heard the back door slam and exited the site immediately like a kid looking at porn instead of doing his homework. I hopped up and headed into the kitchen. Stephanie dropped her backpack onto the counter and shot upstairs.

"Steph!" I followed her up.

"Hi." Stephanie was already in her room, a cozy mix of watercolor florals and stripes in lilac and pistachio.

"Can I ask you something?" I had been determined not to do this, but I couldn't not.

"Uh-oh," said Stephanie.

"No 'uh-oh.' Just a question. Why did you go see Daddy? At the office, I mean."

"You're kidding, right?"

"No," I pretended to be casual. "Just wondering."

"Well," Stephanie began, "I went to see him because he's my father. And he wanted to see my prom dress."

It took a minute for me to process. First, there was the dig. Of course, he was her father. Second, what was with this prom dress thing?

"Wait a minute...Your prom dress?"

"Yeah, you know, the fancy dress you wear to prom. Which is in, like, two weeks."

So she had bought a dress. My daughter had gone shopping and picked out a dress without me. Wasn't I supposed to sit in the corner of the dressing room poised to button and zip?

"You went without me?"

"Yeah, you were, you know..."

"I don't know. What was I?"

Stephanie stared at me. Her phone chimed. She typed a return message.

"What was I?" I asked again.

"You were kind of out of it. You've been kind of out of it. Actually, on that very day, I think you were in bed with the shades down pretending to be asleep when I came in to ask you if you wanted to go with me."

"If you knew I was pretending, why didn't you say something?"

"Because..." Stephanie spoke slowly as you would to a child, "...you were pretending to be asleep. If you'd really been asleep, I would have woken you up. You were kind of a wreck."

There had been several days exactly like that, a string of them. Me, bundled under the comforter in a darkened room, giving in to the medication that my internist had prescribed. The Antivert made me loopy (loopier)—foggy, drugged, heavy-lidded. The doctor had dismissed me with a pill. But the pill had only whisked me farther away from my life. I'd summoned enough sense to stop taking them, but too late. Now, here I was weeks later, having missed my daughter's life, too—the one life I still cared about.

"May I see the dress?" I asked.

"You're going to love it, Mommy." Stephanie bolted for the closet. *There's my girl.* "Close your eyes." She stepped into the bathroom to slip on the dress, not out of modesty, but for the surprise. I sat on her bed, waiting.

"I used the emergency credit card," Stephanie said.

"But that's for emergencies."

"This was an emergency," Stephanie submitted. "My mother was lying in a dark room pretending to be asleep at three in the afternoon."

I nodded. "How are you going to wear your hair?"

"I'm not sure yet. We'll have to experiment."

"Sure." *We* will have to experiment. Thank God, I thought, she's giving me another chance. We would fiddle with updos and tousled waves. I would redeem myself.

There had been a week, years ago, when Adam had taken over all of Stephanie's care and feeding. Stephanie was four years old, and I'd had a miscarriage. I spent one night in the hospital, then a few days lying around the house, giving in to bouts of weeping that came from a deep hormonal place. I shuffled by Stephanie's bedroom one morning, wrapped in my flannel bathrobe, and peeked in.

Adam was bent over Stephanie, struggling with her pigtails. She was complaining that they were not even. Adam gently, patiently, slid out the elastics and set to brushing Stephanie's hair again. Then he gathered half the hair onto one side of her head and slid it through one of the elastics, doubling the stretchy thing to secure it.

"That's good, Daddy," Stephanie said. "Do the other one just like that."

Adam gathered the other half of Stephanie's hair into his hand and repeated the procedure. Then he examined the pigtails for symmetry with such care that I would not have been surprised had he run to fetch the level from his toolkit.

I didn't cry over the baby lost anymore after that.

Now, these many years later, Stephanie stepped out of the bathroom wearing a burgundy silk strapless dress that made her waist look the size of a headband.

"What do you think? I can take it back if you hate it."

"You couldn't have done better," I said. Stephanie closed the bedroom door to look at herself in the full-length mirror.

"I'm obsessed with this dress!" she said.

She, like all her girlfriends, was always "obsessed" with something—some new pastry hybrid (muffin meet donut, croissant meet cookie), tidying up Marie Kondo style, the latest Kreation Juicery green drink. So many obsessions.

Obsession—these girls had no idea. Lifting the needle on a record in the brain over and over and over again, lowering it onto the exact spot over and over and over again—that particular spot on the brain vinyl—until you wear a groove in the thing so deep, it skips all on its own. And then it skips forever. On its own. No more lifting the needle. No more raising it over the spot. No more lowering it. Only skipping, over and over and over. All by itself. Like growing a reflex.

Obsessed with this dress. Kid stuff.

But because I was overcome by the sight of my daughter standing there in the dress, and because I was riddled with guilt over not having held my daughter's hand through the prom dress rite of passage, and because a generosity of spirit suddenly washed over me unlike anything I'd felt in months, I said, "I bet Daddy beamed from ear to ear."

But mostly, I said it because I wanted to send a message to the ghost lurking in the corner of my daughter's Shabby Chic bedroom. It was the ghost of our family, and I wanted to let it know I saw it there. I wasn't sure, however, whether I wanted to send it packing or give it mouth-to-mouth.

# CHAPTER TWENTY-EIGHT

EIGHTEEN KIDS WERE LINED up on the Turneys' front lawn as though they were posing for the paparazzi on a red carpet. Boy, girl, boy, girl. Their parents, standing opposite, snapped photos and commented to one another that so much, but somehow nothing much, had changed in all the decades of prom nights. The limos were longer. The dresses were skimpier. The cameras were phones.

Adam and I stood at opposite sides of the lawn avoiding one another's gaze, staring at our daughter. Most of the other girls were in black, trying to look older. It made several of them look younger. And several looked like hookers. A few others wore sherbet tones that made them look like little girls gone scavenging in their dress-up trunks. Stephanie had nailed it with the burgundy. Sophisticated but not somber. Unique. If anyone should ask, "Who is Stephanie Fielder?" the answer would be, "The girl in the burgundy dress."

Matt Turney and Stephanie were pals, nothing more. He was a lanky kid with a slight wall eye. Stephanie and Matt had been in the same class since kindergarten. Seaview "lifers." Going to prom together was a bit like going with a second cousin. But they'd had an understanding that they would serve as each other's Plan B (though Stephanie had confided to me that she knew she was secretly Matt's Plan A). One night well after midnight, Matt had texted Stephanie to come to her window. He stood below, holding a sign: "Stephanie + Turney = PROM."

Now, I watched as Matt pulled a white orchid from its box. His hands hovered inches from her chest—one clutching the flower, the other the pin with which to secure it, unsure of where to land. Stephanie nodded me over.

"It might work right here." I tapped my daughter's waist, off center. It was the perfect spot, what the dress would have ordered.

I pinned it on and retreated—now to Adam's side of the lawn as the driver threw open the doors of the Hummer on steroids. The kids made their way to the limo, the girls teetering on stilettos that splooshed into the sod with each step. One of the boys, Max Porter, approached the driver and slipped him a bill as though he were Frank Sinatra palming a C-note to a maître d'.

"I don't like that," I said to Adam.

"Calm down," he admonished.

"I've never liked that Max Porter," I said.

Adam shushed me.

"I'm telling you," I whispered. "No good can come from that."

"You're freaking out," Adam insisted. "It's prom for Christ's sake!"

Just then Stephanie turned and dashed back to us.

"I'm so happy you're both here."

"Of course we're here," Adam said. He left out the "both," though that was her point. Then he whispered in Stephanie's ear, "You're the most beautiful girl here."

There had been a moment at Mommy-and-Me when a mother, stationed on the Mommy bench, had tried to get her little girl's attention. The three-year-old was pouring corn meal from one container to another. "Pretty girl!" the mother called. And every single little girl on that playground turned to face her own Mommy. I could not recall a time when my head would have turned if someone called "Pretty girl!" Must every girl migrate from the Age of Look-At-Me to the Age of Oh-Please-Don't?

"Have a good time," Adam said.

And Stephanie was gone. Back across the lawn, into the limo, swept into prom.

"What's with all this 'Are you going to prom' thing? When did they stop saying 'the prom?'" I chattered, trying to make conversation with Adam.

"I don't know," he said. "It's sort of the end of civilization as we know it, isn't it?"

He was only half kidding. Only Adam would have known my simple grammar question spoke to my very real fear that civilization was indeed deteriorating.

In the first grade at Ridgepoint, I had been trained to stand immediately to the side of my desk when an adult entered the classroom and then, like all the little Ridgepoint girls at the sides of their desks, to curtsy. We practiced this procedure often, a sort of etiquette fire drill.

I never wanted my baby to curtsy to a dour headmistress who patrolled the school like a floorwalker at an old department store. However I rejected the curtsying and the nunnery silence in the halls, I could never quite overcome my decided preference for manners and general politesse. Grammar reflected those things. Its erosion reflected their erosion. Civilization was deteriorating; there was no denying it.

So, when I pondered "prom" as opposed to "the prom," Adam knew what I meant. Adam knew all those things about me. He knew all my subtexts.

"It's going to be a long night," I said.

"I know," said Adam.

"Want to come over?"

♦♦♦

ADAM BEAT ME HOME. I pulled into the right side of the garage slowly, having grown accustomed to hogging the entire space. Adam was waiting in his car. We walked together through the back door into the kitchen.

Wordlessly, Adam filled the kettle as I grabbed a couple of mugs from the cupboard.

"She's so beautiful," Adam said. Safe territory. Shared territory. I nodded. My mind had wandered to Stephanie as well. Where else on prom night?

"She'll be fine," Adam assured me. "I'm glad we named her Stephanie," he said. "It suits her."

He was trying so hard, even apologizing for a tiff from the distant past when baby naming books littered the house. "It was that whole Stephen Dedalus thing."

"My James Joyce obsession."

"I was afraid it was going to be so weighty. I mean…James Joyce."

"I knew she'd be up to it," I said.

"You ask a lot of people."

"Only of the people I love," I said. "I expect nothing from everyone else in the entire world."

We drank our tea at the kitchen table. Neither of us mentioned the last time we sat there, uneaten corned beef and pastrami between us. The crossword puzzle in today's newspaper lay semi-completed on the table. I slid it in front of Adam and scooted my chair next to his.

"I need help," I said. "You'll know this one...." I searched the puzzle. "Here it is. Twenty-nine down." I pointed to the single filled-in square in the line; the second letter—a "P." We leaned over the puzzle, shoulder to shoulder, head to head.

"British portrait painter," Adam read. He filled in the three blank squares. The word was OPIE.

"Opie?" I said. "Opie is a British portrait painter?"

"John Opie," asserted Adam.

"Well, that's just not right," I contested. "Opie is Andy Taylor's little boy. Ronny Howard. Mayberry sheriff's son. I've used Opie a thousand times. Those are the OPIE clues."

"I know," Adam agreed. "It's one of those words."

"Like OBI. Or..."

"ITE," offered Adam.

"ITE?"

"The suffix for minerals."

"ATTA."

"ATTA?"

"Atta boy. Atta girl. I had it a couple of days ago."

"Or ASIN."

"ASIN?"

"A as in apple. Z as in zebra."

"Oh!" said Adam. "ASIN. Why didn't you say so?" I laughed. Adam laughed. The sight of Adam laughing delighted me more than my own laughter. I didn't want him to ever stop.

"There's always ULEE," I said.

Adam furrowed his brow.

"You know," I explained. "*Ulee's Gold*. We use it all the time. The Peter Fonda bee-keeper movie."

"Right. *Ulee's Gold*."

"According to crossword puzzles, that's Peter Fonda's one and only movie."

Adam laughed, shaking his head at the truth of it. "No *Easy Rider*. No *The Trip*." He was on a roll. "No *3:10 to Yuma*."

"Peter Fonda was in *3:10 to Yuma*?"

"He was."

"They should use that one then," I insisted. "YUMA. How could they have missed YUMA? We should write to the crossword puzzle people."

"I think we should," Adam said. "YUMA's been overlooked. It's a dreadful oversight."

"Egregious."

Adam smiled at my wordsmithing one-upsmanship. I smiled because we were saying "we."

"And, of course, the ever-popular ÉTÉ," submitted Adam.

"ÉTÉ?"

"You know, French for summer."

Both country and season had been contaminated in my imagination. Now they were conflated into one three-letter crossword favorite. France. Summer. Adam's summer in France. My stomach gripped.

Adam and I fell silent over the puzzle. I leaned in again, body to body, willing the warmth of his body to calm the churning deep in my gut whipped up by one three-letter word.

"Echo," I said after a minute, tapping forty-three across.

"Nymph of unrequited love?" read Adam.

"It's Echo," I said. "I'm pretty sure."

"No, Echo loved the sound of her own voice," Adam contended.

"When no one loves you, that's what happens—you start talking to yourself."

Adam filled in the squares. "It fits."

"I know my nymphs," I said.

I carried the mugs to the sink. Adam stood behind me, one hand on either side, so that when I turned around, my back was pressed against the countertop.

I rested my head on Adam's chest and let him fold me in his arms. I would have hoped there would be comfort there. I could not have guessed there would be a jolt as well. When was the last time that kind of current had flowed between us? I knew that some couples fought regularly so they could collide with the jolt waiting at the other end, a heady cocktail of pheromones and adrenaline and honey. Suddenly I understood how it could be addictive.

Adam let go of me for a moment, long enough to take my face in his hands. I looked at him. This was my husband. I did not have to play some game whose rules I had long ago forgotten, if I had ever known them at all. I did not have to play at being coy. All I had to do was kiss him.

There had been a time when I could not come within ten feet of Adam without kissing him.

"I'm going to kiss you," I would say.

"You can't resist me, can you?" he'd joke. But it wasn't a joke. I couldn't resist him. Twenty-plus years had turned down the volume. I assumed it had gone silent forever. But tonight, here in the kitchen, it was back.

I pulled him to me and kissed his mouth. Still, he held my face in his hands while I pressed my body against his, as close as possible. Closer. I wanted to touch him everywhere at once, to revisit every inch of a landscape warm with memory. I yanked at his shirttail, freeing it, so that I could reach under and touch him.

Adam had always known how to kiss me. Even when we were young, he had never been one of those guys who shoved the whole of his tongue into my mouth as though he were spelunking. He offered the breathless pull of wanting more.

My back pressed against the counter, I held him closer. He released my face and slipped one hand up under my T-shirt while the other unbuckled his own belt. Then he slid his hand down my arm and stroked the hollow in the crook of my elbow. Once, so long ago, he had told me that spot excited him. Ever since, when he touched me there, it excited me, too. Our own private erotic symbiosis.

"Let's go upstairs," he suggested.

"No." I didn't want to risk weakening the charge between us even for a moment. Besides, his jeans were already puddled around his ankles. I fumbled with my own J Brands, shimmying them down. I wished I had on some silky thing underneath instead of the all-cotton I normally wore under my yoga gear. But who cared? Surely not Adam. His fingers found their way under the cotton. With his other hand, he took mine and gently placed it on himself as if to remind me: this is how we do this, you and I—as if to send us back in time to when we were first learning how to make love to each other. I wiggled my hand under the elastic waistband of his Jockeys and touched him. A shudder twitched through him—involuntary and sweet, so sweet.

With my other hand, I cupped the side of his neck to pull him closer still. His heartbeat pounded in his throat, matching the rhythm of my own. Adam swung an arm around my upper back as though he were going to dip me in a ballroom, trying to lower me to the kitchen floor. I resisted, pulling him closer to me instead. No. Change nothing about this moment.

I scooched back on the counter, shoving the espresso machine out of the way, thinking: *We're going to have sex on the kitchen counter. Like in the movies.* I tried to delete the word from my brain. But it was too late. Movies. Sex. Sex in the movies. French Girl was always just off screen these days, and now, suddenly, she was ready for her close-up.

*Leave me alone.* I wanted to shout. But that would be impossible. French Girl had laid claim to my imagination. She would insert herself where she damn well pleased, and I was powerless against that dark corner of my own psyche where the girl now lurked.

"Adam...," I whispered, hoping that the sound of his name—of my voice saying his name—would wither the French girl. I ached to tell him I loved him. It was the truth. "I love you, Adam.... I love you...I love you...," but French Girl held the words hostage and would not release them.

I struggled to put my brain on pause and let my body take over. I zoomed in on sensation after sensation. But even when I managed to bring each pinpoint into focus, I could not connect the dots to ride them all the way to abandon.

Adam's voice was husky. "Oh, God...."

I was going for a "God, yes!" He owed me a "God, yes!" and I would do whatever it took to exact one. I reached behind him, up over his shoulder blade to the base of his neck. I expected to find hair flipping there, hair that I could twirl around my index finger. I didn't know which Adam I was making love to anymore—the one from the video or my husband. My fingers reminded me; this hair was short and close-cropped—coarser, more wiry because of the silver woven into the wheat.

Again he grunted, "Oh, God." And then his grip on my back relaxed and his head dropped to my shoulder. I could feel his breath against my neck. Something like a laugh escaped his lips. Mine too. Sudden self-conscious acknowledgment of us, longtime marrieds, having just had sex on the kitchen counter. And relief. We were home again.

Adam bent down to pull up his pants, still crumpled at his feet, sending his cell phone sliding from his pocket and skittering across the floor. Fly still unzipped, he scooped it up and crossed the kitchen to the little desk where the charging station lived, but could not find the right cord. iPhone 7, iPhone 11. Built-in obsolescence that could give a person brain freeze.

I pulled up my panties but did not bother to gather up my jeans from where they lay on the floor next to me. Rather than rehook my bra, I wriggled out of it under my T-shirt and tossed it on the floor as well.

"Verona or Bordeaux?" I asked as I stared into the pantry.

Adam did not answer.

"Pepperidge Farm," I explained. "Verona or Bordeaux?"

"What's this?" Adam was holding a small, white card. At first, I wasn't sure what it was. Then my knees turned to jelly and a rush of heat lurched to my cheeks.

"It's nothing."

"'I'm so glad this has happened,'" Adam read. "'Love, Peter.' That would be Peter Lafferty, Peter?"

"Yes."

"He's so glad what has happened?"

"Nothing."

"Nothing isn't a 'this.' What is 'this?' This 'this' that has happened?"

"Nothing," I insisted. "Nothing happened." I wasn't even convincing myself.

"Oh my God." Adam sat down, elbows on the kitchen table, head in his hands. "Oh my God," he said again.

"It was nothing. You know Peter. He's…"

"He's what?"

"He's…"

"He's a man you slept with. That's what men mean when they say that. That's what the 'this' is. The 'this' that happened."

"No…Adam…"

"No, it didn't happen?"

"Just no."

"No, it did happen? But I'm supposed to ignore it."

"No," I said. "No. Don't do this. You don't want to do this."

"You don't get to tell me what I want to do." Adam waved the card in my face.

"Please don't do this," I begged.

"I'm not supposed to do this? I've felt guilty and ashamed and miserable day after day, week after week."

"It meant nothing."

"You did sleep with him!" Adam shouted, flattened by the truth. Fury reconfigured his face, hardened his eyes in a way I had never seen before. I stopped breathing.

"Well, you…you were having a sort of an affair."

"It was email! Email doesn't count. It's not real."

"It seemed real to me when I read it."

"But it wasn't," he said. "You slept with Peter fucking Lafferty!" Adam spat out the words. He picked up one of our mugs from the kitchen table and hurled it against the counter where we had just had sex. The Victorian milk glass basket sitting there happened to be one of my prized pieces. It shattered across the countertop, gouging the Caesarstone. It shattered across the floor. It shattered everywhere. My hands flew to cover my face.

"Goddamn you!" Adam roared. He stormed out the back door into the garage.

I wanted to run after him, but felt planted there, surrounded by milk glass shrapnel. Then I heard Adam's car backing out of the garage, yanked on my jeans, and ran through the house out the front door. I kept running, across the lawn into the street until I was right in front of his car. Adam slammed on the brakes, screeching to a halt inches from me. He flung open the door and came at me.

"It meant nothing to you?" he demanded. "It means something to me. It meant something to Peter."

The sudden force of my sobs doubled me over at a right angle. I clutched my rib cage. "It wasn't me," I managed to say.

"What the hell...?"

"I wasn't myself. The thing with that Aimee girl..." There was no finishing that sentence.

"Are you insane? You can't compare fucking another man to a couple of silly emails." It dawned on him anew: "Jesus Christ, Peter fucking Lafferty."

"I'm not asking you what you've done since you've been out of the house," I ventured.

Adam stared at me in disbelief. Maybe I had gone insane.

"You know...we were on a break, like they say..." I vamped.

"A break? Like in *Friends*? Life is not a sitcom." Adam's voice broke. "Our marriage is not a sitcom." He let out a constricted wail.

"Can't we start over?" I pleaded. "You hurt my feelings. I hurt your feelings. It's all over. We're even."

"Are you out of your mind?" He was crying now, too. "I'm such an idiot," he muttered. "I felt so guilty, so ashamed. For what? For nothing. But that can't touch the shame I feel now."

"I know. I'm ashamed, too. You have the right to be ashamed of me. You have every right."

"Don't flatter yourself. I'm ashamed of myself for thinking I knew who you were. For not knowing you were capable of something like this. It's me I'm ashamed of. Ashamed that I was a fucking fool." He turned away from me and got back in the car.

"I love you, Adam. You know that. I love you." I couldn't remember the last time I had told him that. Or the last time I had really known it with such certainty.

Adam pulled away and shot down the street. I ran after him, but I gave up when he turned left onto Beverly Glen. For a long moment, I stood there alone in the middle of the late night street, then dragged myself back to the house, spent from sobbing but unable to stop.

It was only when I walked back into the house that I noticed the red streaks leading from the kitchen to the front door. I had cut my foot on a milk glass shard, a remnant of one of my favorite things.

# CHAPTER TWENTY-NINE

THERE MIGHT BE SLEEP *in my future*, I thought, *but not tonight.*

I sat motionless in the overstuffed easy chair in the bedroom. The same chair that held me prisoner that afternoon when this nightmare first began.

Tonight, my brain wandered to an even more awful place: the realm of second chances come and gone. I had missed more than one opportunity that night when I had discovered Adam watching himself making love to the French Girl. If I had it to do over again, would I go back to bed and forget about it? End of story? Would I leave the emails in the cloud like so much vapor? If I had it to do over again, would I laugh at the Top Ten List? One thing I knew for sure: if I had it to do over again, I would instruct Peter Lafferty to go straight on Sunset Blvd. instead of turning right up into the bird streets. It was exhausting to relive that first moment over and over again. Each of those moments over and over again. Exhausting.

A vision of Adam haunted me. He was turning slowly in his desk chair, away from the computer, to stare at me. With hard eyes. Eyes filled with disgust. But then I realized it wasn't Adam in his chair. It was Peter Lafferty wearing an unbuttoned double-breasted suit and grinning like David Letterman. Lafferty/Letterman wheeled his chair closer to me and whispered in my ear, "This is the end. My only friend, the end." Lafferty was no Jim Morrison. He was no Dave. And he was certainly no Adam.

The ringing phone yanked me from my dream. There would be no second chance after all. No do-overs.

I picked up the phone. "Adam?"

A girl's voice—not Stephanie's. "Maura?" It was Mallory, Stephanie's best friend. "I'm sorry to call so late."

"What's wrong?" I was on my feet.

"One sec...The nurse asked me something."

"Is Stephanie okay?" I shouted into the phone. "What happened? Where are you?"

Mallory came back on the line. "Stephanie started throwing up and she couldn't stop. Then she sort of fainted. We're at the hospital. I think maybe she drank too much."

"Let me talk to her."

"Adam is here," Mallory said. "He said to tell you everything's under control."

"Adam is there?"

"Yeah, he says you don't need to come or anything."

"Let me talk to him."

"I'll see if I can find him," Mallory said. "It's kind of crazy here."

It's kind of crazy here, too, I thought. You've made me even crazier if that were possible. It's kind of crazy everywhere. Crazy.

I hung up and dialed Adam's cell. It rang once, then went straight to voice mail. I called Mallory back.

"Hello." A boy's voice.

"Who is this?" I demanded.

"Oh, hi, this is Matt. How are you, Mrs. Fielder?" Matt asked, borderline Eddie Haskell.

"Where are you?" I asked. "Which hospital?"

I could hear Matt shouting to no one in particular. "What hospital is this?" Two or three voices in the background shouted back, "St. John's." I hung up before Matt could repeat the name.

The next thing I knew I was pulling into Emergency Room Parking at St. John's in Santa Monica. The valet was nowhere in sight. I threw the keys on the passenger seat and blasted through the entrance, barely waiting for the door to swing open. Mallory fluttered over to me in her meringue of a dress.

"Why did you call Adam?" I asked.

Mallory looked at me, perplexed.

"I mean...never mind," I said, embarrassed to be fixated on where I numbered on the list of Who-To-Call-In-Case-Of Emergency.

Mallory led me through the waiting room. Several patients dotted the Naugahyde couches, staring at the muted flat screen bolted high on the far wall. As we approached the entrance to the emergency room, Mallory smiled at the nurse behind the window as though they were already old friends and pointed at me: she's the mother.

Mallory led me to the second partitioned area on the left. I slid the curtain along its aluminum rod, flinching at the fingernails-on-blackboard squeak.

"Here you are," said Mallory as though she were a cruise director escorting me to the Lido deck.

Stephanie lay resting, eyes closed, on a narrow bed, her dress blotched with dried vomit. Adam sat on a metal chair at her side. Like me, he was still wearing the same clothes—the clothes we had on at the beginning of the evening when we sent Stephanie off in the limo, the jeans that were shoved down around our ankles when we were pressed up against the kitchen counter a few hours ago.

Mallory headed out, but I stopped her. "Mallory, how was the prom?"

"It was super fun. The after party kind of sucked. Me and Stephanie were really sad we didn't stay at prom longer. Everyone was in such a hurry to get to the stupid after party."

I nodded. Sounded about right.

There was no place for me to sit, but Adam did not get up. Nor did he release Stephanie's hand where an IV was inserted into a slender vein.

"What happened?" I asked Adam.

"Shush," Adam snipped.

"I have alcohol poisoning," Stephanie muttered, not opening her eyes. "So dumb…"

I plucked several strands of hair away from where they were stuck to the side of Stephanie's face. She managed a wan smile.

"Leave her alone," ordered Adam.

I smoothed the thin blue blanket bunched around Stephanie's calves.

"I said leave her alone," Adam barked.

Stephanie's eyes sprung open.

I picked up the washrag crumpled on the stainless steel bedside table, moistened it in the pitcher of water, and began sponging at the largest patch of crusted vomit on the skirt of her dress.

As if electrocuted, Adam shot from his chair and snatched the washcloth from my hand. "Stop it!"

Stephanie's gaze darted between her father and me. Whoa. "You're supposed to be mad at me," she proposed. "I'm the one who drank too much."

"Don't worry, young lady, your turn will come," said Adam, wagging his finger in her face. He returned to the chair. It was his. He was there first.

"Tough night," said the doctor as she entered the cubicle. "I'm Dr. Colton." Barely five feet tall, the doctor wore turquoise leggings under a purple dress. Her white coat hung inches longer than the dress. Doctors used to be older than me, I thought. What happened?

"We're lucky she didn't seize," said young Dr. Colton.

I had learned the term in pastry class at Williams-Sonoma. Now, I could only think of chocolate, improperly tended in a double boiler, coagulating into an unusable mass.

"She's going to be fine," continued the doctor. "We're hydrating her. It's all good."

Hardly, I thought. "Can we take her home?" I asked.

"We'll see how she's doing when the IV is done. I'll check back in a couple hours." Dr. Colton patted Stephanie on the leg. "Where was prom?"

"Shutters," answered Stephanie.

"Cool," said the doctor before disappearing into the hall.

I stood at the foot of the bed, swaying back and forth like I used to when I held baby Stephanie in my arms.

"You guys don't have to sit here," said Stephanie. "Go get something to eat or something."

"No," I said. I grabbed hold of the railing on the side of the bed, staking my claim.

Adam stood and kissed Stephanie on the cheek. "You're going to be fine." Then he slid the curtain open, walked out, and slid it back. Again, the awful squeak sent a shiver up my spine like my old nemesis, the nightmare witch.

"Young lady?" Stephanie said snidely, repeating her father's words, even wagging her finger exaggeratedly—an expression and gesture that were so not her father. "I mean…really. What's up with that?"

I shrugged.

"I guess it's going to be just me and Daddy for the college trip."

"What?" I asked. These days there were so many conversations in my absence.

"Just the two of us are going, Daddy says."

"Okay," I agreed. "Sure."

Of course it couldn't be the three of us, not anymore, but that had not yet occurred to me. I lifted Stephanie's hand—the one without the IV—and kissed her palm. I had kissed that palm every morning when I dropped her off at preschool, folding Stephanie's dimpled fingers tightly over the spot—secret code for Mommy's always with you. Tonight I was the one who needed to be reminded.

# CHAPTER THIRTY

THE THREE OF US had done a first pass the previous year over spring break, hitting the east coast where Ivies and hidden Ivies awaited like so many petals to be plucked. The collegiate version of he-loves-me-he-loves-me-not.

A whirlwind of walking tours. And info sessions. Single nights passed in college town inns where upkeep was less of a priority than the free breakfast needed to fuel that day's round of walking tours and info sessions and driving to the next town.

Twelve schools in eleven days. Mile after mile of quad after quad. Student reps leading the pack, walking backward through the campus so the assembled group could hear their spiel. Heads poked into tiny dorm rooms. I, jotting notes in a special journal purchased for the occasion: spiral bound with a Buddha on the cover. (I'd hoped it would nudge me toward inner peace about the whole college thing.) Bolting pizza, cold and congealed, no matter if the dining hall was split level Brady Brunch or Harry Potter Gothic.

And driving. So much driving. We nicknamed the GPS voice "Dolores." Stephanie slept in the back seat of the rental car, a metallic blue Chevy Malibu. More than once, I glanced over my shoulder to discover our girl slumped, head slung forward, face hidden by the hood of her coat. Only her mouth peeked out from under the faux fur, just enough for me to see that she was drooling.

I dug in my tote for a Kleenex and rummaged past a miniature sewing kit, a collapsible steamer, and a tiny nightlight. I'd gone a little nuts at the travel store. The proprietor, a Lebanese gentleman, had asked my destination.

"We're taking our daughter to visit colleges."

"Is she your first or your last?" he'd asked.

"Both. She's my only."

"Oh. You will miss her."

"Yes," I said, "I will."

"Mothers and daughters," he declared.

The shopkeeper took my armful of stuff and carried it to the cash register.

"Do you have children?" I asked him.

"No. But I remember how it was for my mother when my sister went to study at the Sorbonne." He smiled as though he could see my future in a crystal ball. "Like a fish in a frying pan."

I paid for my items—all these Lilliputian versions of things I never used in the first place. I could feel the cast iron skillet heating up.

Over the intervening year, I steeled myself as I sculpted the itinerary for this second trip. This time I would be prepared for the coming attraction of loss. It would not blindside me. What I could never have foreseen is that it would be Stephanie in the front seat of the rental, next to her father, while I stayed home in a house, empty and airless.

♦♦♦

"DON'T HURT YOUR BACK!" I called to Adam. A reflex. As though his potentially herniated discs were still my purview. He raised an arm and waved dismissively, hefting Stephanie's suitcase into the trunk of the Town Car.

Barbara had promised she would arrive at the house before Adam to act as a buffer, but she pulled up just as I wrapped Stephanie in my arms for my goodbye.

"I'm nervous," Stephanie whispered into my ear.

"To go with Daddy?"

"No. Why would I be nervous for that?"

Of course—Stephanie would have no reason to be nervous about that. I was the one who would be nervous to be alone with Adam.

"I'm afraid I won't know for sure. Which school."

"I think you will." How was she supposed to know anyway? She was seventeen. I had been taught so much and so well, but still, I had yet to figure out how to really know anything about anything.

"You know what?" I stepped back from Stephanie's embrace so I could look her in the eye. "It doesn't matter if you don't know for sure. You can always transfer. It's not the biggest decision you'll ever make in your life. It's supposed to be fun."

Stephanie looked at me as though I were speaking in tongues.

"I don't want to transfer. I want to get it right the first time." There was an urgency in her voice that made me realize how very much this girl was my daughter. Get it right. And get it right the first time.

I held her close. "There's too much life to get it all right the first time, sweetheart." Stephanie held me tightly—maybe she could squeeze her old mother back into this alien creature.

"Call me tonight," I said.

"I will," Stephanie promised. Now there was her mother—the woman reminding her to call.

Stephanie got into the car where Adam already sat waiting. Then they were gone.

# CHAPTER THIRTY-ONE

BARBARA WASTED NO TIME. "I've got big news."

We plopped onto the couch in the living room. I never spent any time to speak of in the living room and had forgotten how comfortable that couch was. I had grown tired of the chenille, a cappuccino-colored shadow stripe, and had driven from showroom to showroom six or seven months ago, gathering fabric samples. Today, as I tucked one foot under me, I couldn't imagine why I ever wanted to have the thing reupholstered.

"What do you think about this couch?"

"Didn't you hear me?" Barbara asked.

"Yeah, sorry. Big news."

"I'm making a professional change." Barbara took off her velvet headband and tossed it onto the coffee table. It clanked against a cloisonné bowl filled with seashells. "I've become a travel agent."

"How come?"

"What do you mean, 'How come?'"

"Why are you becoming a travel agent?"

"I was thinking about what I really love. And the answer was..." Barbara floundered, her bubble of enthusiasm burst as though I had taken a hatpin to it.

"Traveling?"

"Of course! Traveling."

"I didn't know you liked to travel that much. When was the last time you went anywhere?"

"That's beside the point. I would have gone if I'd had someplace to go."

No energy to address her circular non-logic.

"Anyway, it wasn't really traveling I was thinking about, so much as…hotels. I absolutely love hotels. Always have. Remember when we were little, the first time we stayed in a hotel where they have those brass…I think they're brass…those things that they put the luggage on…you know, with the arches over them? Remember how I was so fascinated by those things? I pushed you all over the lobby."

"You pushed me down the stairs on one of those things."

"Whatever. I've always been fascinated by all things hotel."

"So why not work in a hotel?"

Barbara picked up the headband and twirled it in lopsided orbits around her index finger.

"I don't want to wait on people. Are you out of your mind? But if I'm a travel agent, I get to go to all kinds of fabulous hotels and get the royal treatment."

"Really?"

"Don't you think so?"

"I guess."

"Your enthusiasm is underwhelming," Barbara sniped.

"I think it's great," I commented weakly. "Go, you. When did all this happen anyway?"

"It's all happened really fast. You remember Liz Banning? A couple of classes ahead of me at Ridgepoint? I ran into her last week and she's been a travel agent for years and her assistant suddenly moved to Missouri or something and…I don't know…I started thinking about how you feel like anything can happen when you walk into a really gorgeous hotel and how it would be so nice to give people that feeling…"

Barbara seemed close to tears. Was it the thought of a well-run concierge desk and impeccable turndown service? Or was it because, at this stage in her life, Barbara Locke found herself working under Liz Banning?

Barbara had been Liz's slave for freshman initiation at Ridgepoint, an annual tradition that allowed the seniors to torment the freshmen in any way they saw fit. The more unfit the better. Like all her fellow freshmen, Barbara had sectioned her hair into forty-three braids, representing the number of girls in the senior class. As commanded, she wore her uniform backward and inside out. She carried Liz's books, delivered her a lunch of cracked crab and peeled grapes, and recited a poem about Liz at the initiation assembly. Tanning, fanning, Carol Channing. It had not been an easy ditty to compose. For most of Barbara's classmates, it ended there. But Liz had pushed the envelope of freshman slavery.

Tradition called for the seniors to treat the freshmen to dinner at the end of their day of humiliation. They took over a section of the Hamburger Hamlet in Westwood, toasting the plebes with root beer. Liz Banning, however, had one last demand. She thought it would be amusing to foist Barbara onto a lone diner—a guy— at a booth in the corner. This kid was the kind of handsome that made young girls look away, as in "Don't look into the light." Before Barbara had to invite herself to sit at his table, Liz instructed her to go into the ladies room, take off her bra and put it on over her uniform (still backward and inside out). That was Liz Banning's idea of funny.

A small patch of chenille on the couch began to pill. I picked at it. I remembered how Barbara had sobbed that night, swearing she would never go back to school again.

"You're going to be really good at this travel agent business," I said to my sister. "You won't be her assistant for long."

Barbara knew I remembered. The braids, the grapes, the exquisite boy, the bra.

"She's gotten really thick around the middle," Barbara said, not without glee.

"I love it," I said. I was staring at the brown velvet headband swinging around Barbara's finger like a hula hoop. I couldn't stand it anymore and grabbed it away.

"What's wrong with you?" Barbara asked.

"I've never stayed in the house alone. I hate it."

"It's been fifteen minutes."

"I hate it. I just hate it." I slid the headband onto my head. It dug instantly into my temples. I snatched it off. "How can you wear this thing? It's like a vise."

# CHAPTER THIRTY-TWO

I ARRIVED AT ST. Christina's twenty minutes early on the off chance that I needed to fill out paperwork for next year's move to third grade. The administration secretary pretended to have processed my request. Maybe she had. Either way, she told me, "Ms. Barcraft really wants you back in second." I doubted Ms. Barcraft cared one way or the other as long as she had an extra adult in the room.

I almost said, "What about Ernesto?" but I was afraid an outburst like that would get me booted from the program altogether. The next thing I knew, they'd be pulling my file and cross-checking my fingerprints against a federal database of pedophiles. So I nodded at the secretary and said, "Second grade is fine."

I found the second graders on the playground. Most of the boys were chasing one another and shouting. A few were playing handball against a wall. Four or five girls huddled in a corner near the tetherball, whispering and casting glances at the boys. One of the girls looked like she was about to cry. *And so it begins*, I thought.

There was Ernesto. He was seated at a low picnic table munching a bag of Cheetos. He spotted me and waved. His Day-Glo orange fingertips made him look like he'd been helping a bee deliver pollen.

"Want one?" he asked, raising the bag to me as I sat down across from him.

Out of the corner of my eye, I noticed a beefy man in a dark suit headed in our direction. When his shadow darkened Ernesto's face, I looked up, squinting. He was backlit against the mid-morning sun.

Oh no, I thought, not another foster home for Ernesto. Or worse. Please don't let the state take my Ernesto. I wondered if I should adopt him. Would I have the energy to mother a teenaged boy in another ten years? Could I raise a boy without a husband to help? Of course, Adam would be home by then…wouldn't he?

"Are you Maura Locke Fielder?" the man in the suit asked.

"What?"

"Maura Locke Fielder?" he repeated.

"Yes. What can I do for you?" I asked.

"I have something for you," he said. An envelope appeared in his hand. I half expected him to say, "Voila!"

Instead, he said, "You've been served."

*Served? Like everybody's got to serve somebody?*

Ernesto washed down the last of the Cheetos with strawberry milk.

"I don't understand," I said to the man. But all he did was nod toward the envelope now in my hand. Then he turned and walked away like a tertiary character in a Coen Brothers movie.

"How did you get on school grounds?" I called after him.

The man turned to face me over his shoulder. "I walked."

Great, I thought. So much for security at St. Christina's. You couldn't even rely on a saint to keep crazies in check these days.

I slid my finger under the stickum of the envelope. Inside was a packet of papers. On top, a letter with a lawyer's letterhead. My eyes darted around the paper, landing on the phrase: "Automatic restraining orders." The next sentence was underlined: "You are now subject to these Orders." What was going on? Who on earth wanted me restrained? And why would I of all people need restraining? Self-restraint was my specialty. At the top of the letter in all caps were the words: "VIA HAND DELIVERY." I looked at the man in the dark suit, the hand deliverer. He was already out the gate and sliding behind the wheel of his Ford Explorer.

"Mrs. Maura?" said Ernesto. But I didn't answer. I lifted the cover letter to look at what came next. Maybe that piece of paper would make some sense. It was an official-looking document: gobbledygook stamped by the Los Angeles Superior Court. A box at the top said in bold: YOU ARE BEING SUED. LO ESTA DEMANDANDO.

I searched my mind for what I might have done. Could you be sued for an unpaid parking ticket? Had I ever in my life not paid a parking ticket? Had I ever not paid a parking ticket in Mexico?

And then I saw it. "Re: Marriage of Fielder." On a line of its own. In bold. And underlined. My marriage wasn't anyone's business. How dare someone write to me re: my marriage. It belonged to me. To Adam and me. I managed to focus long enough to read the first line of the actual letter: "This office represents your husband, Adam David Fielder in a Dissolution of Marriage action…"

I felt the lure of the Tilt-A-Whirl. I grabbed hold of the edge of the table. Steady…steady…

"Mrs. Maura," said Ernesto, "this is our last Monday. My teacher told me."

His little voice sounded far off and plaintive, but I couldn't answer him. As though in a dream, I did not know how to get to him.

I resumed scanning the sheaf of papers. Below the summons was a multi-page petition with check boxes. The box next to "Dissolution of Marriage" had been x'ed.

The cyclone of weirdness that had started to swirl at 2:00 a.m. that night in Adam's study irised into that box. There was another series of check boxes. Next to: "Dissolution of marriage based on:" the option, "irreconcilable differences" had been x'ed. He got that wrong, I thought. He should have checked "Other: incurable insanity." Mine.

I let the papers fall on the table next to the empty bag of Cheetos. Ernesto was trying to tug me back. "Mrs. Maura…?" He pointed his finger at a word. "Dis…" He started again. "Dis…so…"

I stared at the paper. "Dissolution," I read. Normally I would have helped him sound out the whole word, patiently, one syllable at a time, but there was no normally anymore.

"What does that mean?" he asked.

"It means…" I said. "It means…when something solid turns into liquid. Like melting. Like turning into nothing."

Ernesto nodded. He understood. "This is our last Monday," he said again.

"I know," I said. "This is our last Monday."

"What will I do without you?" asked Ernesto.

His mouth was coated with cheesy orange powder, his eyes watery. I wanted to scoop him onto my lap and rock him. I wanted to assure him that Santa would find his way to his house next year and the year after that. I wanted to explain to him that I had tried to go with him to third grade. Mostly, I wanted to tell him that I had no clue what I was going to do without him.

"You will do fine without me," I said. "You'll see."

◆◆◆

I CRUISED THE FROZEN food aisle, clutching my shopping list as though it held some meaning, as though it were more than a string of words. Determined to accomplish the errands of the day, I'd headed from St. Christina's straight to Gelson's. But the divorce papers stuffed in my purse changed everything. This marital moment was not going to be a blip—a crazy episode when the Fielders temporarily lost their footing, but were living happily ever after by the final commercial break. This was now something official, something that had been stamped and filed and case numbered.

I pushed my cart past the Hungry Mans, past the Amy's organics, past the DiGiorno. Nothing appealed. More than that—I could not remember what you were supposed to do with food. I continued down the aisle, walloped by an Arctic blast as another shopper opened a freezer door. She took her time deciding between Chocolate Therapy and Chubby Hubby. Even so, I was pushing through gelatin, the supermarket air thick and viscous. Suffocating. There were divorce papers in my purse. I'd been served. I'd been served what I had dished out.

I stared at the list in my hand. Cereal. Yogurt. Brazil Nuts. (Barbara had read that vertigo could be triggered by a magnesium deficiency. Google: High Magnesium Foods. Result: Brazil nuts.) I rested the side of my forehead against the freezer door. The jolly Green Giant smiled at me. Maybe I could appropriate some of his hands-on-hips confidence. Instead, I abandoned my cart and made my way back through the Jell-O atmosphere, outside, and into my car.

I reached into my purse to feel for the papers, to make sure they were real. They were. Did Adam think so little of our marriage that he could reduce it to this stack of documents containing words like "petitioner" and "pursuant?"

Before I knew it, I was driving along the palisade to Adam's office. I was building up a good head of steam. How dare he order the papers served at my place of employment…well, non-employment…my place of volunteerism? How dare he humiliate me in front of all the other teachers, in front of Ernesto? And finally, how dare he watch himself having sex with another woman, write to her, and blame me for everything?

My left-turn signal was already blinking when I remembered. I would not find him at the office. He was at a small liberal arts college somewhere in Ohio. He had engineered this *coup de grace* precisely so that I could not show up at his office and boil over, scorching its blonde wood furnishings with rage. I would not even be able to confront him at his parents' house where he was now living.

I could hear him instructing his lawyer: "Do it on Monday. Do it when I'm listening to a college kid field questions about the Greek system. Do it when I've got Stephanie with me. Do it in front of that little boy she loves." Of course. I could not even phone him. There was no way we could have this conversation within eavesdrop range of, as the papers described her, "the minor child."

Instead of turning into the driveway for FCM, I headed straight on Ocean Avenue, then turned east on Santa Monica Boulevard, the ocean glinting in my rear view mirror.

◆◆◆

"I WANT TO GO away," I said to Barbara. I showed up at her office without calling.

"What are you talking about?

"I want to go someplace," I repeated. "I've got to get out of here."

"By yourself?"

"By myself."

"You can't do that."

"Of course I can."

"How can you go away all by yourself?"

"Very easily."

"You've never gone anywhere all by yourself."

"And that's just plain crazy," I countered. "I'm a grown woman."

"That's debatable," Barbara cracked wise, a big sister obligation.

"You're a travel agent. Book me a trip."

"You've lost your mind."

"Where should I go?" Barbara played along. "Laguna?"

I shook my head.

"Santa Barbara?"

"No place beachy. Couples walking along the sand..."

"Napa?"

I shot her a look. "You've got to be kidding. Wine country? How much more reeking of romance can you get?"

"San Francisco," Barbara ventured.

I squinted as though I were gazing through mist. "London," I declared.

"London!"

"London."

"That's across the ocean."

"I know where London is."

"You can't go to London by yourself."

"Of course I can."

"All by yourself?"

"Stop saying that!" I shouted. "We've established I'm all by myself. You have no idea how all by myself I am! Adam served me with divorce papers." I regretted it instantly, both because saying the words made the fact of it real and because I was not up to Barbara's reaction.

But Barbara had no reaction. Not for a long minute. Then she swiveled in her chair to face me square in the eye. "You're going to London. And while you're gone, I'll find you a lawyer."

"I don't need a lawyer," I bristled. "Do I need a lawyer?"

"I think you might."

I nodded. "Okay. You find me a lawyer. And you know what else you can do for me?"

"Anything."

"You can tell Mother and Daddy."

Barbara inhaled sharply, her hands flying to the hollow at the base of her neck, mimicking our mother's go-to response. "I'll pass on that one," she said. "Maybe we'll never have to," she hoped.

"Do you think?" I hoped.

"I do. I think that's very possible." Barbara was not so convincing, but I pretended I was convinced.

"I wanted to go to London on our honeymoon, you know," I said.

"So why didn't you?"

"'Cause Adam wanted to go to Paris," I responded. The realization clubbed me. Paris. Pain au chocolat. The Louvre. Summer-Abroad French Girl.

"I never knew that," said Barbara.

"Yeah, well…There's a lot you don't know." The connection blindsided me. I remembered our second afternoon there. I was suddenly stricken with jet lag and Adam left me napping in the hotel to take a long walk and visit his old haunts. Suddenly, all these years later, I wondered where that walk had led him, to whom it had led him. I was about to blurt out: "Adam slept with this young, beautiful, evil French girl on our honeymoon!" But I stopped myself. I had no proof of the young lovers' reunion, stolen and intoxicating, overheated by the poignancy that he was newly wedded to someone else—an ordinary American girl.

Barbara studied my face. "You are going to have the most fabulous time," she said. Then she spun back to face her computer and click-click-clicked. "I am going to get you the most amazing deal."

♦♦♦

By the time I got home, five emails were waiting for me, all from Barbara. Airline reservation and hotel reservation. A link to a list of the best restaurants in London, another to the hottest West End shows. I clicked my way through. Good for her. Barbara might be good at this travel agent thing after all.

I opened the fifth email and clicked on the link. It took a second for my brain to register. Match.com. Barbara must have made a mistake. I checked her message: *Might as well see what's out there.*

What was wrong with my sister? After an entire lifetime, did she not know me at all? I was grateful not to have ever had to play that game. I didn't want to learn the rules now. No winks. No matches. Not me.

But then it occurred to me—maybe I should give it a shot. I'd be buying a cosmic insurance policy. I could answer the questions. I knew my height, my hair color, my eye color. I knew how to shop. Shoes...men...how different could it be? You try them on, you send them back. Absolutely, I could do this. More to the point, if I went through with it—filled out the questionnaire, created a profile—I was bound not to need it. Isn't that the way the universe works?

But if the universe had been holding up its end of the bargain, there would be no divorce papers in my purse. Lip gloss, a pen, stray pennies, but no divorce papers. I was going to be a single person. I was a single-person-in-waiting. *Click here to meet singles.* I was one of them, dog-paddling through a sea of candidates with only an algorithm as a lifeline.

I needed a lifeline. Maybe someone out there—someone who owned an island in the South Pacific—would want to take me away from all this. Would I go? I rested my fingers on the keyboard and let them loose on automatic pilot. Zip code—easy. I am a...woman, I clicked...looking for.... I clicked again...a man.

Of course, it was unlikely that this man would be an island owner. He was more likely to be...I didn't even know what. Someone I knew? If we showed up at Starbucks and recognized each other, could I laugh nonchalantly at the who'd-a-thunk-it coincidence? What if he turned out to be Randy Cochran from cotillion, all grown up, bald and paunchy? What if he's that weird guy who was always throwing a Frisbee in the quad at USC? Or one of the divorced dads from Stephanie's school? How about those work-at-home dads who were always hanging around, staple gunning banners on back-to-school night?

What if he's one of Gwen's exes—the architect, for instance. There I am, supposedly enjoying Mahler's Ninth at Disney Hall, obsessing over what I secretly know about this guy and his hour spent with Gwen reassuring him that this happens to everyone at one time or another.

The nightmare scenarios kept on coming. What could be worse than finding myself matched with someone I already knew? Only one thing: finding myself matched with someone I didn't know.

A stranger who says "between you and I?" and I can't stop myself from correcting him? Or barks at the busboy and demands the waiter remove his sub-par steak from the check? What if he tells me to meet him at end of the Santa Monica Pier and I don't know if he means the land end or the sea end?

What if he has some weird fetish—feet or nostrils or armpits? Or he can't stop talking about how his wife screwed him over? What if he still has a wife who thinks she's happily married?

My finger hovered over "Submit."

And then it hit me, what if no one picks me?

No one at all.

# CHAPTER THIRTY-THREE

IT WAS MORE OF a pod than a seat. I settled in, exchanging half-smiles with the other passengers. At the last minute—either through kismet or an adolescent urge to outmaneuver Liz Banning—Barbara had gotten me a deal on a first class ticket. As it turned out, Barbara really did have this travel agent thing nailed. She had a breezy phone manner cultivated in her breezy Mel's Diner years. I wondered what the airline agents, concierges, and tour guides would think if they could see the woman on the other end of the phone. Barbara was so not the hip Angeleno they must have pictured—that delightful Barbara Locke who would get them in to all the trendy restaurants where they might see a Ryan or a Jennifer or maybe, with some luck, a Rynifer sneaking out through the kitchen door. Maybe, by then, she really could swing a reservation or two. She was already working points-miles magic.

So I found myself in a seat that was more than a seat. It was a lifestyle. A cocoon containing a private TV and a multi-purpose desk. I swiveled a full three-sixty, executing one full rotation before the vertigo panic kicked in. I would stick to minimal swivels, a few degrees one direction or another, as necessitated by the various activities—eating, movie-watching, window gazing—that would occupy the next ten-and-a-half hours.

I accepted the flute of champagne offered by the flight attendant before takeoff. It seemed the thing to do. I worried that vertigo would lie at the bottom of the glass, but took a sip in the spirit of a first class traveler. The bubbles sparkled with promise. Besides, a few sips might help me forget the papers stowed in the drawer of my bedside table.

I had read and reread them a hundred times since the man in the dark suit had thrust them into my hand. Once in the last twenty-four hours, I had simply held them without looking at the words, distinguishing between the slight pebbling of the attorney's high-quality stationery and the thinner, slicker, government issue summons. I had considered packing them in my suitcase, but opted against it. Sitting here, in seat 2B, I could pretend the papers, both textured and smooth, had never happened.

There was a young couple in the center section. Blatant honeymooners. In order to interlace their fingers, they had to reach over the mini-wall that separated them. This position could not have been comfortable, but they seemed happy to pay the small price to remain connected.

A couple in their seventies occupied the two seats behind the newlyweds. As soon as the plane hit cruising altitude, the wife pulled out two sleep masks, handed one to her husband and snapped the other around her own head.

I scanned the other passengers: assorted singles—like myself, I thought, incredulous. Business travelers, both male and female. A teenaged boy who spoke with an English accent. An elderly man wearing a navy blazer with a crest on the breast pocket. He was reading a book about World War II.

At first, I had not taken particular notice of the man sitting in the pod next to mine, but when I glanced at him a second time, I thought I recognized him. Had I gone to college with this man? Had he been a parent at Stephanie's preschool? Or, for that matter, was he famous? A sidekick on a cop drama or the investigative journalist on that cable show about vampires? I studied his face out of the corner of my eye. I did not know him after all, I decided. Nor was he an actor. He was just a type. Tall—maybe six-two, a bit lined, and pleasant. Approachable. He was the kind of man you would ask for directions, the kind of man who might even walk you part way. He caught me looking at him and smiled.

I shifted in my seat, playing with all the buttons like a teenager in a limo. Finally, I settled on head back, feet elevated at a forty-five degree angle. I dozed off until the flight attendant tapped me gently, asking for my dinner order. I went for the pasta primavera. It turned out to be a dried-out knot of fettuccini doused in sauce meant to be creamy, but was instead weirdly granular. I stabbed the specks of zucchini and carrot out of the glop, but left the rest. When the flight attendant appeared pushing a trolley with sundae fixings, I declined.

"Have a few bites," she prodded.

"Well...okay." I studied the toppings. "Butterscotch, please."

I wolfed down the whole thing by the time she had served the rest of the passengers.

"Would you like another one?"

"I would actually," I said. "It was really good."

I ate most of the second sundae as well, leaving what I considered a respectable few bites at the bottom of the schooner.

The man in the next pod was on his way to the bathroom up front. "I went for the hot fudge," he said to me.

"Butterscotch," I countered, raising my spoon for show-and-tell. A sticky golden thread trailed off.

I pushed the buttons on the side of my seat, but could not find the comfortable position. I settled on full reclining and unfolded the blanket over me. The cabin was dark now—officially bedtime within the capsule.

Several hours later, the flight attendant leaned over and whispered, "Rise and shine." I had told her earlier that yes, I wished to be awakened for breakfast. I had not slept at all, but apparently had feigned sleep convincingly enough.

"I'm awake," I said. "Completely awake."

The man next door was returning to his seat, shaving kit in hand. "Good morning," he said.

"Good morning."

"Did you sleep?" he asked.

"Not really. No."

"That makes for a long night."

"Oh well. It's morning now." I raised my window shade as if to prove my point. Sunlight blasted in.

"That's the attitude," he said. It took me a beat to realize he meant that my attitude was good—something I did not expect to be accused of.

Breakfast was not as anemic as dinner. I ate the *omelette fines herbes* and spread my croissant with coarse-cut marmalade from a tiny jar. I was sipping the last of my coffee when the man next door leaned over the little dividing wall. "I'm Gavin."

"Maura Fielder," I answered.

"Gavin Duke," he submitted, extending his hand.

"That's a great name," I commented. "It's like a name the studio would give you if you wanted to be an actor in 1959."

I thought better of adding, "Or a name a hack screenwriter would make up for the guy who meets the girl on a plane."

He was better looking than I had realized, handsome really, despite the brutal cabin lighting. His saddle-colored suede jacket picked up the tawny in his hair, but he managed to keep the overall effect from appearing studied. He was younger than I had first thought, probably about my age. He was on his way to visit his son, he said, who was working toward his PhD in philosophy at Oxford.

"Wow." I meant it.

"It sounds impressive, but sooner or later he's going to have to get a job. He keeps choosing later."

"Does he want to be a professor?"

"I don't think so. He'll probably end up at McDonald's asking if you want fries with that, but he'll be able to make a mighty good case for exactly why it's a Happy Meal."

I explained that my own daughter was in the throes of deciding which colleges to apply to, touring some last minute candidates as we spoke. "With her dad."

"That's nice."

My sitting here in seat 2B while my husband and daughter trotted from campus to campus was anything but nice. "We're...."

"Divorced?" he prodded.

I shook my head.

"Separated?"

I shrugged. "I don't know what we are."

The flight attendant whisked away my breakfast tray.

"I'm a widower," Gavin remarked.

"I'm so sorry."

"It's been seven years, and it still sounds weird when I say it..."

"I understand."

He smiled at me in a way that suggested I could not possibly understand. Then he raised a finger to his right ear, wiggling as he pressed, to release the pressure as the plane began to descend.

Through the window, The London Eye looked like a Tinkertoy revolving below. We fell silent for the rest of the descent, but when wheels touched down, Gavin turned to me again. "Where are you staying?"

I hesitated.

"I'm at the Dorchester," he volunteered.

Part of my brain screamed, Stranger Danger! Then I figured: why not? "The Athenaeum," I said.

"I know it," he said. "It's not far from my hotel. I've got a car waiting if you need a ride."

"No, that's okay." I was almost sorry he didn't persist. "That was a really stupid thing to say," I said. "What I said before. Of course I don't understand what it's like to lose your wife. How could I possibly? I try not to be one of those people who says stupid things just because you don't know what else to say. I don't know how it must feel, but I'm sorry. Really. I'm so sorry."

Gavin stared at me for a long moment. Then he said, "Please may I give you a ride into the city?"

◆◆◆

THE DOORMAN OPENED THE back door of the high-gloss Mercedes and extended a gloved hand.

"Thank you so much," I said to Gavin as I stepped out. "I hope you have a good time with your son."

"I never asked what brings you to London," he said as he too stepped out of the car.

"It's sort of a belated honeymoon," I submitted.

"But I thought you were..."

"I am."

"Well...Good for you," Gavin said with a brusque nod of the head that was suddenly very British, very stiff upper lip.

"Thanks again," I waved.

"You're welcome," he said as he slipped into the back seat. The car pulled away from the curb and was swallowed up into Piccadilly gridlock.

It turned out that Barbara had booked one of the apartments that occupied a row of Edwardian townhouses connected to the hotel proper. The bellhop led me around the corner to the brick buildings with the transomed doors and arched windows. Here in this flat, I could pretend I was "That Girl" adventuring out on my own.

I unpacked at once—hanging the hangings, placing the foldeds in the walnut chest of drawers, depositing toiletries along the narrow rim of the pedestal sink. The bedding looked to be from a collection designed to conjure an English country garden: all cornflower blue and maize—a cheery mix of plaids and precise florals, the kind of thing Barbara would wear to a summer wedding.

I phoned Stephanie to let her know I had arrived safely, but got sent to voice mail. "Hey, this is Stephanie. You know what to do."

"It's Mom. I'm here." And then I could not think of what else to say. Here I was indeed—drifting in limbo between married and unmarried, between full-time parenthood and parenthood-on-demand, between youth and not-so-youth. Alone on a king-size bed draped in the colors of summer.

I explored the living room. It was more space than I needed. There was a sitting area complete with an old-fashioned fax machine for the business traveler. I wished I were one of those, my days peppered with meetings. The kitchenette was both efficient and welcoming—containing everything one could need, notably a kettle and an assortment of teas. I would stock the kitchen with breakfast fare so that I would not have to be a single diner in the hotel restaurant in the morning. I would watch the BBC while I sipped Earl Grey and ate a crumpet at my very own dining table. I could pretend it was the Swinging Sixties and I had crossed the pond in search of all things mod: mop-topped pop stars sporting lace cravats pouring out of trendy boutiques on King's Road; psychedelically swirled Rolls Royces sharing the road with double-decker buses; and music everywhere.

As it happened, today when I stepped outside, taking care to lock the door of my flat and making my way down four flights of corkscrew stairs, there was no music, only the press of traffic and the lung-squeezing odor of diesel fuel.

I wandered the tangle of streets behind Piccadilly until I came upon Shepherd Market—a cluster of shops and bistros, practically the Disneyland version of London. I roamed the enclave past a florist and a tobacconist and a shop specializing in the art of English leathercraft. I passed the more mundane dry cleaners, hairdresser, and Mail Boxes Etc. Even a café advertising Mexican-Polish cuisine. Kielbasa nachos?

I stopped into a small chemist's. Everything from lipstick to tooth powder seemed quaint. I wanted to buy something I could not find at home. I had brought plenty of shampoo and body lotion, and the hotel supplied its own array of Caswell and Massey minis, so I made do with a tube of lavender-scented hand cream.

The morning of my flight, I had rushed to a foreign exchange merchant in Brentwood and stuffed some oversized bills into my wallet. Now, I paid for my purchase with money bearing a picture of the queen—the pursed lips, the pin-curled hair, the crown, for heaven's sake, which her expression seems to insist trumps her plainness. When I pulled out that five pound note and used it so casually, as if it were the legal tender I had grown up with, my old life turned to smoke. Suddenly, there was no stash of documents in the drawer of my bedside table.

By the time I'd reached the next corner, I felt like I was entirely someone else. The sensation of transformation took my breath away. I would not have guessed it was still possible. On that first day of summer vacation all those years ago, Gwen and I stepped out of that Westwood head shop different girls from who we had been when we had stepped in. "Girl school girls," that delicious guy had said, cracking open the chrysalis that encased us; we believed we could elbow our way out in one deft motion.

I felt like that now in Shepherd Market.

Up ahead, I spotted a scrawny figure in an exquisitely tailored violet pin-striped suit. I watched him from the back. Something about this guy was familiar, though strangely odd, oddly strange. I lived in LA I knew what it was like to see a movie star across a restaurant. There was always that moment: Oh, that's so him, but a little bit not the him I might have expected. I watched this man from the back. Something about the walk—the way he sprang off the balls of his feet. Something about the perfect layers of his perfect haircut bouncing as he moved. Something about the force field around him. He turned ever so slightly. Just enough for me to catch a glimpse of his face. The crags of a generation were etched deep into his cheek. And then he turned completely. I reached to grab a hand—Adam's— but no one was there. I would have to have this moment alone. This moment when I stopped in my tracks to stare at Mick Jagger.

Inevitably, he appeared smaller. A decent gust of wind would have its way with him. The Amazon woman on his arm dwarfed him. Not to mention the hulking presence behind. Bodyguard, no doubt. Mick seemed almost spritely. Had it not been for those iconic lips, I might have believed he was some sort of elfin creature rather than Jumpin' Jack Flash. The lips and the electricity.

I dug for my phone in my oversized purse. I called Adam. Then cancelled. Then Stephanie. And cancelled. I would tell someone sometime about this sighting, but it would have to wait. It didn't really matter whether it was now or later. It would always be second-hand. Or would I forget this moment altogether without someone there to share it? Would it evaporate and become as apocryphal as happily-ever-after?

I moved on through the village, its charm suddenly anachronistic in the wake of the Jagger sighting. There were two or three tables waiting for patrons outside a little restaurant called The Only Running Footman. I sat down and stared at my phone. I had four new emails. The only one I cared about was from Stephanie. The subject line read: "Drum roll, please!"

It took a while for the message to open. I stared at the round gear thingie, spinning, spinning, spinning, and wondered what Stephanie's drum roll could be announcing. Had she fallen in love with a school? Had she decided to forestall the whole thing and take a gap year? What would she do with a gap year—backpack through Europe with Mallory? At eighteen years old? I don't think so. Or, had she talked her father into returning home to his family? Had she convinced him she needed him in the house, with her, every single day, not just on the phone? Had she mentioned that I was moving about the house like a phantom, distracted and vacant? "Drum roll, please"—whatever it meant—was being provided by my syncopated heart.

Finally, the message opened.

*"Alert the media! I wrote my essay. Mamasita, could you please proofread this thing? I miss you. P.S. Surprise! I went with #5."*

I clicked on the attachment and waited for it to download, staring as the megabytes ticked off their progress.

We had discussed the various essay prompts ad nauseum, swinging between #2 with its focus on identity, and #4, the ever-popular lesson learned from failure. We'd dismissed #5 pretty quickly and yet, there it was, at the top of the page: "Discuss an accomplishment or event, formal or informal, that marked your transition from childhood to adulthood within your culture, community, or family."

How could Stephanie have chosen this topic? There had been no such transition; she was still a child. My child. My baby. And yet, this is what she wrote:

*Let's get this straight from the start. I have no intention of ever achieving the status of a full-blown grown-up. What's the fun in that? Everyone says, "Never stop growing; never stop learning; never strop expanding your comfort zone." I, however, would add, "Never stop playing." Inspiration lies in play, in my opinion.*

*All that said, something happened to me when my grandfather died. It was a subtle change, but it was a still a change—a shift somewhere so deep as to be almost imperceptible. It was a passage, neither cultural nor communal, but definitely familial, and for me, family trumps (can a person still use that word???) culture and community. What this change really was was (fix that, Mommy—the double "was" problem—okay?) an ascension, though not entirely welcome. If life were a ladder, I moved up a rung. With my grandfather gone, my father became the patriarch of the family, but he also became the next in line for you-know-what. That realization made me leapfrog (too cutesy?) over adolescence into adulthood. It was like I landed on a new square without passing GO because there were suddenly fewer players. I resented being launched into adulthood. I wasn't finished in the sandbox.*

*My grandfather was not an easy man. To be blunt, a lot of people hated him. He built a business on equal parts intimidation and "smarts," as he would say. But he never had to prove anything with me, so he just loved me. "Love that girl," he would say when he looked at me, and I knew he meant it because he would smile a goofy smile as though he just couldn't help himself. I never said, "Love that grandpa," back, but I should have. When my grandfather died, I realized that there aren't ("are not" or "aren't"???) a limitless number of chances to say that to people. Clichés abound about grabbing the here and now. We find them in poetry, film, and song. Carpe diem has become so ubiquitous an aphorism (maxim? adage? principle?) as to join the white noise of generally accepted truths. (Mom, does that make sense? But you know what I'm trying to say.) Even so, it embodies a grown-up concept and it hit me like a runaway freight train (too cliché??). Childhood depends on tomorrows. Adulthood knows they are not guaranteed.*

*I will always grow and learn and push the boundaries of my comfort zone. At least I hope I will. I will build castles in the sandbox even when I'm supposedly too old. But I will also tell people I'm glad they are in my life. I will thank them for making me think. I will laugh with them. I will tell them I love them. That's the best part of "owning" being a grown-up. (better word or way to put that please??) No matter how ruthless Sam Fielder may have been in the business world, as a grandpa, he knew enough to tell me he loved me all the time. And he always had time to play with me.*

*Love that grandpa.*

I read the essay again, more slowly. I would answer her questions. I could fix the double "was" problem. I'd crack open my mental thesaurus for a better word where she asked for it. Those were easy fixes. The harder part would be earning her forgiveness. Could she forgive me for shattering her final year at home, for yanking her out of that sandbox? Sure, Sam had died. But who was I kidding? I had been the one who'd taken a battering ram to her innocence.

# CHAPTER THIRTY-FOUR

I READ THE ESSAY a few more times, wowed by the person glowing there. Then I made my way out of Shepherd Market and headed for the Burlington Arcade. I passed a full hour there, running my hand over cashmere sweaters and eyeing fine silver "objects of vertu." I paused in every shop, each a fine antique unto itself. In Hancocks, jeweler to the queen (aren't they all?), I became transfixed by a necklace and matching earrings. The proprietor, an elegant man with ruddy cheeks, fingered the chain of his pocket watch as I peered through the glass case.

"Yes," he said, "Burmese rubies with diamonds en suite."

"Beautiful," I muttered. "I love the earrings."

"The ear clips are unusually lovely," he corrected me—remarkably, without a hint of condescension. "And you'll notice the cushion cut of the rubies. Extraordinary."

I had no clue what a cushion cut was, but I wanted to buy the suite of gems right there and then. Truthfully, I wanted to be transformed by it, to inhabit it as though it were not a suite of gems, but a suite of rooms in a Noel Coward play. I settled for a ring: a trio of opals, Stephanie's birthstone, with garnet specks nestled between in a Victorian setting. It was a splurge, but I would give it to Stephanie for her eighteenth birthday in October—an occasion that merited a splurge.

I dangled the little bag from my wrist as I continued down the Arcade. I had entered from the Piccadilly side and now exited at the far end on to Bond Street where I continued wandering past high-end boutiques. Might as well have been Rodeo Drive. Louis Vuitton, Dolce & Gabbana, Hermes. They were all there. But, thankfully, also Boodles and Smythson with a "y"—ultra-British enough to remind me I was far from home.

Before I knew it, I found myself on Savile Row. Window after window of bespoke men's haberdashery. I picked up speed, striding past the flannels and tweeds.

Gradually, galleries appeared among the storefronts. I paused to look at a series of black and white photographs printed with some sort of cross-hatching overlaid on the images. Body parts shot so extremely close up as to be rendered landscapes or, more aptly, moonscapes. I squinted at them, trying to identify the scenery.

Art was serious business on Savile Row. Galleries had names like hedge fund companies. Waterhouse & Dodd; James Hyman; Erskine, Hall & Coe. Then a funkier one called Shout!

In the window, a video was playing on a retro TV, more of a piece of furniture really—a giant eyeball of a thing balancing atop a tapered faux wood base. I paused to admire the set. A Predicta. So aptly named, providing a wide-open window into the future, as opposed to the palm-held voyeuristic peek into other people's lives used to entice viewers these days. I admired the Atomic Age contours of the set and was about to continue on down the Row when, suddenly, the TV jerked me back. On screen: the face of a middle-aged woman. Heart-shaped, high cheekboned, eyes wide-set. I stared at the face, trying to place it as I had the macro body parts in the gallery a few doors down.

An off-screen interviewer asked: "What do you look for in an emerging artist?"

The woman answered: "That is difficult to say…" The accent was French. "Originality, bien sûr…more than technique. I should not mean that. As much as technique is what I should say." Her less-than-perfect English was so fetching. As was the way she made eye contact with the camera. I had seen that gaze into a camera lens before.

At two o'clock am on a Tuesday.

I studied the face. It was her. And she was still beautiful. Despite all the years. She had that French woman thing going for her. People were writing best sellers about it—what it is and how to get it. She had it. Despite the fact that she had aged. Despite the smoker's lines around her lips and the pouches under her eyes. Despite the gray in her hair. French Girl was still something.

I pulled open the heavy glass door to the gallery. A stick-thin hipster in skinny black jeans rushed over to me. "We're hanging," he said.

"I beg your pardon."

"For tonight. We're still hanging." His arms swept about, indicating the blank walls.

"Oh, I'm sorry."

He waited for me to leave, but I did not.

"I know her," I said, nodding toward the set.

"Aimee?" The kid went wide-eyed, suddenly eager and charming. "She's brilliant, isn't she? Truly brilliant. We're all mad for her."

He thrust a postcard in my hand. "Come back tonight. There'll be nibbles. And champagne."

"Nibbles," I repeated—then, realizing I should act like a person, I nodded toward a painting already hung on the far wall and added, "I love that one." The piece was mammoth, sans frame, depicting a noose and a Barcalounger. I hated it to the point of revulsion.

I stared at the card in my hand.

NEW WORKS by Simon Chitlaw-Leeds
ARTIST'S RECEPTION
Wednesday, 24 May
Half Eight

In smaller print across the bottom: *Courtesy of Galerie Laroche, 32 rue Louise Weiss, Paris, France*. The hipster nudged me toward the door. "Tonight then?"

"Tonight," I said.

As I emerged back onto the street, the video started up again. That voice, sultry and cool—from now on it would join the perfect face in hijacking my brain. "Finding a new artist..." said that voice steeped in the Seine, "is not unlike the falling in love." *Oh, please.*

"Bien sûr," she added, just to remind me that she was French.

"Bien sûr," I said aloud to no one. Suddenly, my mission was clear: to find something magnificent to wear when, later that evening, I would find myself face to face with that face.

I stepped off the curb and hailed a taxi.

"Where to?" asked the driver as I climbed in.

"I need to buy a dress."

"Well, then…Harvey Nick's or Harrods?"

"Harrods, I suppose," I said.

Within a few blocks, the taxi was ensnarled in traffic. The driver nodded toward an elegant building with black iron railings. "Brown's up ahead there," he volunteered.

"I beg your pardon?"

"Best tea in London," he explained. "Tourists hear about the Savoy and the Ritz, mind you, but they're past their prime if you ask me. And a might stuffy. 'No trackers, no trainers,' and all that."

"No trackers, no trainers?"

"Yeah, that's right. But Brown's, that's where all the Mayfair ladies take their tea. You might want a cuppa before venturing into Harrod's."

"Well, then…" I said, "Brown's it is." I paid the driver, got out of the cab and smiled at the hotel doorman as he swung open a burnished mahogany door with leaded glass windows like faceted diamonds.

◆◆◆

I WAS LUXURIATING IN a mouthful of clotted cream when he walked in. I had been seated ten minutes earlier, engaging my server in conversation as people traveling alone are inclined to do.

"I love the ceiling," I said, gazing up at the stamped white tin.

"It's lovely, isn't it?" chimed the young woman. Her hair was pulled back into a low chignon to go with her conservative black suit, but she was warmer than her appearance suggested, and brimming with information.

"We were named the top London tea, you know" she declared with such pride she might as well have owned the joint. "By the Tea Guild."

"How wonderful," I said. "The Tea Guild!" Like the Lollipop Guild in *The Wizard of Oz*.

When the tea arrived—tiers of crustless sandwiches, glossy scones, pastries like tiny presents—the young woman poured Brown's house blend through an etched silver strainer into my cup. The fine porcelain was decorated with an ivy pattern, a lone leaf at the bottom of the cup. As the server poured, I broke off a piece of currant scone and slathered it with Devon cream.

Gavin Duke spotted me, my mouth full, and raised a hand in greeting, cutting around the baby grand. Then, there he was, standing beside my table.

"I guess everyone who is anyone has tea at Brown's," he said.

I swallowed hard, the scone suddenly dust in my throat. "Apparently."

"Are you waiting for someone?" he asked.

I shook my head.

"May I join you?"

"Of course."

He thought better of it even as he sat. "Did you want to be alone?"

"No, not at all," I said. I never would have eaten in a restaurant alone at home, but here, rules didn't seem to apply.

"It's so funny I should run into you," he said, swallowing an egg sandwich in two bites as the server materialized with another cup. "I was thinking about calling. I really wanted to call you, but...." He ate a raspberry tart the size of a quarter or, more fittingly, a shilling. He segued back and forth between savories and sweets. So disconcerting. Anyone could see that although the middle tier—the scone layer—was fair game at any point in the ritual, you were supposed to work your way from bottom to top, sandwich to pastry. I ate a smoked salmon on wheat as he popped a mini éclair.

"Would you like to come to a gallery thing with me tonight?" I asked, surprising myself.

"That'd be great." He licked chocolate glaze from his upper lip. "Oh no...Not tonight. I've got theater tickets with my son."

"No problem," I said, suddenly embarrassed for having invited him. My cheeks flushed with rejection. *How do men put themselves through this? It's too awful.* "You must be looking forward to seeing your son," I regrouped. "What's the play?"

"Something called *Blood Brothers*. It's about twins separated at birth."

I snorted.

"I'm serious," he said. "Twins from Liverpool no less."

He reached across the table to refill my tea. The perfect inch-and-a-half of crisp shirt sleeve stuck out beyond his navy cashmere jacket. I had always been a sucker for that inch-and-a-half. He forgot to use the little silver strainer when he poured. The leaves sloshed into my cup.

"I'm sorry. You can't take me anywhere," he said. "Can you tell fortunes?"

"Not very well," I said. "Not my own anyway."

He peered into my cup. The leaves gathered at the bottom.

"I got nothing," he said. "I'll have a funny comeback in an hour or so." He had an easy charm. And porcelain blue eyes. I hadn't noticed how blue until this moment. The crinkles spraying from their corners made him look well-lived rather than middle-aged. Men were lucky that way.

I removed the top piece of wafer-thin white bread from a chicken and watercress sandwich—force of habit. Gavin bit into an Empire biscuit. The shortbread shed crumbs down his front. He brushed them away unselfconsciously.

The server silently replenished the sandwiches on the bottom tier. My hands flew to my stomach to indicate I was too full already, but Gavin helped himself to a prawn-mayonnaise. I poked at the remnants of a lemon curd tartlet with my fork and cocked my head toward the pianist. He had been moving through the old standards and landed on "The Way You Look Tonight." I sang along in my head: "Lovely, never ever change / Keep that breathless charm / Won't you please arrange it? / 'Cause I love you, just the way you look tonight."

Although I had just eaten the corner of a petit four, I picked up the last remaining sandwich—mature cheddar and chutney—and took a bite.

◆◆◆

I SAT IN THE back of another taxi and dug in my bag for the travel guide overnighted from Amazon. I flipped to the pages about Harrods. *Omnia Omnibus Ubique*. That was the store's motto. As if all department stores had mottos. All Things for All People Everywhere. I only needed one thing: a dress for meeting Aimee Laroche.

As the green awnings grew closer, my Circadian rhythm lost its groove. Despite having worked my way through an entire pot of tea, I almost nodded off. I was desperate for a coffee kickstart.

"Is there an entrance near the Food Court?" I asked the driver. Then, remembering what I had read: "I mean the Food Hall. Halls. Can you drop me near the Food Halls?"

The opulence of the halls gobsmacked me—all that marble, gold, and stained glass. And the culinary options, staggeringly vast and varied, displayed as though they were precious jewels in spotlit cases. I spotted a gleaming roaster, edged my way toward it through the crowd—past the European butters in their rainbow foils, past the mini marzipan sculptures, past the ubiquitous tea—and ordered a double espresso. I downed it fast while admiring a gargantuan coffee bean dispenser. It reminded me of the pipe organ in the silent movie house on Fairfax Avenue, its golden cylinders topped with copper caps. The caffeine mainlined through my system. Instant buzz. More than a buzz. I was wired, propelled out of the Food Halls in search of the dress.

I moved on to the Perfumery Hall where too many fragrances waged war. They made me cough, a sputter in my trachea. A young woman approached. She was holding a silver tray bearing a crystal bottle shaped like a crest. She caressed its purple stopper.

"Two Thousand Fleurs?" She waved a white stick drenched with scent under my nose. "By Creed?"

"No, thank you," I said. I hurried away from the perfume into the handbag salon. So many handbags. So much of *everything*. I had not practiced the fine art of real-world shopping since the bathing suit hunt with Gwen. And here I was, in the ultimate anti-cyber store.

I regretted having not packed a dress, figuring I'd make do with jeans and a pair of black slacks, which I could dress up or down as needed. I had not envisioned a scenario that could not be met with black slacks and a sweater. Who was I going to see anyway? Who was going to see me? As it turned out: French Couture Girl. I needed to look like a woman who did not make do with black slacks and a sweater.

But how to find the women's department…one of the many? There was an app for that, my guidebook informed me. I pulled out my phone.

Match.com had a match for me. Even though I had never uploaded a photo, paid a dime, or hit "submit," the site still stalked me, bombarding me with messages relentlessly and undeterred. "He shares the same birth month!" I sent the exclamation into the trash.

I had missed a text from Barbara. "Found lawyer."

I stared at the words, seemingly so innocuous, suspended in their little thought bubble. Barbara had signed off with an emoticon: a round-eyed face with the mouth spread wide revealing rows of teeth. What was that supposed to mean? This lawyer was a shark? I should prepare to do battle? Or time to grin and bear it?

A second text from Barbara appeared: "Oops. Wrong one." Up popped another face, equally inscrutable: winking eye, dangling tongue. What could this signify? You might as well start drinking? The ambiguity of these wacky cartoons filled me with self-doubt. Was I the only person who did not know how to decode these totems, this telecommunication version of the mood ring? And then another emoticon popped up. A sad face. That, I understood.

I gave up on downloading the Harrods app and forged ahead, but ended up having circled back to the Food Halls. I scanned the mosaic frieze of a hunting scene. As if to drive home the tally-ho, the gilt case below presented a rabbit—whole, skinned, ready for roasting.

"I'm looking for women's wear," I said to the butcher, a rotund fellow wearing a straw boater.

"First floor," he said.

I backed away from the bunny.

"Up one flight then, tiddly-i, tiddly-i-o," he added. "We're ground."

I nodded. The rabbit, the perfume, the coffee. The muchness. Too muchness.

"May I suggest the Egyptian Escalator?" the butcher called after. "You can't miss it. Right in the middle of it all."

I raised a hand and nodded.

I headed for the center of the store but was led astray, attracted to the cosmetics department like a magpie to shiny things. I wandered past the counters bearing the names of old friends: Bobbi Brown, Estee Lauder, Laura Mercier. I ended up in front of my standby:

Clinique. The words on the bottles and tubes made promises I needed to hear. Solution, Corrector, Turnaround. Flaws were easy to fix if you could wait six weeks for improvement and landed in the lucky eighty-four percent who saw results (which may vary).

I swiped a lip gloss across the back of my hand.

"Glamour-full," said the girl behind the counter.

"Not really, but thank you," I said.

"That's the color. It's a lovely nude. Goes with everything."

I smudged another stripe next to the first.

"Play-full. They're both Full Potential. Plump the lips, a bit of collagen building. Shouldn't really say building, can't guarantee—they like us to say stimulating."

"Which one do you like?" I asked, thrusting my hand under the girl's eyes. "This is one of those nights where I have to look great. Or at least feel like I do."

"Someone special," suggested the girl.

"She is, in a way…"

"I see."

It took me a second. "Oh, no…I'm not gay. Not that there's anything wrong with that."

The girl raised an eyebrow.

"You know, like in *Seinfeld*."

The girl was baffled.

"Never mind," I said. "I'm going to meet my husband's old girlfriend tonight."

"Oh my goodness! Say no more," said the Clinique girl. With that, she began opening drawers, producing sample after sample. "Brilliant! We're going to make you gorgeous."

"Thank you," I said. "Thank you so much."

"Absolutely gorgeous," the girl reiterated. "Your husband won't even look at her."

"Oh, he's not here with me. We're sort of…I don't really know what we are. It's a long story."

"I love long stories," said the girl as she tossed a mini mascara into the goodie bag. "Double your lashes, this will. You'll be amazed."

I checked my lashes in the mirror. Doubling wouldn't hurt.

"Go on," the girl prodded. She added a sample-sized eye shadow. "Martini," she said. I thought for a moment that my cosmetics friend was offering me a drink, but realized that was the name of the color. The girl nodded: go on.

"Well, a few months ago, I woke up in the middle of the night and my husband wasn't in bed, so I went downstairs. And there he was, in his study, in front of the computer…"

The girl shook her head. No matter which side of the pond you resided on, a story beginning with a man in front of a computer in the middle of the night would not end well.

"He was watching a tape of himself…you know…having sex," I whispered that part, "with an old girlfriend. Some French girl. In Paris. When he was young."

I wasn't sure how to continue. I wasn't sure I could continue. Though I'd repeated it to myself like a litany, I had never told the story out loud. Not in order, not from start to finish. The video. The emails. The packed suitcase. The espresso had kicked in full force. My heart raced and the back of my neck was slick with sweat.

"And he's been shaggin' her all this time?"

"Oh no," I said. "She lives in Paris. We live in Los Angeles. But still, it's not right. A grown man watching his younger self having sex and corresponding…"

"No, of course not," said the girl. She held a tiny square of green plastic in her hand. The girl tapped the apple of my cheek. "Dab a bit of this right here."

I studied my face in the mirror, touching my own cheek to mark the spot.

"So…?" the girl prodded.

"So, basically, I kicked him out. I wasn't going to stand for that in my home. I have a seventeen year old daughter…"

"No way," said the Clinique girl. "You couldn't possibly."

"I do. And what if she walked in on her father watching a tape like that?"

"That'd be dodgy, wouldn't it?"

"Dodgy," I said. "Not to mention, how could I be sure he was really done with this online affair sort of thing?"

The girl tossed a sample of foundation in the bag. "Photoshop in a bottle, they call this. It'll make your complexion amazingly youthful. Brilliant."

"So you can see why I showed him the door?"

"What else could you do?"

"Exactly," I concurred. "What else could I possibly do?"

The girl studied the contents of the bag, rummaged in a drawer for one last thing and dropped it in. She held my hand in her two. "You're all set," she said.

I paid for the lip gloss and took the bag, now weighted with samples.

"Thank you," I said. I stepped away from the counter, but paused. "So you'd do the same thing?" I asked.

"Absolutely."

"Thank you so much."

"Cheers," said the Clinique girl. "Keep your pecker up."

I laughed. I'd look that one up later. There was an app for that, too.

I weaved through a string of halls, following the signs until I found myself at the base of the Egyptian Escalator. A life-sized statue of Princess Di and Dodi Fayed greeted me. I stared at the couple, immortalized in bronze, dancing beneath the wings of an albatross. I wondered if they had really been in love or if the princess had simply been giddy with relief to be rid of the royals.

A crush of tourists squished me onto the escalator. The air took on a mugginess I imagined would hang over the Nile. How'd they do that, recreate the actual atmosphere like that?

The escalator made the espresso swirl in my stomach. A wave of seasickness. By the time I arrived at the top, I could not find my land legs. I stumbled to lean against a column. Fayed's face carved onto a sphinx stared down at me. There was his face again…and again—on several pharaonic busts. Why wouldn't he leave me alone? And there was so much gold: golden sculpture, golden sarcophagus, golden figures floating in the Zodiac tableau overhead. So much golden light.

And then the spinning began.

Gilt palm fronds seemed suddenly to be waving in an absent breeze. Asps carved in stone began to undulate. Countless Egyptian masks stared down at me like so many King Tuts. I felt entombed in a pyramid while everything else reeled around me.

I fanned myself with the tails of my cardigan. Even so, sweat beaded on my upper lip and at my temples. There was no stopping the dam. In another minute I was drenched. I mopped my spine with my T-shirt. It came away sopping wet. Clammy and bone-chilled, I shivered uncontrollably, clenching my jaw to keep my teeth from chattering.

All I wanted was stillness, but there was only motion. Escalators up and down. Shoppers rushing. Tourists milling all around. I closed my eyes against the onslaught, but crazy chevron patterns zapped across my brain as though I were the bride of Frankenstein.

I went down.

A twinge of embarrassment, but too rocked by the vertigo for humiliation. I opened my eyes. A sail of yellow swooped before them. I heard a voice.

"Oh dear, are you all right?" The words had a lovely lilt.

"I'm fine," I heard myself say as if from far away.

"I don't believe so." The accent was British, but East Indian British. I looked up into the face of an older woman with caramel skin, lineless and with a slight sheen beneath wisps of jet-black hair. Her wire-rimmed glasses gave her a professorial air. She wore a saffron colored sari. An azure shawl shot through with gold threads rested across her shoulders.

"I am, I'm fine," I insisted.

"Are you going to be sick, dear?"

"I hope not," I checked in with my stomach.

"Let's get you some air." The woman's voice calmed me, slowed my hummingbird heart. With one hand, she gripped me under the armpit. The other she wrapped around my waist.

"Come on, then," she said soothingly, "I'm going to help you get outside."

She steered me to the nearest exit, steadying me through all the people among all the merchandise in all the halls. I allowed myself to slump against the sunflower silk, the flesh beneath it pillowy and smelling of anise and something else I could not identify.

We made it out onto the street. The woman placed her shawl around my shoulders against the chill. "Take a deep breath," she instructed me. I did as I was told.

"I feel better," I assured her. "I can go back inside now."

"Oh no, dear, I wouldn't."

"I'm looking for a dress," I protested. "It's very important."

"A dress is never critical," declared the woman.

She ushered me into a taxi. Just as she was about to close the door, I removed the shawl. "Don't forget this."

"No, you keep it," urged the woman.

"I couldn't possibly," I said.

"It's a gift. You must learn to accept the things that you are given." Then she closed the taxi door. "Take good care of yourself, dear."

"I will," I promised, leaving several acres of women's wear unscoured.

"I will," I said again as the taxi headed for the hotel.

# CHAPTER THIRTY-FIVE

THERE WAS NO ROMANCE to the fourth floor walk-up on the way up the stairs. Still reeling from my episode at Harrods, I dragged myself up, step after step, sick and tired and jet-lagged. I dragged Gallery Girl with me, her face calm and cool on that television screen. I dragged my absence on Stephanie's college tour, as palpable as any presence. I dragged the burden of her childhood declared gone. I dragged the divorce papers waiting for me in the drawer of my bedside table.

Inside the flat, I slumped on the bed. I had a voicemail. I must have missed the call while embarrassing myself by having a spell at the world's grandest department store.

"Hi, Mom. We're two states down and three to go. So far, I kind of liked Oberlin. I don't know. Denison maybe? I've got to go. I can't believe you're in London. That's, like, so weird."

It was indeed, like, so weird. Stephanie and Adam—doing the Midwestern sweep, cocooned in a rental car with inadequate ventilation. *Who needed it?* Following a student tour guide weaving in reverse through campus after campus. Interrogating seniors about dorm security. Scoping out the graffiti in campus ladies' rooms. Deciphering Stephanie's mumbled comments—"too crunchy granola," "too Abercrombie," "meh." *Who needed it? I did.*

I lay in bed for an hour, unable to lift my head from the pillow. While my daughter and husband slept in a Holiday Inn Express in Mount Vernon, Ohio, I granted myself ten more minutes like a teenager making a Monday morning bargain with the alarm clock. Finally I showered and dressed.

When the phone rang, I was absorbed in adding an extra swipe of Martini eyeshadow to the crease of my eyelid.

It was Gavin. "There are girlfriend issues," he said.

"I beg your pardon."

"My son. He's in the middle of some drama. He bailed."

"I'm sorry," I said.

"I'm not," he said. It might have sounded smarmy, but it didn't.

By the time I got off the phone, I was dressing for more than a possible showdown.

◆◆◆

THE TALE OF THE Liverpudlian twins turned out to be both melodrama and musical. A gaggle of teenaged girls seated in front of us clutched one another at the heartbreak of it all. I glanced at Gavin, his eyebrows arched in disbelief. We smiled simultaneously, stifling giggles, pleased we were in agreement. And then Gavin reached over and took my hand. I didn't dare look at him. By the next scene, he had intertwined his fingers with mine and was ever so slightly stroking the valleys between my fingers; I could barely concentrate on anything beyond that whisper of sensation.

When the lights came up at intermission, we agreed that Act II could only mean more torture. We gathered our things and made our way through the lobby out into the night air. I had grabbed the good Samaritan's royal blue scarf—a last minute addition on my way out the door. It was not something I normally would have owned, but the Indian woman was right. The length of silk worked magic, its opalescence elevating my mood as I wrapped it around me.

"I'm sorry the play was so...I don't even know what to call it." Gavin shook his head.

"You've got to love a good 'nature versus nurture' musical," I joked.

Gavin chuckled. "Don't forget 'separated at birth.'"

"And a song that requires rhyming 'Marilyn Monroe' at the end of every line.'"

"Should we go back?" teased Gavin.

"Nah," I said.

"You're right. One of them's bound to die in the end."

"Oh, they're both goners," I asserted.

"You think?"

"Definitely."

We were out of play banter. I nodded toward the Palace Theatre across the street. "Is that where the Beatles played for the queen?" I asked. "You know, 'People in the cheaper seats, clap your hands. And the rest of you, just rattle your jewelry.'"

Gavin looked at me quizzically. He didn't know the reference.

"John," I said. "Of course it would be John."

Gavin nodded, but he couldn't click into Beatles lore. Adam knew it all. "Did you grow up in LA?" he asked.

I nodded. "Born and bred. How about you?"

"My father was a doctor with the Public Health, so we moved around a lot."

"Sort of the medical version of an army brat?"

"That's right."

I was about to ask him if he'd ever considered becoming a doctor himself, but suddenly realized that he might actually be a doctor for all I knew.

"What do you do?" I asked.

"I own a chain of shopping centers."

"Duke's Shopping World!" I realized.

"That's me."

"I've seen the commercials, but I don't think I've ever been to one."

"So far we're in what they like to call 'outlying areas.' But if you ever find yourself in Pacoima or West Covina. The Inland Empire. We buy where the land is cheap. Closer to civilization, land is expensive so it gets subdivided into single family homes." He was losing me. "It's not really very interesting."

"Duke's Shopping World," I said. Then, suddenly emboldened, "I hate to tell you this, but your commercials could use a little classing up."

"They're stupid, aren't they?"

"Pretty stupid." I had never been so candid with a stranger.

"I think so, too. But everyone tells me they're doing the trick," said Gavin as he hailed a cab.

"But you're Duke," I said.

"Where's your gallery thing?" Gavin asked.

"What?"

"The art opening. It's still early, let's go."

♦♦♦

THE GALLERY'S RESIDENT HIPSTER had added a fedora to his ensemble. (*How to go from day to evening with one signature accessory!* I had clicked on that link once or twice.) The kid was air kissing his way through the throng.

Gavin and I zigzagged through the waiters circulating with trays of blini and skewered shrimp, through the collectors flipping through price lists, past the paintings depicting odd couplings of household objects. We paused in front of the noose dangling off the Barcalounger and shot each other a look.

The hipster appeared at my side. "Brilliant! You made it," he chirped.

"I did," I said.

"Have you said hello to Aimee?" he asked breathlessly.

I shook my head.

"Well, let's just fix that, shall we?" He clamped a hand on my shoulder and steered me through the crowd. Gavin followed. Hipster Kid air kissed a young man also wearing a fedora—right cheek, left cheek—then stood on tiptoe to whisper something to a six-foot-tall woman with chopsticks plunged through her perfectly messy bun.

In the same way that a celebrity sighting can be confusing at first, a movie star appearing small and unsparkly while pushing a shopping cart through Whole Foods, I did not immediately grok that it was French Girl. The real-life LinkedIn, Orange-Tasting, Home-Wrecker Girl, not the one who reigned over my imagination.

She was still attractive, but more because she believed she was—a sort of habit, the party favor left over after having led the life of a stunning woman. Not to mention that French thing again—an attitude embedded in her national heritage that, in the wake of Gauloises and Camembert and vintage Bordeaux, still proclaimed its superiority and seductiveness.

But her looks had morphed. The hair that had fanned across the pillow in the video had lost its luster and was now cut chin length in a practical, if stylish, bob. Her skin, luminescent even in the video's feeble lamplight, was no longer porcelain. A furrow creased between her brows. There was a thickness at her waist that the draping of her dress could not camouflage. French Girl wasn't a girl anymore; she was middle-aged.

As much as this was a happy revelation, it also disappointed me, as though I myself were somehow less-than because of the diminution of my rival, even if that rivalry was…whatever it was… part words on a screen, part moving picture, part fantasy. She had been Adam's once-and-again fantasy, but then I had taken over the job of fantasizer-in-chief. There was an expression for that: *folie à deux*—shared madness. French, of course. I wanted to turn and run, but I was fixated by the sight of this woman a few feet away, this woman who had beguiled my husband long distance, then haunted me, capsizing my life in the process.

Hipster Boy maneuvered me into position for my audience with her. He waved his hand in front of my face with a pivot of the wrist as though he were presenting a set of Samsonite on a game show. But Aimee was not interested in me. Her gaze was fixed on Gavin.

Gavin had changed into a suit and tie since teatime. Even in this artsier-than-thou crowd, he looked so at home in pin stripes that he did not seem overdressed. The suit made him look like his own man, like a grown-up.

Aimee extended a hand. "Aimee Laroche," she said. "A pleasure to meet you."

He shook her hand and when he did, she reached out her other hand and took hold of his bicep. Her left hand remained there, her thumb stroking the inside of his arm.

"And who are you?" she asked.

"Gavin Duke," he said. "My friend brought me." He gently nudged me toward her. "This is Maura Fielder."

"Oh," she said. She smiled wanly. She was only interested in Gavin, and he had said "friend," not "wife," not that she would have cared. "You are American."

"Yes," he said.

"I'm so lucky you happen to be on holiday."

He smiled in response, then rested a palm between my shoulder blades, nodding toward the bar. "I'm going to get us a drink."

Aimee watched him retreat, then looked back to me.

"Your name," she said. "Did he say Fielder?"

"Yes. Maura Fielder." I draped the shawl over my shoulder. The gold thread prickled my neck.

"This is an unusual name, yes?"

"I don't know. It came with my husband. His name is Adam Fielder."

Finally, she looked at me.

"I know an Adam Fielder. From Los Angeles. You are the wife of that Adam Fielder?"

"I am. I am the wife of that Adam Fielder." I repeated the words as though they were the secret phrase that would gain me entrance to a speak-easy.

"So, Adam is here as well," she said, scanning the crowd. "I was afraid he did not receive my invitation. I thought perhaps my assistant forgot to send it, though I think I may have written something on his...how do you say?..."

"Personally. You say 'personally.' And..." I added, "I have no doubt that you did. But I have no idea whether he got it. And he's not here."

I should have acted like I knew about the invitation. On the other hand, she hadn't heard from him. Maybe he was telling the truth. Maybe the emails really had stopped. "I'm here in London alone."

"I think not," she said, cocking her head toward Gavin in the crush at the bar.

"It doesn't matter what you think," I said, surprising myself. I needed her to know that I was nobody's fool, especially hers. "I saw your movie, by the way."

"Pardon?"

"Your movie."

"Mon Dieu! You saw my movie?"

"I saw *a* movie you were in," I said. "From a long time ago." I looked her up and down as if to calculate the number of years. "A very, very long time ago." I had never gone out of my way to be rude. Who knew it could be so energizing?

She took a sip of her red wine. "So you came all this way to meet me?" she asked. "How very...how do you say?...assertive of you. How very American."

"It was pure coincidence. But I don't expect you to believe that. I suspect you're someone who plans her attack many moves in advance."

"Attack?" She was good at many things, this woman, but not at playing dumb. "You are here to make an attack?" She feigned horror, raising her hands, palms outward.

I had envisaged this moment, even though I never believed it would come. I had written and rewritten its dialogue, alternately cutting, condescending and cool. Occasionally, I threw in a threat or two, riffs on "Keep your hands off…"

Gavin returned with our wine, handed me a glass. I took a sip, my heart thrumming in my ears against the cacophony. Here she was—I could have at her—but suddenly, she seemed so not worth the effort. I wanted nothing but to be done with her.

She touched Gavin again, this time clutching his hand between her two.

"Are you enjoying the show?" she asked him. "Are you interested in anything…*comment dit-on?*…in particular?" She took a step toward him, forcing me to take a step back…right into a waiter.

He lost his footing, tripped, slid on the black-and-white checkered floor, struggling to maintain the tray of hors d'oeuvres balanced on his outstretched palm. He nearly succeeded. A stumble. A save. Then a moment in slo-mo. The tray flew from his hand. I was just out of range. Most of the spring rolls landed on the floor, but Aimee was a direct hit for the dipping sauce, her couture creation suddenly a Jackson Pollack.

"*Merde!*" spat Aimee. "*Connarde maladroite!*"

I didn't have to remember my French to know the woman was calling me names. She let loose. "*Allez-vous en, salope!*" That, I had gotten precisely. I'd just been called a bitch. Though most assuredly the word had never been on any ninth grade vocabulary list.

Hipster Boy, who fled with the first shower of sweet and sour, reappeared with a bottle of Perrier and a fistful of napkins. He stood paralysed, trying to figure out what to do with his arsenal. I took the bottle from him and doused the napkins with soda, then blotted Aimee's dress gently.

"Give that to me," Aimee demanded and set about dabbing at the sticky spots.

I removed the blue shawl from my shoulders, the shawl given to me by the Indian woman who had shown me the kindness of strangers. While moist splotches spread like bacteria on Aimee's crepe de Chine, I extended the shawl to her. "This will cover everything."

Aimee composed herself, embarrassed by her outburst. "I cannot take this. It belongs to you," she said.

It was the perfect straight line, but I was through crafting punchlines. I looked Aimee Laroche in the eye. "Consider it a farewell gift."

I wrapped the length of silk around her, inhaling one last time its perfume of anise and...cardamom. Yes, it was cardamom. Sweet, spicy, pungent—with an undertone of something deeper, the scent that had eased me back into my own skin when the Indian woman cradled me. An aroma something like earth.

♦♦♦

When we stepped outside, a fine mist hung in the air, just enough to make finding a cab impossible. I huddled beneath Gavin's umbrella and leaned into him. Gavin asked if I'd like to stop into a pub for a drink, but I said no. I wanted to keep walking. Saying goodbye to Aimee Laroche made me feel shot out of a cannon. I had to keep moving.

"Are you a collector?" Gavin asked.

"My husband...," I stopped myself. You never talk about an ex on a date, Gwen once told me. But Adam wasn't my ex.

"I have to tell you something," Gavin said. "I know it's been a long time, but I haven't really dated much since my wife died. I went through a period a few years ago where all my friends kept trying to fix me up. I'd go out to dinner with these women—nice women, all of them—but by dessert...I don't know...I guess you're not ready until you're ready. Nobody can tell you when that is. It just happens." He paused a moment. I paused with him. "When you least expect it," he smiled.

We kept walking and he kept talking. It reminded me of when Stephanie was little and rode in the backseat of the car. She was always more forthcoming with juicy tidbits about her day when she didn't have to look me in the eye. She would relax open like a tulip, and I would learn who had elbowed her away from the shapes corner or slighted her at snack time. Because of the London drizzle, Gavin and I were forced to cozy under an umbrella. He told me things he would not have had we been facing each other over dinner at a posh restaurant. Like Stephanie buckled into her booster seat, it seemed as though he could not help himself.

"Early on...you know, shortly after...my sister-in-law kept giving me books. And advice. Join a support group. Volunteer. Go to the supermarket in the evening when all the single women are there on their way home from work."

"That's a good one," I said.

Gavin chuckled. "And, of course, everyone's favorite: take a class. I signed up for a string of them. Ceramics. The Psychology of Human Motivation. How To Talk To Anybody."

"I bet you did well in that."

"I'm talking too much, aren't I?"

"Not at all. I didn't mean that." I suspected it was my turn to talk about myself. Instead, I asked, "Not that it's any of my business, but you didn't mention internet dating. Didn't anyone suggest that?"

"Everyone suggested that. My sister-in-law, the same one, went so far as to make me a profile. But when I read it, it didn't feel like me at all. All the facts were right—the data points, as they say—but it wasn't me. And I couldn't figure out how to fix it. I fiddled with the damn thing for an hour before realizing I had no interest in the whole enterprise. It couldn't have been less interesting to me. An imaginary version of yourself getting matched with someone else's imaginary version of themselves. No thank you. There's no there there. Not for me anyway."

"Better to be fixed up by a friend than an algorithm," I said.

"Yes," he said. "I guess some people actually find algorithms friendly. I'm afraid I'm not one of them." He took a beat, then, "What about you?"

"Me?"

"Have you tried the internet?"

"Oh, I'm not dating."

He fell silent.

"But I would never do the internet thing. In fact," I said, "I'm officially done with the internet as of an hour ago."

"It's easier to be alone than to deal with that stress," he said.

"Did you know stress didn't even exist as a concept until the 1950s?" I said. "I read that recently."

"Wow," he said. "And now we spend half our lives trying to figure out how to deal with it."

"And the other half creating it," I said.

We fell silent as we continued along Piccadilly. I was about to ask him if he knew where the word "Piccadilly" came from because I had read that recently, too, in my guidebook, but thought better of it. I didn't want to sound like a *Jeopardy* contestant. Instead, I said, "What did you make?"

"I'm sorry?" he said.

"In Ceramics? What did you make?"

"A napkin holder."

"How ambitious!" I poked fun. "No simple ashtray for you."

"You'll see it. It's prominently displayed in my kitchen."

An available cab passed. We both noticed its yellow for-hire light, but neither of us hailed it. "You're right about my commercials. I'm going to make a change."

"Oh, what do I know?" I said.

"You know a stupid commercial when you see one."

We waited for the light to change in front of the Ritz Hotel. It turned green and we started to cross, but I looked the wrong way to check for oncoming traffic. Gavin grabbed my arm to stop me from getting hit by a tiny Smartcar. He held onto me for more than an instant, then moved his hand to rest on my shoulder, holding me back from the curb. He let his hand rest there for several heartbeats longer than necessary. The feel of his hand electrified me, yet relaxed me at the same time. Not because he was protecting me, not even because he might have been sending a signal, but simply because the lingering weight of his hand on my body evoked something old and familiar—the sense of belonging. I might have hoped he was sending a signal. I might have wanted more. Maybe I wanted him. I definitely wanted him to want me.

"Do you still miss her every single day?" I asked. "That's a stupid question. Of course you do."

He nodded. "I do. But sometimes I think I miss the her I've made up in my mind since she's been gone."

"Maybe it's hard to tell the difference," I said.

"Exactly," he said. "She wasn't perfect, obviously."

"But you were perfect together," I suggested.

"Honestly? Far from it."

We passed a men's club. Gentlemen in tuxedoes gathered out front smoking and clapping one another on the back, like extras directed to suggest the winding up of a convivial evening in the background of a scene. The smell of whiskey hung over the group. The rain had stopped and Gavin struggled to close the umbrella, focusing hard on the task, more than was required. He finally Velcroed the closure strip around. It took a moment for us to recalibrate the distance between us now that we no longer needed to huddle. Suddenly we were just two people walking in a foreign city.

"My friend, Gwen, tells me I should get over myself. She thinks I'm not hip."

"I'm sure you're very hip."

"I'm not. I can't swipe through people. I don't even know how to swipe a thing out of my mind. Also…" I could feel his eyes on me. "Also, I seem not to be able to lower my expectations. People say, 'Accept me with all my flaws,' but then accepting my flaw—my inability to lower the bar—I guess that's a toughie."

"Maybe it's not a flaw," he said. "Maybe it's your version of love."

My breath caught, forcing a strangled sound from my throat.

"Who knew we'd be middle-aged and having to figure out how to move on?" he said.

"How do you do that with a hole in your heart?" I wondered.

"I was kind of hoping you'd help me figure that out," he said. I felt his hand at my waist as we turned onto Down Street. My building lay ahead on the right. I paused in the middle of the block. Hardy bonhomie drifted past us from the tables outside a tapas café.

"I can't," I said. "I'm sorry, but I can't."

We walked the half-block to my building. "I'll just see you to your room…," Gavin said. Or maybe come in. I wanted him to come in—part of me did anyway. It would not be a replay of my night with Peter Lafferty. It would be good with this man, great maybe. The inch of air separating us already zapped with electrical charge. I unlocked the front door of the building and stepped inside. He followed.

"I can get to my room myself," I said.

"Are you sure?"

"I'm sure."

I let go of the door, but grabbed it before it closed. Gavin turned around, momentarily hopeful. He moved closer to me.

"You know what?" I said. "I'm in love with my husband."

Gavin nodded. It was not much of a revelation. He might have known all along.

"I'm not sure I've ever said that out loud before," I said.

"It sounded good." He took a half a step back.

I smiled, too, then let go of the door, allowing it to close between us with the faintest thud.

# CHAPTER THIRTY-SIX

I STUDIED THE CUSTOMS form for several minutes before deciding to declare the antique ring. The cracked leather box—as old as the ring itself—lay buried in my purse. I considered slipping the ring onto my own finger and leaving the declaration form blank, but I could never do that. The guilt would explode all over my face like an allergic rash and probably land me in an interrogation cubicle where I'd become a little too familiar with the feel of latex gloves stretched over the beefy hands of a customs agent. I filled in the form accurately, wondering if I were the only person on the plane declaring the full amount of her purchase. It was worth it to avoid those latex gloves.

I felt guilty anyway as I dragged my suitcase toward the customs desk. I assumed everyone felt that way—guilt by virtue of situation. Was guilt in all our genes or just mine? As if to prove my particular susceptibility, I could have sworn I heard someone calling my name. There it was again. "Maura!"

I glanced around. Yes, there was a woman waving wildly at me. I smiled and nodded. I had no clue who it was—this person who was making her way through the crowd, annoying everyone in her path.

"Maura!" she said. "It's me! Pamela."

Pamela Simpson. To be precise, I assumed Pamela Simpson was lurking in there somewhere. She was one of those Ridgepoint girls I ran into periodically, but it had been several years now. She didn't look old exactly—just older—and unmistakably larger. Pamela had never been one of those girls—a skinny, nobby-kneed child harboring a plus-sized matron waiting to burst out, like the Incredible Hulk, in mom jeans. Surprise!

She threw her arms around me. "Where are you coming from?" Pamela trilled.

"London."

"I was in Florence for a week," Pamela said. "Oh my God—the gelato!"

I wondered if it were possible to gain that much weight in one week. Probably not, even in Italy. And could it be some sort of protracted sugar high that was responsible for this manic version of my eleventh grade Chem lab partner?

"You think you couldn't possibly eat any more gelato and then you turn a corner and there's another gelateria and these trays of the stuff are calling to you from the window. Chocolate hazelnut like you can't believe. This one place has a flavor called Fantasia. It's positively orgasmic."

"Sounds great. Where's...?" I couldn't remember the new husband's name. I'd heard Pamela was on number three. Maybe four.

"Neil? We're divorced."

"I had no idea," I said.

"It's brand new. Not even signed, sealed, or delivered yet."

"I'm sorry," I said. And, really, I was.

"It's okay. Really. It's so much easier the third time."

*Yes, it would be.*

"Almost painless," Pamela said. "That's why I went to Italy. You know that book, *Eat, Pray, Love*? After my first divorce, I did all three, but this time I figured all that freakin' ashram got me last time was another ex-husband, so I might as well stick with the 'eat' and pray I'm not stupid enough to fall in love again. So...two weeks in Italy. I ate pasta in shapes I've never heard of!"

I felt an ode to trofiette coming on.

"I looked for you on Facebook," Pamela segued, "I thought we could be 'friends.'" Pamela did the air quote thing. The gesture annoyed me with its one-two punch of ubiquity and misuse. Air quotes or no air quotes, I didn't think I wanted to be friends with Pamela Simpson at this point in our lives. I had no time for rekindling ancient friendships, virtual or otherwise. There was only one relationship I could think about. The one I had broken. The one I needed to fix.

While Pamela made noises about sharing a taxi to the west side, I began composing my dialogue. I needed to talk to Adam. A-SAP as Stephanie would say.

I also needed to compose myself. Barbara had arranged a car and driver, but I would not offer a ride to Pamela. More guilt. There could be no gathering of thoughts with Pamela Simpson in the back seat of a Towncar. I pretended to shift to a faster-moving customs line and maneuvered my suitcase behind a Middle Eastern family. With still more guilt, I hoped that racial profiling was alive and well at LAX. Sure enough, Pamela sailed through the checkpoint several lines to the right as my line ground to a halt. I waved to Pamela, frantically gesturing for her to go on without me. Pamela did the "call me" thing, thumb and pinkie outstretched at ear and mouth. Then she shouted, "See you at the reunion!" I didn't even know we had one coming up.

I settled into the backseat and pulled out my phone. Another greeting from Match.com. "Like you, he's a non-smoker!" Delete.

I phoned Adam. No answer. It took the driver twenty-five minutes just to make the loop out of the airport. In that time, I phoned Adam twice more. Still no answer. I discussed routes with the driver. Avoid the freeway. Sepulveda, just as bad. Exposition, even worse. Going northeast was impossible. The guy assured me he knew a shortcut through the Marina. I called Adam again. Still no answer. So easy—too easy—these Smart Phone calls. No dialing, just a whisper of a tap on the screen. So much nothing between impulse and execution. Irresistible.

Since the driver was taking me west to go east, I was tempted to be dropped off at Adam's office—to have it out with Adam once and for all. To rail against the desktop invader that had laid siege to our home; to rail against the papers stowed in my bedside table; to rail against the folly of it all. And to beg for his forgiveness. But I was too travel-grimy for a scene like that.

So the driver inched on, through Westwood. I had heard rumors that a developer was trying to revive the village, but as I gazed out at street after street, the rows of vacated shops looked pretty sorry.

I thought about the time before the village had degenerated into an architectural hodge-podge, when a Mediterranean theme had unified these five square miles with clay roofs and Spanish tiles, with paseos and courtyards. All that had changed when the first high-rise went up, followed by its inevitable clones. But it had been a gang shootout in the late eighties that ended Westwood's reign as a hangout. Everyone said it was an art student caught in the crossfire, but I was never sure. Urban myths sprang up around that night like toadstools after a downpour. All I knew was that "the village"—one of the places that made this city mine—had been sacrificed in a hail of gunfire.

Now, I discovered that even The Gardens had closed. When had that happened? I had just eaten lunch there with Barbara. Next time the two of us strolled around Westwood, it would be added to our list of ghosts. The hot fudge sundae from the building's original ice cream parlor and the tostada grande from the Mexican restaurant that followed would be joined by the soup they called the Bowl of the Sun. It would shine so much brighter in my memory than it had when the waitress placed it in front of me, its parmesan spike waiting to crumble into dust.

As dusk settled, I watched the neon sign flicker to life on the Bruin Theater. My thumb twitched over Adam's name on my iPhone. I tapped the number.

Four rings and then: "What?" Adam's voice was gruff. He knew it was me, of course. Caller ID. But there was no "Hi." Only: "What?"

"It's me."

"I know."

"I wanted to let you know I'm home." My voice came out in a high squeak. "And I want to hear all about the college trip. Every little thing."

There was a pause. A long one. The kind Sam would have said you could drive a truck through.

Then, "My lawyer says I'm not supposed to talk to you. Your lawyer can talk to my lawyer."

"I don't have a lawyer."

"Then get one," Adam ordered. And hung up.

I tapped his phone number again, but hit "END" before it could ring. There was nothing for me to say. An hour earlier I had been prepared to fix this mess. I thought I'd be able to fix it as easily as I had left that defiled oven behind in my college apartment.

♦♦♦

FINALLY, I FOUND MYSELF in the foyer of my house, my Tumi T-Tech at my side. Muffled sounds of movement were coming from the darkened family room.

"Stephanie?" I called as I flipped on the lights.

Stephanie leapt from the couch. Her hair hung mussed over one eye. She tucked it behind her ear as she ran to give me a hug.

"I missed you so much," I said, breathing deep the coconut scent of her hair. "I want to hear everything about your trip. What's the leading contender?"

"I'm not sure," she said. "I'll tell you all about it." Then, "You remember Josh."

A figure rose from the couch, a pair of legs that took several seconds to unfold. His hair was cut short, like a little boy from the fifties, making the tuft of soul patch beneath his lower lip seem pasted on. But there was something in the face that did strike me as familiar. The high forehead, the broad mouth, the gray eyes against the olive skin. Of course. Cindy Lafferty's olive complexion. Peter Lafferty's steel eyes.

"Joshua Lafferty!"

"Hi," said the boy. "Nice to see you," he added, as though prompted by a parent.

What was Joshua Lafferty doing in my house? Peter Lafferty's son? I studied him, almost squinting, searching for the preschooler in there—the projected aging of a face on a milk carton but in reverse. He was a good-looking kid. I caught Stephanie looking at him, too. Yes, he was a really good-looking kid.

We all stared at each other.

"We're a little pressed for time actually," Josh said.

"Where are you off to?" I asked.

"Going to get some dinner. Maybe see a movie," Stephanie said, edging the boy toward the door. "I didn't know you were going to be home."

"Go," I said. "It's okay.

They both wanted out of there. Stephanie and this boy who—hadn't it been mere months ago?—had toddled across this very floor wearing a dragon costume under Stephanie's pink tutu.

"I'll hear about the schools later," I said.

"Totally," said Stephanie. "But you know…Good ones, bad ones."

The kids headed out, Josh placing a hand on Stephanie's hip.

"Tell your dad I say hello," I said to Josh. Take that back. I wanted to say, "Tell him I specifically did not say hello. That I sent him no message whatsoever." Instead, I smiled and waved. Josh Lafferty waved back. I resisted the urge to clap my hands encouragingly as though he were still that little boy who had just learned to wave bye-bye, flashing a proud grin that revealed two seed pearl teeth.

Did it have to be Joshua Lafferty? Peter's Josh?

Enough karmic punishment. I got it already. Enough.

I was exhausted. The kind of exhausted that makes it impossible to sleep. It was more than my off-kilter body clock. More than Josh's hand an inch from Stephanie's tush. It was Adam. Adam bypassing hello. Adam barking at me to get a lawyer. Adam making it clear: he was playing for keeps.

I was pulled into Adam's den. I stared at the computer, the invader. It had not been so long ago that it was the new techno kid in town, like the VHS machine and its older sibling, the Betamax. Like the microwave oven. Like the phonograph. Like all those contrivances that made people ask, *How did we ever get along without this?* But somehow the computer was different. It had presence. It had intelligence. It contained the world—www, for heaven's sake—and it served it up, vivid yet surreptitious, in whatever form your personal weakness found solace.

Bluefly. Chickdowntown. Shopittome. I started with the sale items, ticking off a striped T-shirt and a pair of bejeweled ballet flats. Before long I entered the "Just Arrived" zone. I clicked on an Ella Moss blouse—the Enchantress—into my cyber shopping cart. A jersey cardigan that fell to bat wing points. A military jacket with a notched collar and pewter buttons. A silk top with a beaded panel running down the center, the kind of thing you'd wear with slacks to a hip dinner party—hipper than I would ever go to.

I hit "Continue Shopping." I could always edit the contents of my cart before submitting the order. I could, but I would not. I never did. I would order it all. I knew my Amex number by heart. Its expiration date. Its CVV number. (Need help finding this? I most certainly did not.) I filled in the numbers one after the other wherever a little asterisk demanded, numbed by the ritual.

I paused on a gunmetal bracelet, its chunky oval links connected by braided strands of white gold. At the last minute, I added the bracelet to my cart even though I had practiced a lifelong policy of never buying jewelry for myself. I justified the purchase as an offering. The bracelet was called Lover's Links. Not until I finalized the order, confirming credit card information and mailing address, did I realize that I would never be able to fasten the toggle clasp onto my own wrist. Adam always did that for me.

# CHAPTER THIRTY-SEVEN

I AWOKE AT 4:00 a.m., ravenous. I scrambled two eggs, crumbling in a handful of shredded mozzarella, and ate every bite. Though I rarely made coffee for myself, this morning I did—a whole pot—and drank two cups. I needed to be well caffeinated. I was going to put the pieces of my marriage back together today.

I showered and began putting on my makeup before remembering the Clinique wonder-workers buried in my suitcase. I dug for them, offering silent thanks to the counter girl who listened and, as it turned out, knew her stuff. The high impact mascara performed as touted. My lashes alone would melt Adam's frost.

By the time Stephanie was up, I was on my third cup of coffee. I dropped a slice of bread into the toaster for Stephanie, but she breezed through the kitchen, saying only, "Josh is here." For one horrible instant I though she meant he had spent the night, but then I realized he was outside in his car, waiting to drive her to school. She was almost out the door when she bounced over and threw her arms around me. "I didn't want to wake you up last night. It was too late. I'll tell you all about the trip later." And she was gone.

She had spent the last several days with her father. Of course she couldn't shift gears immediately, Team Daddy to Team Mommy. It would require a reentry period, back into my orbit. Very soon, the three of us would no longer be planets colliding. I was going to make it my business.

◆◆◆

WHEN THE ELEVATOR DOORS slid open to the lobby of Fielder Creative Management, I spotted the two men immediately. They stood about three feet apart from one another. The muscles in Adam's forearms flexed and relaxed as though he were pumping veins to have blood drawn. I followed the line of the motion down to clenched fists. The tips of his ears flushed bright red and he kept folding his lower lip over his teeth. A constellation of signals I knew well. They sprang into action whenever his father quizzed him about the state of his life.

I knew the other man, too. From the square of his shoulders. I knew those shoulders. Unfortunately. They belonged to Peter Lafferty.

Get me out of here.

I considered pushing a button, any button, and stepping back into the elevator. But Adam spotted me over Peter's shoulder. I spotted him spotting me. I stepped off the elevator—like a grown-up, I thought, as in "we're all adults here"—and headed across the lobby. I rarely wore heels, but I had today; their click-click-clicking sharp against the Carrera marble. I circled around a nine-foot plexiglass column bisected by a cobalt plexi plane. The sunlight struck the piece through the skylight so that it cast everyone in its orbit crayon blue.

"It's a bit much," Adam had warned his father when the old man purchased the sculpture. Sam didn't care. In fact, he had a domed skylight installed directly above the thing at the apex of the four-story atrium.

"It's sort of psychedelic," Adam had added.

"Psychedelic shmychedelic," Sam had retorted.

Now here it was, turning Adam and Peter Lafferty into overgrown Smurfs.

For a moment, I took in the tableau as though I were plastered flat on the roof gazing down through that skylight. I saw myself approaching the two blue men. I watched Adam watching me. He had been watching me from the instant the elevator doors parted. I watched myself hesitate, triangulating my position vis a vis the two men. I watched myself step between them, Adam and Peter, to create a semicircle, as though sidling into a conversation at a cocktail party. I inched closer to Adam, throwing the arc off balance. I was making a statement. Declaring my allegiance.

Peter spoke first, prompting me to zoom back into my body.

"Maura! Wow, great to see you."

Adam locked eyes with me.

"I was telling Adam he and I should have lunch some time," Peter continued.

What? Was this French farce or *Fatal Attraction*? I took the temperature of the air between the two men. Okay, I suddenly realized, Peter didn't know that Adam knew. Or worse still, he was lording it over Adam who said nothing, just kept curling his lip over his teeth and clenching his fists. Clenching everything.

"Well," Peter finally said, "I guess I better get to my meeting."

Peter extended his hand to Adam, but Adam ignored it. So Peter leaned in and clamped a hand on his shoulder. Like an old pal. Then he turned to me and said, "Good to see you, kiddo." And he placed his hand between my shoulder blades like someone who had been there before. Then he strutted through the lobby toward the main conference room, glass-enclosed and providing a full view of the players awaiting Peter's arrival—agents, lawyers, and the two surviving Doors. He stepped into the room like he owned the place.

"Kiddo?" Adam snarled.

"He's an idiot." I tried to sound casual, but my voice was shrill.

"You slept with a man who calls you 'kiddo'!"

Adam turned on his heels and headed for his office. I followed him, skittering along, picking up speed.

He passed the conference room where Peter Lafferty was laughing too loudly. He moved quickly, not once looking over his shoulder to see if I was behind him. I was nearly running now, sliding really, to catch him.

"Adam!" I called, "we need to talk!"

I didn't dare yell any louder. Business was being conducted. The deal factory Sam had built was chugging away. Movies being packaged on their way to manufacturing. I strode past the conference room. Peter glanced through the glass just as I was passing. And winked at me.

Instantly, I veered off my path, throwing open the heavy glass door. I stood in the doorway.

"Don't do that," I said to Peter.

Heads snapped in my direction.

"What?" asked Peter.

"I said, don't do that."

I paused to catch my breath, taking in the scene. A Lalique chandelier hung over a rosewood racetrack of a table. I scanned the group. All the biggies from the music department were in attendance. And a couple of house lawyers. There was a famous producer, too—heavy-set with a heart-attack-in-waiting flush across his cheeks. He was cracking open pistachios mounded in a Baccarat compote dish. He had a rhythm going, discarding the shells with one hand while tossing the nuts into his mouth with the other. But even *his* head turned to me.

I looked directly at Peter. "And don't call me kiddo."

"Um…" Peter hemmed.

"I am not your kiddo," I said, my voice louder this time.

"I don't…," he said.

"That's all I wanted to say," I said. And then once more with stunning authority: "No winking. And. No. Kiddo."

I spun around to continue on to Adam's office. I was wearing new shoes; I had neglected to scuff their soles. My feet scooted out from under me cartoon-style, and I landed, splat, on my ass right in front of the supersized glassed-in conference room. A passing agent—subsidiary rights—swooped to my side, offering a hand.

"Are you okay?"

I was not. Ouch.

"Sam had a thing about keeping the floors polished. It's like an ice rink in here," the agent said. Adam reappeared around the corner, having heard the thump of my fall.

"We need to talk," I pleaded.

"What about?" said Adam.

"About Stephanie. About your trip. About my trip. About everything."

"Not here," said Adam. "Not now."

"We need to talk about us."

I reached into my purse and pulled out the divorce papers. I held them away from my body like they were contaminated. Which they were. I stared at them for a moment, then I ripped them into piece after piece after piece and watched them rain onto Sam Fielder's Carrera marble floor.

Adam glared at me. *Who was this woman?* I would never make a scene in a public place. I reserved that kind of spectacle for the kitchen.

A flutter of hysteria bubbled in my stomach, but I didn't know if I was going to guffaw or weep. I studied Adam's face to help me decide. He shook his head in disgust or disbelief or both, then headed toward his office.

I stood frozen, eyes fixed on my husband's back moving down the hall. A damp hissing made me wonder if I had entered a parallel universe, a movie universe, where any worthwhile exit means disappearing into the steam of a departing train. Then I realized the sound was coming from a cappuccino machine. I turned the corner into the lobby and headed not for the elevator down to the garage, but for the front door.

I could feel a bruise already blooming on my butt where I'd landed hard. It throbbed. My walk took on the cadence of Tiny Tim, my three-inch heels click-*click*, click-*click*, click-*clicking*.

There was more than the usual buzz around the reception desk. I could hear the young receptionists giggling—Heidi and…was it Ashley? Tiffany? I glanced toward the desk. Matt Damon was chatting with the girls. I remembered when Sam had fired a receptionist for not demonstrating the proper degree of solicitousness to Tony Curtis.

"Jesus, Dad," Adam had said, "the girl's twenty-three years old. She's probably never seen a black and white movie."

"*Spartacus* is in color," Sam said. "One of the greats. 'I love you, Spartacus,' for Christsakes."

Now Sam was dead.

As I approached the bank of tittering receptionists, I wondered how he would have rated their treatment of Matt Damon. I had to hand it to the old man. When it came to stars' egos, he always knew the precise note to hit without pandering, or at least without the appearance of pandering.

Matt Damon smiled at me as I passed, acting as though he hadn't noticed that I had just made a fool of myself.

I pushed open the front door. It swung onto the wide thoroughfare of Ocean Avenue, a stretch of promenade dotted with chunky palms, then dropping off to the ocean beyond. I crossed the boulevard and walked south toward the pier, drawn by the slow spin of its Ferris wheel.

It was easy to feel that I had somehow left LA. Foreign languages swirled around me. Farsi, Lebanese, French. Travelers eager to see the water. Transplants picnicking with their families. These were the people who gravitated toward the bluffs, accustomed as they were to living their lives in public spaces—not Americans. Not Angelenos anyway. Angelenos were accustomed to living their lives in their cars.

I walked along the promenade, gasping to stretch my lungs. I could feel the rub of a blister beginning on the back of my heel, so I took off my pumps and slung them over my shoulder hooked on two fingers. The grass was not soft and springy—rather, spiky against my soles as though each blade had been razor sharpened.

I had almost reached the pier when my cell phone rang. It was Barbara.

"They're on their way," she said.

# CHAPTER THIRTY-EIGHT

THAT'S THE WAY IT had been for the last several years. No advance warning. Only our mother shouting into the cell phone, announcing their imminent arrival, while our father turned the two hour drive from Palm Springs into three.

"We're on our way," Mother would say, not only too loudly, but with the exaggerated enunciation that suggested an abiding suspicion of using a phone in the car.

The vise grip on my temples tightened as I pictured my parents tooling along the far right lane of the San Bernardino Freeway—my dad behind the wheel of the '08 Volvo, my mother buckled into the passenger seat, reminding him every five minutes to keep a decent distance from the car in front. At least twice during the trip, Elliot would recite the rule, "I know, Joan, one car length per ten miles of speed."

"Just because you read the driver's handbook doesn't mean you're following it properly," Mother would say. It was one of their routines. During the past several visits, I had noticed that my parents' conversations tended to be a string of such routines. Their marriage had gone into reruns.

I hadn't seen my parents since Adam moved out. It had not been difficult to present a lighthearted version of the situation over the phone.

"It's nothing."

"You know how these things are."

"Don't worry about it."

My mother did not press for details, though chances were she had logged major phone time with Barbara speculating, criticizing, accusing—me, never Adam. Joan Locke had spent her married life swathing her husband in the cotton batting of blissful ignorance. She expected me to do the same. If it came to divorce...well, the Lockes didn't do divorce.

When I heard the Volvo chug into the driveway, I rearranged my features into a facsimile of all-is-well and trotted out front.

"I guess your sister's at the office," Joan said as I opened the car door. Of course my mother's opening remark would be about Barbara. Everything was always about Barbara. That's the way it had been ever since Barbara hit puberty with a vengeance and claimed center stage.

I offered my mother a hand out of the car, but she waved me away. I had forgotten how completely my mother had transformed from Westside mom to desert retiree. Her hair was now so very all one shade—country club ash. She wore it in a stiff bob that pointed at her jaw. Today she was sporting a lime-and-turquoise ensemble that would have screamed like a banshee from the closet that once contained the sedate clothing of the Ridgepoint Mothers' Club secretary. Her striped blouse felt crispy in my arms when we hugged.

"We're only staying one night," Mother declared.

Okay.

Glancing over my mother's shoulder, I noticed that my father was moving in slo-mo. He took some time straightening himself out from behind the wheel, but never seemed to reach his full height. I really wanted a hug from my father today. I wanted to rest my head against his chest and close my eyes and be the little girl who could never have imagined having a tantrum in the corridor of a chrome and glass office building overlooking the ocean. But when I embraced him, my head did not rest against his chest as it used to. In fact, I could lower it to his shoulder. He had become the incredible shrinking father.

"How was the drive?" I asked.

"We had to crank up the AC," my father said. "It'll affect my mileage."

"Yeah, I guess it might," I said.

"Is Stephanie home?" Mother asked.

"It's a school day," I said.

"Well, I know that," Mother responded, though I wasn't so sure. Didn't Palm Springs days all sweat together?

"I've hardly seen her since I've been back," I added.

"Oh yes, how was your trip?"

"Good," I said.

"That's good," echoed Mother.

"I'm sorry we didn't make it to the old man's funeral," Dad said.

"Dad wasn't feeling well. You were congested, Elliot, remember?" Mom said. "So much phlegm," she added to me.

"It's okay. Really," I said.

"We should have been there," Dad asserted.

"Nobody missed us, Elliot," Mother said. "They had movie stars."

My father had no respect for the business of entertainment. He was a man ahead of his time. An environmental scientist before there was such a thing, he dedicated his life to erasing the handwriting on the wall before it had ever been scribbled. He worked in a think tank and lived in his head. His daughters baffled him and we knew it.

One July afternoon, our father came upon us in the backyard squeezing lemon juice onto the tendrils of hair surrounding our faces as per the diagram in *Seventeen* magazine. We listened while he explained the mechanics of the bleaching process. After several minutes Barbara asked, "But, Daddy, do you think Chad will notice?" He was at a loss for an answer. That was Dad.

Our mother, on the other hand, always had a comment.

"You could use a little trim," she said now, sweeping my hair behind my shoulders. It was longer than it had been in years, below my collarbone. Mom slid a section between her fingers as though they were scissors, as if providing a template for a stylist. The extra two inches of length violated my mother's rule about hair past the age of forty. She cast an eye down my body, a quick once-over well-practiced.

"Those are some tight jeans."

"That's the style." I wore a long tunic that ended well below my rear. Skinny jeans were okay if you wore a long enough top over them, even at my age. I'd read that in *More* magazine, the grown-up version of *Seventeen*. I had dropped five pounds since Adam had gone and the top masked that, too. I would escape a comment about my looking a little scrawny. They came together like Macbeth's three witches: Mom's remarks on hair, weight, and attire. The mother-daughter trifecta.

I busied myself unloading suitcases and bags of groceries. "You didn't need to bring all this food," I said.

"You can't get grapefruit like this here," Dad insisted.

"And we stopped at Hadley's," Mother added. "I know how you girls love those dates."

In fact, I had always loved the date milk shakes served at the roadside place twenty minutes west of Palm Springs. The plain dates—not such a thrill. But I would exclaim over them. Even if it meant that all future visits would bring more of the same.

It took my parents nearly an hour to settle in. I tried to help with the unpacking, but Mom insisted, "How will I know where things are if you put them away?"

I wondered why they'd brought so much for an overnight, but when I looked more closely, I realized they had brought very little. The unpacking just took a really long time. My parents were moving slowly, so much more slowly than they used to.

At one point, Dad sat on the edge of the bed in the guest room. He pretended to be testing the mattress, but I could see that he was out of breath. I sat next to him and took his hand. It was the slightest bit clammy. I caught my father's eye and he winked at me.

"Do you want to leave your shaving gear in your Dopp kit, Elliot?" Mom asked from the bathroom.

"Sure," he said, standing slowly.

Mother emerged from the bathroom and eyed the eight or nine UPS boxes stacked in the corner of the room. When Barbara had called to say our parents were on their way, I made a mental note to remove the boxes, but I'd misplaced that note the minute I walked into the house. In fact, when I went to hang clean towels in the guest room bath, I had not even noticed the boxes. They didn't register anymore.

"What's all that?" Mother asked.

"Just some stuff," I said.

"What kind of stuff?"

"Stuff I ordered. Clothes and stuff."

"My goodness," said Mother. "Who are they for?"

I pretended not to have heard the question while folding a lime-and-turquoise striped polo shirt pulled from my father's suitcase. Lately, my parents came as a matched set. "Wow, Dad, this is some shirt," I said.

"Pretty snazzy, huh?" He handed me a worn Members Only jacket for me to hang up. It needed to be laundered, or better yet, thrown out.

"Are they all for you?" Mother persisted.

I nodded.

"Why do you need so many new clothes?"

"I don't know."

"Don't you want to open them at least?"

"I will. I haven't gotten around to it."

"Well, I don't get it. You buy all these new things but you can't really need them or they wouldn't still be sitting in their boxes. Seems a horrible waste of money to me."

I slipped my father's windbreaker onto a hanger.

My mother was not finished. "I mean, honestly, you weren't raised that way."

"What way is that, Mother?"

"To be such a spendthrift." She spat out the word as though she were accusing me of shooting heroin.

"Frankly, the way I was raised doesn't seem to be relevant anymore," I proposed.

"Relevant? What does that have to do with anything? Relevant to what?"

"I think Mother and I better take our afternoon nap," said Dad.

"I better start dinner," I said and left my father hanging up a pair of well-pressed pajamas.

But I did not head for the kitchen. I retreated to my bedroom and closed the door behind me. I stood there, trying to remember exactly how I had been raised. My mother was right. It hadn't been this way, whatever this way was.

Sure, there were girls at Ridgepoint who came from old Los Angeles money. Girls whose fathers were captains of industry; fathers who oversaw holdings that dated back a generation or two;

fathers whose first names appeared in the school roster as a string of initials, mysteriously suggestive of power. There was the Lower School girl who was picked up by a chauffeur every afternoon and the Upper School girl who lived four houses down the street but drove a carnation pink T-bird to school—the sporty model with the porthole.

I thought back to the time when Prudence Horsfall came over to play. After an hour or so of Barbies, we headed down to the kitchen to make root beer floats. My mother was stationed behind the ironing board, gliding the pale blue Sunbeam over one of my uniforms. Pru's eyes widened.

"Do Mommies iron?" she asked, incredulous.

"Well," said my mother, "this one does."

No, I had not been raised that way. In fact, my parents were frugal. My mother spent countless afternoons pasting S & H Green Stamps into book after book. Barbara and I joined her in the kitchen, sitting at the pumpkin-colored Formica counter, poring over the Green Stamp catalogue. Earnestly, we debated the relative merits of a Chemex coffee pot or that most exotic of new appliances, a Salton yogurt-maker. It didn't matter that we neither drank coffee nor had ever tasted yogurt—the white goo pictured in a small glass container, a sort of mason jar-cum-petri dish. It was fun to study the catalogue. It was fun to ooh and aah over the latest, the greatest, the shiniest. It was fun to get something for free.

Suddenly, standing there in the middle of my bedroom, behind its closed door, I knew that my gallivanting from shopping site to shopping site was not in pursuit of the perfect pair of jeans or the cutest top. What I had been chasing was the thrill I had known hunched over that Green Stamp catalogue, the thrill of picking something out and knowing that, in time, the precise thing I had chosen would arrive.

When the doorbell rang now, I could not remember what might be arriving. I had become accustomed to forgetting what I'd ordered, but I usually had a vague memory of ordering *something*. Today, I couldn't even remember clicking on "Place Order."

It was not Doug, the UPS man. Or Juan, the FedEx guy. It was a messenger. He checked his e-clipboard. "Maura Fielder?"

"Yes."

He handed me an envelope. It was from Fielder Creative Management. I signed for the delivery, then ripped open the tab. Inside: the torn-up pieces that had been the divorce papers...and a roll of Scotch tape. I carried the divorce confetti to the kitchen where I sprinkled it across the top of the table. It took me twenty minutes, give or take, to reconstruct the deconstruction document, piece by piece, like a jigsaw puzzle. But I didn't read it again after it was put back together. Why bother? I knew it by heart. Then I picked up a pen, turned the paper over and began to write.

♦♦♦

MOTHER COUNTED OUT THE silverware. "We're dying to see your new office," she said to Barbara who was tearing lettuce into a salad bowl. I basted the roast chicken. It was the first proper dinner I'd made in ages, since the week of the Crockpot. I tended to the bird nervously—an odd recipe, calling for both milk and lemons. I smashed at the little curds with the back of my wooden spoon.

"What floor did you say it's on?" Mother asked.

"Seventeenth," Barbara said.

"That should be okay," Mother answered. "My ears give me trouble if I go above twenty floors. I'd be deaf as a doornail for the rest of the day."

"It would be worth it," I insisted, trying to make my big sister's life shimmer. "Barbara's office is spectacular."

"I was watching 20/20 the other day," said Mother, "or maybe Dateline, one of those."

"They all keep your mother up at night," Dad chimed in from the dining room. "I have no idea why she insists on watching them. All they do is give her something to stew about for days."

"Your father doesn't know what he's talking about," she said.

I carried the silverware into the dining room, clutching it like a bouquet. "As it so happens, this show...it's the one with the pretty young woman with the dark hair...great haircut, chin length..."

Barbara and I locked eyes: message received.

Mother continued, "20/20, I think...it was all about the happiest jobs. And they said that travel agent ranks as one of the happiest professions. That's why you're a natural. You've always had a special gift for happiness, for finding the happy in things."

I turned my back on my mother to maneuver the chicken out of the oven. Did that mean that I myself had a particular gift for unhappiness? I set to carving the chicken. As I disjointed a thigh, I wondered why it felt like every single statement my mother made about Barbara carried an equal and opposite statement about me, like a law of physics.

Mother mounded rice pilaf into a serving dish. A grain of rice fell under the metal grate on a burner of the cooktop. She set aside her task to remove the grate and dig out the grain, using her Conga Line Coral nails as tongs.

"That's some color, Mother," said Barbara.

"It's from the Caribbean collection."

"Wow," said Barbara.

"Wow," said I.

"Where's Stephanie?" Mother asked for the fifth time since they'd arrived.

"She's at school," I said. "She works on the school paper. It's a production night."

"What does that mean?"

"It means she won't be home 'til really late."

With the naked burners exposed, Mother spotted a splotch where some butter had scorched on the stove. She grabbed a scrubby sponge from the sink and began to scour, leaving me to finish ladling the pilaf into its serving dish. I carried the dishes into the dining room. That's the way Joan Locke served dinner. *Father Knows Best* style. As I placed them on the linen runner, my father crooked a finger, beckoning. I stepped closer.

"You know, honey," he whispered, "your mother gave me strict orders not to mention anything…about anything. You know her. 'No unpleasantness, Elliot.' But are you okay?"

I threw my arms around my father's neck. He patted my back stiffly, like he was burping me.

"I'm trying to be," I said.

"Good girl," said Daddy. "That's my good girl."

It was the first time we had been around a dinner table, the four of us, in no one could remember how long. After the last time Adam and I had entertained, I neglected to remove the leaves that extended the dining room table, so now the four Lockes sat around the table with vast distances between us.

Barbara set about composing her dinner plate. She painstakingly separated the skin from a few slices of chicken breast, leaving it behind on the serving platter. She shuffled through the pilaf with the serving spoon, trying to manage a scoop containing neither pine nuts nor currants, but plentiful with snippets of dried apricot. Finally, she served herself some green beans, scraping any traces of butter off each bean with her fork. Of these, she created a distinct pile to one side of her plate.

"Whatever are you doing?" Mother asked.

"I'm on an elimination diet," Barbara replied.

"Why would you be doing such a thing?" Mother wondered.

"I think I may have food allergies that are hindering my performance."

"Performance?" Dad said.

"You know, optimal health, energy, well-being."

My mother stared at Barbara's plate. "You kept the apricots."

"Orange foods are our friends. Beta-carotene."

Joan shook her head. "We forgot drinks," she said.

It took me a moment to realize this was my house and not my mother's. I hopped up and returned with a pitcher of water.

We ate in silence for several minutes, Dad nodding his approval of the food with every bite. Adam was good at filling these conversational holes. I realized I had not spent any significant time with my parents without Adam in twenty years. I no longer knew how to navigate that relationship without him. He smoothed out the jagged edges. The way I had done for him with Sam. This evening, without Adam, I found myself impaled. Even on the silence.

Finally, Mother said, "Are you girls going to the Ridgepoint reunion?"

"I don't think so," I said.

"You have to go," Joan insisted.

"Actually, I don't have to," I countered.

"I might want to go," said Barbara.

"I really don't want to see all those girls right now," I said.

I passed the salad to my father. He helped himself and passed it on to Barbara.

"You should go," Mother reiterated. "You never know if it's your last chance to see some of those girls."

"That's cheery," I said.

"I'm just saying, life is unpredictable," my mother said.

"I guess we should go," Barbara suggested, then she broke into song: "Ridgepoint, thy daughters bring homage to thee…"

I joined her in singing the alma mater, but we petered out at the end of the first chorus. "We pledge our loyal love, Ridgepoint to thee."

"Who do you think might show up?" I asked.

"The usual suspects," Barbara said.

"Who were those twins that looked like the girl from *The Bad Seed*?"

"Oh God, I know who you mean. What were their names?"

I bolted from the table to fetch the Ridgepoint yearbook. I knew exactly where it was—on a shelf in the den. It was covered in ecru linen. A dark green laurel wreath dotted the second "i" in "Ridgepoint."

Dad glanced at the words meant to appear stitched on the cover in forest green. *Lux Puellarum.* "Light of the girls," he translated.

I placed the book in front of Barbara. "After my time," Barbara said.

"It's from my senior year." I flipped through the pages. "Here they are. Sally and Susan Van Port."

"Of course," Barbara said. "Any Van Port in a storm."

I laughed. Mother looked at us quizzically. "It's a long story," I said.

"Having to do with the autumn mixer with Black Fox Military School," Barbara explained.

Mother raised both hands, palms forward. Spare her the details.

I opened the book to my senior page. A full page was devoted to every senior girl, each featuring a black and white portrait. Mine— my face half-shadowed by a tree branch, arms folded across my chest, my uniform blazer buttoned just so over my white Oxford shirt. I gazed into the distance, toward my future.

"Very author's photo from the back flap of a book jacket," said Barbara, holding the picture for all to see as though she were showing an illustration to a group of children. She read off the vital statistics summing up my Ridgepoint career. Cum Laude Society. Assistant Editor, Literary Magazine. Lux Copy Editor. Class Historian. French Club. Proctor Committee. Uniform Committee Chairman.

"See what a good time you had?" Mother said. "You should go."

"Oh yeah," I quipped, "a great time. I'd give anything to relive those laugh-a-minute days on the Proctor Committee."

"How about etiquette class?" Barbara chimed in.

"They taught you lovely posture," Mother said.

"They taught us how to stifle a sneeze," Barbara said.

"They took us on a field trip to Geary's to teach us how to pick out wedding china," I remembered.

Mother picked up the salad tongs, struggling to manipulate them, and served my father another helping of salad even though there was still plenty on his plate. "Do what you want," she said.

"How's Gwen?" Dad piped up.

"Gwen's a piece of work," Barbara volunteered.

"She's fine," I said.

"I always liked her. Smart girl," Dad said.

"Very polite," said Mother.

"Well, she's fine," I reiterated. "Her brother had his gall bladder out, but he's fine now, too."

"Oh my goodness," Mother said, "so young."

"I think it happens a lot in middle age," Barbara said.

"Oh, you girls aren't middle-aged," Mother protested.

"Well, one of us isn't," I said.

Barbara threw a green bean at me. I picked up a piece of charred lemon baked with the chicken and prepared to launch.

"Girls!" Mother gasped. "Honestly."

I returned the lemon to my plate. "You didn't behave this way when you were little, for heaven's sake. Dinner time was always the nicest time of the day and you were both perfectly well-mannered."

"Yeah, we were fine. You were the one who was always storming away from the table," Barbara said to my mother.

"What are you talking about?" Mother asked.

"You know, one of us would say something that rubbed you the wrong way and you'd get up and go to your room and close the door and that would be the last we'd see of you for the night."

"I always figured it was your sneaky way of getting us to do the dishes," I added.

"I have absolutely no idea what you're talking about," Mother said, resting her knife and fork, tines up, diagonally on the side of her plate, indicating she was quite finished, thank you very much.

"It happened all the time," I insisted. "Remember, Daddy?"

All three of us turned to my father. He finished chewing a bite of chicken. "I vaguely remember something like that. Once or twice."

"Once or twice?" Barbara laughed.

"It was practically a nightly occurrence for two years," I said. "When Mom was...you know, going through the change, shall we say?"

"Maura!" Mother pushed her chair away from the table.

"It's true, Mom. And believe me, I totally get it. Hormones are the root of all evil."

"I never went through any such thing. I never did any such thing. You must be thinking of your other mother." With that, she stood from the table and began clearing the dishes, sliding Dad's plate out from under him as he was about to spear a green bean.

I grabbed the bowl of pilaf and followed her into the kitchen.

"I'm sorry, Mother. I didn't mean anything. It's funny after all these years, don't you think?"

I dumped the rice down the garbage disposal.

"Well," she said, "that's a sin and a crime. Throwing away perfectly decent food like that." She shook her head longer than required in honor of a clod of rice sucked down the disposal.

"What is it, Mother?' I asked.

"What is what?"

"What's on your mind?"

"I have no clue what you're talking about."

"Please," I demanded, "just say it. It'll make all our lives so much easier."

"Okay, then," she acquiesced, "Do you want to be a divorcee? Is that what you really want? Remember Dorothy Davison? Miss High-and-Mighty? Ended up having to drive herself to chemotherapy."

"You don't automatically get cancer because you get divorced," I asserted. I turned to Barbara. "Do you?" I asked. Twinge of panic.

Barbara shrugged: don't ask me—I'm just a spectator.

"Make fun all you like," Mother huffed. Barbara and I did the simultaneous eye roll. Mother had "that tone" as in *Mother's got that tone*. "I'd like to know exactly what it is that you expect. What do you expect, Maura?"

"I wish people would stop asking me that!" I jammed the last of the pilaf down the disposal with the wooden spoon.

"She insisted I say what was on my mind," Mother reminded Barbara as though I were no longer present.

Left alone in the dining room, Dad was thumbing through the yearbook. He paused to examine a photograph of the arch that marked the Ridgepoint Great Hall. He read the inscription aloud: "Prestolatio Excellentiatum."

"What did you say, Dad?" Barbara asked.

"Your motto. Expectation of excellence."

"Okay, I'll go," I said.

"Only if you want to," Mother replied.

I wished I didn't even know there was going to be a stupid reunion. The simple knowledge that it was taking place made me feel like I was obliged to go. I could go and be anxious ahead of time and depressed after. Or not go and feel guilty.

"I'll leave it in the hands of the wardrobe gods," I said, wandering off to Adam's study. In the search box, I typed "cocktail dress."

Wikipedia informed me that the length of the cocktail dress varies depending on fashion and local custom. I wondered what constituted the local custom of the Ridgepoint girl. Were we all so much a type? Like DAR ladies in their St. John knits or Jungian therapists in flowing earth mother skirts and massive turquoise jewelry? What were the sartorial hallmarks of a Ridgepoint girl? And would I be caught dead wearing them?

My eyes wandered down the page, scanning links to prom dresses, homecoming dresses, beaded dresses, fashion dresses (whatever that meant), the little black dress, and the promise of "more than just a cocktail dress" cocktail dresses. I almost clicked on "party dresses." It felt like the most fitting category for revisiting the population of my childhood, but I continued to scroll down. I did not pause on sites hawking dresses labeled "funktional" or "sex-a-delic." I was tempted to click on "rockabilly" dresses if only to see what they could possibly be. With one click of the mouse, I could travel anywhere from JCPenney to Bergdorf's.

Perhaps the designer route would prove less daunting.

I navigated to my fallback shopping site, then clicked my way through a series of steps with championship speed. Given the bargain I had made with myself—wardrobe determining attendance—I barely scanned each screen as it appeared, half-hoping I would come up empty.

But then, there it was. One of those dresses that had my name on it—a flattering wrap with a three-quarter sleeve that would hide the weird crepiness recently developing on my upper arms. (At first, I had thought a sweater had left the slightest shadow of its weave, but no, it seemed to be my actual skin.) The website offered the dress in several colors. I was immediately attracted to the green. They called it Irish Jade. I forgave the cultural mixed metaphor and went for it, because it was, in fact, funktional and even slightly sex-a-delic while, mercifully, lacking any tinge of rockabilly.

I bought it with one click. And paid extra for overnight shipping.

◆◆◆

BARBARA HUNG AROUND UNTIL bedtime—our parents' bedtime. We knew the drill. *Don't leave me alone with them. Please.* Then I put my parents to bed, placed a decanter of water on the bedside table, and plugged in a bathroom nightlight.

"I'll leave the door open a crack," I said as I left the room. "Good night, Mother. Good night, Daddy."

"Why is Stephanie out so late?" Mother asked again. "Especially on a school night."

"The yearbook, Joan," my father reminded her. "She works on the school yearbook."

"The newspaper," I muttered.

I plodded upstairs to my bedroom. I'd give Stephen Colbert a chance to wipe away the day. He was doing his straight-legged high kicks when Stephanie appeared at the door, sniffling.

"Are you catching a cold?" I asked.

Stephanie shook her head no, but sniffled again. Then she erupted in great, heaving sobs.

"What is it?" *Oh no.*

Stephanie launched herself from the doorway onto the bed. She buried her face in my chest, sobbing as Colbert introduced his house band, Stay Human.

"What is it?" I cried again. "Tell me!"

Finally, Stephanie caught enough breath to manage, "Josh slept with Mallory." Another paroxysm of sobs.

"I don't understand," I said. "You're interested in Josh? I mean, you like him?" And I silently cursed Mallory for upping the ante. Would Stephanie now feel like she had to sleep with someone, too?

I took a breath. We'd had the talks. Diseases. Protection. Things you can't take back, things you can't undo. Now was not the time for a refresher.

"Mom," said Stephanie, exasperated between sobs, "he's my boyfriend. Where have you been?"

MIA.

"Okay," I said, "Josh and Mallory were going out and sleeping together and then he started seeing you?"

Stephanie pulled back and looked at me. "What?"

"I'm trying to get this straight. If Mallory's angry with you for going out with him…"

"Why would *she* be mad at *me*?"

"It sounds complicated." I was still struggling to fit the pieces. "You don't want to lose Mallory as a friend."

"It's not complicated," Stephanie declared. "It just sucks. I was going with Josh and then while I was away with Daddy looking at a bunch of stupid schools, he slept with my best friend." Another wail from somewhere primal.

"You and Josh…you already…" My mouth turned to cotton. Stephen Colbert was lying on a plaid blanket pondering the mysteries of the universe, doing his "Big Questions with Even Bigger Stars" thing. Robert DeNiro lay next to him.

"Can I ask you something, Bobby D.?" said Colbert.

Stephanie burrowed into me again. I stroked her hair. "It's okay. It's okay," I murmured.

She wiped her nose on the sleeve of my nightgown.

"You should never stand for that. Cheating is unacceptable," I choked out.

"I know," whimpered Stephanie. We stayed like that, mother and daughter, curled into one another on my bed, keening. Suddenly, the image in my brain was no longer of Josh Lafferty resting his hand on Stephanie's hip proprietarily. The image was of his father. And the silver-blue halo cast around him by the swimming pool light as he lowered himself onto me.

I began to wail with such ferocity that now Stephanie was the one cradling my head in her arms. There, there.

"You know, Stevie…" said DeNiro, as though he didn't get what was funny about this bit at all.

# CHAPTER THIRTY-NINE

I DESCENDED INTO THE bowels of the parking structure, winding down, down, down, the crackling flicker of the fluorescents overhead. I had tamped down the dread of this moment ever since the man in the suit thrust the papers in my hand on the schoolyard. I had traveled to London to quash the dread. But now it came rising up like bile, reminding me that it had been there all along, a psychic walking pneumonia you can no longer pretend does not require antibiotics. As I corkscrewed down, level after level, my guilt welled up. I deserved this. I did this. Adam may have lit the fuse, but I was the bomb who exploded.

I checked the scrap of paper with the lawyer's information. Thirty-second floor. The express elevator shot me up. I stopped short at the door to the suite. The plaque said "Family Law." Who were they kidding? It was end-of-family law.

I announced myself at the reception desk and sat on the Eames couch. There was no getting comfy on this thing, but then again, this was an office in the business of dismantling households.

Jonathan Granville's assistant escorted me to a corner office. Granville was on the phone, but motioned me in, nodding toward the couch. I was fairly certain the Miro hanging above it was the real deal. Surrealism—how very appropriate for this passage into the alternate universe of divorce.

I studied the man behind the desk—a massive chrome tree trunk of a base, two-inch glass slab atop, green-edged and glowing like neon. Granville was all whippet angles. He looked like he used one of those hair products that promise the look of an afternoon spent at the beach. He offered me an exaggerated shrug: sorry, trying my best to get off this call. But he was in the middle of making a point.

"Listen," he said, "your client has a twenty-two-year-old pregnant girlfriend in Shanghai..." Granville's face lit up. Score! "Oh. This is news to you...Well, let's talk after you've had a little chat with your guy." Granville hung up and smiled at me. "Like they don't have private eyes in China," he chuckled.

He stood and extended his hand. "Jonathan Granville. So nice to meet you, Maura."

He touch-latched a section of built-in cabinetry to reveal a mini fridge and handed me a Fiji water. "I had a good conversation with your sister. Nice lady. She filled me in..."

*What had Barbara told him?*

"She wants only the best for you," said Attorney Granville as he perched on the corner of his desk and uncapped his own bottle of water. He took a swig. "Do you have the papers?" he asked.

I handed over a manila envelope. "They're a little worse for wear," I explained. Granville pulled out the papers taped together like a jigsaw puzzle. No reaction. There were no surprises left in his business.

"I know what you're hoping for," Granville segued.

I leaned forward, eager to be clued in.

"You're hoping for a nice, amicable divorce. You'll stay buddies. He'll carve the turkey at Thanksgiving. Your friends won't have to sit you in different times zones at weddings and bar mitzvahs. You'll smile at each other over cake at the grandkids' birthday parties." My eyes welled with tears. As much at the sudden image of grandchildren as anything else.

"It's not going to happen," said Granville matter-of-factly.

I shook my head. No?

"That's not your situation," he began. "Your father-in-law left your husband a business worth millions. Tens and tens of millions. Maybe more. That's the good news. For him. For you, not such good news. Inheritance is not community property. Worse, you were already separated when the old man died. Your sister mentioned that you're the one who packed your husband's bags. Not what I would have advised."

I struggled to focus on what he was saying.

"I'm not going to sugarcoat anything," he continued. "You're living in a neighborhood you can't afford. You need a take-no-prisoners strategy and that's what we do here. We audit your husband. We sic a forensic accountant on Fielder Creative Management… Your Scotch tape or his?" he asked, waving the papers in my face.

"Um…his actually."

"There you go. He used a business asset for personal expenses."

My eyes widened. Partly because this was crazy. Partly because this guy was scary good.

"No matter what you may think," he said, looking directly into my eyes. "Every divorce is kill or be killed. The truth is someone is going to end up in a two-bedroom apartment in the Valley. North of the boulevard. And you don't want that someone to be you."

No, I shook my head again, I did not want that someone to be me. I did not want that someone to be Adam either.

Granville had more. "The truth is…when it comes to the kids… they follow the money."

"I have one child. A daughter."

"But with luck, you'll have grandkids. And they'll follow the money also." Granville kept going. "If you're not the one who ends up with the house…if you're not the one taking the kids to Maui for spring break…if you're not the one who can afford to buy them cars, to pay their college tuition, to make the down payment on their first homes, and to help them out with private school tuitions for those grandkids you're going to have, and God willing, great-grandkids, what you'll get from them are excuses at Christmas and a text on your birthday."

"My daughter…" I ventured, my voice hitching. Stephanie would never do that.

"As for your friends," Granville was gaining speed. "They'll proclaim neutrality like fucking Switzerland, excuse my French, but sooner or later, they'll take sides. And you know where that side is?"

I shook my head.

"This side of Mulholland Drive. Your best friend is not going to sit in canyon traffic, or worse yet, that parking lot known as the 405, to listen to you whine about your divorce over a hot dog at Art's Deli. Which spouse gets the hot dog at Nate'n Al's?"

"Which?"

"The spouse I represent," Granville crowed. He chugged his water, downing the whole eight ounces, suggesting the task ahead was going to require a great deal of hydration. "Listen, I get it. This isn't how you expected your life to look. It doesn't match the picture you had in your head. But trust me. We're going to have fun. By the time we're done, your son will never speak to him again."

"You've got your facts wrong, Mr. Granville," I said. Granville opened his mouth to interrupt, but I raised a hand to silence him. My turn. "First of all, I've got a daughter. Not a son. Second, my best friend would go to Pacoima to have a hot dog with me. And finally, my husband is a nice man."

Again, Granville started to jump in. This time I held up my index finger while I considered precisely how to phrase what it was I wanted to say. "My husband is a good man. I don't want to punish him. I want to be married to him."

◆◆◆

I SPENT THE NEXT twenty minutes searching for my car in the parking structure. I wandered from floor to floor, aisle to aisle, pressing the key fob clutched in my hand in a one-sided game of Marco Polo. Finally, my car beeped in reply, a distant chirp that I followed—warmer, warmer.

I headed west from Century City on Pico Blvd. I did not want to go home, could not face the empty house. I was even strangely repulsed by the notion of roaming my favorite shopping sites. I did not want to see Barbara. I was proud of the way she had embraced her new job, but now was not the time to hear about how she had upgraded an amenities package.

I continued west past Fox Studios where there were no reminders of the old New York street backlot, only massive billboards for TV shows I had never heard of. I thought of calling Gwen to meet for coffee, but an update on her beau-du-jour would exhaust me. I wished I could see Ernesto. I wished he could sit next to me and read *Frog and Toad Together*, but it wasn't a Monday, and besides, the volunteer term had ended. Worse still, when the new school year began, I was not going to be his third grade Reading Lady.

I loved these people. All of them. But Adam was my person.

With no place to go, I did what girls who grew up in LA do. I drove. Side street after side street, anywhere that bypassed the gridlock. It didn't matter where the smoother-flowing tributaries took me.

Today, at five o'clock, they happened to take me to Daniel Lilliani.

♦♦♦

DANIEL USHERED ME IN and led me down to the studio where he was doodling a still life haphazardly arranged on a card table in the corner. I sat on the couch, a low-slung banquette attached to two walls so that when you were seated, eye level lined up precisely with the ideal view of the neighboring hillsides. Daniel poured some sherry into a cut crystal glass as though I were an aged auntie come to call. He commented that he had been working on my portrait that morning, but I did not ask how it was coming along.

"To what do I owe the pleasure of your company?" he asked.

All I could do was shake my head.

"How can I help?" he asked.

"I don't know what to do."

"Well, that's always a good place to start," Daniel said, his mid-Atlantic affectation calming me.

"Things have gone from bad to worse," I said.

"They do that, don't they? Usually before they get better."

"Not this time. Adam's responsible for the bad. But I'm the idiot who made them worse. And there's no going back to just plain bad. Better's a whole other planet."

Daniel poured himself a sherry.

"I was thinking how you have the best stories," I said. "How they always make me feel...I don't know...hopeful."

"That's the nicest thing anyone's ever said to me," said Daniel. He took my hand between his two.

My tears blurred the canyon view sprawling beyond the plate glass window, transforming it from hyperrealism to Impressionism.

Daniel raised his glass to his lips, holding it by its stem. The sunlight boomeranged off a chiseled diamond in the crystal and sliced through my retina, exploding into a starburst. I had a second or two to realize it was coming. Then, sure enough, it hit. Through the window, across the canyon, a swimming pool—moments before tranquil and glassy—appeared suddenly whisked by an unseen eddy.

I slumped back onto the couch and closed my eyes. Dampness was already gathering at my hairline and beneath my lower lip.

"What is it, dear?" Daniel asked.

I raised a hand to answer: it's nothing—it will pass. But my hand dropped so limply that Daniel was alarmed.

"Should I call a doctor?"

I was afraid to shake my head. No movement of the head. No movement at all. No movement. No.

"Vertigo," I whispered.

"Oh my goodness," he said. "Oh my goodness."

My eyes closed. I did not even know that Daniel had left the room when he returned with a damp cloth.

"I'm going to put a cool cloth on your forehead," he told me, like a doctor warning of a slight pressure before a minor procedure. I wanted to tell him that wouldn't work, but did not have the energy; the roiling was too far beneath the surface to be stilled by a cloth.

I was still lying there, just there, as the afternoon turned to evening. Daniel described to me the metamorphosis—the stripes of glare dimming, gradually soft focused around the edges until the clouds turned to wisps of cotton candy against the ombre sky. He spoke softly, seated next to me, holding my hand. Not stroking it, not tapping it—no motion, no motion. Just holding. Then he fell silent.

The room was dark when I opened my eyes. I was not sure where I was until I noticed Daniel's battered thermos, lid off, resting against the chipped enamel sheet pan he used as a palette. They formed a still life of their own, suggesting a story far more intriguing than the artichokes and lemons positioned on the card table.

"I'm so sorry," I said.

"Not at all," said Daniel.

"I ruined your day."

Now he patted my hand. "My days are not so important."

I sat up. The room stayed put. "I'm okay."

"I'm glad."

I leaned against the couch, adjusting a pillow at the small of my back. "This isn't what I ordered," I said.

"Vertigo can be quite debilitating."

"No. I mean for my life. This isn't what I ordered."

"I don't think anyone gets precisely what they ordered. There's always some mix-up in the kitchen."

I chuckled as I sat up slowly, leaning against the cool, well-worn leather of the banquette.

"You've spoken to Adam, I'm guessing," I said.

"Yes," he said simply.

"If I hadn't kept digging, would it have run its course and been over with on its own? If I'd left it all alone, would it have gone away? Evaporated?"

"I don't know, dear," he said.

I nodded. No one would ever know.

"But that's not who you are," he said. "And that's okay."

"Is it?" I said.

"It is. That's all any of us can be."

"Would you tell me if you knew Adam was cheating on me? I mean not just this email thing, but for real? Would you tell me if he'd ever cheated on me?"

He didn't answer right away. Daniel was not given to knee-jerk responses. "I'm not sure," he said finally. "I suppose it would depend on how I found out and if I'd made a promise to him."

Not the answer I wanted to hear.

"But I can tell you this. Of all the men I know...of all the men I've ever known, Adam is the least likely to cheat. Now that I think about it, I would be stunned to find out that he had cheated on you, Maura. Positively stunned."

"Sort of like the neighbor next door that everyone says was so nice and quiet until he bursts into a Burger King with an AK-47."

He chuckled, but shook his head. "No. Nothing like that at all, Maura. Besides, you didn't ask me if I thought he was capable of mass murder."

I slumped back again, head resting against the top of the banquette.

"What can I do for you, Maura?" he asked.

"Tell me the story of the Chagall."

Of all the stories about her parents that Daniel used to tell Stephanie when she was little, this had been her favorite.

"Very well." Daniel sifted through the collection of stories in his brain.

"You and Adam were taking an Art History class. He was a senior..."

"And I was a sophomore," I chimed in.

"Adam had noticed you over the course of the semester. You sat in front and were always bent over your notebook scribbling furiously. He sat behind you, so mostly all he saw was the back of your head. But there was something about that back of the head."

I smiled.

Daniel continued. "It was the end of the term. May."

"May thirteenth," I interjected.

"For your final paper of the year, the professor required that you analyze a painting of your choice. You and Adam both chose the Chagall."

"*The Birthday*," I specified.

"Yes. *The Birthday*. A lovely piece. It has such a dreamy quality. All of Chagall does, of course, but there's something about that one. Some people say the woman is in mourning because of her black dress and that it's her lover's spirit descending to kiss her. But I don't think so..."

"Oh no, neither do I. He's leaping to kiss her."

"With ordinary daily life hovering all around the edges and there they are—a couple floating in the center. He's bending to her, twisting really. He'll do anything to kiss her."

"Anything," I said. "He'll shape shift in any way he needs to just to kiss her."

"Precisely."

I opened my eyes. Continue please.

"So Adam approached you and he said, 'You're doing the Chagall, too.'" I nodded. "And you started talking. You intended to do a research paper and Adam had in mind more of a personal essay. And you started talking, and Adam had never felt so comfortable with someone before."

"Neither had I."

"You know," said Daniel. "There's more to that story. Surely Adam must have told you by now—why he chose the Chagall."

"Because there was so much to say about it."

"No," said Daniel. "Because you had already chosen it."

I sat up fully, leaning forward. "Because I chose it? I thought it was because he loved it."

"Same difference, as they say. He waited for you to pick first. If you had chosen the Rembrandt, he would have chosen the Rembrandt. If you had chosen the Matisse, he would have chosen the Matisse."

"But he loved the Chagall," I said.

"He loved *you*," Daniel insisted. "Already."

# CHAPTER FORTY

THE RIDGEPOINT SCHOOL FOR Girls was no longer. Sort of. It was about to be corrupted. By boys. The school was merging with the one remaining boys' school in Los Angeles. Ridgepoint alumnae protested passionately, writing letters and attending meetings, voicing their existential concern that it would be the girls who would sink in the impending estrogen/testosterone soup. To no effect. The merger was on. This final pre-merger reunion would be a last hurrah before male cooties permeated the halls.

I didn't want to go. Fabulous wrap dress or no. I phoned Barbara early that morning.

"I can't go to this thing. I just can't." My voice broke. "A person can't go to a reunion when their life is this big a mess."

"I get it," she said. "I wouldn't have wanted to go if I didn't have this great job."

"But you go," I said.

"No, I can't go without you. It's okay. There'll be another one."

"No, I'll go," I said. "We'll go. It'll be a hoot." Because Barbara— worshipped wild child turned gluten-free matron—was still my big sister and she deserved to have a really good wingman in a roomful of Ridgepoint girls.

I told Barbara to head over as I stared at the snow globe collection across the room. They had become so much visual white noise like the life truths in Stephanie's essay. Alternately exquisite, silly, and kitsch, they all deserved their due. I opened the glass doors of the cabinet and picked one up—San Francisco's fog globe. I shook it and watched the glitter obscure the Golden Gate Bridge. I held a few more in my hands—Sedona's pink jeep, Vienna's ferris wheel. Then I opened the drawer below the cabinet and took out the Big Apple.

It took me a minute to find the crack, but there it was. Even so, I placed it back on the shelf with the others. It wasn't my collection without it.

♦♦♦

BARBARA ARRIVED AT MY house with her outfit zippered into a plastic garment bag as well as a tote full of stuff, including panty hose.

"Remember Cinnamon panty hose?" she asked as she pulled out her own nude pair.

"I was partial to Harvest," I said.

"Why did we want to make our legs look orange?"

"We were covering flaws we didn't have," I considered. "Can you imagine if we'd known about the real ones waiting for us?"

Stephanie flitted between us, acting as handmaiden, makeup artist, ego-booster. She sifted through my jewelry box. "Aunt Bopper..." she said, holding up a sterling pin in the shape of a comma. "You should wear this."

Barbara held the pin high against her collarbone. It gave some pop to the cream-colored dress that fit her closely at the bodice—being the kind of dress that had a bodice. Adam had given me the pin years ago. Birthday or anniversary, wasn't sure which. I nodded. Yes, Barbara should wear it. Even so, she still looked like she was trying out for the part of Wife #4 on *Sister Wives*. A look that was not acceptable. Not today.

"You know," I ventured, "I think I've got a belt that would look great with that."

I dashed out of the room and returned, moments later, with a pile of boxes—Zappos, Shopbop, Neiman's. I dropped them on the bed, grabbed a letter opener from the bedside table and began slicing.

"What's all this?" asked Barbara.

"I have absolutely no memory of buying this," I remarked. I held up a charcoal T-shirt with leather sleeves.

"You've got a problem," Barbara said clinically. "Like a Dr. Phil–worthy problem."

I slit open all the boxes and dug through blouses, jeans, and sweaters that I tossed onto the bed like so much swag.

"Here it is!" I declared finally, extracting a wide snakeskin belt with a double ring buckle. It was a statement piece—the kind of accessory that might just make Barbara's vanilla dress look like it had attitude. Barbara held it for a long moment. Then, just when I thought she was going to toss it back onto the pile, she buckled it around her waist.

"Oh my God, Aunt Bopper," said Stephanie. "Perfecti-ono!"

Barbara looked to me for confirmation. "Perfecti-ono," I concurred.

Barbara stood in front of the full-length mirror. Stephanie and I held our breath.

"Perfecti-ono," she said finally. And then, "What else have you got there?"

"All kinds of stuff!" I enthused. "It's yours. It's all yours. Whatever fits. Whatever you want." I set about creating piles, giving myself over to the purge phase of my shopping bulimia. It had been a long time coming.

Barbara picked up a long camel-colored sweater. She held it up against her body. "I might have some pants I can wear with this."

"They've got to be tight," instructed Stephanie. "It's long and baggy. The bottoms have to be tight."

Barbara nodded, processing the information. She could learn this material.

I found a pair of black leggings, still encased in their plastic bag, and ripped it open. I handed them to Barbara. She laid them on the bed, then laid the sweater over them for the full effect.

"That might look good on me," she said.

"That would look spectacular on you," I said.

"You're sure you're not going to wear this stuff?"

"It's yours."

"Too casual for the office?" Barbara asked, suddenly eager to learn.

"Great for the office," Stephanie and I said in unison.

"Are you sure?" Barbara pressed.

"It's meant for you!" I said, elated. "It really was. All of it. I think I was buying it for you all along."

Stephanie pitched herself across my bed to reach the iPad fitted into its dock. She slid her index finger across the screen, animating it. *Suite: Judy Blue Eyes* blasted out. Stephanie bobble-headed in time to the harmonies of Crosby, Stills & Nash.

I reached for Barbara's hands. I wanted to dance with my sister like we used to when we were girls and an irresistible beat pulsated from the radio. But Barbara was sifting through the clothes.

So there was Stephanie, slipping her hands into mine, doing the shuffle-two-three, shuffle-two-three, break-step I had taught her when she was small and we played dance party, just the two of us, between nap time and dinner. Now we were dancing, then singing, then singing full-throttle.

"Tuesday morning, please be gone I'm tired of you / What have you got to lose? / Can I tell it like it is? / Listen to me baby. / It's my heart that's a-sufferin', it's a-dyin' / That's what I have to lose..."

The chorus rose. I let go of Stephanie's hands. We twirled around the room, arms weaving, wrists following arms, feet following hips, hips merging with beat. The song ended. Stephanie and I touched down to earth.

"I slept with David Crosby, you know," said Barbara as though she were announcing what she'd eaten for breakfast.

Stephanie's eyes popped.

"At least he said he was David Crosby," Barbara added.

"Aunt Bopper! Scandalabra!" Stephanie screeched. "I can't believe you never told me that."

"Your mother told me not to."

"That's right," I said. "And thank you very much. I don't remember rescinding that request."

"Oh, she's old enough. It was a long time ago anyway. When all you had to worry about was herpes and getting pregnant."

Stephanie turned to me. This was not her Aunt Bopper of the peculiarly modest frocks. This was not her Aunt Bopper, keeper of dogs and cats. Not Aunt Bopper who, as long as Stephanie could remember, had had only one boyfriend, the short-lived Hugh Marshy whose name Stephanie heard Adam and me bandy about along with words like "tedious" and "humorless."

"When was this David Crosby thing?" Stephanie asked.

"Oh, you know, " said Barbara, "eons ago. When he was starting to get a little large, but not quite the full Cowardly Lion."

Stephanie looked to me to make sense of it all.

"We were young once," I said.

"What else have you never told me?" Stephanie demanded.

Barbara and I locked eyes. I could see Stephanie struggle to decipher exactly what was passing between us. Was there too much for us to remember or nothing more at all? Maybe David Crosby had been it. A single electric moment in her aunt's life. She had to be wondering: had there been such a moment in her own mother's life? But she swept the notion from her mind like so much detritus, scraps of dreams forgotten in the morning.

# CHAPTER FORTY-ONE

"THE FIRST TIME I ever saw the word FUCK, it was carved into a tree on the nature trails behind school," I said. My palms moistened on the steering wheel as I turned off Sunset Blvd. onto Beverly Glen. The approach to Ridgepoint did that to me. "We were gathering some kind of pods and looking for pinnate leaves with Mrs. Guthrie..."

"Fourth grade," Barbara said.

"Third," I corrected her. "Mrs. Guthrie was third grade. I know that because in the third grade when you had to multiply by ten, you moved the decimal point toward the windows. In the fourth grade, you moved it toward the door."

Barbara nodded.

"It was traumatic," I recalled. "We had our little bags of nature stuff and we looked up and there it was on the tree. Two trees actually. The F-U were on one tree and the C-K were on another. So Caroline Maloney—she was the one who said it out loud... she pronounced it funny. Fewk. That's how she said it. Fewk. Mrs. Guthrie got all discombobulated and said, 'Well now, that's not a very nice word, is it?' And then she pointed out some sort of bark we were supposed to find fascinating. But she couldn't stand it, I guess, because after we walked a little farther she suddenly said, 'Not that you girls will ever, ever say it, but the U is short."

"Mrs. Guthrie?"

"Mrs. Guthrie. With the mole."

"Oh my God. The mole. That thing could have had its own zip code."

"I don't think I ever saw those FUCK trees," Barbara said. "And I spent a lot of hours down there. When I was in tenth grade, Mimi Burnside and I were going through our Byronic phase and we used to walk the nature trails and recite *The Love Song of J. Alfred Prufrock.* 'Let us go then, you and I, when the evening is spread out against the sky…'"

"Like a patient etherized upon a table." I said.

"Miss Zipser would be so proud."

"Not technically a Byronic phase if you're reciting T. S. Eliot," I said as I turned into the school parking lot. It was easily twice the size it had been when we had gone to school there. A conifer grove had been sacrificed.

"Do you suppose Miss Zipser will be here?" Barbara asked.

"Oh my God," I said. "I hadn't thought about teachers being here." I felt like I hadn't kept up with the reading and a pop quiz was on its way.

"What do you care? All the teachers loved you."

"That doesn't mean I want to see them." I turned off the engine. It took us a minute to get out of the car.

The reunion was in the Great Hall. It used to be the centerpiece of the campus. Now it was dwarfed by a steel and glass science complex surrounding it on three sides. The Great Hall was no longer great.

Inside, the heavy velvet drapery was gone. The room was sunnier. But the surrounding science building refracted the sunlight into severe angles. They splintered through, making the massive room look more like a menacing laboratory than the site of somber Christmas programs and end-of-the-year rites of passage. And it smelled funny. I remembered precisely how it used to smell—of pine furniture polish and old ladies' Jungle Gardenia. Today it smelled of second rate catering.

I wondered why the room was full of old women. Then I realized: they were my classmates. So much salt in the salt-and-pepper hair. Hillary Watson had pulled her wiry scrub back into an I-give-up ponytail. And there was a good deal of spread. Hips had widened and buttocks dropped. Breasts had grown heavy, now draped rather than cupped. Even feet—once begrudgingly laced into saddle shoes—pancaked out in squat-heeled pumps. Ineluctably, there'd been a whole lot of settling going on.

There was also the aging-be-damned group. Women who relegated their sagging faces to a portrait in the attic or the doctor's office. As for their bodies, whatever cardio pop, pilates, and spinning didn't take care of, liposuction did. It was a tough town to grow old in. You had to claim a camp.

I ran the back of my right hand down the side of my torso and over my hip, a familiar path, calibrating my current self against my previous self. Did all the girls in this room—women, they were women now—did they trace the outlines of their bodies to see if they still felt like themselves?

"Maura Locke!" I heard from a distance. I scanned the room in the general direction of the voice. Luanne Forester weaved through the crowd waving wildly. I raised my hand hello. Luanne's eyes bulged, making her appear weirdly excited to see me. (This eyeball thing was not new. Already quite pronounced when she was young, it had prompted Gwen and me to leaf through our Physiology text in search of an explanation. We had referred to Luanne ever after as "TC" for thyroid case. What had our nicknames been, I wondered.)

"I was hoping you'd be here," Luanne said. She lowered her voice. "I mean, really, what do you and I have in common with these people?"

I wracked my brain for what it was I might have in common with Luanne.

"So how's your daughter? She must be about sixteen?"

"Seventeen," I said.

"I keep up through Mandy Hunt who talks to Gwen every now and then," Luanne explained. I nodded. Had Gwen let slip to Mandy Hunt that Adam had filed for divorce? I wondered how many women in the room were divorced. If only I had known how desperately I didn't want to be one of them that morning in the kitchen when I refused to laugh at Adam's Top Ten List.

"Mandy couldn't come." Luanne lowered her voice again. "Hysterectomy." Then, cheerfully, "We should all get together some time."

I waved over Luanne's shoulder to no one in particular and headed into the thick of it to join Barbara and a cluster of girls from her class. Disappointingly, not one of them gave me a dirty look or signaled Barbara to get rid of me. So disconcerting. My role with that group had always been eager interloper. Now I was just another grown-up.

Cecilia Winsett was holding court, describing in minute detail her latest project as a landscape architect. She was going full throttle on the rhododendron obtusum when Gwen appeared. Dale Baron was about to jump in, but Cecilia didn't give her an opening. She pulled out an iPad from a leather case, and with a press of her thumb zoomed in on a photo. In truth, the garden was spectacular. The photo circulated. Everyone oohed and aahed.

I was about to mention that Barbara was a hotshot travel agent when Dale Baron called up a photo on her phone and passed it around. "Alex is nineteen. He goes to school in New Haven." Code for Yale.

"Let's go claim a table and get some food," Gwen suggested.

"Creamed hard-boiled eggs perhaps?"

"Oh, God," said Gwen. "Flashback."

As we scoped out the table situation, Gwen and I reminisced about the lunchtimes of our childhood. As Lower School Ridgepoint girls, every day at 11:45 a.m. we lined up single file and marched from our classroom to the dining hall where we, these very little girls—first, second, third graders—sat in our assigned spots at our assigned tables with our assigned teachers making sure voices never crept too high, elbows never grazed the table, mouths remained closed while chewing. All while a string of ancient women in starched uniforms waited on us, delivering plates of limp fish sticks, runny hot tamale pie, or on those most dreaded of days, creamed hard-boiled eggs ladled over soggy toast points.

There were indeed eggs today—but these were deviled and dotted with the tiniest speck of caviar. The yolk mixture had already gone inky. "I wonder how long these have been out," Barbara said as she joined Gwen and me at the buffet.

The three of us made a beeline for an empty table and staked our claim. "If TC asks if she can sit here, say no," said Gwen.

"It's official," I said. "We're back in high school."

"By the way," Gwen whispered, "Mandy Hunt's so-called hysterectomy? Reunion facelift gone awry."

My hands flew to my jaw, index and middle fingers tugging slightly. I looked at Gwen quizzically. "Not yet," Gwen said. "I'll tell you when. I promise."

"It's really loud in here," I said.

"It's a party," Barbara said.

Karen Schulter and Melanie Fareed sat down at our table. That was okay. Gwen and I had liked them. They were always nice girls. How had I forgotten so many of the nice girls? Why had I only remembered the annoying girls and why had I found so many of them annoying when all they were doing was wading through adolescence with the rest of us? I was ashamed of myself.

"Have you seen Miss Zipser?" asked Melanie.

"She's still alive?" asked Karen. "I thought she was, like, ninety-five when we had her in seventh grade."

Gwen pointed her out. "She's still alive...in a manner of speaking," she said.

There she was. Miss Flag Salute herself. Miss Zipser was old. Really old. Still rocking the ramrod posture, her hair still lacquered into a sort of crescent roll. She had retired her A-bomb bra, but still teetered on the spike heels she'd always favored, which, with her diminished height, made her look like a child on stilts. A cadre of acolytes swarmed her. She smiled at them and engaged in conversation, but every now and then, her eyes darted around the room. An old habit. Scanning for infractions. I would not have been at all surprised if the pocketbook dangling from the crook of her arm contained demerit slips at the ready. When she glanced in my general direction, I slid my elbow off the table.

"Oh my God," I said, "Miss Zipser—coming this way."

Miss Zipser cut through the crowd, pausing to stiffly return the occasional hug. We all stood when she reached our table.

"Hello, girls," she said.

"Hello, Miss Zipser," we said, voices sing-song. I stifled a curtsy.

The old woman bestowed a smile upon us. "My special group," she said.

Melanie jumped in. "What's new with you, Miss Zipser?"

"I stopped teaching six years ago. I miss it, of course. Girls like you were getting harder and harder to come across. I have my Pomeranians. Homer and Virgil. You remember how I've always loved Pomeranians."

Miss Zipser assumed we had absorbed every detail of the life she divulged in discreet morsels over the course of the school year.

Indeed, I had. I remembered: the Pomeranians, the nephew who played the flute, the spelling champ Friday afternoons at that old-timey ice cream parlor. I remembered the look on Miss Zipser's face when Candace Holoman asked if she ever wanted to get married. And her answer. "It's something we girls all think about, Candace. But not while we're solving for X." How she turned back to the equation on the blackboard, but took an extra second to straighten her shoulders, which had slumped ever so slightly, before raising the chalk to the board and resuming the calculations.

Now, here stood Miss Zipser. She turned her gaze on me. "Maura Locke. Tell me about your life."

I hadn't studied for that question. "I have a daughter," I began. "She's seventeen."

"Oh, that's a difficult age. I tried it once," mused Miss Zipser. For a moment, I thought she meant she had taken a stab at being seventeen and found it distasteful, which may well have been the case, but then I realized she meant she had once tried teaching that age group. No doubt she preferred her minions less driven by hormones and more eager to please authority. Looking at this woman now, I supposed that authority might have been the biggest perk of Miss Zipser's job, the thing that gave her real satisfaction. Her sense of accomplishment lay not so much in molding young girls' minds—though God knows she considered that her sacred duty—but more in having the power to do so.

I deflected. "Do you miss teaching?" I asked.

"It was my whole life." We all nodded sympathetically. "But no, I don't miss it. Now I have time to grind my own coffee in the morning." She smiled. Clearly this was a fair trade: lifelong avocation for a fresher cup of joe. She turned back to me. "Tell me more, dear."

I knew she wanted to hear what I was doing with myself. What I was. Not in my house, but in the world. What I called myself. Doctor, lawyer, Indian chief. (After all, Ridgepoint had produced an astronaut.) I deflected again, gesturing toward Barbara with a flourish. "My sister is a travel agent."

"How delightful," said Miss Zipser. "Of course I can't leave my doggies, but there are so many places to go."

Barbara suggested a cruise might be something Miss Zipser should consider. Barbara said that ships these days were "floating hotels" and you couldn't underestimate the advantages of having to unpack only once. Her eyes widened with enthusiasm as she described the impressive variety of enlightening lectures and endless buffets. "You can have sushi for breakfast!"

Barbara lost Miss Zipser with that one, but even so, I was astounded by this incarnation of my sister. Not long before, the two of us had been walking through the cosmetics department of Bloomingdales when Barbara had preempted a spritz of perfume with a biting "Don't even think about it." Now here she was doing the hawking—a four-day-three-night, seven-ports-of-call version of a spray of Cristalle by Chanel. To Miss Zipser no less.

I volunteered to make a reconnaissance trip to the dessert table. As I headed off, there were several remarks about calories and carbs and glycemic indexes. Melanie said that this very morning she had read an article declaring the BMI passé. Karen wondered how many minutes on the elliptical would cancel out a lemon bar. Barbara explained that she'd recently added sugar back into her diet and felt the better for it.

I took the polar route to the desserts, intent on avoiding any other teachers, but found myself commandeered by Wendy Poe. "Maura! Maura Locke!" Wendy shrieked as she threw her arms around me. "I haven't seen you in forever! When was the last time...?" It was a rhetorical question. "Not since your wedding! Is that possible?"

I had never really been friends with Wendy Poe, but I had run into her at Trader Vic's one evening a month or so before the wedding. It was Kathy Fielder's birthday and that was one of the Fielder family special occasion restaurants, now extinct. It was the first time I had been included in a Fielder celebration and my nerves were jangled. I was relieved to see a familiar face beyond the pu-pus. It happened to belong to Wendy Poe. I chattered anxiously to her and, before I could stop myself, I'd invited her to the wedding.

The Wendy Poe that stood before me now fixed her gaze on me. (She must have had her makeup professionally done. There were probably eight products on her eyes, but she looked like she had barely been sprinkled with fairy dust.)

"I can't tell you how many times I've thought about your wedding," Wendy said dreamily. "The way your husband looked at you when you came down the aisle. That look spoiled me for a really long time."

Suddenly I envied Wendy Poe. Not because of her flawless non-makeup makeup or her spaghettini-thin strands of brown sugar highlights. I envied her because unlike Wendy Poe, I had let that image of Adam recede while she held onto it. "He looked at you like there was no one else in the room, no one else in the world really," Wendy rhapsodized. "And then he smiled the biggest smile. Like a little boy. Like he couldn't contain how lucky he was."

Yes—that smile. The moment racked into focus. Adam's smile. How he kissed the side of my head when I took my place at his side because he simply could not wait for the judge to give him the go-ahead.

"Thank you, Wendy," I said. I threw my arms around her and hugged her for a long moment.

"What for?" she asked.

"For reminding me," I said. "Thank you for that."

I let her go, her memory of that moment at my wedding now, once again, my memory. Wendy waved at someone across the room and headed off, leaving me to continue on to the dessert table. It was particularly noisy near the bar. All that glass and ice and piercing hoots of laughter. Denise Harmon was drunk. She was saying something about "that dyke Spanish teacher." Nancy Rand was trying in vain to shut her up.

The desserts were not a thrill. A few cookie platters, largely piled with underbaked snickerdoodles; a Bundt cake—lemon, I guessed; and a tray of brownies swirled with something the color of Pepto-Bismol. The caterer had put no effort here. No need. It would be unseemly for a roomful of women to complain about not enough sweets. I dropped a brownie onto a plate, then some cookies. The snickerdoodles left a greasy coating on my fingertips. They would taste of lard.

Someone clanked a knife against a glass. No one paid attention. I took a bite of the brownie. The pink swirl tasted like toothpaste.

That clanking again. Blade against thick glass. Still no one paid attention.

I was about to head back to my table when: "Mauranimous!"

"Suzanne!" I exclaimed before I even turned to see her. Only Suzanne Bremmer had ever called me that. Wacky Suzanne, a no-bullshit kind of girl. She looked exactly the same. She had been one of those girls who seem lit up from the inside, like she was perpetually on the verge of giggles. A girl ready to burst out. Now, according to her name tag, she was Suzanne Bremmer-Krakorian.

Suzanne picked up a slice of Bundt cake and ripped off a bite. "I hear you're seeing Peter Lafferty," she said. "He used to go with this woman who's always invading my personal space at Zumba."

I stared at her, struggling to make sense of this. I had worried that people might know I was separated. Kid stuff.

"Don't worry," Suzanne continued. "She's really young, but you're way prettier than she is." She popped the bite of cake into her mouth. "And she's got absolutely no rhythm."

It was louder now—the clink-clank—faster and louder.

Across the table, Victoria Trindle was reminding Miss Zipser of the time we'd all made papier-mâché puppets and Victoria opened her desk the next morning to find that during the night, hers had its face eaten away by a rat.

I interrupted. "Miss Zipser?" I said. "I have an answer for you."

"An answer?"

"You asked me what I've been doing with myself. What I am."

Miss Zipser looked at me quizzically from under eyebrows gone sparse and mostly gray.

"My daughter tells me I'm a wreck. And she's right. That's what I am. I'm a wreck."

"Oh my," said Miss Zipser, more horrified by this news flash than by the thought of the grotesquely faceless papier-mâché puppet.

The clinking again. Louder even still. Persistent, demanding.

I turned toward the noise. So did everyone else. Beth Richland stationed herself at the podium directly in front of the massive windows, no longer draped. The sun was beginning to set behind them and the light blasted in. My hand flew to visor my eyes.

Beth began, "I have had so much fun planning this wonderful event."

Whoops went up like flashpots around the room.

"I know how much our Ridgepoint education means to all of us," she went on. "I think it's safe to say that it made us the women we are today."

More cheering. Let's hear it for the women we are today.

Beth nodded. She raised her hand to her chest to play with a double strand of cultured pearls the size of grapes. The microphone picked up the sound. An unnerving click-clacking. "I know. I know," said Beth, "it's true, isn't it? Look at us. Aren't we something?"

Was she running for office? Had Beth Richland always been so full of hot air? Speaking of which, I thought, it was really hot in this room. Really hot. I grabbed the neckline of my dress and flapped it against my skin. I hadn't realized I was so clammy. Fabric was sticking to me in all kinds of places. I plucked at it around my waist. I was so stupid; I should have worn something that breathed. What was the fabric that breathed? Cotton? How did those commercials go? The touch, the feel, of cotton? I should have worn cotton. Like my old Ridgepoint uniforms. Even so, I could get pretty sweaty in those cotton uniforms. Especially on flag salute mornings.

I tried to peer past Beth Richland to the lawn outside and beyond to where the flagpole used to be. It was still there. Right now the late afternoon sun struck the aluminum, slashing a direct path to my optic nerve. I closed my eyes. But the laser beam of sunlight left its imprint, along with a kaleidoscope of violet and yellow. I grabbed the edge of the table to steady myself and tried opening my eyes. That made it worse. Vertigo. Full-blown.

I dropped my head. Maybe fixing on the floor would stabilize me. Otherwise the floating would overtake me and the dizziness would follow, an upper cut at the end of that out-of-body instant. But no. It was too late. The floor was already tottering. The vertigo had me by the scruff of the neck. I tried to set the plate of goodies down on the table, but it crashed to the floor, sanding the parquet with cinnamon sugar. Someone grabbed my arm. "Are you okay?"

"I had a wave."

"Let me get you some water," said a disembodied voice.

"Hold a piece of ice on the inside of her wrist," said another.

"It'll pass," I said, trying to convince myself.

Barbara was there. "The vertigo?"

I nodded ever so slightly.

"She has vertigo," Barbara asserted.

"Is it benign positional?" someone asked.

"I don't know," I said.

"It is," Barbara said. "I'm sure it is. I read all about it. Remember, Maura, I told you?"

"Has she ever tried the Modified Epley Procedure?" asked Ellen Rappaport. I had been assigned as Ellen's buddy when she arrived as a new girl in the ninth grade.

"That's the thing I couldn't remember," Barbara said to me. "That's what I was telling you about."

"No," I insisted. "I'll be okay."

"I'm a chiropractor," said Ellen.

"No kidding," Barbara said. "I've got this pain in my shoulder. A strained rotator cuff, I think. Maybe a little tear actually…"

At the podium, Beth was saying something about how her days as class historian had shaped her life.

"I know how to do the Epley," Ellen Rappaport said to me. "Please let me try. It can't make it worse. I promise."

"No," I insisted.

Ellen Rappaport ignored me. She was a Doctor of Chiropractic; she would exercise the authority conferred upon her by that degree. "We need to clear off this table."

The desserts disappeared in an instant.

"Okay," Ellen instructed me, "lie down."

"You've got to be kidding," I said. She held a palm to my forehead, half covering my eyes. My forehead was drenched with sweat.

"I'm perfectly serious. Lie down on this table with your head hanging off the side."

"We'll help you," coaxed Gwen.

"Don't be a baby," said Barbara.

I looked at the faces staring at mine. The Great Hall was spinning. Enough, I thought. Enough of this. Finally…enough.

"Okay," I said. And, with several supporting hands easing me up, I edged onto the table.

At the other end of the room, Beth Richland realized there was something amiss. "Oh my goodness," she said. "Is everything all right?"

The roomful of Ridgepoint girls turned en masse to watch as I climbed onto the dessert table in the middle of the Great Hall.

"I don't know about this..." I hesitated.

"Just lie back." Ellen placed her hands on either side of my head as I settled onto the table. "Scoot back a little," Ellen prompted.

I did as I was told. I hung my head off the edge of the table. I looked up at Ellen Rappaport. Ellen's skin had cleared up in the past several decades. I was happy about that for her. She smiled down at me so reassuringly that I relaxed and closed my eyes. And as I did, I said to no one in particular, "Fewk it."

Ellen Rappaport held my head in her hands and turned it to the left for thirty seconds, then to the right for thirty seconds. Then she rotated my entire torso to the left for another thirty seconds. After these moves, Ellen instructed me to sit up very slowly to see how the world turned.

It turned—smooth and steady. Barbara had been right about the tiny BB rolling around inside my skull like a handheld puzzle. Ellen Rappaport had managed to roll the ball through the maze to its target.

"Thank you, Ellen," I said when my feet hit the floor and the room remained still. And then I burst into tears. I had no idea why. Was it relief or gratitude? Or the absurd simplicity of the cure?

Barbara suppressed an "I told you so" about the Epley, though her expression said it anyway.

Ellen handed me her card, which I took, gratefully, truth be told. When I put it in my purse, my hand felt a folded piece of paper—a paper held together by countless little lengths of Scotch tape. I grabbed Barbara's hand. "We've got to go," I said.

"Are you okay?" Barbara asked.

"I'm fine. Now I've got to go make everything else fine."

"Let's get out of here," Barbara said. "Finally!" she added. I wasn't really sure if it was an editorial comment on walking out on the Ridgepoint proceedings or on my coming to my senses.

We were exiting the Great Hall as Beth Richland called Miss Zipser to the stage to receive a lifetime achievement award.

I didn't care. I had already spent too much of my own lifetime worrying about Miss Zipser. Now, riding the high of proprioception restored, I knew it was time to get rid of the Miss Zipser in my head. Why the hell not? I was going to go for my own lifetime achievement award. Fewk it.

# CHAPTER FORTY-TWO

IT WAS MY FAVORITE stretch of Sunset, where it wound leisurely toward the Strip as you headed east. Barbara was behind the wheel. Like teenagers, it felt great to be driving, maybe a little too fast, blasting the radio and leaning into the curves of Sunset Boulevard. Until we found ourselves behind a Starline tour bus and had to slow.

A snippet of the guide's patter floated our way. "Atop the grassy knoll on the left is the world-famous Beverly Hills Hotel. If you're an Eagles fan, you might recognize it as the Hotel California. If you've got an idea for a movie, stop by its fabled Polo Lounge and take a meeting with a studio mogul." Given the world of revolving doors at the studios these days, I wondered if executives hung around long enough to turn into moguls. And I doubted anyone had taken a meeting on a "grassy knoll" since 1963.

The guide was on to the next point of interest. "On your right is the park where George Michael..." I couldn't make out the rest. The bus slowed to a crawl to let its passengers take Instagrams of the public restroom.

Barbara turned left onto Beverly Drive, passing the hotel, pink against a cloudless robin's egg sky.

"I don't expect anything," I tried to convince myself.

Barbara drove. "Do you forgive him?"

"I do," I said. "It's me I don't forgive. So there's not a reason in the world why Adam should forgive me either."

"You two..." said Barbara.

"We two...what?"

"Nothing," said Barbara. "I just depend on you two being you two, and there are very few things I depend on. You and Adam are one of them." Barbara kept her eyes on the road. This was always the tricky part of getting to Sam's house, winding off of Beverly—a right, then a left.

The Fielders' driveway was coming up on the left. Adam had disarmed the sensor on the electric gate for the funereal after-party. It remained wide open, allowing us to cruise past the intercom.

The gardener's truck was parked at the far end of the driveway. He was unloading flats of impatiens. Sam would have been pleased that the place was being kept up. "Spick-and-span," he would say. Miguel, the gardener, raised a calloused hand in greeting, first wiping it on his mud-streaked jeans.

Barbara nodded toward Adam's car parked in the garage where the Eldorado used to live. Sam had given the Caddy to Wendell when they both retired. "What the hell use have I got for it now?" he said—his way of saying thank you.

Barbara stared through the windshield toward the entrance of the house, a massive six-panel door accented by a brass knocker engraved with the family name.

"You have no idea how hard this has been on me," Barbara said. "Adam and me?"

"Yes."

Not the moment to point out this was my life we were talking about. Instead, I said, "I'm sorry." I opened the car door. "Wait for me here."

"You're on your own," Barbara said. "You can do this." Barbara rounded the bend of the circular driveway and headed out.

I stood there, stuck to the spot where I had been deposited. I stared at the front door, paralyzed. Finally, I climbed the steps to the door and rang the bell. It played the first few notes of the theme from *Lawrence of Arabia*. The first time I visited the house, I asked why *Lawrence of Arabia*? Had the movie figured in Sam's career?

"Nope, he just liked it," Adam explained. What Sam really liked was that his doorbell didn't go ding-dong. It played the theme from the biggest damn movie he could think of, back from when movies delivered your five bucks' worth. Sam Fielder's doorbell won an Academy Award for best score.

I waited for Adam to open the door. But he didn't. It had not occurred to me that he might not be home. His car was there. I rang again. No rustling inside. No hurried footfall. Nothing.

I peered through the little windows bordering the front door. Sidelights, they're called. If only I could delete all the useless information from my brain. Sidelights, metric conversions, Gwen's childhood phone number. Maybe the constant orbiting of all that information had triggered my vertigo, like a computer crashing.

I cupped my hands around my eyes to look inside. The Fielder foyer looked a lot like a swank financial institution with its slate floors and Danish modern furniture, de rigueur when Sam and Eileen bought the house in the fifties. Each time they redecorated, they stuck with the umber palette and the teak. As Sam always said, "If it don't need fixin', don't break it."

And then I saw it. Propped up against the wall on the way up the stairs, my own eyes staring back at me. It took me a moment to realize this was a painting. It was nothing like looking at a photograph, but a bit like looking into a mirror. But a magic mirror, a mirror from a fairy tale. Daniel had been annoyed that he'd missed with the eyes. Yes, the eyes in the portrait were not the eyes I had brought to his studio that day. These were eyes from another time, eyes filled with something I had long ago forgotten. It might have been hope.

I lowered myself to the stoop. That's what Sam called the grand, terraced steps leading up to the front door. The stoop. As if he were still in the Bronx throwing a pink rubber Spaldeen with the kids from the block.

I watched Miguel plant the impatiens. I wondered if he had taken it upon himself to spruce up the yard or if Adam had decided to sell and was planting a cheery border so that the house would show well. To sell or not to sell: that would have been a discussion between us, a decision made together. Maybe my portrait propped against the stairway wall meant we would be having those discussions again. Soon. It had to. What else could it mean? Only that he still loved me.

I closed my eyes. There were so many things I wanted to tell Adam during the time he was gone. Or was it the time when I was gone? I rifled through my mental catalogue.

I wanted to tell him how Barbara had transformed her style and how this travel agent thing seemed like it was actually going to stick.

I wanted to tell him how my parents were calcifying in the desert, slowing and shrinking.

I wanted to tell him how Stephanie had slept with a boy and, more important, had her heart mangled.

I even wanted to tell him how I had stepped out of a chemist's in Shepherd Market and spotted Mick Jagger—but that without him there, Mick Jagger was no Mick Jagger.

Sam used to say that once the lights went out in a movie theater, the chance to sell those empty seats was gone forever. Now, as I sat on Sam's stoop, I realized all those moments in my life were gone forever like the empty movie seats. The college trip. Stephanie's heartbreak. Mick Jagger. Gone.

♦♦♦

I SNAPPED BACK WHEN Miguel clanked the tailgate of his truck shut. He waved again before climbing in behind the wheel, then he drove away.

It had been there all along, hidden by the truck. The glacial blue. The four interlinked rings. The lips-and-tongue decal. The car that belonged to Tara From Literary.

I leapt from the step, snagging my dress on the stone. A run shot through the jersey. How foolish of me to have thought that just maybe my portrait inside the house where Adam was living meant something more than a polite nod to Daniel. How foolish of me to think that he was waiting for me to apologize, that he had hit the pause button on his life in the meantime. Adam had probably lured Tara From Literary upstairs right past the portrait. Did he lead her to his teenage bedroom or did he unwrap her one button at a time on Sam's California King? The Brooks Brothers shirt…the narrow skirt… the impossibly high pumps. My imagination panned along these items strewn across the floor, a trail invoking eagerness and ardor.

I had not been surprised when I spotted Henry Boswell that day in the garage falling under the spell cast by Tara From Literary. But Adam? Could he have fallen under her spell, too? Spell-proofing was supposed to come with marriage, wasn't it? We were still married, weren't we?

I had not fallen under Peter Lafferty's spell. What I had done was something stupid. And spiteful. Now my punishment took the form of this Audi parked in Adam's driveway. My punishment and my penance.

I crossed the driveway to the car, to get an up-close-and-personal look at the thing, as if Tara's particular animal scent might be lingering there and would explain so many things I had spent a lifetime trying to decode. But the car was just a car. I slumped against its hood, defeated.

I hardly looked up when I heard chatting. Adam and Stephanie strolling up the driveway.

"Well, this is a surprise," said Adam when he saw me.

"What do you think?" Stephanie patted the little blue coupe lovingly, bouncing on her toes, hyper with first car infatuation. "That wacky Tara from Literary was selling it and Daddy thought it would be perfect for me. Don't you love it?"

"I do," I said. "I love it. I'm just surprised."

"We took a walk, and I understand about what a big responsibility this is," Stephanie assured me.

Adam had always been big on the walk-and-talk whenever he had something important to discuss. I exhaled; Tara was not on the premises. Clothes were not strewn. Bodies were not grinding and sweating. My mind got it. But my nervous system did not rebound so quickly. I had run out of rebound long ago. I burst into great, heaving sobs.

"Daddy told me all the rules. I promise I'll never text. Ever. Not even at stoplights. I'm going to be super careful and take really good care of this car. I'm going to wash it myself every single week. Probably twice a week. You're going to be amazed at how responsible I'm going to be. Isn't it the cutest car you've ever seen?"

I nodded.

"Don't cry, Mommy," Stephanie said. "I'm going to be such a good driver. I'm going to be so careful."

"Are you okay?" Adam asked.

"I'm fine," I said. "I think this is great. It's adorable. So adorable."

"Isn't it?" Stephanie gushed. "It's absolutely faboosh!"

"Are you sure you're okay?" Adam asked.

"I'm fine. Actually, I'm really good. Ellen Rappaport fixed me. I've had a little vertigo."

"Stephanie told me," said Adam.

"Who's Ellen Rappaport?" Stephanie asked, flicking a rogue leaf off the hood of the Audi.

"A girl in my class," I answered.

"This color's called quartz," Stephanie bubbled.

"What's this cure?" Adam asked.

"It's a maneuver. Barbara told me about it when I first got hit… you know, when I first started getting dizzy, but, I don't know, it sounded kind of weird. It was weird, I guess. But it worked."

"I don't know the official color of the interior," Stephanie said as she slid behind the wheel. "What do you think, Mom?"

"Ivory, maybe? Ecru?" I volunteered.

"What is it?" Adam asked. "This maneuver?"

"Well, she had me lie down on a table…and she twisted my head this way, then that way, then my whole body…She's going to email me a link to the exact technique."

"Cool," said Stephanie. "Can I drive it over to show Mallory?"

"Mallory?" I was stunned. "You're still friends?"

Stephanie shrugged and twisted the corners of her mouth. "She apologized. And she's my best friend. "

"You can't drive with Mallory in the car, you know," Adam said.

"I know, I know. I'm going to be the very soul of law-abidingness. I'll drive there, at like twenty-five miles per hour. Then straight home. By midnight."

Stephanie turned to me for approval. I looked at my daughter behind the wheel of the car. She was seventeen. It was her turn to drive Sunset Boulevard singing at the top of her lungs.

"Okay," I said. "Straight there. But home by eleven."

"I promise!" Stephanie leapt from the car and threw her arms around my neck. I extended an arm out, inviting Adam into the hug. He stepped forward hesitantly, but then it was the three of us, for real.

"No drag racing on Sunset Boulevard," Adam half-joked as Stephanie slid back into the driver's seat. She revved the engine a little, the sound mimicking her own excitement, then circled around and back down the driveway to the gate. She stuck her arm out the window and waved wildly.

"Both hands on the wheel!" I called.

Adam placed a hand on the small of my back to coax me off the ledge of motherhood. His palm landed precisely on the spot where my single dimple lay. He jerked it back as though he had burned himself. He wanted to let me know it meant nothing. Less than nothing.

"Are you thinking of selling the house?" I asked.

He shrugged. "I haven't decided."

I nodded. He wasn't going to ask what I thought.

"I got everything wrong," I said. "I did everything wrong."

"Yes, you did," he agreed, easily, quickly. Coolly.

"I don't have a lot of practice with that. I'm not good at doing the wrong thing." I hoped it would be a joke. But it didn't land like one. "I've always done what everyone else told me was the right thing. In fact, I was so busy worrying about everyone else's right thing that I never gave myself a chance to figure out what the right thing for me was. Until I did the wrong thing. The biggest wrong thing. And I know it. I knew it right away. I knew it before I did it. And the worst part is, I did it to you. It's not an excuse, but everything was so topsy-turvy. Everywhere I turned everything was changing. Everything was letting me down. All those things that are supposed to be constant in life are disappearing or have already disappeared. Stupid franchises keep going in where great restaurants used to be. There's traffic on Sunset at one in the afternoon. The sun doesn't come out until September. David Letterman's been replaced by someone who comes out grinning...and twirls. And then you... that night...the video...and the emails...All of a sudden, I couldn't count on you to be you. I didn't know who you were anymore. I didn't know who you were if you were a you who didn't love me anymore. And that was too scary for me. I admit it—I wanted to punish you for that."

Adam listened.

"Actually it was scarier than that. I didn't know who I was if you didn't love me anymore. I'm not me if you don't love me."

"I don't believe you thought I didn't love you," he said.

"How could I not? You were writing these crazy intimate things to another woman."

"That had nothing to do with us. I'm not making an excuse. Honestly. But that had nothing to do with loving you. Which I do, by the way. And always did. I tried to explain this to you. It had to do with wanting to feel something different...feeling alive... It was stupid, but it was a sort of a lifeline. What you did..." His voice trailed off.

"What I did had to do with wanting to feel the opposite of alive...with wanting to feel nothing."

"You thought I didn't love you?" Adam said, as though maybe he finally understood what that might feel like. He opened the front door, motioning me into the house.

"Nothing. I just wanted to feel nothing," I said. I paused in the doorway. "I'm sorry. I'm so sorry."

"Something happened to your dress," said Adam.

"I know."

"Too bad," he said.

"A dress is never critical," I said.

◆◆◆

ADAM POINTED TO THE painting where it leaned against the wall about halfway up the sweeping staircase. "What do you think of it?"

"What do *you* think of it?" I asked back.

"I asked you first," Adam nudged.

"I asked you most recently," I said, trying to earn a smile, even a small one.

Adam led the way across the foyer to Sam's study.

The room smelled of brittle old books, stale cigars, and cheap Bay Rum, the first aftershave Sam could ever afford and the only one he ever used. A slight variation in color mottled the luggage-toned leather of his chair, leaving the faintest silhouette of Sam's sturdy body, as though he had just been called from his desk.

Adam swiveled the chair toward me and pulled me down to it. Facing me on the desktop was a double folding sterling frame, a gift from me and Adam for one of Sam's birthdays—eightieth, perhaps. On the left side was a photo of Adam, Stephanie, and me, snapped on Sam's boat. On the right, a photo so old that I did not remember it at first. Adam, head cocked, wearing a paint-splattered smock and brandishing a paintbrush like the Statue of Liberty's torch. Me, holding an enormous palette. Between us, Sam, extending his thumb and squinting as though straining to find perspective, a parody of a parody. I leaned in to get a closer look—the three of us in Adam's studio, playing dress-up and mugging for the camera, Adam's mother urging us on from behind the lens.

"Wow," I said.

"I know," Adam agreed.

"When was that?"

"I can't remember," he said.

"How can we not remember?" I said.

I sat back in the chair, settling into the ghost of Sam's outline in the leather. A brown cardboard manuscript box sat on the corner of the desk. Adam slid it over to me and lifted off the top, uncovering a three-inch stack of pages. On the top page, in Helvetica bold: *SELL IT, DON'T SMELL IT*. Beneath that: *The Autobiography of Sam Fielder.*

"Oh my God!" I said. "Did you know about this?"

"No. He never said anything to me."

"Unbelievable," I muttered as I lifted the stack from the box.

"It's unfinished. I think. Unless he thought nothing of interest happened after the mid-eighties."

"A very real possibility," I said.

"Here's the shocker," Adam said as he lifted the title page. The next page was the dedication. It read: "For my son, Adam, who saved the two most important things in my life: my business and my marriage." My eyes darted between Adam and the page, the page and Adam.

"I'm speechless," I said.

"Well, I'm pissed," Adam said. "My dad never said anything like that to me. He never told anyone he thought I was doing a good job, let alone saving his business."

"You're wrong."

Adam furrowed his brow.

"After the funeral…" I explained, "Wendell told me exactly that. He said your father bragged about you all the time. To anyone riding in the car." I mimicked Wendell mimicking Sam, "At any given time, twenty-five percent of the people in this business hate me…"

"More like fifty," Adam interrupted.

"That would be your father. He said twenty-five. He said twenty-five percent hate me. But I never know which twenty-five. Adam knows. And he knows how to make it right with them. Without Adam, FCM would have been kaput long ago."

Adam shook his head in disbelief.

"'Mr. F. knew what was what.' That's exactly what Wendell said."

"I wish he'd said something to me," Adam said, his voice catching.

I picked up the dedication and offered it to Adam. "He did." Then, glancing at the page, I added, "Why would he say you saved his marriage?"

Adam exhaled loudly. "He cheated on my mother. With a script supervisor he met when he was visiting a location in New Mexico. Some stupid Western. Big flop. Served him right." Adam shook his head, chuckling, "Starlets were always throwing themselves at him and he went for below the line."

"Did your mother know?"

"It's a company town. Of course, she knew. She kicked him out for a little while. But I went to her. I was sixteen. I told her how much Dad loved her. Which he did. She knew that, I think, but I had to convince her. I personally guaranteed her that he'd never do anything like that again."

"And she believed you?"

"Because it was the truth. I told my father I'd given Mom my word. And he gave me his." Adam shook his head. "I guess that was the first package I ever put together."

"I can't believe you never told me this."

"Ancient history."

I picked up the picture frame, studied the photo, but still could not place the moment when it was snapped. "I thought I remembered everything."

"It's impossible to remember everything," Adam said. "That's why you have to choose what you remember very carefully."

I nodded. Deleting whole files from my brain. I was going to have to learn to cultivate that skill, though I'd spent a lifetime grooving all kinds of things—events, snippets of conversation, sidelong looks— so deeply into my brain that they became part of me.

"It just so happens that I wrote something, too," I said. I removed the taped piece of paper from my purse and handed it to Adam. He stared at the reassembled divorce jigsaw.

"What's this?"

"Turn it over," I said. And he did. "It's a new, improved Top Ten List," I explained.

He didn't smile.

"Read it," I said. "Out loud." I wanted to be able to hear his voice saying these things. I wanted to hear if they sounded as true for him as they were for me.

"The Top Ten Reasons To Save A Marriage"

10. Because we know what to order for each other in a restaurant.

9. Because you've got the Across and I've got the Down.

8. Because you hold my head when I throw up.

7. Because when you look at me, I feel like I don't need Botox.

6. Because you're the one who put those laugh lines there.

5. Because it doesn't matter what color the walls are painted— it's not home unless we're both in it.

4. Because ain't nothin' like the real thing, baby.

3. Because becoming a Hollywood statistic is so clichéd .

2. Because sometimes the harder you try to break something, the more you learn it's unbreakable. (a.k.a....If it don't need fixin', don't break it.)

1. Because of why you chose the Chagall.

Adam put the paper down next to his father's manuscript on the desk. "Have you always known why I chose that painting?"

"No," I said. "I just found out. Daniel told me. Why didn't you?"

"Because fate seemed more romantic," he said. "And because you loved that story so much."

"Well, as fate would have it," I said, "I love the real story even more."

He stared at me for a long moment. But I had nothing. I was out of tricks.

I turned to replace the photo on the desk, inadvertently setting the chair revolving. I grabbed the desk to stop the spin, then froze for a moment to check in with my body. No equilibrium coup d'etat. I was okay. I was on solid ground.

"So this maneuver thing," Adam said to me. "Maybe I should learn how to do it in case the vertigo ever comes back."

◆◆◆

LATER, IN BED, I rested the side of my face in the hollow above Adam's collarbone. There was nothing new about this spot. It just happened to be my spot. A spot that really was, quite simply, all good things. It had taken me a minute or two to readjust to the slope of the bed, but now it was home again. It was no wonder I spent so much of the past few months with my head spinning. The tug of gravity had not anchored me to the earth.

"So," Adam said, "you never told me what you thought of the painting of you."

"It kind of blew me away," I said.

"In a good way?"

"In a really good way. It captured something I thought was long gone. Which is weird because that's the exact opposite of how I felt when I sat for Daniel. I was dizzy and sort of untethered. Lost. I was lost."

"You sat for Daniel?"

"Of course. How else could he have painted me?"

"That's not the painting I showed you. I painted that one."

"You?" I propped myself on an elbow to look at Adam eye to eye.

"Yeah, me. After I sent back the pieces of the divorce papers, I was useless. I couldn't work, I couldn't sleep, I couldn't think. I didn't know what to do with myself. So I decided to try to paint. I went to see Daniel as a sort of safe haven, but I was still frozen."

I nodded. I got it. Finally, I got it. For me, the world had spun off kilter. For Adam, it had gotten stuck. Flip sides of the same heartache.

"I was about to give up," Adam went on, "but then Daniel said… you know how he is…he said, 'Dear boy, it's very simple really. Paint what you love.'"

"You painted that painting?" I wanted to make sure I had it straight.

"I did."

"Of course," I finally got it. "Daniel couldn't possibly have. Because it's how I feel when I'm with you."

Adam kissed me. "It's a painting of us."

"You and me," I said. A complete sentence. More than that. A complete story—with a beginning, a middle, and…a beginning.

# ACKNOWLEDGMENTS

MY THANKS TO MARIANNE Moloney, literary manager, steadfast believer, and respository of countless stories from the wonderful worlds of books and movies.

To my daughter, Cami: you inspire me every day. I want to be just like you when I grow up. And to Moshe, the man lucky enough to be her husband: I cannot imagine what would have become of our family without you.

To my husband, Norman: my thanks for believing in this book ever since its first, messy incarnation, long before (like the Beatles) we was what we was. For that, and so much more, I will be hugely grateful all the way to the end of the line.